INTUITION

Allegra Goodman
INTUITION

A NOVEL

THE DIAL PRESS

INTUITION
A Dial Press Book / March 2006

Published by
The Dial Press
A Division of Random House, Inc.
New York, New York

This is a work of fiction. Names, characters, places, and incidents
either are the product of the author's imagination or are used fictitiously.
Any resemblance to actual persons, living or dead, events, or locales is
entirely coincidental.

ISBN-10: 0-7394-7190-2
ISBN-13: 978-0-7394-7190-6

Printed in the United States of America

To my grandparents
Calvin and Florence Goodman
Who love the good, the true, and the beautiful

Part I
The Lab

1

ALL DAY the snow had been falling. Snow muffled every store and
church; drifts erased streets and sidewalks. The punks at the new Harvard Square T stop had tramped off, bright as winter cardinals with
their purple tufted hair and orange Mohawks. The sober Vietnam vet
on Mass Ave had retreated to Au Bon Pain for coffee. Harvard Yard
was quiet with snow. The undergraduates camping there for Harvard's
divestment from South Africa had packed up their cardboard boxes,
tents, and sleeping bags and begun building snow people. Cambridge
schools were closed, but the Philpott Institute was open as usual. In the
Mendelssohn-Glass lab, four postdocs and a couple of lab techs were
working.

Two to a bench, like cooks crammed into a restaurant kitchen, the
postdocs were extracting DNA in solution, examining cells, washing
cells with chemicals, bursting cells open, changing cells forever by in-
serting new genetic material. They were operating sinks with foot ped-
als, measuring and moving solutions milliliter by milliliter with
pipettes, their exacting eyedroppers. They were preparing liquids, ices,
gels.

There was scarcely an inch of counter space. Lab benches were covered with ruled notebooks and plastic trays, some blue, some green,
some red, each holding dozens of test tubes. Glass beakers stood above
on shelves, each beaker filled with red medium for growing cells. The
glass beakers were foil topped, like milk bottles sealed for home delivery.

Peeling walls and undercounter incubators were covered with postcards, yellowing Doonesbury cartoons, photographs from a long-ago lab picnic at Walden Pond. The laminar flow hood was shared, as was the good microscope. In 1985, the Philpott was famous, but it was full of old instruments. Dials and needle indicators looked like stereo components from the early sixties. The centrifuge, designed for spinning down cells in solution, was clunky as an ancient washing machine. There wasn't enough money to buy new equipment. There was scarcely enough to pay the postdocs.

On ordinary days, the researchers darted into and out of the lab to the common areas on the floor. The cold room, warm room, and stockroom were shared with the other third-floor labs, as was the small conference room with its cheap chrome and wood-grain furniture, good for meetings and naps. But this Friday no one left the lab, not even the lab techs, Aidan and Natalya. Gofers and factotums for the postdocs, these two belonged to a scientific service class, but no one dared treat them like servants. They were strong-willed and politically aware, attuned to every power struggle. They kept darting looks at each other, as if to say "It's time to go downstairs," but they delayed going to the animal facility for fear of missing something. The lab directors, Marion Mendelssohn and Sandy Glass, were meeting in the office down the hall. They had been conferring for half an hour, and this did not bode well. One of the postdocs was in trouble.

How bad was it? No one spoke. Prithwish kept his head down over a tray of plastic tubes, eyes almost level with the avocado plant he'd grown from seed. "My most successful experiment," he often said ruefully. Robin ducked out to look up and down the hall, then brushed past Feng as she hurried back inside. The black and white clock on the wall was ticking past three, but like the clocks in grade school, this one was always slow. Natalya glared at Aidan, as if to say "I went downstairs last time; it's really your turn now," but Aidan turned airily away. It might have been funny, but no one joked at the techs' pantomime.

"Cliff." Suddenly, Marion Mendelssohn was standing in the doorway. She stood there, fearsome, implacable, dark eyes glowering. "Could we have a word with you?" Cliff smiled tightly and shrugged, a desperate little show of nonchalance.

The others looked everywhere else, as their lab director led Cliff away to the office she shared with Sandy Glass.

Cliff's cheeks were already burning as he followed Marion down the corridor. At six foot three, he was more than a foot taller than Marion. Still, he was entirely in her power, and he dreaded what she and Glass were about to say. For years he'd been developing a variant of Respiratory Syncytial Virus and had dreamed of using his modified RSV to transform cancer cells into normal cells. His experiments were not working; Sandy and Marion had ordered him to give them up, and he had disobeyed.

The door closed behind him, and Cliff was standing in the tight, cluttered office.

"Now, Cliff," said Glass, "did we or did we not have a discussion about your continuing trials with RSV?"

Cliff stood silent.

"Maybe you don't remember our conversation," said Glass, smiling.

Cliff did remember, and he knew better than to smile back. Always cheerful, brimming with the irrepressible joy of his own intelligence, Sandy Glass smiled most when he was angry.

"I said you had to stop using RSV," Sandy reminded Cliff. "You said you understood."

Cliff nodded.

"We established RSV has some effect *in vitro*," Glass said. "Congratulations. You're on your way to curing cancer in a petri dish. But what have we established when we try injecting RSV into living mice?"

Cliff looked away.

"You've established *nothing*. You injected fifty-six mice with RSV, with no effect on tumors whatsoever. Therefore, Marion and I asked you to stop. We asked you nicely to move on. What did you do next?"

"I tried again," Cliff said, staring down at the floor.

"Yes, you did. You tried again."

"I'm sorry."

Sandy ignored this. "We told you to stop wasting resources on RSV."

"I didn't want to give up," Cliff said.

"Look, I realize RSV was your baby," Sandy said. "I realize this was two years' work developing the virus."

Two and a half years, Cliff amended silently.

"We understand you put your heart and soul into this project." Sandy glanced at Marion, who looked anything but understanding. "The point is, RSV does not work. And now, yet another set of experiments—against all advice, against our specific instructions. What were you thinking, Cliff? Don't say anything. Perseverance can be a valuable trait, particularly when you're *right*. But we see now that this third trial is showing every sign of failing spectacularly. No, don't apologize. Just tell us what you were thinking. Tell us your thoughts, because we really want to know."

Why had he tried twice more with the virus after it had failed? They were expecting an answer, but Cliff could not speak. The truth shamed him; it was so simple: he could not bear to jettison work that had taken so much time. The hours, the thousands of hours he'd spent, sickened him. How could he confess to that? The scientific method was precise and calibrated. A scientist was, by definition, impassive. He cut his losses and moved on to something else; he was exhausted, perhaps, but never defiant with exhaustion. A scientist did not allow emotion to govern his experiments.

And yet Cliff had been emotional and unrealistic about his work. He had behaved unprofessionally, taking his long shot again, and yet again. How could he explain that? There was only one reasonable explanation: he was not a scientist. This was what Mendelssohn and Glass were driving at.

"Did we or did we not agree," said Glass, "that you would end the wholesale extermination of our lab animals?"

"We don't have the money," said Mendelssohn, and she didn't mean funds for the mice themselves, which cost about fifteen dollars each, but the money for the infinite care the delicate animals required. "You'll recall we asked you to work with Robin."

"She could still use another pair of hands," Glass said, and Cliff hated him for that, and for the patronizing, slightly prurient tone in Glass's voice.

"I deserve my own project," Cliff said, raising his eyes.

"There is no such thing as your own project in this lab," Mendelssohn declared.

"Look, this is a team," Glass said, "and you need to pull your weight, not drag everyone else down with your personal flights of fancy."

Down the hall, in the lab, the others gathered like near relations at a funeral.

"They wouldn't fire him," Prithwish said loyally. He was Cliff's roommate, after all.

"They will not fire him," Feng agreed.

Natalya thought about this. "My feeling is Mendelssohn would not, but Glass would." She was Russian and had been a doctor herself, before coming to America. Natalya had never taken to Glass.

"They'll be arguing, then," said Prithwish.

"They'll let him stay," Aidan predicted, "and make him so miserable he'll leave by himself."

"He was miserable before," Prithwish pointed out, but the others hushed him. Cliff was coming back down the corridor.

Instantly his friends scattered, vanishing into the clutter of glassware and instruments like rabbits in the brush. All but Robin, who pulled at Cliff's sleeve. Silently they slipped into the adjoining stockroom, the lab's poisonous pharmacological pantry.

She closed the door behind her. "Are you all right?"

His cheeks were flushed, his eyes unusually bright. "I'm fine."

She drew closer, but he turned away.

"What are you going to do?"

"I don't know," he said. "They've already tried to pawn me off on you."

"They suggested that you work with me?"

"Six months ago, but I said no."

She was surprised, and hurt. "You never told me that."

"What was the point? I didn't want to work on your stuff."

She folded her arms. "What's wrong with my stuff?"

"Nothing!" he lied.

She had spent five years working on what had once been considered a dazzling project, an analysis of frozen samples of blood, collected over the years from cancer patients who had died of various forms of the disease. Sandy Glass had been convinced that somewhere in these samples was a common marker, a significant tag that would suddenly reveal a unifying syndrome underlying his patients' tragic and diverse conditions. Glass had presented the project to Robin in her first year with a flourish, as if he were bestowing upon her a great gift. He'd told Robin he was convinced there was a Nobel Prize in this work; that this above all was the research he himself had hoped to do if his clinical duties had allowed. Then, having bestowed his blood collection along with a great deal of disorganized documentation about each donor's illness and death, he'd left her to work alone.

He'd chosen her for her fierce intelligence, her passion for discovery, her ambition—and, of course, Glass had always liked a beautiful postdoc. Robin's eyes were a warm brown, brilliant under pale lashes, her blond hair silken, although she tied it back unceremoniously with any old rubber band she happened to find. Her features were delicate and easily flushed, her teeth were small and almost, but not quite, straight. On the upper right side, one tooth overlapped another slightly, like a page turned down in a book. With her fine eyes and shining hair, she'd always seemed to Cliff like a girl out of a fairy tale. Still, even she could not spin Glass's dross into gold.

"So there's nothing wrong with my work, but it's not good enough for you," she challenged Cliff.

"No, I didn't say that."

"That's what you were thinking."

"Look, if I ever thought that, I'm sorry. Just, please . . ."

Gravely, she turned on him. "But you aren't sorry."

"Stop!"

"I just thought . . ." she began.

"Don't think anything. Just leave me alone."

He strode back through the lab and out into the hall. How could Robin expect him to talk to her? What did she want from him? To beg her to let him work on her dismal black hole of a project? To break down sobbing on her shoulder so she could comfort him? He still heard the humorous disdain in Glass's voice. He saw the hard disappointment in Mendelssohn's eyes. They had not ordered him to leave; they'd even allowed that he might stay, but they had made him suffer. They had held up the evidence of his disobedience and failure, then tossed whatever scrap of a scientist he'd been upon the garbage heap and all but called out "Next!" There was Prithwish coming after him down the corridor. Cliff was not going to suffer his condolences. He escaped into the stairwell and bolted down the stairs.

Outside the institute, the snow had stopped. The December sun was setting, and the world was strangely still. He'd run down four flights of stairs, and stood for a moment, breathing hard. Then he caught his breath and his anger flared again. He kicked his way through the snow, mouthing retorts. *Who do you think you are? Who do you think I am?*

He walked without noticing distance or direction. Startled, he saw a red neon sign, *LIBBY'S IQUORS,* and realized he was in Central Square. A bus swept past, but there were scarcely any cars on the road. Stores were closed, and clean snow blew over the empty taxi stands. All alone, Cliff walked on.

He walked over a mile, as far as MIT, and then turned around and started back again past shuttered Victorian factories converted into warehouses, redbrick ramparts lowering in the shadows of taller office buildings. He thought about calling his parents, but what could they say to him? They owned a stationery store in West Los Angeles. They'd always encouraged Cliff. He'd attended University High School, gone to science camp in summers, practiced triangulation on sunbaked tennis courts, built his own weather station, cooked homemade versions of Silly Putty, toothpaste, and glue. His parents had paid for chemistry sets, and student microscopes, and even Stanford. They were well educated; both had gone to college, but Cliff was the first person in his family to earn a PhD. His parents knew nothing about bench work or lab politics. He thought of his thesis advisor, now dead. What would Professor Oppenheimer have said? He'd have laughed, of course, showing off his yellow teeth. He'd say, "What do you expect? You don't listen to the lab director, you get busted. You screw around with someone in the lab; of course you're gonna end up fighting later. You get what you deserve. How many times do I have to tell you? Don't shit where you eat."

His hands were cold, even in his pockets. He walked and walked up Mass Ave, and then along the Charles River, and his heart began to calm. The cold air began to smooth and smother his angry pride; numb despair overtook indignation.

He imagined he would keep walking forever in ever-widening circles, but as the river curved, he came upon the Weeks Footbridge, and there on the bridge he stopped. The Charles stretched out in the dark; pure, white, frosted with snow, like an ancient road now forgotten.

Cliff was overcome with a profound idea. He would walk across the river. Invisibly he would walk across the invisible river and leave his own footprints in the white snow on the frozen water. In the middle of the city, he would wander alone as if in the country, the slight crunch of the ice under his feet. He would walk to the other side.

He ran down the cement stairs of the Weeks Footbridge and then more cautiously found his way down the frozen muck of the riverbank. He put one foot onto the white ice and felt a complete peace come over him, a total forgetfulness. Then he put his weight on the foot. The ice sank beneath him. Viselike, the cold of the water seized him, soaking his sneaker and sock, burning through to his skin. With a yelp, Cliff pulled back onto the bank. Instinctively he clambered up to the sidewalk on Memorial Drive. Faster than ever, he walked on, but now the cold burned his ears, and he couldn't feel his right foot. A single rational thought rang in his ears. He had now demonstrated that he was an idiot.

He found some money in his pocket and stopped at Nini's Corner, the little store crammed with magazines and waxy apples and oranges stacked high up inside the windows. He bought a bag of honey-roasted almonds, which he ate as he strode up Brattle Street. He licked the sugar mixed with salt from his cold-numbed fingers, and he wondered where his gloves were, and whether he would have to teach high school.

He might have walked forever if it were not for his frozen foot. With a Californian's horror he began to wonder whether he had frostbite. How long did it take for necrosis to set in?

The phrase "personal flights of fancy" had lost some of its initial horror. The ringing of Glass's disapproval in his ears was just a little softer. He imagined Prithwish was still at the lab; Cliff wouldn't have to see him when he got to the apartment. But then, what did he care? Cliff had already had his humiliation, and he felt, with some relief, that his capacity for embarrassment, at least for this evening, was used up. What did it matter if he'd wasted years? What did he care if he'd ruined

INTUITION   11

his chances in research? Realistically, what had been the odds that he'd succeed?

As he began trudging north to Somerville, the balm of apathy began to soothe Cliff's wounds. His despair seemed to melt and pool inside him, until he could almost congratulate himself that he was no longer desperate, but simply demoralized and depressed—emotions entirely accepted, even expected, in the lab.

2

"YOU CAN'T just crawl under a rock," Aidan told Cliff on the eve of Sandy Glass's Christmas party. Aidan and Natalya and Robin had come to pick him and Prithwish up, and they stood in the doorway of the apartment, like a bunch of carolers.

"I'm not crawling under a rock. I just don't feel like going," Cliff said.

"Ta ta ta *tum*." Aidan sang out the theme from Zeffirelli's *Romeo and Juliet* while playing air violin. Aidan was an impossible ham, and improbably handsome as well, an aging young swain with his curly blond locks and pale blue eyes. The lab tech position was just Aidan's day job. He was really a baritone and soloed all around Boston. He worked with Emmanuel Music, among other groups, and sang cantatas at every opportunity, even to the mice in the animal facility. "Ta ta ta tummmm, ta ta ta tum," he serenaded Cliff.

"Very funny," Cliff said.

"You'll need letters of recommendation," Robin reminded Cliff. She took his hand, and he smiled a little. Only she could be so earnest in such a low-cut black dress.

"You need to work," said Prithwish as he knotted his red tie.

"You need to eat," said Natalya.

"You can't turn away from all that free food," added Prithwish.

"I'll drink to that," said Aidan, and he produced a bottle of champagne from inside his dress coat, and plastic champagne flutes as well.

"Let's stay here," Cliff said to Robin.

"No, no, you aren't going to burn your bridges like that. You're going to work this out," she told him. "Here, see, we brought you a drink to get you started."

Cliff wasn't the only one who needed fortification before the Christmas party. Even in the best of times the researchers approached this event with trepidation. Sandy's house was so grand, his polished floors so perfect, his Persian carpets so rich and delicate, they never knew quite where to put their feet. Glass lived in Chestnut Hill in a brick Tudor with a turret and a wrought iron balcony and a slate roof like the armored plates of a prehistoric beast. Inside, the rooms were draped with damask curtains. The rosewood piano gleamed, and though the leather library chairs were cracked with age, though the radiators hissed, and the first floor was rather drafty, everything in Glass's home seemed precious, and historic.

Shy on arrival, the postdocs stood in the entryway, until Ann Glass took their coats and ushered them into the living room crowded with people from Sandy's other life, the medical practice where he made his money.

"Who is that? Robin?" Sandy embraced her and kissed her on the cheek. "I didn't recognize you all dressed up. I never recognize any of you," he said to the assembled: Aidan, Prithwish, Cliff, Feng, and his wife, Mei. "Go get yourselves some drinks." He shooed them to the bar. "Watch out for the mistletoe!"

Glass didn't mind overwhelming his researchers with hospitality and intimidating them with his prosperity. He liked to show his postdocs what could be done with money and talent and imagination. His house was an object lesson in that respect. After all, he'd been poor at their age too.

Glass loved the satin touch of fine woods, the patina of cracked leather, the ring of certain words. Appearances were not superficial, but of substantive importance to him. Thus, years ago, Glass had discarded Sam, his given name, and nicknamed himself Sandy. His last name was invented too. Toward the end of medical school, he'd changed it from Glazeroff. This he'd done not just to forget that his grandparents were Eastern European Jews, but for aesthetic reasons. He could not countenance living and working in such a Russian bear-coat of a last name, and so he'd distilled Glazeroff to its purer form.

Christmas appealed to him. Each year he adorned a tree with blown-glass ornaments. He appreciated lovely things, and over the years he collected more and more of them. He well recalled the cheap suits he'd worn when he was younger, the slip-covered furniture in his parents' house and the greasy potato latkes his mother fried for Hanukkah. In fact, he remembered these things with a certain nostalgia. Nevertheless, as soon as he could afford fine clothes and food and more elegant traditions, he availed himself of them. It was, of course, his wife, Ann, raised Episcopalian, who read books about Jewish history. It was she who lit a little silver menorah that Saturday night for the Christmas party. Nine slender candles were melting fast among the greens and pinecones on the dessert table. She lit the menorah every year because she felt it was important for the children.

The children were scarcely that anymore. There were three daughters. Louisa, who was twenty-four, and refused to go to medical school. Charlotte, a sophomore at Harvard, who wouldn't be a doctor either. And then there was the little one, Kate. She had come home from the John Parrish Hill Academy for winter break, only to disappear into her room with her books.

Even after the party had begun, Kate was upstairs reading John Donne's *Devotions upon Emergent Occasions*. With the kind of feverish, imaginative sympathy that won her the English award each year, she had begun living and breathing less and less like a fifteen-year-old girl and more like a Protestant divine.

Glassy-eyed, she read Donne's account of the illness that brought him close to death. She lay with her head propped up on pillows and imagined herself John Donne in bed, his illness overtaking her, swamping her like a flood covering her body, drowning her, as she read each section: "'*Medicusque vocatur*. The physician is sent for'. . . . '*Metuit*. He is afraid.'" She read the words aloud, like one obsessed—but this was practical as well. She was memorizing Donne's Fourth Meditation for the Southern New England Speech and Debate Festival.

Her mother appeared in the doorway several times and told her to change and come downstairs. When Kate finally threw on a red plaid wool dress and wandered down, the house was hot and made her strangely itchy. The crimson walls in the library seemed too bright, the caterers' silver platters too shiny. The dining table was covered with an array of pfeffernuesse, gingersnaps, madeleines, miniature napoleons, and bite-size chocolate mousses in sweating chocolate shells.

Her father's old doctor friends wore black and navy. Wiry, white-haired Dr. Hoffbauer, with his narrow blue eyes, and fat Dr. Krieger from South Africa, and bald Dr. Bier all shook Kate's hand and examined her, and said she'd grown, as if this were an important clinical observation and not a cliché. Her mother's colleagues wore purple and houndstooth, and teal knits and gold buttons, and they smiled at her and complained among themselves about "the administration," and they smoked. At a slight distance, clutching their drinks, stood the small contingent from her father's lab. They huddled together for mutual protection, the women spindly in high heels, the men trussed up in crimson neckties. Only one postdoc had wandered off.

He was clearly a lab rat, although she couldn't quite place him. He was tall and jittery, his dirty-blond hair too long, his suit jacket too short in the arms. Still, he had an air of nobility about him as he leaned against the mantel in the library. He had dark, disillusioned eyes, and fine features scuffed with the beginnings of a beard, as if he were a prince in disguise.

"Are you new?" Kate asked politely.

"No," he said, flustered. He hadn't noticed her before. "Are you?"

"Not really." She liked him for not figuring out who she was.

He scanned her face, her ash brown hair and bemused blue eyes. Suddenly he understood she was Glass's youngest daughter. "Oh," he said miserably.

"Yeah, I'm Kate," she said.

"You've grown," he said, defending himself.

She drew herself up, self-conscious, annoyed. "So I hear."

"That's why I didn't recognize you."

"Well, we're even." She relented. "I didn't remember you either."

"I've been at the lab almost three years."

"That's nothing," Kate told him. "Some of you guys have been coming here half my life."

"Hmm." He smiled fleetingly at his shoes. "I doubt I'll last that long."

"Why?" Kate asked. "Are you not producing?"

Nervously, but with a glint of humor, Cliff's dark eyes darted over her, and Kate felt flustered, herself, to be looked at. "How old are you?" he asked her.

"How old are you?"

"Thirty," he said.

"Are you a Mud-Phud?"

"Just a PhD," he said. "I was at MIT before this."

"So you must really like research."

"Oh, yeah," he said. "I really like research. I really, really do."

She stared at him. She would have died rather than ask, but "really, really"? Was that irony? Or was he serious? He looked unhappy enough, standing there all alone. "It'll get better," Kate said earnestly.

He shrugged.

"You know," she told him, "when John Donne was thirty, he was imprisoned."

In the dining room, Kate's mother was helping along the conversation here, urging miniature mince pies there. Ann Glass was an associate professor at Boston College and had published a book on George Eliot. Still, she tended everything in the house. She shepherded the party along, consulting with the caterer, introducing Marion's husband, Jacob, to a linguist she thought he might find interesting. She thought of the guests even when Sandy forgot them and talked shop in the bay window of the living room.

He was debating some point with Marion, and his blue eyes sparkled as his hands sliced the air. Ann's husband was not a handsome man. His features were coarse, his mouth wide, his forehead the more prominent because he had so little hair left. His nose began well, but drooped at the end. His cheeks were red with rosacea. With Sandy, however, the rules of attraction did not apply. He had a quality that went much farther than youth or beauty—an irresistible liveliness that seemed to override cynicism and doubt, a self-confidence occasionally unbearable, but in many cases deeply reassuring. Had he not enjoyed the benefit of a medical education, it's doubtless Sandy would have been an extraordinary salesman like his father, Irving. Shoes, hardware, large appliances, and Israel bonds would have flown like doves from his hands. As it happened, Sandy's sparkling savoir faire made him a stellar oncologist. He radiated hope to every patient. Instead of death, he dwelt on baseball games and the Boston Marathon. He asked terminally ill investment bankers about the stock market; joked that they should give him tips. He focused on the day-to-day, never on the eternal, and his patients loved him for it. He wasn't going to give up on them and turn spiritual. He was an old-fashioned doctor, fighting tooth and nail against disease. Patients came to him from all over the world. Tycoons and Saudi princes, even other doctors. His overworked residents called him a VIP-ologist, and there was some truth to this. Still, no one could deny his gifts. No one played the end game against cancer as Sandy did. He set himself squarely against every cancerous cell, and so inspired his patients into battle that, magically, even the most sophisticated believed that he could never fail them. Their worry was that in dying they might fail him.

Naturally, Sandy's colleagues hated him, yet he had come to thrive on the brine of their dislike. At forty-nine, Sandy didn't just endure, he adored his job. His ambition was not corrosive, but creative, a by-product of his buoyant spirit. Egotist, optimist, Sandy was a force of nature, and Ann resented but also loved him for it. She shook her head and smiled at her husband holding forth, wineglass in hand, his scant gray hair bristling with a kind of static energy.

"We'll have to scrape something together," he told Marion.

"We don't have the results," she replied.

"Well, we'll just have to find them, won't we?" Sandy said.

"I've come to think," Marion said, "it's more a question of which results find us."

"Passivity is not the answer," Sandy snapped.

Marion looked at him reproachfully. She knew as well as he that their old grant from the National Institutes of Health was ending, that last year's research gambit had failed, and that they desperately needed funding. She knew they had to pull together a resoundingly good grant proposal for NIH by April first or contemplate folding. The Philpott Institute was governed by strict Darwinian principles. Investigators broke even or went bankrupt, losing staff and space and equipment to their rivals. Peter Hawking, the institute's director, was saddened when his researchers failed, but, preferring to dwell on happier laboratories, he averted his eyes from their distress. Lab directors without funding had little recourse; they took desperate measures: they switched fields, or retired, or sometimes left science altogether. Marion knew her position was precarious, but she took it stoically. Unlike her research partner, she was a staunch pessimist. Armed with the constant expectation of setbacks and disasters, she took catastrophe in stride.

"We're going to have to make a fresh start." Sandy's voice was low. "And the first thing we should work on is replacing Cliff."

"Sandy!" whispered Marion, drawing closer. "First of all, he's fully funded through June . . ."

"Then in June, he's leaving. If he can't get with the program, I want someone else."

"You can't just boot him out." Marion bristled at Sandy's authoritarian approach, but as a clinician, Sandy came from a world where those who were younger or less experienced did exactly as they were told, or faced the consequences.

"Watch me," Sandy said.

"If he wants to stick it out, then I think we should reassess the situation six months from now . . ."

"Are you actually defending him?" Sandy asked.

"I hired him," she pointed out. She did feel responsible for Cliff. Three years ago he'd been a hot prospect from MIT. His professors had raved about his technical ability, his insight, his gift for seeking out and cracking intractable problems. Max Oppenheimer declared Cliff the brightest student he had ever seen. And Marion had known Oppenheimer for twenty years and never heard him speak that way. She had not just hired Cliff, she'd insisted to Sandy that he would be a key player, a star in the making. Together they had welcomed Cliff with open arms. And then? Perhaps their expectations had been too much for him to bear. Tacitly, she and Sandy had taught Cliff to be unrealistic. "He's talented," she said.

"So what?"

They both knew that in the end, talent hardly mattered if you couldn't get results. Lots of people were talented. Talent and intelligence, not to mention tireless hard work, got lab scientists through the door, but—this was the dirty secret—you needed luck. You might be prepared and bright and diligent, and fail and fail and fail. The gene you sought to isolate, the phenomenon you thought significant, could still elude you; the trend and significant pattern of disease could devolve into an endless hell of ambiguities.

"I still think he has potential," Marion pressed.

"Potential for what?"

She said nothing. Sandy was probably right. Still, she would not simply cut Cliff loose. She knew what it was like to struggle. At the Philpott she had fought for her scientific life, foraged and competed for every last piece of equipment in her lab. After years of ceaseless competition, she'd grown thin and patient, critical of herself and others. Anyone who worked for Marion tensed at her glance and dreaded her questions—never rhetorical, never dramatic, but quietly devastating in their acuity. With one pointed query she could lift the paint off the best ideas to reveal the rotting suppositions underneath.

"You know he has to go," Sandy said.

Still, she frowned and ever so slightly shook her head.

Marion had been a lithe young scientist once, a beautiful, impulsive girl who earned a PhD at twenty-five and imagined Harvard would hire her just for her elegant work in crystallography. She had been quick to smile, joyous in her facility as carbon structures opened up to her, each in turn, lovely and elliptical. The scientific world had seemed to her then translucent, sparkling, orderly as the Peabody Museum's collection of glass flowers. But there was no job for her at Harvard. A sly postdoc named Arthur Ginsburg got a position there instead, and Marion almost came to believe what others said of her: that her papers were repetitive, descriptive, and nothing more. She scrambled to find a place for herself and the means to carry on her work, and when she ended up at the Philpott Institute, she came as a pauper and had to switch fields. She knew the misery of starting over.

"'It is too little to call Man a little World,'" Kate recited in the library. Cliff sat in a brown leather chair and Kate perched on the matching brass-studded ottoman. "'Except God, Man is a diminutive to nothing. Man consistes of more parts—'"

"'More pieces,'" corrected Cliff. Kate had brought down Donne's *Devotions* so he could check her.

"'Man consists of more pieces . . .'"

"Right."

"'And if those pieces were extended, and stretched out in Man, as they are in the world, Man would be the gyant, and the Worlde the

Dwarfe, the World but the Map, and the Man the World.'" She stopped for a moment, and Cliff thought she'd forgotten her lines again, but she shook her head, interjecting, "He makes man a microcosm of the earth, and then he just explodes the metaphor! Because man is more complex than the world, more subtle, and more . . . vast." Kate beamed for a moment, radiant, pedantic. She was herself a secret poet, essayist, dedicated humanist—her mother's child.

"Hmm." Cliff stared at the open page before him. Truth be told, until now, he hadn't heard of John Donne. He hadn't learned much about seventeenth-century poets during his years of chemistry and biology and graduate school. It occurred to him now that he'd spent his whole adult life in a prison workshop. Years and years of manual labor went by. New results filtered through only on the rarest occasions, and always to other people. Miracles didn't happen, but Cliff and his friends kept on working. Like scientific sharecroppers, they slaved all day. They were too highly trained to stop. Overeducated for other work, they kept repeating their experiments. They kept trying to live on their seventeen-thousand-dollar salaries. There was not much poetry in that, or if there was, Cliff had certainly not been privileged to see it.

"Kate, what are you doing?"

"Are you reciting poems to the guests again?"

Kate's older sisters had come to rescue Cliff. They burst into the library laughing, impudently underdressed in jeans. The young women were like Ann, tall and auburn-haired, their arms elegantly slender, their complexions fair. They looked nothing like Sandy, but they possessed something of his frenetic energy and self-confidence. They laughed because they knew that when they whirled into the room they changed the weather; they were the magician's daughters.

"It's not poetry," Kate said, "and he asked."

"Be honest, did you really ask her to recite for you?" inquired Louisa.

"I did," said Cliff. "And I like it."

"Oh, really!" Louisa pulled up a straight-back chair and sat down on it backward, long legs straddling the seat. "It must be good stuff, then."

"What is it? Let me see." Laughing, Charlotte leaned over to read the title of the book in Cliff's hands.

"Don't tease her." Louisa was protective, gentle-hearted, though frighteningly accomplished.

Cliff ignored all this and turned to Kate with such warmth and pleasure she nearly blushed. "Where were you?" He turned back to the *Devotions*.

"'If all the Veines in our bodies, were extended to Rivers,'" Kate recited, "'and all the Sinewes, to Vaines of Mines, and all the Muscles, that lye upon one another, to Hilles, and all the Bones to Quarries of stones, and all the other pieces, to the proportion of those which correspond to them in the world, Aire would be too little for this Orbe of Man to move in . . .'"

Sipping his drink, Cliff kept listening, prompting Kate when she forgot a word. Her sisters left, but he stayed on, letting his mind wander in Donne's ever-evolving conceits. Man was like a world, but so much greater, so much more complex. The world was plagued with caterpillars, serpents, and vipers. Man's diseases were like giants. Monsters. Through the library's great square doorway he could view the others standing in the dining room, feasting at the long table. Robin was playing her part, listening intently to Ann Glass. He could not see Marion or Sandy, but could easily imagine them somewhere in the house, plotting some punishment for him in the guise of a new research program. It was good to take refuge in the library with Kate. Cliff felt himself covered by metaphors there, safe, as if he were hidden behind old tapestries. "'And can the other world name so many venimous, so many consuming, so many monstrous creatures, as we can diseases . . . ?'" Kate read, and he smiled at her for bestowing her unexpected archaic self upon him, for reciting instead of forcing him to make conversation. He laughed softly at the words—really not a bad description of a postdoc's life: "'O miserable abundance, O beggarly riches!'"

3

THE GUARD at the institute barely looked up from his *Boston Globe* the next morning as Marion headed for the back stairs to the underground animal facility. She came in almost every Sunday to look in on the mice, her lab's tiny livestock.

On the Philpott's lowest level, she made her way through a labyrinth of white-tiled hallways cluttered with rolling carts and bins. There were bins of rumpled lab coats, which would go out Monday to the laundry service, and carts of clear plastic cages replete with smudged water bottles and soiled pine shavings, all stacked up like a thousand dirty dishes at the door of the equipment room. Lab techs would sterilize and return them, sparkling clean. This institute had never suffered sabotage from animal rights activists. Still, there were locks on every door. There was the unspoken sentiment that this work was safer here, under the earth.

At a bank of lockers in the hall, Marion donned a clean pale blue lab coat. All personnel had to wear them in the animal facility. She slipped aqua disposable paper booties over her shoes and a matching cap over her hair. Then, briskly, she made her way toward the numbered doors where the Philpott's mice were kept. Each door had a window tinted red. From the outside looking in, each holding area looked like a little room in hell, but the devilish red glow in Philpott's animal rooms was actually a precaution. The animals needed rest, and the red windows shielded them from the hall lights at night.

Marion was an attentive and compassionate investigator, almost fond of her small charges, proud and careful of them—not as if they had rights or souls, but as a craftsman might treat precious tools. She had worked with many strains of mice in her time and knew their particular traits. She knew the sleek albinos, their fine white hair and timid manner, their ruby eyes like the tiny birthstones in children's jewelry. She knew a particular strain of black mice, always agitated, jumping and flipping over constantly, like dark socks in a Laundromat dryer. Those animals knocked food pellets from their wire holders. Their fur was spiked and greasy with their rations, their manner mischievous. They looked like little punks. She knew a gray strain that fought, and others that wouldn't breed. She knew the strains that habitually ate their own pups—although all the mice ate their young to some extent. She had seen mice rip each other to pieces, and watched, as well, as three or four slept together, breathing delicately, in one soft mossy heap. These and others lived at the Philpott: some thin, some fat, some drug addicted, some healthy, some sick by design. She knew them all well, but these days she worked with mice the color of pink rubber erasers; they lacked a thymus gland, and because of this condition, they were hairless. They were called nude.

Nude mice lack a normal immune system. They cannot reject grafts of foreign tissue. Like quivering pink agar they would accept tissue from a lizard or a cat or even a patch of chicken skin complete with tiny feathers. Nude mice accept these xenografts and support the tissue as if it were their own. Marion's mice harbored human cancer cells. With her athymic mice, she could study tumors in vivo.

Nude mice were, in many ways, ideal vessels for Marion's experiments, but their great utility was also their weakness. They could not fight off contaminants as ordinary mice might, and so they were a target for disease. The Philpott maintained strict rules for the care of these animals. Their water and food, bottles and cages, were all sterilized. Food pellets for nudes had a soggy, cooked texture from the autoclave. Entering the athymic mouse room after handling other animals was strictly prohibited.

Peering through the red window in the door of the lab's animal room, she was pleased to see that Feng had come in before her. Each postdoc had lab duties, and Feng managed the colony record keeping.

He often came in on weekends, and, like her, he'd come to check up on each group of the lab's experimental mice.

His full name was Xiang Feng, but he went by Feng, which Marion only gradually realized was pronounced Fung. Feng himself had been too polite to correct her. He'd been born in Beijing, but had grown up in the north, where his professor parents had been reeducated to grow soybeans. Despite his father's transformation from molecular biologist to farmer, and his mother's parallel metamorphosis from historian to productive member of the proletariat, Feng had excelled in academic subjects and placed high enough on his national exams to earn admittance to Beijing University. In his graduate work he had excelled again, and after several years of research and teaching had petitioned successfully to come to the United States to train with Marion. He had arrived in Cambridge with a Pan Am flight bag, one suitcase, and a formidable arsenal of lab techniques.

Feng kept a punishing schedule. He chose his problems well, and he worked constantly. He seemed to live the life of a scientific ascetic—except that he was so funny. That was the odd thing about Feng. He was driven like few Marion had ever seen, but his manner was entirely bubbly. He wore glasses, but he also sported a mustache. A demon for accuracy, he kept meticulous records but downplayed the effort. He'd spent years beating his head against intractable problems, but this did not discourage him. He did more than any other postdoc in the lab, but he expected nothing. He worked with a kind of gallows humor to which the others could only aspire. Deliciously self-deprecating, he dismissed his own results as minor, or even accidental. "It's random luck," he'd say whenever he published an article or research note, and this, along with myriad other sayings of Feng's, had become a catchphrase in the lab. "Fungi," the other postdocs called them. To Marion's secret amusement, the researchers collected Fungi in their lab books. For the past six months or so the postdocs had been compiling a lexicon that included such classic definitions as:

> Successful grant proposal (idiom): "major disaster, long-term"
> Analyze (verb): "to flounder"
> Hypothesis (noun): "highly flawed thinking"
> Conference (noun): "cancer junket"

Government Appropriations for Cancer Research: GAC
   (acronym): "sick tax"
Breakthrough (noun): "artifact"

Feng kept his sense of humor, and he stayed calm. When progress stalled and it seemed to Marion the others wallowed in self-pity, Feng persevered.

He nodded to her as she opened the door, and together they faced the cages that filled the windowless white room. Five steel racks held between twenty and thirty cages each. Over one hundred cages, almost three hundred mice. A living library of the hairless creatures. And yet the room was almost silent. The animals had been bred for quiet, as they had been bred for so many other conveniences. Only once in a great while did the faintest squeak escape from any of the mice living there together.

"What did you find?" Marion asked Feng.

"We'll see." Feng opened his record book. Cage number, mouse number, weight, condition. Each was neatly marked in columns on the pale green and white page. Finding his place in the record, Feng took two of Cliff's cages from their rack and carried them to the high stainless steel worktable. Then Feng turned on the laminar flow hood, a mechanism that blew a constant stream of air over his work surface and sucked away contaminants. Under the hood, Feng picked up and turned the experimental mice one by one. Their skin rippled and wrinkled with every move. The creatures seemed nearly transparent under the examining light. Their organs showed lavender and purple through their thin skin, and the blood vessels in their ears were clearly visible, like the red veins in budding leaves. In some ways the animals acted like normal mice, nosing their food curiously, standing up on hind legs and cleaning their front paws—but without fur, the mice looked like wizened little men. They seemed fussy and careful. They strained to reach the edges of their cages when the lids were removed; they tried to chin themselves up over the side; but it never occurred to them to dash around wildly, spring into the air, and make a break for it, as an ordinary mouse would do. The nudes were rarefied creatures. Outside the animal facility, no field mouse would recognize them.

These animals were already quite sick. Tumors bulged grotesquely, as if the mice had swallowed marbles. By Marion's reckoning, most of the tumors were close to the institute's mandated one-centimeter limit. Cancer had deformed the animals entirely. Indeed, there was the first fatality, a small body lying in the corner of a cage. As Marion recorded the death, Feng sealed the dead mouse in a black plastic bag. He would put the corpse in the refrigerator that served as the animal facility's morgue.

As Feng examined the mice in one cage, Marion studied those in another. In silence Feng and Marion held each mouse gently, with gloved thumb and forefinger grasping the fold of skin behind the neck. Positioned on their backs, the mice flailed their legs helplessly and could not turn or bite while Feng and Marion measured their tumors with tiny calipers. Cliff had injected six groups of mice with breast cancer cells. Nine mice in each group. Fifty-four in all. After the tumors developed, he'd injected three groups with his virus, and set three groups aside for his control. Each experimental group had received a different genetic variant of the virus. The mice in two groups with the virus had already died, and those in the third group were close to death as well. Marion couldn't help tsking for a moment at the waste. She wasn't proud of sacrificing living creatures for the idle repetition of failed experiments.

"Marion," Feng said.

He rarely spoke while working, and she started, surprised to hear his voice.

"What is this?" He was turning a mouse slowly in his hand. "Is this mouse correct?"

"What do you mean?"

"Is it from the protocol?" Feng asked.

"I've already checked that. This is the correct mouse. This is number three hundred sixty-three," she said, pointing to the metal tag on the mouse's translucent ear.

"Then where is it?" Feng asked.

"Where is what?"

"The tumor," he said.

She took the mouse herself and turned and felt the wriggling body in her hands. Instinctively, the creature flexed its feet as Marion pal-

pated the first set of mammary glands. The tumor was barely percepti-
ble, scarcely protruding on the animal's neck.

"Now look at this one. Three-sixty-five." Feng lifted another
mouse from the cage. "This one last week had a tumor point five cen-
timeters in diameter. Where is it now?"

They began to examine all the mice, comparing tumor size with
the records in Feng's lab book. Nearly all had tumors as big as, or
slightly bigger than, they had been before. Three mice, however, had
tumors significantly smaller. How could this be? Somehow three tumors had actually shrunk.

Marion and Feng looked at each other. After repeated failure,
could one of Cliff's viral variants actually have some effect? What had
changed here? What had Cliff done? The variation of the virus was
R-7. Cliff had scrawled a note on the blue index card labeling this cage
of mice. But he'd never gotten R-7 to work effectively in live animals
before. Were these three mice significant? Or were they outliers of some
kind—tainted by some other condition? This was the difficulty with
animal research: so many different things could go wrong. Cancer cells
would not grow or grew too slowly, blood work was inconclusive, animals died of some extraneous illness. Despite all Marion's precautions,
there had been an outbreak in the colony years before. Only a few animals had died, but Marion had terminated all her experiments anyway.
"The mice were exposed to pathogens, and they're tainted," she'd announced at the lab meeting. "Obviously, we can't study cancer and
some other unknown infection as well. What would we be looking at?"

What were they looking at now? Probably nothing. And yet . . .
What were the chances that Cliff had actually happened onto something? If there was a real cause and effect, if R-7 actually reversed the
progress of cancer growth, then they must find out how. Marion was
not excited; she would never pin her hopes on one such observation,
but she could not let it pass either.

She knew Feng was making the same calculations she was. The
odds were against them. Still, there was the slight chance of some significance, that Cliff's technique might have had some effect on these
three mice. If that was the case, the ramifications could be huge. Holding a mouse on its back, Marion accidentally pinched the loose skin of

its neck. The mouse's eyes bulged, its mouth popped open, exposing sharp white teeth. The animal's pink face started into a tiny mask of surprise.

"I don't think there's anything here," Marion said.

"I doubt it," Feng agreed.

"We'll observe them, in any case," Marion said. "We'll watch to see if the cancer grows again, or if for some reason tumors on other mice decrease. We can see if anything more happens here."

"I don't think anything will," Feng said cheerfully. When it came to nonchalance and scientific pessimism, he outmatched even Marion. The difference was, Marion's pessimism had been earned, while Feng was a natural.

Marion arrived home to find Jacob playing speed chess at the kitchen table with their son, Aaron. Jacob pushed his knight forward and slapped down the button on his side of the time clock with his hand; Aaron countered with his bishop, then slapped the clock in turn. At fourteen, Aaron had his father's lanky body, messy brown hair, and craggy nose. He was a nationally ranked chess player in the under-eighteen category, but his father still beat him on occasion. Although Jacob no longer practiced seriously, he was a wily competitor.

Marion's husband had been that rarest of creatures, a child prodigy. Growing up in Cincinnati, Jacob spoke late, but his first word, according to family lore, was "delicious." He could read A. A. Milne to himself at the age of four, Dickens by six and a half. At seven, he made his concert debut, playing Mozart's second violin concerto with the local youth orchestra. At age nine he matriculated at the University of Cincinnati. He graduated with a degree in biology just before his bar mitzvah, and then stayed on for his doctorate. By the time he was seventeen he had left home for a postdoc with Franz Applebaum at Columbia. He arrived with glowing recommendations from all his professors, and three publications. Like an academic red carpet, his future seemed to unroll before him.

In Applebaum's lab, however, Jacob's apparently inexorable path toward scientific glory took a startling turn. Away from home, with only the minimal supervision for which Applebaum was famous, Jacob began, for the first time in his life, to reflect critically on the nature of his accomplishments. As he solved myriad minor problems in cell biology, and studied the scientific literature—as he watched Applebaum direct his lab, choosing investigative paths, deciding where to invest his time and experimental energy—Jacob identified in himself a fatal inability to generate new problems. He mastered techniques and processes, absorbed methods, systems, languages with amazing speed, but he could not derive systems of his own. With the tremendous clarity of his seventeen-year-old mind, Jacob recognized this deficiency. Applebaum gave him the run of his lab, and yet Jacob found himself incapable of devising his own investigative program. In short, Jacob realized that he was not creative.

This was the most important discovery of Jacob's life, and characteristically, he made the determination with ruthless accuracy. He had been groomed to think of himself as the next Pasteur—if not the next Heifetz. He had been raised by a science-mad rabbinical father and a pianist mother to understand that life's glory lay in molecular structures and medical research. Now he realized, for the first time, that he was not one of the chosen few; that he was probably incapable of anything more than incremental advances. He lacked the second sight to shape new paradigms and shake up the world with revolutionary propositions.

The discovery shocked and saddened him, and yet with the newfound understanding of his limitations, he also felt profound relief. Young as he was, Jacob had been exercising his mind since babyhood. And now, suddenly, he saw that he could stop. He could simply get a job, and read and play. He could abandon his prodigious expectations and begin to live.

His parents were baffled by this turn of events, and some of his Cincinnati professors were heartbroken, but Jacob did not waste much time pining for what might have been. He was busy now with growing up, and he had just fallen in love with Marion.

They'd met in Applebaum's lab when she arrived from Barnard to do her initial crystallography research. He was a postdoc, and she a freshman in college, but they were just the same age. Jacob saw in Marion everything he was not. He saw the way she pursued her work, taking her own direction in the lab. She was small, with curly brown hair and snapping black eyes, and she worked with a baggy lab coat thrown over her dress. The sleeves were too long on her, so her fingers just peeped out. Jacob had hardly noticed women before, but in his eighteenth year, when he gave up being a genius, he gave his heart to Marion, and more than that, he laid his formidable mind at her feet. When they were twenty he asked her to marry him. She was only a girl, but he believed she would make radical discoveries.

This was why Jacob dedicated himself to Marion. He was not trying to be a feminist, or to sacrifice himself. He did not particularly resent his teaching career at Tufts. He believed in Marion. He proofread every paper she wrote, and discussed every nuance of her work in the lab. Friends and colleagues thought him saintly and quite strange. Some felt secretly that he emasculated himself in his devotion to his wife's career. He had been a preternaturally gifted boy, and was now a highly unusual man. His mind was still agile, his reasoning frighteningly quick. He was a microbiology lecturer known for his clarity and his passion for the subject. He was famous, as well, for his dedication to those undergraduates who came to him for help. Patiently, during office hours, he tried to explain his course material, even while privately he wondered if some of his students had been mistakenly admitted to college, because they seemed to him mildly retarded. He was a happy man, for he had grown up. Indeed, he had grown out of himself, as many child prodigies fail to do. He was happy because he had discovered early, rather than late, that he would not be winning a Nobel Prize. And he had been granted an insight many of his scientific peers lacked—that when it came to Nobels, he himself did not need one. No, someday that distinction would belong to his wife.

"Is something wrong?" he asked Marion without looking up from the chessboard. Instead of joining them, she had been standing silently in the doorway of the kitchen. "What is it?"

"Something strange with the mice," she said.

"Cliff's?"

"Yes." She described to him what she and Feng had seen.

"Suddenly the virus is working?"

"Well, it's probably not."

"You'll have to test it out," Jacob said. "Then you'll see."

"Of course."

He nodded matter-of-factly, eyes on his queen.

"I don't know if we should tell Sandy yet," Marion said.

"Because he'll put out a press release that you've cured cancer."

"I didn't mean that . . ."

"Check," said Jacob. "Well, I think you're right not to tell him."

"That's the thing." Marion fretted. "I don't think it's right at all to keep information from him, but I'm worried . . ."

"He'll go off half-cocked," said Jacob.

"Your turn," said Aaron, extricating himself.

Unhappily, Marion came over to the table and set down her worn brown briefcase with the small gold initials MJM. The *J* was for Joyce—a fact that amused Sandy greatly. He'd teased, "Suspicious would be a better middle name for you. Or Doubtful."

"You know I'm right," Jacob said, frowning at the board.

She did know. Sandy went off half-cocked: that was the danger, but it was also entirely the good of him. You could set him off like a firecracker. She knew no one else so flammable. He was incautious. Imprudent. And yet Cliff, and Prithwish, and Robin—especially Robin—had been working so long without relief. They needed some change, or at least some news. They needed a little of Sandy's excitement.

"I think sometimes his timing . . ." Jacob began.

"He has an excellent sense of timing."

Jacob moved a piece and slapped his time clock. "He's a terrific publicist. He's a great fund-raiser. But I'm not talking about how well he speaks at conferences, or how he can charm money from NIH."

"Don't you think those are important qualities?"

"No question." Jacob's dark eyes darted over the chessboard. "I give him all the credit he deserves. Particularly when it comes to charming money. But those aren't scientific qualities, are they?"

"That's not entirely fair."

"Why not?"

Aaron looked up, curious. His parents kept no secrets from him, but they seemed at times to speak in private code, hiding their meaning in plain sight.

"Look," said Marion, "you know how he is."

"Yes, I know exactly how he is."

Distracted by their serious, almost sparring, voices, Aaron made a careless mistake.

"Aha!" His father pounced. "Check."

Aaron stopped eavesdropping instantly; now he had to scramble to find a way out again.

"You'll have to use your own judgment," Jacob told Marion.

He liked Sandy. He would say that to anybody. Sandy was a wonderful storyteller, and had a great ear for satire. He loved to argue—argued brilliantly about everything from global warming to Reagan's Star Wars defense system—and often took a contrarian's point of view, a great virtue in Jacob's mind. Sandy was musical, literate, and a mean Scrabble player. He was almost everything one could ask. And yet, Jacob did not entirely respect him.

He did not begrudge Marion her friendship. When Sandy had first approached Marion, Jacob had encouraged her to collaborate with him. He had immediately appreciated the money and publicity that the doctor would bring in. Nor did Jacob resent Marion's loyalty to Sandy, and her increasing closeness to him over the past ten years. Perhaps some husbands would be jealous, but Jacob found nothing interesting in the idea that jealousy is a natural counterpart to love, or that when men and women work together there inevitably are sexual undercurrents. These sentimental notions—reductive, clichéd, ingrained in the cultural fantasies of romance—were utterly foreign to him, and had no relevance, as far as Jacob saw, to anyone offscreen, or offstage, or outside the pages of books.

Jacob's reservations about Sandy were scientific, and thus, far more profound. When it came to science, Sandy's motives were not entirely pure. True, Sandy was excited by discovery. Captured by a research program, no one touted that program so well. But Sandy was not Marion. Sandy's work was not about giving of himself, but about building up himself, his ego, and his persona. Sandy lacked humility; he lacked respect for the complexity of the problems before him, and attacked research with evangelical zeal. Given any encouragement, Sandy would go off rampaging for bold new results, sometimes forgetting what might be small and diffident, and difficult to describe—the truth.

"I wouldn't tell him anything yet." Jacob couldn't help warning one last time.

"But I should," Marion concluded, in such a decided voice that Aaron looked up again.

"The less he knows, the better."

"That's not true," said Marion.

"It's mostly true."

"It's a *little* true," she conceded.

But now Jacob was back in the game, eyes sparkling with competitive fire. "Checkmate."

4

SANDY HAD a trick, honed from the earliest days of residency, of waking without an alarm clock. Right before he went to sleep, Sandy told himself what time he wanted to wake up. Then he closed his eyes and settled back onto his pillow. The next day, sometimes to the minute on the clock, Sandy's eyes would pop open. He loved to get up early. At five in the morning, he slipped from bed while Ann still slept, dressed in running clothes, and padded downstairs. Then off he ran. Up and over the hilly streets, breathing hard, watching for ice, he took his route past brick houses and treacherously steep driveways. He ran and ran, drinking in the cold air. This was his preparation for Monday clinic. Up earlier than anyone, fueled by morning energy, this was Sandy's secret time before he went to see his patients. He was girding himself with all his skill and cunning and humor. As he ran, he wrapped himself in his cloak of invincibility.

By the time he arrived at the hospital, he had showered and shaved, breakfasted and dressed, donned his dazzling white coat. Presidentially, then, Glass strode down the wide polished corridors while his residents briefed him on the crises of the day. Interns tried to keep up, while a medical student scampered here and there, pushing the wall buttons for the automatic doors so that Sandy could sweep along without breaking stride.

"Lucia Fiorelli is going home today," a tiny resident named Asha told Sandy.

"No she's not," Sandy said. "She needs her biopsy."

"She wants to be discharged," Asha said nervously.

"She's got something like fifteen family members here," another resident piped up.

"And they're very angry," said Asha.

Sandy looked at her quizzically.

"They are insisting she go home," Asha said, increasingly agitated.

Sandy snorted. "Where are they? The lounge?"

The relatives, arrayed on chairs, had a pallor Sandy recognized, a particular shade of gray that came of desperate fear and too many hours under sickening fluorescent lights. They'd been up all night.

Sandy saw this, but revealed nothing. He ambushed the family with smiles and handshakes all around. "Mr. Fiorelli! Mrs. Fiorelli! How are you?"

They had been crying. Their daughter was just twenty-one.

"And you're Lucia's aunt? Nice to meet you . . . You're Nana! I've heard about you."

His warmth threw them off guard; the family roused themselves from the peach upholstered chairs. Brothers, cousins—they all shook off sleep and bagel crumbs. Still, Lucia's father turned on Sandy. "I want my daughter home," he said. He'd been waiting all night to say his piece. "She's been poked and prodded. . . . She's suffering here. She's in pain from the procedures. She wants to go home, and she needs to go home."

"I understand, Mr. Fiorelli. I know exactly what you mean," Sandy murmured. "She needs to rest."

"That's right."

"She needs to live without needles. You know, there is nothing like a hospital to make you feel worse. You just come in the door and you feel ten times worse. And you can't get a decent meal here. I'll bet there is nothing Lucia needs more right now than some of Nana's good home cooking. . . ."

Behind his back, Sandy's residents cringed at the familiarity in his voice. In the hospital Sandy could walk from room to room and pull out language tailored for every ethnic or socioeconomic background. Like the magician's endless chain of knotted handkerchiefs, he could evoke Italian meatballs, baseball statistics, sailing stories, even sentimental childhood memories of the High Holidays. No one could Jew a patient like Sandy Glass.

"No one can take good care like Nana . . ."

The Fiorellis were already softening. They were angry, but they were also vulnerable: desperate to do something for Lucia; desperate as well, after their long vigil, for some human contact with a doctor—some normal words, a message from the everyday world.

"Let's talk about getting Lucia some of Nana's cooking," said Sandy. "Some pasta, some meatballs, some soup. Red bean soup. Minestrone. What does she like? What does she love?"

And the family laughed a little. They knew that Dr. Glass had changed the subject, shifting the issue from discharging Lucia to how they'd manage while she stayed. They didn't mind. Giving in seemed a fair trade for speaking about her as a person who still had likes and dislikes and would actually benefit from minestrone. Dr. Glass never spoke of Lucia as a patient, only as herself—their daughter and granddaughter. A young woman still very much alive.

The residents looked on in disbelief. They did not entirely understand the alchemy of authority, charm, and chutzpah that Glass employed. Clutching their empty notebooks, they followed him out of the lounge. There were few notes to take when Glass rounded in the hospital. He breezed through the corridors; never dwelt too long on patients' charts. He let his residents grapple with medications, doses, side effects—and delivering bad news. They hated him for the way he sent them in with test results—the tumors were back; the cancer had spread; the chemo was not working—while he breezed in later, after the storm. He was nothing if not smooth. The young doctors followed him down the hall in silence, still stunned by how quickly he'd won the Fiorellis over. This was Glass's magic, but unfortunately it was unteachable. As all residents who trained with Glass soon learned, his lessons were of the most ethereal kind.

He could not cure his patients. He rarely changed a prognosis in the long term. Perhaps, in the end, he would not save lives, but he always knew what tone to take.

"Look, we're all terminal," he told one breast cancer patient. "We're all predead."

"Time? What is time?" he opined to an elderly man, a professor

emeritus from MIT who demanded to know how much time he had
left. "Who knows how much time any of us has?" Sandy shrugged.
"Haven't the physicists been bending time for years? Isn't it true the
Hopi Indians think time is space? See, that's why I don't like the question. I could give you a number—but then you'd have to call me a liar
later on."

"Give me a ballpark," the professor growled at Sandy from his bed.

"That's my point," said Sandy. "Once you start talking about ball-
parks—there's no difference in life expectancy between you and anybody else. We're all in the same ballpark together."

Sandy conned his patients, but he also spoke the truth. He embraced the truth of mortality, along with the deep-held fallacy that you
and I are exceptions to the rule. He acknowledged that the idea of
death would be terrifying, if life itself were not so absorbing. He im-
plied that, moment to moment, even time in the hospital might bend
and stretch into something longer, better, happier. He demonstrated
this in the huge impact he made in just a few minutes with each patient on rounds. A direct look in the eye, a warm handshake—he always treated the deathly ill as if they were still among the living. This
above all: he never looked away as though his heart might break.

By noon, Sandy was powering out of the hospital and across BU
Bridge. He'd had a productive morning, given Asha and the rest their
marching orders. But now, driving into Cambridge, as the winter sun
was silvering the Charles, Sandy could only think about the lab and
Marion. She'd called and told him about Cliff's mice.

He parked his white Mercedes tenderly in the pocked and muddy
Philpott lot, and hurried up the front steps of the Victorian building, its
arches and turrets faced in ruddy stone. Could this be the day they'd
been waiting for? He looked for Marion in the office, but she wasn't
there. After years of slow progress and false starts, had they finally found
a better path?

He burst into the lab, which was gloriously lit with afternoon sun.
The arching tops of two great windows graced the space, along with part
of an inscription that had been painted in 1887: KEEP BACK THY SERVANT
ALSO. The building had once been the Cambridge Manual Training
School for boys, and it was full of such vermilion words, fragments of

scripture selected to inspire and at the same time chasten the vocational students, to raise and reform the spirit. Years later, however, as the Philpott subdivided each floor, and hanging ducts and light fixtures multiplied, the biblical inscriptions had been broken up as well, so that cryptic partial phases popped up in offices and passageways: WETH HIS, or THE GLORY OF GO. No one at the institute read the writing on the walls.

"Marion," Sandy said.

She looked up, startled, from the microscope. She hadn't expected him so early.

"Come on." He motioned her into the hall.

"What was that about?" Robin asked, after the two disappeared.

Feng shrugged, although he had a fairly good idea.

"He seemed so secretive. Didn't you think that was strange?"

"No," said Feng.

"Maybe he was looking for Cliff," Natalya said.

Cliff drifted in an hour later. Mechanically, he opened the door of the incubator, opened the second glass door, took out his petri dishes, studied his breast cancer cells under the microscope, their irregular clumps like clustered sesame seeds. He stared at each batch of cells, took his notes as usual. He did his time.

He sensed Feng standing at his shoulder, but Cliff did not look up from the microscope.

"Cliff," Feng said.

"Yeah."

"I came in yesterday. Marion and I came to look at your mice."

"Great."

"The ones injected with R-7 . . ." Feng said. "It looks like maybe something happened there."

"What was that?" Cliff asked.

"Maybe something is going on," said Feng.

If Cliff hadn't been so down and so detached, if he had not been cultivating a Zen calm, he might have recognized this statement for what it was. He might have copied Feng's words into his lab book as a classic Fungi:

"Maybe something is going on" = sudden, life-changing event.

* * *

"We've got some news," Glass began at the lab meeting that afternoon. The researchers sat at attention, galvanized by what they knew he was about to say. Feng had told them all about what he and Mendelssohn had seen. The postdocs had rushed down to see the mice themselves. They'd been talking about nothing else. Now Glass made it official. "There is a possibility we've got a result here, at last, with Cliff's virus and some small number of mice."

At last. Those were the words that struck Cliff. He felt the irony acutely. Sandy spoke as if he had been waiting patiently for months and months, watching and hoping for this day to come. The words were odd, and also sweet. Cliff swung his legs off the table in the third-floor conference room and sat up straight. The other postdocs' excitement brushed against him, as their pity had burned him days before. Cliff looked at Robin, and her eyes were filled with such fierce longing, he turned away in confusion.

The researchers were all staring: intent, admiring, jealous. Prithwish smiled broadly, but his good cheer was slightly forced. Feng sat composed and quiet. These were Cliff's siblings. They had been his peers here at the wood-grain table; they'd drunk bad coffee with him at these meetings. They had winced with him as Marion chided everyone for inadequate record keeping, or insisted each of them read a journal article and then present the results to the group, demonstrating the published work of other labs. They had all striven to ask the right questions, to look sharp at certain times and nonchalant at others. They were never closer than in commiseration. The longer their hours, the worse the odds of their success, the closer the postdocs had been. Empathically, the others had felt Cliff's embarrassment and hopelessness in their own hearts. Now his status was changing before their eyes, and their emotions became much more complex.

Clearly, R-7 had had a dramatic effect on three mice, and Sandy was enthralled. Marion kept putting her hand on his arm as he spoke, cautioning him, as if he were driving too fast, but Sandy was in his element, announcing a new set of trials and putting Cliff and Feng in charge. It was as if Sandy had never spoken a harsh word to Cliff about circling mindlessly on cold, dead trails. All that was forgotten. Cliff's unwillingness to cut his losses and move on to something new had now borne fruit.

Sandy did not hold grudges, nor did he necessarily remember when he hurt people. He was unreflective, even about the very recent past. History did not interest him. Negotiation, reciprocity, settling old scores bored him. Always he was grappling with the problem at hand, and for some time, the problem had been the need for major new funding. Now, suddenly, seizing on Marion and Feng's observations, Sandy found value in Cliff's work.

Marion had done some thinking about the genetic strains of mice that Cliff had used and how the genetic material in R-7 might have worked with these particular animals. But Sandy broke in to preview his plan of attack. They would seize on Cliff's slim results as the linchpin for the lab's new grant proposal. Prithwish and Robin would prepare new cells for analysis. "Meanwhile, Cliff and Feng will prepare four new groups of mice for injection." Sandy beamed at them all, and Cliff and Feng and Prithwish could not help beaming a bit back at him, reflecting a little of his radiant imagination.

It was up to Marion to douse them with disclaimers. "As you know," she said, "connections like this can be tenuous at best. Myriad other factors can come into play. This set of experiments could amount to nothing. And there is always an opportunity cost when we—"

"Yeah, yeah, yeah," Sandy interrupted. He met Marion's skeptical look with a nearly irresistible expression of warmth and mischief. He actually put his arm around her shoulders and gave her a hug and a shake. "Nothing ventured, nothing gained."

Sandy swept back to the office, and Marion stayed to clarify the methods and procedures the postdocs should follow. She spoke soberly, with characteristic gravity. Still, Cliff could not calm down enough to listen. His position had changed too radically. How strange the way neither Sandy nor Marion acknowledged the violence of the change. Did they expect him to shift from failure to success so easily? He might have been a man in Stalinist Russia, suddenly rehabilitated by mysterious powers from above: his work, for the moment, all the rage.

Naturally, Cliff felt Sandy and Marion were manipulating him. He understood that their whole attention was captured by the research potential of three tiny creatures whose tumors had receded. He knew he was being used, and still he didn't care. He had begun something with the mice, set events in motion that might lead to real results. He saw it in the other postdocs' eyes: tremendous discoveries befalling him. The field had opened up for him; the whole world was ringing in his ears.

All day he worked with the others, preparing cells for the new trials. He dashed from the cold room to the lab, then into the stockroom and across the hall. By evening, the others were swirling all around him and debating where to go to dinner, arguing about where to celebrate, all except for Robin, who was silent. In the midst of that bustle, he pulled Robin into the hall.

"Well?" he asked delightedly, and drew her close.

She reached around him and thrust her hands into his back pockets. "Congratulations," she whispered.

He knew how hard and how long she'd worked. He understood that she despaired of ever triumphing as he had that day. Still, he wished she would let herself celebrate, jump and dance down the empty corridor.

"Robin," he chided her. He wanted to tell her all this would happen to her, too, that her luck would turn as well. But he had no good arguments for this, and she had no reason to believe him. Such luck as his was far too rare.

"I hope it all works out," she said, looking up, and then, as if afraid to sound too stingy, she added, "I'm sure it will."

He bent down to kiss her, but she turned away slightly, and his lips brushed her ear as he whispered, "Please be happy for me."

Part II
Mice

1

THAT WINTER Cliff worked longer hours than anyone. Even Feng went home by eight or nine o'clock so he could eat dinner with Mei. Cliff would dash out to Store 24.

Ambition, long dormant, had awakened in him, and where he had been weak from lack of hope, now his appetite for science revived. Was Feng's observation significant? Cliff knew this was his question to address. These were his experiments, his years of preparation yielding a possible bonanza. This was the crucial moment. If he was lazy or lost focus, someone else would take up the charge and seize the credit. Now, in the darkest season of the year, he lived and breathed and dreamed about his new batch of three dozen hairless mice.

"Unfortunately," said Feng one January night, "I think this will all turn out to be an artifact, and the virus will have no effect."

Cliff looked up, hurt. He knew Feng always spoke that way, but the dark logic wounded him nonetheless.

The two of them were working side by side in the animal facility, injecting human cancer cells into the new mice. The work was tricky and tedious, and it was late. Cliff and Feng were both exhausted. They didn't use the laminar flow hood, because Marion wasn't around to see them. She would have been horrified, but they injected the mice on paper towels spread right on the stainless steel table. None of the postdocs really believed in Marion's extra precautions with the animals. Experience showed them the nudes were not nearly as fragile as she assumed. Peculiar as they appeared, the creatures were surprisingly hardy. In fact, Cliff had irradiated these mice the day before so that the cancer cells would have a better chance to thrive. Even when they were supposed to sicken and die, nude mice did not drop dead as easily as everyone supposed.

They were trying to work quickly. Feng had carried the cells downstairs in orange-capped tubes stuck into a plastic bucket full of ice. Seven tubes of cancerous cells, and two tubes of normal cells for the controls. To all the cells, Feng added a special gel that promoted tumor growth.

As Feng prepared the syringes, Cliff wadded up a paper towel, stuffed it in a mason jar, then poured in a capful of anesthetic from a brown bottle. Anesthesia ready, Cliff moved two cages from their rack to the tabletop. He removed the lid of the first, sloshing water from the animals' water bottle. Suddenly uncovered, the mice stood up on their hind legs and strained upward, noses swelling, bodies swaying. Cliff plucked up the first mouse by its tail and placed it in the mason jar. The tail kept popping out, so Cliff didn't screw the lid on all the way. The lid jiggled as the mouse tried to escape, but in a few seconds the little animal succumbed and slept. Cliff laid out the mouse on its belly, nose down, tail loose, utterly limp except for the ears, which fanned out, rigid and erect on top of the head.

Even now, after all these years, the mice sometimes spooked Cliff. The anesthetic was intense, but brief. Thirty seconds in the jar yielded just about thirty seconds' time for the injections. Occasionally an animal woke up, twitching. Startled, Cliff could misdirect his needle, poke all the way through the skin, or hit an organ. A big mouse might need a second dose of anesthetic, or even a third.

This animal lay still, however. Cliff took his syringe, and in three different places he inserted the needle just under the skin, gently depressed the plunger, and then drew back. The skin swelled and bubbled up where the cells and gel went in. In one place, as Cliff withdrew the needle, a drop of blood emerged. Just one drop, the size and color of the animal's own red eyes. Then it was over. Cliff restored the mouse to its cage and crushed corncob bedding. The three injections oozed like nasty insect bites, and the animal lay still for a few seconds, but after a few pokes with Cliff's gloved finger the mouse was up and about again, nosing for food.

"This stuff never works like it's supposed to," Feng said companionably.

For the first time, working with Feng, Cliff felt a superstitious chill come over him. "Hey, man, don't bet against me like that." He stuffed another mouse into the mason jar.

Puzzled, Feng turned to Cliff as he handed him a fresh syringe.

"It's bad luck to bet against people." Cliff was wrought up, or he would have remembered that Feng believed the opposite was true. "Anyway, this is partly your work too. You shouldn't bet against yourself."

"If this doesn't work," Feng said, "there will be more experiments."

"For you, there will be," said Cliff. "Not for me. For you, it doesn't really matter as much. Shit!" He realized he'd left the mouse in the jar. He rushed to unscrew the top and set the mouse down on the table. The animal lay still.

Cliff bent down over the tiny body. Almost imperceptibly, the mouse's rib cage expanded and contracted. It was breathing.

"Cliff," Feng chided, "you're talking like the unlucky one now. You shouldn't think that way."

"How am I supposed to think?" Cliff exploded. He poked and prodded the mouse's wrinkly skin. His needle slipped into the loose folds. "This has to work. It has to!"

It was childish, Cliff knew, to stand there and will experiments to work, throwing a tantrum and expecting results to come. The forces of disease arrayed themselves in the experimental mice and all the lab's glassware and machines, just as they did outside in the world. Shouting about it was as futile as standing outside and raging against a thunderstorm. There were no imperatives in research. Even for Marion, there was no experiment that would succeed because it ought. No line of inquiry had to be right just because it matched the investigator's intuition. Cliff knew all this, but he'd been up almost twenty-four hours, and he couldn't think straight.

He was frightened sometimes by the intensity of his emotions. There were days when he envisioned such success that he felt a kind of awe, as though the lab were already covered with clouds of glory. There were days when he could almost taste the future before him: the results, the publications, the prizes. But there were times, as well, when Cliff imagined all his good fortune evaporating; the remission of the mice nothing more than a freak occurrence; the idea of using R-7 only a beautiful dream. He swung sickeningly between delight and despair.

He had never felt this way about research before. He worked on tenterhooks, alert to the slightest changes in the mice, nervous about even discussing his experiments. He had seen this in other people, but never felt it fully himself: the propulsive energy of scientific questions, the relentless force of an investigation that might succeed. He began to forget about winter: the slush, the outside world; the city out there, cloaked in white. He stopped reading the newspaper or listening to the news. He wore the same blue jeans and brown sweater every single day. He paced restlessly, feverish with calculations, touchy, paranoid. He lost track of time, but he was obsessed with time. He was the victim of his changing moods, run ragged by his own imagination. Jubilant, confused. Lovesick.

He could not tell exactly when it happened—whether it began when he despaired, or when he'd been called back into favor—but this winter a fraying chord, his own perception of himself, had broken inside of him. It seemed to him now that all his previous work had given him nothing, and that he, in his thirty years, had given nothing to the world. This was his chance now, and with it came a weight of hope and expectation that he could hardly bear.

By early February tumors had begun to form on the mice in the experimental groups. Pale and smooth, the size of pimples, tiny bumps had emerged on the flanks of the animals. Five weeks after injection with the cancer cells, the tumors were bulging, swollen knobs of flesh unbalancing the nudes' pink bodies. Cliff recorded the tumor sizes in his lab notebook. Carefully, more carefully than he ever had before, he kept and copied his records. He still scrawled notes and numbers on scratch paper, but his lab book was sacrosanct. He lined up his figures in neat columns, printing every number with the utmost care. His previous experiments had been rehearsals; his trials and errors just dry runs. Now he checked his animals night and day. He placed his cages on certain shelves of the isolator rack and posted signs: DO NOT MOVE! These were his mice, his proprietary tumors swelling just under the skin of the busy, unknowing animals.

"Good. Good. Good," he whispered as he examined the tumor-burdened mice, lifting up the creatures by their tails.

He would buy a box of powdered donuts and a quart of chocolate milk, and that was dinner. The sudden blue sky between the trees, a glimpse of messy shrubs, the wafer-thin tombstones in the cemetery on Garden Street as they poked at rakish angles through the snow—that was all he had of daylight. A few hours' rest on the couch in the lounge or, sometimes, in his own tangled, stale sheets served as a night's sleep.

Waking up one morning, he was half surprised to find himself in Robin's apartment. She lay face down with her pillow over her head, her hair streaming over her bare back and shoulders.

"Robin," he whispered.

She stirred and sighed.

"Are you sleeping?"

"Yes, obviously I'm sleeping," she groused, even as she turned toward him. He closed his eyes again and wrapped his arms around her bare body. She was deliciously warm; he felt as though he were sinking underground, escaping chilly air, wind, and all the work on land. But such work! What work awaited him! He was injecting his mice that morning with R-7. The virus was prepared, the animals ready, their tumors developed. This was the day. He kicked off the blanket.

"You aren't really getting up."

"I have to hurry."

"Don't be ridiculous." She pulled him back down and curled up next to him with her head on his shoulder.

"I'm injecting today."

"Saving lives, huh?" Her voice was muffled.

"Yeah, saving mice, anyway."

She looked at him, sleepy and satirical. "Small lives."

"Small for now." He was entirely awake and eager, tense with the possibilities of the day's experiments, already begrudging himself the night's sleep.

"Today the mouse, tomorrow the world," she said.

"Are you making fun of me?"

"Just so you don't become a complete asshole," she explained.

"Prophylactic teasing?"

"Right. I have to inoculate you." She lifted her head and kissed him on the lips. "So stay."

He slipped out from under her. Absentmindedly, almost reminiscently, he touched her face.

"It's not even six." She sat up with the sheet covering her and pulled her knees up to her chin. "Why don't we have breakfast and go in together?"

"No, you don't understand . . ."

"Right, how could I?" she shot back, offended.

"I'm sorry. I'm sorry," he murmured, even as he pulled on his clothes. "Please, Robin." But, unspoken, the facts forced their way between them. He had results and she didn't. His experiments were like Christmas; every morning he had new questions to unwrap, but Robin had no new world to conquer.

"I'll see you soon?" he asked her.

"Just go," she said.

"Don't be that way."

"I'm not that way. I'm fine."

He hesitated. He understood, even as she pretended otherwise, that she was angry with him. Chasing his results, he had left her far behind, and she feared she would never catch up. He felt her watching him as he hunted for his old gray sweater, first one balled-up sock and then another. He knelt on the bed and kissed her good-bye, but she was no longer warm. "Let's go out tonight to the worst movie we can find," he said.

"You're working tonight," she reminded him.

"I'm not. I'm not," he said as he ran out the door. But he was working that night, and every night. "We'll make the time," he called. He just didn't know what else to say.

As soon as Feng got to the institute, he hurried down to the animal facility to meet Cliff.

"Are you ready to inject?" Feng asked.

Cliff looked up from the stainless steel table. He'd already replaced his cages on the rack, gathered his syringes, cleaned out the anesthetic jar. "I'm just packing up."

Feng stood for a moment in silence, astonished that Cliff had come in so early and worked so fast. The plan had been for Feng to help with these crucial injections, and especially with the record keeping. Marion liked Feng to keep an independent record of dates, procedures, and deaths in the colony. But Cliff had already recorded the injections in his own lab book; he'd noted the date of R-7 injections on the cage cards in black pen. As Cliff took a proprietary interest in his virus and his mice, he'd appropriated more and more of the record keeping as well. Marion had questioned this at the last lab meeting, but neither she nor Glass had directly told Cliff to ease up. No one chastised him for sprinting forward alone, now that there was a chance he was running in the right direction.

Still, as he threw his used syringes into the plastic biohazard containers, Cliff felt a twinge of guilt to see Feng standing there empty-handed. Cliff could have waited two hours and allowed Feng to inject the mice with him. Being a team player, or a friend, for that matter— these were things Cliff valued. Most days, he tried to show a certain generosity of spirit.

All around them, inside their orderly clear plastic isolators, the pink mice scurried. The injections had gone well. Cliff should have been able to share that with Feng. It was just that Cliff held possible results so tantalizing and so precious that he couldn't, even for an instant, open his hand.

Feng looked for a moment as though he might turn on his heel and go. Instead he walked over to the isolator racks and examined Cliff's mice. He scanned the rows of cages and observed a group on which he and Cliff had tested the potency of the cell line they planned to use in their experiments. Feng and Cliff had injected these mice with cancer cells several weeks before they began their official experiments, and so the tumors on these were much more advanced. These mice had already demonstrated that Cliff's cancer cells were alive and well, dividing viciously. Feng was surprised Cliff had let them linger.

"These guys from the test group," Feng said. "They should be sac'ed."

"Yeah, I'm planning to do that," said Cliff.

"I'll do it for you," Feng said.

"You don't have to." They all hated sacrificing the animals. Euthanizing the mice with CO_2 was clean and relatively easy, as was lethal injection. However, Marion disliked both these methods. She felt that gassing mice caused unnecessary suffering by prolonging death and making the animals frantic. She did not allow injections because the barbiturates used could infiltrate blood and tissue, and compromise later analysis. Instead, Marion hewed to the Philpott veterinarian's guidelines for decapitating experimental mice. The method was messy; but it was the quickest and therefore, she felt, most humane. Robin and Feng were fairly adept. Prithwish managed well with the nude mice, but couldn't bring himself to break the necks of mice with fur. "They are like real animals," he said. "I can't explain it." But Cliff had a real phobia. "I'll do it later," he told Feng.

"No, it's okay." Feng took out the cages and pulled on a pair of latex gloves. Bad form, he thought, to keep these mice around. On humans their tumors would have been unimaginable in scale, the size of cantaloupes.

Cliff's stomach lurched as Feng plucked the first mouse from its cage. Still, he was too proud and too possessive of his animals to leave the room.

Feng held the mouse just above the fine metal bars of the isolator's water bottle and food pellet holder. Instinctively, the mouse's feet opened and the creature clutched the bars with its pink toes. Feng took a pencil from his pocket and placed it on the back of the mouse's neck. Then, with a sharp pull, he tugged the animal's tail. In one clean jerk, the mouse's head snapped back against the pencil. Small, heavy, lifeless, the head fell forward, limp. Feng laid the body on a clean paper towel.

Swallowing, Cliff forced himself to look as Feng picked up the next mouse by the tail. For a moment, irrationally, frantically, Cliff felt that Feng was getting back at him, pointing up and preying on his weakness. At the same time, Cliff felt ashamed. He felt the reproach in Feng's actions—the suggestion that he had been careless with his animals, the aggressive humility in Feng's insistence on doing Cliff's dirty work.

The room was clean but close, stinking faintly of food pellets, urine, and turds—a smell like overripe granola. Already a small row of nudes lay on the counter. In death their heads had wilted; their delicate sense organs had collapsed. Where their necks were broken, right through their pink translucent skin, Cliff could see the dark blood pooling.

Mouth set, hands quick, Feng worked intently. Once, just as he was about to sacrifice a mouse, his glasses slipped a little down his nose. Still, he did not flinch or break his rhythm.

"I've been a selfish jerk," said Cliff.

Feng laid out the mouse's body and plucked the next one by the tail.

"Look, it's a collaboration," Cliff said. "We're working together, and you deserve a share in whatever comes out of this as much as me."

"As much as *I*," Feng corrected.

Cliff grinned hopefully. Feng loved to correct Cliff's English. Feng had studied grammar seriously in school, and knew all the parts of speech by their proper names.

The top of Feng's blue cap was all Cliff could see as Feng bent down again for the next animal.

"I'm sorry," Cliff said.

Feng had emptied two cages now of their inhabitants. He stuck the plastic lids back on, and placed the empty cages just outside the door to be picked up for autoclaving.

"I'm sorry," Cliff said again. "Okay?"

"Okay," Feng said calmly.

For a moment, Cliff was confused enough to wonder if he'd actually invented this whole conflict. Was Feng's silent anger just some figment of Cliff's imagination? His surge of energy on waking had now dissipated, and sleep, the black nothingness of sleep, attacked Cliff from every side.

"Why don't you go get some sleep?" Feng said, echoing Cliff's own thought.

He sighed with relief. "Thanks, Feng." He picked up his bucket of supplies and ice. "Listen," Cliff mumbled, contradicting what he'd said before about collaboration. "I owe you, and I promise I'll sac the next group myself."

2

Serene in the midst of the lunch rush at Harvest restaurant in Harvard Square, Sandy sat at his table with a glass of ice water. He was skimming *The New England Journal of Medicine* as Louisa rushed in, coat unbuttoned, backpack hanging off one shoulder. She was the rare mythical graduate student who enjoyed her work, took required courses cheerfully, and prepared for area exams by covering three-by-five cards with copious notes. Sandy's daughter loved to learn, and he couldn't have been prouder of her—except that she was studying the history of science! That entirely descriptive field. Why would anyone want to read about discoveries instead of making them? Why would anyone as capable as Louisa write about other people's inventions? Glass fervently hoped this doctoral program of hers was just a passing fancy.

"Where are the menus?" she asked.

"I already ordered."

"You ordered for me too?"

"You were late," he pointed out.

"Just five minutes!"

He grinned. "The early bird orders the entrée. You're having the roast breast of Bombay duck with bing cherries."

"What if I didn't want duck?"

"But I knew you would want it," he said.

She shook her head at him, but couldn't argue. He knew duck was her favorite.

"How are things?" He leaned forward in his chair.

"I know what I want to study," she said. "I've found the thing I want to do."

"Medicine!" he exclaimed.

"No. No, no. I've just come from Houghton Library. I finally got my visitor's card. I think this is it: this is what I want to do. I want to study Robert Hooke."

Sandy's mouth twisted slightly in distaste. "Robert Hooke."

"He's neglected," she said.

"Wonderful."

"He fought with Newton. He's probably the most neglected early modern biologist—"

"Great."

"Despite the fact that he invented the word *cell* and saw the first cells under a compound microscope. And his book, *Micrographia*—have you seen it, Dad?"

"No."

"It's unbelievable. I was sitting there in Houghton with the book and I could not believe this stuff. Look. I've got some photocopies under here." She rooted in the backpack full of papers and books under her chair. "Look at this one. The eye and head of a great drone fly. And this one, a blue fly." She thrust an inky illustration in front of her father, the exquisite black engraving of an insect enlarged to monstrous full-page size: its hairs, its folded wings, its hideous face.

"Not before lunch," Sandy said.

"I mean, what do you think it was like to see a fly under a microscope, magnified like this for the first time?" asked Louisa. She wanted to open her father's mind, to make him understand what it was like to see these tiny insects rise up from the pages of Hooke's book like great flying machines, to unfold Hooke's illustrations: the ant in all its armored glory. "Did you know this book was a huge best seller? Do you know how many copies were sold?"

"No," said Sandy.

"Neither do I—but I'm going to find out," Louisa said. "This is what I'm going to do for my dissertation. This book has everything I love: early instrumentation, natural history, art . . ."

"But have you been thinking about what we discussed?" Sandy asked.

"Daddy," she said. "You may have noticed by now—I don't want to be a doctor."

"A couple of hours a day," he said. "You run over to Central Square. They've got a Stanley Kaplan right there."

"But just listen," Louisa said, "I don't want to take the MCATs. What's the point in paying hundreds and hundreds of dollars to study for them?"

"I could pay," her father said sweetly.

"No."

"Taking the test doesn't mean you'll be a physician," he said. "All it means is you're keeping your options open. You'll get a sense of how you'd do; brush up on skills. Give your brain a little exercise . . ."

"Great, I'll be the only person taking the MCATs for fun," Louisa said.

"You'd ace them."

"But-I-don't-want-to-do-it," she intoned, tapping the table with her spoon.

He yielded then, holding up his hands. Still, he murmured, "But you should."

"Why?" she burst out in exasperation.

"Because you *can*," he said. And that was the truth. He thought she should go into medicine because she could, because she had everything necessary. Because she had him. He could take her into the Boston medical community and clear the way before her; he could escort her down the polished white halls, past the gatekeepers and competitors, all the while whispering in her ear—beware of this one, don't go anywhere near that one, smile here, say nothing there, watch your back. Louisa should choose medicine because it was the greatest profession; that went without saying. But his motivation was also simpler than that. He wanted her to become a doctor because it would be easy for her, while it had been hard for him.

"The cassoulet of lamb, sir?" said the waiter. "The duck for you?"

"Thank you," Sandy told the waiter, even as his daughter turned on him.

"Why do you think," Louisa said to Sandy, "that people should do things because they can? Whatever happened to doing things because you want to, or because you love them?"

"But the history of science?" Sandy groaned. Just a few years before, he'd sent his daughter off to Swarthmore, and of all the myriad fields she might have chosen, this subdiscipline of the humanities was the one that she brought home.

"You don't like it," Louisa taunted him, "because you don't understand it."

"It's details," Sandy said, shuffling Louisa's photocopies together and handing them back to her. "Arcane details. The blue fly. The feet of the fly. The tufted gnat. Christ."

"But you've got it backward," said Louisa. "I'm not talking about details. I'm talking about the big picture, the historical context of discovery, the nature of creativity, the changing cultural patterns of the way human beings see . . ."

So she'd get her master's degree in the history of science, Sandy mused. She'd finish up her little project and apply for medical school the year after. Robert Hooke was fine; he was eccentric; eccentricity was all the rage in med school applications. English majors, musicians, writers. Sandy had served his time on the committees. Harvard loved that kind of thing. She would be a doctor in the end. He knew it. Louisa was no soft-spoken library researcher. No math-fearing patsy. She was his son.

"You should see Hooke's silverfish."

Sandy raised his water glass, almost as if he were going to make a toast. But he was just gesturing to the waiter.

"Dad, you aren't listening," said Louisa.

"I am listening, and I'm utterly fascinated," he replied.

"You could at least pretend to be interested."

"I *was* pretending!" Sandy protested.

Sighing, she put down her fork and knife.

"Weasel," Sandy said, "you can see any of the stuff in this book with a child's microscope. You don't even need a good one."

"But that's not the point," she told him. "This was 1665! They were seeing this invisible world for the first time. It was like going to the moon! It was all new."

"So what? Now it's old. It's old news. Look, you're young, you're bright, you're full of energy. Look around you!" He waved his hands expansively at the tables nearby, the other diners laughing, talking, tucking into Quahog chowder. "The world is full of questions to be answered, diseases to investigate, not to mention—God forbid—money to be made. There are problems screaming to be solved. I just don't want to see you throw yourself away on this historical stuff. I'm telling you—you won't have a job, your twenties will be gone . . ."

"That sounds like your postdocs. That sounds like Cliff, not me," said Louisa.

"Oh, no, you've got it all wrong," Sandy said. "Cliff is going to have any job he wants. He's got the world on a plate. Cliff, more than anyone—he's got a tremendous future ahead of him."

The virus had begun to take effect. Two weeks after injection, Cliff was sure the tumors on several experimental mice were smaller. Three weeks after injection, Marion herself admitted a measurable difference in four mice. Six weeks after injection, Marion turned to Sandy in their office and said, "I want you to swear to me that you won't talk about this."

"Talk about what?" he asked airily.

"The experiments," she said.

"But which part do you want me to keep secret?" He wanted to hear her say the words aloud: we have results; R-7 is actually working in sixty percent of the mice. Marion was never going to get up and tap-dance on her desk, but Glass wanted the pleasure of hearing they might be right about something. He scooted his swivel chair over and directed all his persuasive thoughts at Marion: Say it; say it. Say that somehow in all the mess of experimental ambiguity we might have stumbled upon something true.

"You know what I'm talking about, and don't you dare," she said.

He scooted his chair back to his corner of the office and smiled. Marion was getting nervous, and this was a good sign. She came to the

lab at all hours and looked suspiciously at everyone who came in and
out—even the techs from the labs next door.

"I can't tell you how happy I am to hear you sound this defensive,"
Sandy said.

She answered wryly, "Yes, well, it's been such a long time since
we've had anything to defend."

Sandy himself was growing calmer by the minute. He had a good
temperament for grand discoveries and impending fame. The grant
proposal for NIH would be a knockout, an utter masterpiece. How
could he be sure of this? He'd already written it. Marion didn't know.
She would have been scandalized, but Sandy had drafted the whole
thing. He'd left out the numbers, of course, the actual tables and figures.
The data were still to come, but secretly, Sandy had crafted all the fili-
gree for the proposal. He'd extrapolated from Cliff's preliminary results,
and discussed their significance at length. The data would come; Marion would come around. Craftily, Sandy did his work in the meantime,
forecasting the future. Language was important when it came to winning large sums of money; style was essential. By April first, Sandy's
statements of purpose and declarations of intent would be polished to
such a sheen the reviewers would see themselves reflected there. He was
a poet of the NIH form.

This was entirely out of order. Marion would never hear of drafting grants prematurely in this way, but in Sandy's mind, there was
nothing wrong with it as long as he kept the process to himself—and
he kept his own counsel scrupulously. He wished he could tell Marion
the level of discretion of which he was capable. How he wished he
could show off his work to her so she might admire his writing. But he
knew better. He kept the draft close and quiet, like a lucky silver dollar
in his pocket.

"I swear to you I won't breathe a word," he promised, and at last
she sat back, satisfied, and took out her lunch.

They ate brown-bag lunches in the office almost every day he was
in town. No one dared even knock on the door. Staff, and even some
colleagues, tittered about these mysterious meetings, speculating that
they were trysts, the expressions of some strange love affair. Few scientists at the institute were too high-minded to snicker on occasion. But

Mendelssohn and Glass's own postdocs were closer to the truth when they imagined their mentors putting their heads together to pass judgment, to plan and parcel out work and punishment. Glass and Mendelssohn thought only of the lab. They never dreamed they might spend too much time together, or enjoy each other too much. Best of colleagues, they remained best of friends, creators of a rare world unto themselves: a peaceable kingdom where the lion might lie down with the leopard. (Marion was no lamb.)

3

MARCH TWENTY-FIRST, the first day of spring, more than half the mice in Cliff's experimental group were in remission. Daily, Cliff could see the bulbous tumors melt away. Once grotesque, the mice were now pink and sleek, their bodies unburdened of the humps they had carried. The change in Cliff was equally dramatic. His own anxiety had all but disappeared. His eyes were hopeful, his movements quick and confident, and while his hair and beard badly needed trimming, he seemed dashing in his scruffiness—devil-may-care and pirate-like.

Robin invited him to come home with her that night for dinner, but he begged off and prowled the halls with quarters for the vending machines, instead. Mendelssohn walked home and Glass drove off; the others unlocked their bikes, clipped on their lights, and rode away; but Cliff bought two packets of orange peanut butter crackers, a bottle of Veryfine apple juice, and a cellophane-wrapped brownie. He ate all this in minutes, washing down the gluey brownie and crumbly crackers with the cool, metallic juice. Then he sped downstairs to the animal facility. As he'd promised Feng, Cliff was going to sacrifice this group of mice alone.

In the animal holding room a blurry mix of classical music and commercials streamed from the black radio perched on top of the paper towel holder. A Mozart piano concerto followed an ad for Persian carpets. Cliff scarcely noticed as he took his cages from the rack. He'd been up so long, he was on his third wind now.

Turning toward the bench top with his hands full, he saw the door open. "Robin, what are you doing here?"

"What kind of question is that?"

"You went home."

"I came back," she said.

"Oh, okay. Good." He spun around gaily and held up his mice. "Do you want to look at these with me?"

She hesitated, as if trying to think of a polite reply. "Not really," she said at last.

"What's wrong?" Standing before him, she looked small and almost dejected—not wired, as he was, from lack of sleep, but worn out.

"I'm thinking about switching projects."

He took this in.

"It's been five years," she said. "And I've been patient."

"I know," he told her.

"And I've had some little leads, but nothing . . . nothing to write home about, and I know no one else thinks my stuff is going anywhere. I tried to ignore it before, but then I realized no one really thinks I'll make a go of it—not even you."

"Oh, Robin." He put his arms around her.

"Here's the thing," she told him, looking up into his eyes. "I want to work on my bone tumor idea. I've got a cell line, and I want to pursue it. But when I went to Marion, she said there wasn't time for me to start. I'm supposed to be a team player and pull the line for you."

"The bone tumors?" He looked dubious, and she broke from his embrace. "But you'd be starting from scratch."

"I know."

"Why don't you wait until we hear about the grant?"

"That's what they said."

"Well, they're right."

"Except I don't want to wait. I don't want to work on the grant."

"Why not, Robin? This one's going to get funded."

"But what if I don't want to work on your stuff?"

He shook his head at her, trying to understand. "Is this because I didn't want to work with you? Do you still think I looked down on your project?"

"I'm senior to you," she reminded him.

"Senior? What does that matter?"

"But it does . . ."

"What does that matter between us?"

"I've been here much longer." She pressed on. "Why do you assume I'm going to jump at the chance to do the scut work on your experiments?"

"I never asked you to do the scut work."

"You don't understand."

"Yes I do," he said, "because I was in your position last year when they wanted me to work with you."

"But that was different," she said.

"How was it different?" he burst out, exasperated.

"Because you could say no, but I can't. I'm expected to do what I'm told."

"The difference is that your experiments weren't working, and mine are," he told her as he put on his latex gloves. "They're asking you to work on R-7 for your own good."

"Hitch your wagon to a star," she said.

"Why don't you just listen to them?" he asked her. "Why do you have to make everything so hard?"

"You think all my ideas are unfeasible, and I shouldn't even try to start something new."

"Oh, please don't start telling me what I think."

"All right," she said slowly, and she turned to leave.

"Robin," he called as the door closed behind her.

She heard him call her name, and hovered a moment just outside the door. But having sought him once, poured out her heart, humbled herself, asking tacitly for his help, she was too proud to turn to him again. She paced the hall instead, half hating him, half longing for him to come out and comfort her.

Robin had been wary of him from the beginning, when he first arrived in the lab. He was eight years younger than she was, his doctorate newly minted, his degrees from Stanford and MIT much fancier than hers from the University of New Hampshire and Boston University. Robin's thesis advisor, John Uppington, was well respected, but Cliff's had been renowned, and his graduate work that much more lustrous.

Cliff's famous advisor and Stanford education reflected his privileged upper-middle-class background, while her less illustrious advisor and state school matched her workaday origins. Cliff never acknowledged the huge difference in their circumstances, but Robin was always conscious of the gap. And there was the class difference—right there.

He had come in as heir apparent to the lab. Once, her project had been of paramount importance, but when Cliff arrived, he came with a new set of plans. He'd usurped Robin's position, beating her out for money, space, time, attention. From the first day he'd had special treatment, and it infuriated her that he would not acknowledge that. She remembered how eager Marion and Sandy were to show him off at conferences. Just after he arrived, the whole lab had gone to a virology meeting at a run-down resort in Maine. Cliff made his debut with a talk in the plenary session. Robin, on the other hand, was relegated to the poster session in a badly lit ballroom.

At night the posters were taken down, and two hundred virologists assembled there for dinner and dancing. A swing band played, and Robin watched Sandy present Cliff to the senior scientists at other tables. Sandy was in high spirits. He swept back to their table with Cliff in tow.

"Behold the conquering hero," Prithwish said. He had to shout to be heard above the music.

Cliff sank into his chair next to Robin and confided, "Yeah, well, I haven't conquered anything yet."

"They liked your talk," Robin pointed out.

He shrugged. "It was all from my dissertation."

She stared at the dance floor and watched one lone couple, husband and wife virologists from Hopkins, trot and spin.

"Do you want to dance?" he asked.

"Yeah, right." She thought he was joking.

"I could show you how," he said.

"I know how," she retorted. She had learned for her father's wedding.

"Marion, it's up to us," Sandy announced. "We'll have to show these kids how it's done."

And to everyone's amazement, the two of them took the floor and began to swing. The postdocs couldn't stop laughing at the two of them—Sandy showing off, trying to spin Marion out wide, while she countered, holding herself upright through every sudden turn. They were all in hysterics by the time Cliff took Robin's hand and dragged her to the floor.

Then suddenly she was embarrassed. She felt herself blushing, heat spreading under her skin. The others were calling out to them from the table, and she would have run away if he hadn't been holding her. She closed her eyes for a second, trying to remember the steps. She listened to the music and counted silently to herself: one, two, one-two, and then plunged in, as she might jump into freezing water.

The pressure of his hand on her waist surprised her.

"What are you doing?" he asked her.

She looked up at him, confused.

"I'll lead," he said.

The hall was dimly lit at night, but the animal room glowed brightly, illuminated from within, and Robin saw Cliff clearly through the red-tinted window. He was blood red, wine red, maraschino red, the red of cell media, the red of stained slides. He'd found his way into the inner chamber of discovery.

But how had he gotten there? What secret door had he unlocked? He had known no more than she. Like Robin, he'd been flailing in the dark. He had suffered, confiding in her that he was paralyzed by the hopes Mendelssohn and Glass placed in him. He'd disarmed her, confessing that he hated the miracle worker role they wanted him to play.

"I wrote a good dissertation. That was all," he'd told her one night at Café Algiers. "They should put a stamp on everyone's dissertation that says 'Current results not necessarily indicative of future performance,' or something like that."

"Like the stock market."

"Yeah. They should call your dissertation a prospectus." He'd sighed. "That would be more accurate."

He'd bucked the starring role thrust upon him, and Robin commiserated with him. They'd suffered together in a sweet fellowship of failure. Secretly they'd mocked Sandy and Marion and called them S&M. They called Marion Madame Defarge for her grim, most ungrannylike way of knitting during her postdocs' presentations. They became such buddies that Aidan called Robin and Cliff the evil twins. But they weren't twins; they were nothing alike; and always Cliff was drawing closer, as close as she would let him.

His first year in the lab, he'd asked her out so many times, her refusals had become a running joke. He'd begun to say, "Okay, tell me the reasons."

"First of all," she'd begin, "I have a boyfriend. Second of all, I'm way too old for you." At that point she was thirty-five and he was twenty-seven. "Third of all, I don't want to."

"But we could change that," he'd say.

"And fourth," she'd remind him, "it would never work out."

But the next year her boyfriend got a plum job at CERN and she didn't follow him to Geneva. She wouldn't give up her experiments in Cambridge. She didn't want to move so far from her family, either. There was no question in her mind she had to stay. Still, she was lonely; she was sad Michel had not considered her position and her future when he decided to move away. Cliff had been stalwart then. He stopped teasing her and worked in silence, companionably at her side. He gave up asking her out and offered simple friendship instead.

And yet their friendship wasn't simple, but fraught, delicious. They worked together, ate together, slumped late in the lounge together. Rousing themselves, they'd race up the institute's back stairs, all the way from the animal facility to the third floor, taking the steps two at a time, careening around corners, until their lungs burst with the effort. Once, he took the lead, but doggedly she followed and overtook him when he stumbled, racing upward even as he called after her, "Wait, Robin! No fair." Adrenaline and giddy fear drove her onward as he scrambled to his feet and sprinted after her. She knew he would pull her down if he caught her. In play, in anger, in sheer frustration, he'd tackle her, so she ran even faster, barely escaping his grasp. And then it was over, all their aggression spent. She collapsed on the top step, and a moment later he sank down next to her. Gasping for air, they gazed back at the stairs as mountain climbers look back at the rocks and precipices they've overcome. Then, glancing over at him, she realized he'd hurt himself, somehow banged and scratched his knuckles, which had begun to bleed. It was strange, confusing, even then, but that was the moment she began to fall in love with him. Nothing was said; he wasn't looking at her. All she did was pick up his hand.

She'd known not to get involved with someone in the lab. She knew better. And his reputation had followed him from MIT. He'd cut a wide swath there in the biology department. He'd been, and still was, a terrible flirt. She'd reminded herself that he was too young for her, armed herself with the hard truth that he cared about her but still wanted to play. She'd always known he'd break her heart and now he had, but not in the way she'd expected. He'd crushed her with his success.

She knew it was irrational, but she could not help looking on his good fortune as a kind of betrayal—as if he'd only pretended to struggle, and slummed with her, affecting nonchalance. Now he'd revealed himself as someone entirely different, and she was shocked by the change in him. She had always been the serious one, the dedicated one; she knew she had always cared for science more. She tried not to begrudge his swift ascent. She strove to understand and even take some pleasure in his brilliance, to transform her mixed feelings into admiration.

Unguarded, oblivious, Cliff stood, examining his mice, holding them up by the tail, each in turn. He had results. She saw that clearly through the tinted window. Those were results he held there by the tail.

He had an almost dazed smile on his face, a smile of utter, innocent joy. She turned away. She'd seen that look before, a gaze as familiar as his tongue, his hands, his fingertips—the realization that he'd finally gotten what he'd wanted.

Cliff saw nothing but his mice. Some were blind now from the radiation he'd used to make them more susceptible to the cancer cells. No glint showed between the folds of pink skin where their ruby eyes had been. Only with careful inspection under the examining light could Cliff even detect the blinded eyes, cloudy white, like seed pearls in their sockets. Apart from this, the six mice affected by the virus were beautiful—active, healthy, their skin unbroken, perfect. Eleven of the twenty mice injected with the virus were still tumor-ridden on their flanks and necks. But these six seemed as good as new.

The evening concert on the radio had begun. The dreamy sounds of Satie. He would have to break their necks, of course, and yet these six mice were absolutely well. He hated the thought of breaking the bodies now so wonderfully cured. He had healed these animals. First he'd brought them close to death, and now he'd brought them back, and he could not wrench them apart that way. An overwhelming, woozy desire came over him to see the mice intact.

He took just one mouse and put it in the clear plastic container that served as the CO_2 chamber. A simple hose fed into the isolator from a spigot on the wall. Cliff depressed the lever and CO_2 filled the sealed chamber. The mouse thrashed against the walls. Bred for timidity, the little creature still fought death; the animal was alive, and it wanted to live. But the thrashing soon ended. The mouse seemed to swell as it expired, growing heavier even as it struggled, until, weighted down, life and color drained. The animal lay still, like a gray mouse statue on the bottom of the cage.

Cliff carried the body gently in his gloved hand to the dissecting room. He turned on the examining light and placed the mouse belly-up on the thick polystyrene dissecting block with its disposable pad. After a hunt for the good instruments—which, as Marion always complained, no one ever put away in the right place—Cliff perched on a stool and went to work. He took four pins and pinned the mouse down, one pin through each paw. The mouse was stretched out now in death, its limbs taut, ears rigid, its two front teeth exposed, fierce in rigor mortis. With tweezers Cliff plucked up the loose pink skin covering the mouse's abdomen, and then with small sharp scissors he snipped one vertical and four horizontal incisions, creating two neat rectangular flaps of skin to open and fold back. Cliff spilled no blood doing this. He had no broken neck to worry about, and he was careful not to snip a major blood vessel. He looked, instead, into a clean, inviolate body. Here was the soft maroon heart, the size of a bean. Here the slippery liver, deep purple, its four flat lobes fanning out enormously as Cliff picked them up with his tweezers. Here the lungs. The kidneys, just the size of lentils. Here were the intestines, curled intricately together. Once Cliff teased them out of the body, he'd never get them all back in again, packed as they had been.

As he might throw back a pair of shutters, Cliff peeled open the flaps of skin and began to pin them to his dissecting pad. Red blood vessels threaded the pink translucent skin, the vessels clustering at the mouse's five pairs of mammary glands. Cliff picked at the skin with his tweezers and exposed each gland, and each gland in turn was normal size, the pattern of the blood vessels normal and undisturbed. There were no tumors visible inside, underneath the skin. Cliff's heart began to beat faster. Over and over, he traced the faint red lines of the mouse's blood vessels, the map of the animal's body, the hairsbreadth rivers that extended from each mammary gland throughout the skin. Over and over he looked, and each time he made the discovery again: his virus worked on cancer cells. He had never seen anything more beautiful or more important than that mouse before him on the table. He had never felt so solemn or so full of joy. It occurred to him that this was the happiest moment in his life—or would have been, if he were fully awake. He had been up since six that morning, and though his hands were steady, sleepiness broke against him in little waves, unbalancing him so that he had to lean against the table. Words bubbled up inside of him, but did not form coherent thoughts. *Mammary, mammary. Blood vessels. Veins.* A phrase kept running through his mind. He couldn't think where it came from: "If all our veins extended . . . If all our veins were extended . . ." The threadlike blood vessels did extend in Cliff's imagination. They seemed to spread and extend into infinite patterns and possibilities, aligning and realigning themselves against cancer. Against death. All his hours in the lab, working with the virus. All the care and ambiguity and blood and shit involved with tumor models in live mice—all that seemed like nothing now as he looked at the normal, healthy corpse before him. Here was the way forward. Here was the human body writ small.

4

Marion had expected Sandy to join her for lunch, but he did not come in at noon, or even by twelve fifteen. Assuming his flight home from Florida was late, she opened her desk drawer and took out her blueberry yogurt, green apple, and bag of carrot sticks. She nibbled the carrots as she trimmed and tweaked the language in the NIH grant proposal to be sent the next day. There was some rhetoric of Sandy's in the introduction. She struck it out, nixing "dramatic results" and "astonishing remission." *Numbers have to speak for themselves,* she wrote in the margin. Sandy had remonstrated with her to stop editing before he left, but she kept on anyway. By the time he burst into the office, she'd slashed his beloved introduction to ribbons.

His flight had not been delayed. He'd come in the night before, slept a few hours, and gone jogging, then rounded at the hospital, talked to a priest who had been admitted overnight, and now, at almost one in the afternoon, without bothering to say hello, Sandy pulled his swivel chair over to Marion's desk and took out his sandwich from its brown paper bag.

"Listen," he began.

She made a face at him. "Tuna fish?"

He glanced down at his sandwich. Marion hated the smell. He shrugged apologetically. If he made his own lunches he would have remembered not to pack tuna.

"Marion," Sandy said, "this is the time to jump on our results."

"What do you mean, jump on them? Aren't we submitting this proposal?" She proffered the draft, ignoring his look of horror as he found his work, even at this late date, covered with red ink.

"We need to announce the results." He swiped the proposal and red pen right out of her hands. "Get Hawking to announce them. The word is getting out."

In the persnickety way he knew so well, she stirred her yogurt with a plastic spoon. "I think you're exaggerating," she said.

"Popper was talking about the virus in Orlando," said Sandy.

She looked startled for just a moment; then her eyes narrowed. "He was talking about it because you were."

"Listen, he brought it up. He confronted me right after the plenary session."

This irritated her, as he knew it would. "How would he know?"

"It's been three weeks—"

"Two," she said.

"Two weeks we've been sitting on these results. We're sending in the grant proposal. The word seeps out. Now is the time, Marion. Either we put out a press release or someone else will."

"It's premature," she said. "We need time to prepare the journal article."

Sandy leaned in, resting his elbows on Marion's desk. "We can wait until we've dotted every *i* and crossed each *t*. We can wait until we reproduce it all and submit it to *Nature*. We can make sure every research note coming from the lab is of archival quality. Or we can seize the moment now. We can announce results that are still preliminary."

"Results that may be incorrect," said Marion.

"Right, we can risk that they're incorrect and stake our claim before someone else does. Before Popper does at UT, or before Yamashita steals our idea. Do you know how much money they have? Do you know how quickly they can run their tests?"

"The grant proposal will date our work and establish our priority," said Marion.

"But it's not enough," Sandy burst out. "We can't afford to wait six months for the review. In the meantime, everyone and his brother is going to try this."

"I don't put out press releases for unfinished work," Marion said.

"No, of course not," Sandy retorted. "You'd rather get scooped."

"We won't be."

"We will. We will! And you know why? Because it's easy."

"You think it's easy to reproduce these experiments? Ask Cliff. Ask Robin."

"No, it's not easy work. That's not the point. Throw enough bodies at the problem and you can tackle that. Our work is reproducible because the idea is simple—once you think of it. Because anyone who hears of it will have to try it. And I'll be damned if I stand by and let you sit on these results, preliminary though they may be."

"Sandy!" She sat up straight behind her desk, and placed her yogurt down before her. He knew better than to press her further.

He let the subject go, but he did not give up. He had collaborated with Marion for ten years. He'd studied her closely, with the same keen look she employed so effectively in her own research, and he knew her heart beat faster when she heard that other labs might copy her techniques. He understood that, despite all pretense and patient labor, Marion was a competitive creature. She was after more than modest gains. She wanted major breakthroughs and serious money, more staff and better equipment. She wanted to conduct a research program that matched and then outmatched the big boys at Dana-Farber and at Harvard, otherwise she would never have chosen to work with him. She had not chosen him as her partner for his charm or lab technique. He understood that. All those years working on her own, she had not pounded the pavement or sought out collaborators, and she had been the poorer for it. She'd not played the money game with NIH or understood the politics at the National Cancer Institute. But she'd found in Sandy the one quality she lacked: the chutzpah to press forward and sell her work. He knew, even as he needled her about capitalizing on their preliminary results, that she was, deep down, susceptible to needling. He understood what Marion herself could never admit. She wanted more than a private sense of accomplishment. She wanted glory.

And yet Sandy struggled to make his case. He could practically taste the inky headlines: "Virus Sends Cancer into Remission: Preliminary Tests on Mice in the Mendelssohn-Glass Lab Show Cancer Tumors Melt Away with Injections of R-7 Virus." Still, Marion refused to allow Sandy to send out a press release, or even to call his friend at *The Boston Globe*. Again and again she refused him, despite the power of his arguments, despite his provocations, his opportunistic knowledge of her very heart. He had the great advantage in that he knew her perfectly. The difficulty was that over the years she had studied him as well. She knew him too.

"I'm not jumping to conclusions," she warned him. "And I'm not going to let you jump to conclusions for me. I won't stake the reputation of this lab on half-baked results."

"You are so damn conservative," he said.

"All right, I'm conservative," she told him.

"We're going to lose our first-strike advantage," he said. "And then we'll have to share credit with copycats at Stanford."

She said nothing.

"Don't you care about that?"

She looked him in the eye and said, "Fine. I'll share the credit if I have to."

Even so, he could not stop thinking about their argument. He was preoccupied at dinner and, still later, at the symphony that night. He sat in Symphony Hall and thought about press releases. He leaned forward in his regular chair, E-3, in the crook of the first balcony, and debated the language he would use. *Treatment with R-7 yields stunning results.* No. *Striking results.* He could not stop considering and reconsidering, even as he gazed at the musicians tuning. Vic Firth, the timpanist, in his black tie and tails, coming out early to check his instruments. So tall and patrician, like an eminent surgeon, laying out his percussive tools. How would the headlines run? Preliminary results in mice show startling effect of modified virus . . .

The black- and white-clad orchestra was massing below. Tendril sounds of violins and oboes filled the hall. Perhaps he'd write a draft. He could write some notes for internal circulation at the institute. Or speak to Lorraine in PR, and suddenly find the press release written, a done deed, without a hint of impropriety on his part. These were just pipe dreams. He would never do such things without Marion's consent. And yet, if her consent were somehow unnecessary? He gazed at the gold pipes of the organ above the stage, pipes that seemed to him like rows of golden sharpened pencils, arrayed in their proscenium pencil box.

The conductor stepped up to the podium. Seiji Ozawa was acknowledging the applause, shaking back his long black hair, ready to begin. He lifted his baton. Where would the musicians be without their conductor? What loose rhythm and wild melodies would emerge without him? Of course Sandy could not push Marion. But could he orchestrate the news? Could he begin the proper, necessary flow of information? He would never hurt her, but he couldn't stand by while she held back. Caution undercut Marion's ambition; worry doomed her to obscure conferences, and articles in esoteric journals.

To make a mark, to see one's name indelibly imprinted on a field! To be a Pasteur, or a von Behring, or a Salk, revered for saving lives, as Beethoven was revered for his profundity! There was the composer's name over the proscenium, inscribed in gold. BEETHOVEN, flanked by gilt cornucopia: double symbols of his fecund gift and overflowing fame. The other gold plaques in Symphony Hall were blank as cuff links without monograms, proof of the fickle politics of history. Other composers were also-rans, their contributions semiprecious; no one had bothered to set their names in gold around the stage. And so it was with science. There were those who triumphed, and those who faded. Marion could succeed; he knew that, if only she chose to compete. And he knew how. He knew how to run a race.

He smiled as the music rose and warmed the hall. The country dance motif began, then the oncoming storm scattering the villagers in the *Pastoral*. Sandy had nothing but admiration for Marion. He had never known anyone, man or woman, so intelligent. But stubborn! He had to find a way around her myopic brilliance. After all, did she want to end up like Rosalyn Franklin or Watson and Crick? Did she want to be Wallace or Darwin? He would not stand by as the partner of an unacknowledged genius.

The orchestra rose below. Applause enveloped them. "Lovely!" Ann exclaimed. Startled, Sandy turned to her. He had completely forgotten his wife at his side. His reverie was ended, and he was back in Boston, on a slushy Thursday night. He sat with Ann in a sea of business suits and jersey dresses, ties, turtlenecks, Fair Isle sweaters. This was Symphony Hall in spring: a scent of damp wool and perfume, a glint of old diamonds, a sweep of stoles, the shimmer of silk scarves and squelch of waterproof boots.

"Sandy," Ann chided during the break. "You're plotting."

"What, me?"

She shook her head at him. She could always tell. Sandy smiled at the orchestra as he schemed and daydreamed. Sometimes he even laughed silently during concerts, the way other people might laugh during sleep.

He stood and stretched. "It's Marion," he confessed.

"She won't do what you want," said Ann, who knew all their latest arguments. Ann was used to hearing Sandy complain, but also accustomed to hearing how he got his way. Perversely, it amused her when Marion stonewalled Sandy. So few people could. Ann herself had given up fighting with him years ago, and chosen more circuitous means to get what she wanted. "You have to pick your battles," she'd explained once to Louisa, and was more than a little hurt by Louisa's reply: "So which battles did you pick?"

"She's got no sense of timing," Sandy growled.

"Do you want my advice?" Ann asked.

"Advise," he said, "advise away."

"Just don't do anything you're going to regret later."

"That's it?"

"Isn't that enough?"

"But what does that mean?"

"You know what it means."

He looked at her glumly.

Ann shook her finger at him. "If you try to send out a press release without Marion, she'll never forgive you."

"If we get scooped, I'll never forgive myself."

"Oh, you forgive yourself all the time," said Ann. "Marion's the one you should worry about." She knew the strictures by which Marion lived. Marion was not given to forgiveness or compromise of any kind. To Ann's mind, Marion had an almost ruthless sense of self and mission. And yet Marion was precious to Sandy, and by extension to his wife. Ann's loyalty and gentleness extended that far. She was old-fashioned in this, more than generous—reading her husband's mind at the symphony, reminding him not to ruin his friendship. Sulkily, Sandy flopped his program face down on the back of his chair and made his way out to the aisle to stretch his legs. Like anyone accustomed to expensive gifts, he took Ann's advice for granted, and simply hated that she was always right.

5

CLIFF CAME to the next lab meeting with his hair still damp from the shower. He wore clean jeans and a T-shirt printed with TOSCANINI'S DARK CHOCOLATE #3. He and Feng were going to present the new results: sixty percent of the cancer-stricken mice injected with R-7 were now in remission. The disease had run its course in the controls, but in the experimental groups the engineered virus seemed to stop cancerous cells from multiplying altogether. The tumors shrank and shrank and seemed to disappear. What might this mean in the future for cancer patients? An alternative to the poisons of chemotherapy? In more than half of the diseased mice, R-7 acted like a heat-seeking missile, entering and subverting only cancerous cells, and skipping cells that were growing normally.

This was a great moment. Even as they gathered in the conference room, Prithwish and Natalya and Aidan were placing bets on how Feng would describe the new developments. Aidan and Natalya both bet on "random luck" as Feng's designated catchphrase, while Prithwish wagered on "some new fluke."

As it happened, Feng did not say a word to downplay the numbers in his lab book. If the work had been his alone, he might have undercut the results. However, Feng deferred to Cliff when it came time to delineate and extrapolate from the numbers of mice in remission and their near-perfect health. He gave Cliff all the glory: the discussion of molecular and genetic issues; the ongoing work to understand where and how the genes infiltrated and subverted each cancer cell.

There were only seven people in the room, but, as Aidan said later, Cliff might have been onstage in front of thousands; he had such presence. Cliff spoke with total mastery. This came of his long hours and late nights. This came of his immersion in the data. Prithwish did not doodle. Aidan did not sprawl across two chairs. Cliff was riveting.

In the silence afterward, Prithwish and Robin stole glances at Sandy and Marion, who sat together enthroned in their chrome chairs. Shrewdly, Sandy examined Marion. The very color of her eyes seemed warmer, a lighter shade of brown. Her features softened, her knitting lay forgotten in her lap. Her lips, usually tight and drawn in concentration, now parted with delight. She turned to him, and for a moment she was so beautiful that Sandy caught his breath. Strangely, he felt as though he were remembering Marion from another time, although he had never known her when she'd been truly young. He felt almost disoriented by the loveliness of the moment. *Now,* she was telling him wordlessly. Now we must collaborate. Now we need to work with Hughes at Stanford, and contact Agarwal at Cornell. We've waited to announce initial results, but now is the time. And aren't you glad?

Jacob was practicing when Marion came home that evening. He stood in the small back bedroom he used as his study and practice studio, and he was working at Bach's Partita in E minor, pouring out the notes and double-stops from his nimble, sweating hands. He had a way of tunneling into Bach that was both expressive and introverted. The theme and variations drew him down distant paths, and he had no sense of the red welt rising on his neck where the violin chafed under his jaw, or the wet patches on his ebony fingerboard. He had no thoughts of these, or bills to pay, or his large and mundane classes, the students with their yellow highlighters and confusion over problem sets.

He did not notice Marion standing in the doorway until he paused a moment and turned the page. Even then, he didn't acknowledge her until he was done.

"I think we'll get a paper out of these results," she said.

Jacob rocked back on his heels, holding his violin in the crook of his arm, the bow swinging slightly from his index finger. "'I think we'll get a . . .'" He echoed her words as if they'd fallen far down inside him. Then, surprised: "Oh, really?"

"Yes," she said.

"They're that good?"

"Better than what we had before."

"But you'll need to reproduce them."

"Of course."

He gazed at the music before him. Was it really time to publish? Was Marion entirely ready? Or was the timing her capitulation to Sandy? Silently he posed these questions, but all he said to Marion was "Are you hungry?"

"Well, that depends."

"Aaron and I were thinking about heating up the pot roast."

"I could keep you company," she said.

He put his hand on her shoulder as he followed her into the hall. The apartment had a stillness about it, as if no wind dared enter. Marion's papers lay exactly where she'd left them, spread over the dining room table and living room sofa. The kitchen seemed empty and unfamiliar. The housekeeper, Philomena, had come and washed the dishes, and put the groceries and chessboard away. Without Jacob's violin, the only sound was the tap-tapping of Aaron typing in his room on his beloved Apple IIe.

In the kitchen Jacob took the pot roast out of the refrigerator. "Why don't you call Aaron," he told Marion.

She felt as though she'd been away longer than a day, as if she'd been gone for weeks and journeyed to far countries. When Aaron came to the table, she thought he might have grown another inch.

"What did you do at school?" she asked him.

"We had a math test."

"And how was it?"

He shrugged, surprised she'd ask such a banal question when so much was happening in the lab. He'd seen the change in his mother; she'd brightened visibly. Her eyes were almost merry, her step quick in the hall; even her voice was slightly different, unguarded and at times excited. "Do you think your paper will get into *Nature*?" he asked her.

"We'll see." The question made her smile.

When he was seven or eight, Aaron used to ask Marion regularly: "Are you going to be famous?"

"We'll see," she'd tell him.

"Are you famous already?"

"No, not yet."

"She will be," Jacob told their son.

"A lot, or just a little bit?"

That always amused her. "At least a little bit," she said.

She ate quickly now; she hadn't realized her appetite. When she finished, she jumped up to clear the plates.

"We can do that," Jacob told her.

"But I was planning to stay home tonight," she said.

"Why?" Aaron asked. "Don't you want to go back?" There was not the slightest resentment in the question. He knew he would have raced back to the lab if he'd been in his mother's position. She was the family traveler, and while Jacob and Aaron missed her, they hoped for gifts on her return. New articles, new observations, the deciphering of hidden codes. They were used to her, and expected these times. Her mind was filling up with experiments; her imagination was rising, and it washed over the rest of her life like a tidal sea.

Sandy's house was not such a sanctuary. The girls were home for the long weekend. Kate was practicing piano in the living room, while Louisa tried to read on the couch. Charlotte was in the library watching the relentless news station, CNN. Smoke filled the kitchen, where Kate had forgotten to take the dessert out of the oven. She'd wandered off and let the meringues burn. Ann came running, straight from the shower in her bathrobe.

Friday was the day Ann didn't teach. She was usually holed up in her little home office, working on her book. For many years, her study on invalidism in Victorian life, *Indisposed*, had been languishing, appropriately enough, in notes and outlines, and three unfinished chapters. Lately, however, the project had a new lease on life. Two daughters grown and nearly independent, and the third away at school, combined with a research leave the year before, had revived Ann's hopes. She turned to her book every moment that she could, and often imagined herself finishing, composing her final acknowledgments to numerous colleagues and librarians, and particularly to Sandy and the girls, *who have diverted me so . . . delightfully? so thoroughly?* Which word to choose?

She snatched an oven mitt and lifted out the tray of black meringues just as Sandy came home.

"Hello, sweetness!" He crushed Kate in his embrace. "Hi, cutie." He hugged Charlotte and turned off the television with his free hand. "There you are, Weasel. Where's your mother?" He bounded into the kitchen, where Ann was scraping chocolate cinder cones into the sink, and came up from behind. "We're going to have our paper."

"Oh, good," she said. "Could you wash this for me?"

"What *was* this?" He chipped at the black cinder cones with a knife.

"Ask your youngest daughter," Ann said. "Those used to be dessert."

"Kate!" he called into the living room. "Come here. You've incinerated our dessert."

"I'm sorry," she began as she stepped into the kitchen. "I—"

But he was already distracted, telling Ann, "Even Marion says we've got results. It nearly killed her to admit it, but she did."

Gaily, still brimming with the events of the day, he took his place at the head of the dining room table and glanced at his daughters— each so bright, and so accomplished. As he looked at them, his pleasure was only slightly tempered by the frivolous choices each had made in pursuit of that folly, that strange-feathered bird, the so-called liberal education. Louisa, with her engravings of gnats' wings. And Charlotte, majoring in art history and women's studies, for God's sake. No one even dreamed of majoring in women's studies when Sandy was in college. No one had heard of such a field. When he was a young man—all right, a nice Jewish boy—there had been business, and there had been law. And then, shining brighter than either of those, so difficult, and so glorious, there was medicine, the trifecta: the promise of economic security, the possibility of greatness, and at the same time, a social good.

Was it the times in which his daughters lived? Their relative affluence, growing up? The famous boarding school that each in turn attended? Their mother's literary influence? Not one of the girls was turning out like him.

"How's school?" he asked Kate as he served himself from the platter of capon.

"My Donne paper won the Parrish Hill prize," she said.

"Attagirl," said Sandy. "What was it about?"

"Macrocosm and microcosm in Donne's *Devotions.*"

"Okay, and what was the point?"

She bristled at the question. "It was just about his conceit that man is a little world, and the world is like man."

"Okay, a conceit," Sandy said. "So what's it good for?"

"His meditations are about his illness taking over his body the way floods cover the earth—"

"What did he have?" Sandy asked immediately. "What was the diagnosis?"

"Well, nobody knows for sure," said Kate.

"Why not?"

"Dad." Louisa defended Kate. "Obviously John Donne's medical records did not survive."

"That's a shame," said Sandy. Then, to Kate: "So, what was the upshot?"

"The upshot?"

"Yeah, what did you find out? What was the point?"

"He was talking about how complex and how vast man is," Kate said, floundering. "And how small and susceptible at the same time."

"Susceptible to what?" he asked with sudden interest.

"To sin," she said.

He laughed at that. The very word was archaic, to his mind. Sin was like some dread medieval contagion long ago contained, some previously invisible microbe carried by rats or fleas. Sandy's ideas about right and wrong were intricate and situational. He injured his subordinates' feelings, overworked his residents, exaggerated on certain occasions, kept silent on others. Professionally, he fought hard and dirty. But he certainly did not sin. "So, that's what it comes down to?" he asked Kate. "People sin?"

Abashed and angry, Kate glared at her plate.

"Sandy," Ann chided him. He provoked the girls with a kind of pride, but Kate was too young to understand him. And already he'd turned his attention to Charlotte.

"Why aren't you eating?"

"I don't eat chicken," Charlotte reminded him.

"It's a capon," Ann pointed out, as if that made a difference.

"I'm applying for a summer research grant," Charlotte said, changing the subject.

"Oh, really? To do what?"

"Go to South America."

"Just go to South America?"

"To do research for my senior thesis."

"Oh, of course—so you'll be wandering all alone through . . ."

"Not alone," she assured him.

"Not with *Jeff,*" Sandy said.

"If you'd just—"

Sandy lifted his hand. "Stop. I don't want to hear it."

"Can I just say one thing?" Charlotte asked.

"No," said Sandy. He was simply in too good a mood. He would not listen to a single word about Charlotte's athletic, ambitious college swain. Jeff from Dunster House. Jeff from the *Crimson*. Jeff the squash player. Jeff Yudelstein. That ridiculous name! Not just an ordinary Jewish name, but an overstuffed knish of an appellation. Yudelstein was halfway between a yodel and a strudel.

"Dad! Could you just *listen*?"

"*No!*" He mimicked her outraged tone exactly. His blue eyes were starry with ferocity and fun.

When the children were small, Ann had done the disciplining at the table. She had taught the girls their manners, their letters, how to count—"Do two twos next to each other make twotee-two?" Louisa had once asked her—and shown the girls how to read people, as well as books. During those years Sandy was rarely home, and she had put in the hours with the girls during the afternoons and evenings, and on the weekends, and in the mornings before school; and perhaps this was why she was the calmer parent now that they were growing up. Lately she couldn't help feeling that she and Sandy were trading places—that he was taking up the enforcer's cudgel. Grateful for his efforts; sometimes dismayed but often amused, she hung back a little from the fray. She placed more confidence in her daughters than Sandy did, because she had raised them herself.

"You think you're so cute," Charlotte rebuked Sandy, "sitting there, controlling the conversation . . ."

"You're like Major Barbara's father," Kate said. Her voice was rebellious, even as she got a little lost in her literary allusion. "You're like what's-his-name . . ."

"Andrew Undershaft," Ann murmured.

"You have this . . . smart-alecky *way*," Charlotte said. "You sit there and start lecturing everyone with this . . ."

"You're like Undershaft when he tells his family whatever they think and do is no good for anything, but manufacturing gunpowder is actually useful," Kate told Sandy.

"And you don't even know what I—" Charlotte said.

"I catch on quickly," Sandy told her.

"You catch on. You can't even let me finish a sentence."

Sandy waved her off. "I know how they're going to end."

The girls were huffy by the end of dinner, but they did appreciate it when he pitched in with the dishes. As soon as they'd finished, Sandy was up, stacking plates. "Bring them in here," he called out to Louisa from the kitchen. He had just thought of a perfect abstract for the paper. He would have to call Marion as soon as he finished washing the plates. He imagined he'd catch her back at the lab.

But the lab was empty. Robin and Natalya had gone home. Cliff and Prithwish, Aidan and Feng, were all heading to the Wursthaus in the Square to celebrate. The young men pushed and shoved as they opened the heavy institute doors. They stepped out into the cold spring evening, teasing Feng about his stocking hat, striped green and white. "Where'd you find that one?" Cliff asked.

Grinning, Feng shrugged. They all knew his odd, frugal taste in clothes.

The four of them tramped over to Francis Avenue and cut through the parking lot there to get to the Harvard bio labs, where they'd pick up Mei.

"Shouldn't we stick to the path?" Prithwish suggested. None of them had boots.

"Nah." Cliff plunged ahead in his sneakers. "Takes too long." The moon was bright; the sky lit up, reflecting light from icy puddles. They jumped over parking-lot chains sparkling with melting snow crystals, and beat a path to the corner of the bio labs' courtyard. There, in summer, the Harvard grad students sometimes challenged the Philpott postdocs to volleyball, but now the net was stowed away, the ropes and pins stuffed into boxes in the redbrick bio labs' basement. The courtyard showed patches of grass and slush in the center, while the edges were still piled with stale snow.

"I'll be right back." Feng headed through grand doors adorned with gold friezes of animal, insect, and plant life: giant wasps, ants, bees, mushrooms, elands. Frisky, joyous from the day, Cliff scooped up an icy snowball. He took careful aim and pelted one of the brass rhinoceroses that guarded the building. Then he shot the other, for good measure. The snow smacked and splattered against the verdigris flanks of the great animals.

"Dare you to climb up there," Aidan said to Cliff.

"Just give me a boost."

"That's cheating."

Cliff looked at the ornamental, but anatomically correct, rhinoceros statues. These were no mere crouching lions; the rhinos stood on brick pedestals, and their height from toe to horn was at least six feet.

Cliff scrambled onto a pedestal and reached upward for a handhold on the brass rhino's ridged back. "Give me a push," he called down.

"It's too high," said Aidan.

"Come on, just push me up."

"Here, I'll help you," said Prithwish, and he tried to push Cliff from below. "Ouch!" Prithwish yelped as Cliff tumbled down onto the slushy ground.

"Once more."

"This is your last chance," said Prithwish with mock severity.

Cliff jumped onto the pedestal, Prithwish pushed, and Cliff flung himself hard onto the rhino's smooth, icy back. "I'm up!" he yelled, triumphant, straddling the beast. He leaned forward, trying to touch the metal horn.

Prithwish and Aidan were laughing at him. Cliff's jeans were soaked through.

"Can you get down?" Prithwish inquired politely as Feng and Mei emerged from the building. Seeing Cliff up there, Mei covered her mouth with her gloved hand.

"Yeah, I'm coming. I'm coming down," Cliff called.

"Well, come on, then," said Aidan.

Cliff should have slid off, or, by rights, he should have fallen. But he did not fall; he swung his legs up and knelt on the statue's back. He crouched there for a moment, and then, in one beautiful movement, found his footing and balanced like a surfer on the back of the rhino. He heard his friends cheering and laughing, but he didn't look down. The night shifted around him. The courtyard was no longer square. Long arms outstretched, he fought to stay upright another moment and then another, until, whooping, he jumped far into the air, far into the soft white night, to land and roll in the matted grass and scant, melting snow.

Part III
Media

1

ONLY ROBIN was unhappy. No one excluded her. No one ignored her. On the contrary, Marion and Cliff asked her daily for progress reports on her experiments. In April, Sandy and Marion submitted the R-7 paper and set Robin to following up Cliff's work. She was supposed to discover whether Cliff's virus was effective on pancreatic cancer cells. Meanwhile, she had no time for her bone tumor work; the new project had fallen by the wayside. She had felt lonely before, toiling in isolation on Sandy's blood collection, but this was worse. This was like being drafted to join a war effort. This was everyone working together in the lab with gung-ho good cheer, and singing Glass's party line. A brutal, jingoistic marshaling of resources for R-7.

There was nothing inappropriate or unexpected here. Cliff had results, and the lab was pursuing them. This was Cliff's time. As a graduate student Robin had waited almost a year to file her dissertation, because the whole lab was concentrating on pushing another student out the door. Stefan had been there longer; his case was more urgent. For a good nine months the lab devoted all its resources to Stefan's project. The techniques were new, the genetic manipulations cutting-edge, but the psychology was utterly traditional. Dutifully, like younger daughters waiting to marry, Robin and the other grad students had worked and waited to finish their own degrees. "Absolutely, after Stefan," Uppington had promised her, "you'll be next."

But Robin was not a graduate student anymore, and she had no assurances at the Philpott that she would be next in anything.

At night Cliff stayed late in the lab, and Robin walked home to Waterhouse Street. She did love her apartment, rent-controlled and right on the Common in an old brick building. Her place managed to be both small and rambling, the bathroom down a long narrow passage, the kitchen right near the bedroom. There was not a single square corner; every wall stood at an angle. She loved to take off her shoes and slide in her socks on the smooth, old hardwood floors.

She had no roommates. There had been a goldfish, but only briefly. A year and a half before, she and Cliff had attended the wedding of a pair of frugal postdocs from one lab down. Instead of flowers, a goldfish in a glass bowl stood as centerpiece for each table. Despite her protests, Cliff had insisted on bringing a fish back to the apartment. He'd named it Linus, for Linus Pauling, and left it right on Robin's bookshelf. For days the fish stared at Robin, bug-eyed, creepily fanning its tail. She was sure it was going to die, and dreaded walking in the door to find it floating belly-up. Finally she made Cliff take Linus back to his place. She often told herself she'd rather live alone.

She sat on the couch and ate pita bread and tabouli salad from the container, showered, changed, and brushed her teeth. In her nightgown she sorted her mail and wrote out a shopping list. Note taker, list maker—inevitably she became secretary for any group to which she belonged. She kept a journal. Nothing fancy, just a blank book of graph paper she had found. She penned her entries in neat black print, sometimes several sentences, sometimes only a few words. She did not try to record all her feelings, as she had when she was younger. She kept a diary for the simplest reason, so the day would not slip away.

She had a quiet fear of vanishing and leaving the world without a trace. She'd published nothing of importance. She had a fear of disappearing when she'd hardly begun. This was not a weepy, sentimental melancholy of hers. She simply suspected she would die young. Her own mother had died at forty-one, when Robin was sixteen. Robin was now thirty-eight. Those were the facts; no cause for existential crisis. She had managed, even at the time. She had been in tenth grade, and missed school the day of the funeral, a Monday. The next day she'd taken a history test on the rise of the city-state of Venice. She'd received the highest score in the class. Her teachers were amazed at this. She actually overheard two of them talking in hushed voices in the hall: "Do you know who got the highest score?" She'd wondered what they took her for, and why they were so surprised she didn't fall apart. The test was easy. She'd prepared. That was all. Her grades had never slipped when her mother was sick. They'd only improved. Her teachers might have understood if they'd thought about it. Her mother was dying of breast cancer, and Robin sat up at night and studied. There was nothing else that she could do.

So now she had a doctorate in biology from BU, and worked and worked in the Mendelssohn-Glass lab, and, naturally, she was a little afraid—not overwhelmingly fearful, but slightly afraid—of dying too soon and wasting her life. It was nothing, really; it hardly showed; it was like claustrophobia, or fear of dogs. She joked about it. "If I ever live that long," she'd say. Or, cheerfully, "I'm planning to be dead by then." The jokes were superstitious, to ward off fate and fear.

Her mother had left her with a feeling of impermanence, and a mission as well. She joked about the one, but never said a word about the other. She had buried the mission deep within her, the rusty desire to combat cancer as a scientist. Valiantly, hopelessly, she felt that even if she could not reclaim her mother, she might make some inroads against the disease. Anyone might have guessed this motive in her, but she tried to hide it, dedicating herself silently to her work.

Time was not on her side. This was true for everyone, but Robin understood it better than most. Because of this, certain people annoyed her. Those whose parents lived to ninety. Middle-aged people with both parents. She tried to be patient with them, but they took such a fey delight in themselves. Disease and disaster happened to other families, while these innocents just burbled along. They just lived and lived, and everyone around them lived forever. World without end. Only very occasionally, disaster struck. A father dropped dead. A boyfriend fell sick. There was an accident. The shock was terrible to these novices; they were so angry at God. They had known in theory, but never *really* known, that anyone could die. They grieved for this. Then, like the stuffed animals in *The Velveteen Rabbit* (a book much quoted at the goldfish wedding), these victims were transformed; they became real.

This was prejudiced, shameful snobbery when it came to misery.

Again, Robin tried not to let it show. How could she fault others for not yet knowing, or learning late, what only tragedy could teach them? Still, secretly, she did fault them. She faulted Cliff. She accused him in her mind of being thoughtless, selfish, young. Clutching her black pen tightly, she bent over her journal and wrote, *He actually asked if I would stay and keep him company tonight to watch him work. Then when I said no, he was surprised.* She might have written more. She could have ranted on, but for Robin that *was* a rant. She'd wrung those few sentences from her heart, and grieved at every word. Somehow Cliff assumed his project would be thrilling for her even from the sidelines. He was that self-centered.

She debated whether he would come to see her, or just go back to his place. She lay awake in bed and asked herself whether it really mattered. She had been weak. She had been lonely. Sternly, a little unfairly, she told herself she shouldn't have been. She prided herself on pragmatism and self-possession, but she had allowed herself to be possessed by him. How was it she fell in love so badly—with the least promising research programs and the luckiest of men? She despised herself, and despaired of him. She must loosen the knots entangling them. How else could she breathe? Over and over, she considered how she might end this foolishness, this needing him, this torturous sense of competition, the secret resentment she felt for him inside the open secret of their love affair.

By midnight, she was livid. Still, in spite of herself, as she heard him open the door, she felt a rush of joy, the quickening of her heart from habit. How stupid her body was, how eager and willingly deceived.

She padded out to the living room and he kissed her. His jacket dripped with rain; his face was lively from his bike ride.

"I want my key back," she said.

"What's wrong now?"

"What's wrong?" she asked. "I don't need you coming and going in the middle of the night. I don't need you constantly waking me up and using me as your personal bed-and-breakfast."

"I've never confused you with a bed-and-breakfast," he said.

"Don't smile at me. Don't ask me what's wrong when you know exactly what's wrong. I was right from the beginning. I knew this was going to happen—all of it."

"All of it."

"Yes! You traipsing in and out at night, and then coming home to me as your long-suffering girlfriend. I'm not long-suffering, and I'm not going to be your girlfriend waiting up while you work late. I don't do that. I never wait up for anyone, and I want my key back, because I'm not waiting up for you."

"Robin," he said, "I never asked you to wait up for me."

"But how can I help it when I'm here and you have my key? Don't you see—you've put me in this ridiculous position."

"I asked you to stay!" he burst out.

"And do you have any idea how that makes me feel when you invite me to watch you work? Is that supposed to be fun? Educational? I know the work, Cliff. I know the experiments. They've got all of us working on your stuff too."

He shook his head at her. If he'd made her so angry, why hadn't she said anything about it at the time? She'd only said "No, thank you" when he asked if she would stay, and then—this was just like her—she'd stewed and steamed and let her anger grow into volcanic rage. He took off his jacket and sank onto the couch. He'd been on his feet since early that morning. "Come here," he said.

She stood instead, like an avenging spirit in her white nightgown.

"If you're working on my stuff, then it's your work, too, and you own some of it," he told her. "Don't pretend you don't."

"No, it's not my work," she contradicted him. "It'll never be my work. I don't have time for my work anymore."

"And is that my fault?" he demanded. "I really want to know, because ever since I've had these results you've been blaming me for your whole career."

She hesitated a moment. "It's not the results," she said. "It's how you act about them."

"And how is that?"

"Selfish," she said.

"Not true!"

"Ask Feng," she told him, for she had heard whisperings from

Natalya that Feng was not happy. "Ask him how he felt when you shut him out of the injections." That was a betrayal of a confidence, but it was effective. For a moment Cliff was stricken. "Ask anyone."

Cliff's eyes narrowed. "Ask you."

"I want my key back."

"Ever since I met you I've tried to be your friend . . ." Cliff began.

"That's one way of putting it."

"And you've always doubted me, and you've always resisted, and you've always competed with me, and I don't understand why."

She was close to tears. "You don't understand because you don't know me. You don't have any idea who I am."

He stared at her, and she was so worked up and her words were so wild that she was indeed a stranger to him. "Who are you, then?" he challenged her.

"Your equal," she said; but fiercely she thought, *better.*

"I know that."

"Just as much a scientist as you." But she was thinking, *I've worked so much longer than you.*

"Don't you think I realize that?"

"I know you don't."

"Look, there's never any arguing with you, so just believe what you want to believe, all right?"

"I said I want my key."

"And when you're done feeling jealous, let me know."

"I am not jealous."

"You're not? No, of course not. You could never admit that. You'd rather just hate me for some imagined crime like . . . belittling you or disrespecting you, or—"

"Give it to me."

He reached into his pocket. "Here, Robin. Here's your goddamn key." He threw his bunch of keys as hard as he could across the room, and they slammed into the wall, narrowly missing a group of framed family pictures before they fell to the floor.

She didn't say another word, not even to ask him to leave. She just walked into the bedroom and shut the door.

For days they didn't speak. They scarcely looked at each other, except when absolutely necessary. The others in the lab tiptoed around them with the utmost care, as though skirting a meteor crater.

Cliff hoped at first that her anger would pass. The first day and then the second, he thought he would be patient and she would come around, but she held tenaciously to her resentment. She advertised the break between them to the others, silently provoking him in the tight lab space. When her tube racks or her paperwork brushed against his, she refused to consolidate her work. Several times Cliff moved out of her way, trying to control his temper.

Then one gray afternoon he snapped. "Could you move? I need the microscope."

Robin froze, shocked to hear his voice.

"Could you?"

And she said slowly, "I was just sorting out these notes."

"Well, could you sort them somewhere else?" Cliff asked, holding his petri dishes. "Because I need to check my cells."

"Of course you do," she murmured under her breath, then turned back to her own bone tumor notes.

"Robin!"

Prithwish and Feng looked up from their bench tops.

"Just a second."

"I said move," he snarled. In the next moment, he shoved Robin and her notes to the other end of the counter.

Her breath caught inside of her, and her ribs hurt. "Don't you dare touch me."

Reproachful, disgusted, he glared at her.

The others were watching. She was behaving badly. She was supposed to back down; his work had priority. He claimed she competed with him. If only she'd had the chance! She took a shuddering breath and walked down the hall to use the ancient ladies' room. She washed her hands at one of the stained white china sinks and splashed her face with cold water. Pulling a brown paper towel from the dispenser, she rubbed her cheeks until they reddened. She told herself he could not hurt her. She was not so thin-skinned. She was overreacting. This is how it goes, she thought. This is just life. Right now his work is more important. He needs the microscope.

*   *   *

That evening she went swimming at Harvard's Malkin Athletic Center, where she'd bought an athletic card. She walked past the weight machines to the women's locker room and changed into her navy one-piece bathing suit. Water streamed over her shoulders in the white-tiled shower. Powdery latex residue streamed off her hands; the stench of the animal facility washed down the drain.

She swam and she swam and she swam in the echoing indoor pool. When she came up for air, she saw a confusion of lane lines and gutters and red kickboards. When she turned her face down again, the blue world through her goggles was private, smooth, and deep. She had been a high school swimmer, and she cut through the water capably, no longer fast, but still strong enough to swim long distances. Twenty laps, forty laps. She flipped and turned underwater until the rhythm of her strokes began to drown out the words in her head. She swam until the other swimmers started to leave. The big pool stilled, and the lifeguards approached and pointed to the clock. Even then, she pulled herself out reluctantly, shivering and dripping on the deck.

He could not hurt her. She would never let him. She showered again and changed into her clothes, pulling on her sweater. Head down, she combed out her wet hair. She told herself she would forget everything about the day. Still, she remembered his hands pushing her away, his sharp voice, her outburst—her unthinking emotional reply. And then, confusingly, she remembered one night almost two years before when they were working late. The memory was just as vivid and returned to her with equal embarrassment.

"Do you want me to walk you home?" he'd asked.

She didn't answer.

"Not such a good idea?"

"Probably not."

He pulled off his gloves and faced her. "All right, give me the list."

"What list?"

"You know," he said. "The reasons. If it makes you feel better."

"All right." She realized she needed a moment to reconstruct them. She had no boyfriend anymore. "First of all, I'm too old for you."

"Okay." He drew a little closer.

She was trembling. "Second of all, it definitely wouldn't work out."
He drew closer still.

"Third of all, I don't want to," she lied.

He kissed her softly, tentatively, on the lips, then drew back and looked at her as if to check that she was all right. She didn't move.

"Come here," he whispered, and drew her into the darkness of the stockroom, and cupped his hands around her face and kissed her, all in a rush, seeking her out with mouth and hands. She wrapped her arms around him as he pulled at the band that held her hair.

"That hurts. Why did you do that?" she chided him as her hair fell around them. She tried to push his hand away, but he ran his fingers through the long strands. "Wait, wait," she whispered.

"I did wait," he said.

Light stabbed their eyes; they froze as Marion opened the door and caught them there in each other's arms.

Marion stood transfixed for a moment, speechless. What had she been thinking, seeing the two of them like that? What terrible thoughts had passed through her mind? "Excuse me," Marion said. She turned the lights off again and shut the door.

"No," Robin whispered as soon as Marion was gone. "I can't believe it." And in that moment she and Cliff were friends again and fellow sufferers. They held each other like guilty teenagers, mortified in the darkness.

"She didn't see anything," reasoned Cliff.

"She did, she did." Robin buried her head in his shoulder even as she laughed at herself and the absurdity of their situation. "She sees everything. She knows everything."

"No, that's not true." He was recovering remarkably fast.

"But what if she . . . ?"

"She won't." He smoothed her hair. "Shh." He was busy reassuring and distracting her, unbuttoning her.

"I think she'll—"

"Worry, worry, worry."

Robin shouldered her bag now and trudged wearily out of the locker room. She tried to blink away those first kisses, the memory of his lips on her bare skin.

"I'm not afraid of Marion Mendelssohn," Cliff had declared then.

"Well, you should be," she told him, but he just teased her, biting her fingers when she covered his mouth with her hand.

The next morning, before Glass arrived, Robin rapped on the office door.

"Come in," Marion called faintly. She was squinting, composing at her black-and-amber computer screen, and she scarcely glanced up as Robin came in. She typed a little more, hunt-and-peck. It was a small vanity of hers that she did not know how to type properly. She came from an era when women typed well, and those women were not scientists.

"Could I talk to you for a minute?" Robin asked.

Marion turned, blinking from her work, to stare at Robin's anguished face. "What is it? What's wrong?"

"I can't make any progress if I'm expected to drop everything for Cliff," Robin said.

Marion took this in. She knew, of course, that Robin and Cliff had fought, that they were no longer speaking. She knew exactly why Robin came to her now. Still, even as she felt the heat of Robin's anger, Marion drew away. Disapproving of Robin's behavior, she would not now reward her by addressing the source of her anger directly.

"We need to work together," Marion said, "or the experiments won't get done."

"Yes, but I was doing a completely different project," Robin said.

"We're studying R-7 now," said Marion.

"But why?" Robin burst out. "Why do I have to work on that?"

"You're suggesting we shift your work to someone else? Everyone here is doing just as much as you."

"I need time for my own research," said Robin.

"You have to be patient," Marion told her.

"I have been patient."

With surprise and some displeasure, Marion saw the set of Robin's lip, the fist tightening unconsciously at her side. Robin, who had always been so quiet, who had toiled in the lab so long, always the worker bee, hardly complaining, even as she dragged her wings. Robin, who had been so disciplined, until she'd gotten involved with Cliff.

Sandy had warned Marion about the two of them early on. Even when Cliff first arrived, Sandy had predicted, "They'll be trouble. You'll see."

But Marion hadn't seen anything of the sort. She saw a bright young man come into the lab full of energy, brimming with new plans.

"You're blind," Sandy told her once.

"And you're a gossip," she chided him. He loved to speculate about who did what to whom, not only in their lab but in other labs as well. "You're terrible."

"I know," he said. "But it's fun."

Marion protested, and he laughed at her, and she'd understood, fleetingly, even as she dismissed the very thought, that such gossip was Sandy's way of flirting with her.

"Look how he's watching her," he'd whispered at a lecture they'd all attended.

She ignored this and concentrated on the guest speaker from Utrecht.

"And she's pretending not to notice," Sandy said.

Marion refused to let him draw her in, even when she began to think that he was right. What if there was something between Cliff and Robin? It was no business of hers. She'd felt a jolt of panic when she walked in on them in the stockroom. She was horrified to find them there, and yet she'd felt protective as well. She'd known even at that moment she would never tell Sandy how she'd discovered them in each other's arms. She remembered her own youth, and how she and Jacob found each other. She remembered late nights and certain darkened passageways, the hiding places in Applebaum's chain of laboratories. She felt, oddly, that to expose Cliff and Robin would have been to betray her younger self. Close as she was to Sandy, free as she was with her ideas, there were some aspects of her life she would not share.

She hated the confusion of public and private life, the self-indulgent mix of work and love. Even as Robin bewailed her research program, begging once again for her bone tumor plan, Marion looked at her with sorrow and disdain.

"I still want to pursue it," Robin said now. "I think I've got a good model there for metastasis. I've got the cell line and everything in place. I just need time."

"That would mean starting from scratch," Marion said.

"I know, but I don't mind," said Robin.

"Yes, but the viral work is well under way. You could be on the paper there." Marion shook her head at her wayward postdoc. How could Robin even suggest something so impractical? What was wrong with her? How could she be so bright and so hardworking and then demonstrate in so many ways such a lack of judgment? Years ago, Marion had advised Robin to stop working on Sandy's blood samples, but Robin hadn't listened. She was a bit like Cliff in this. She kept on working, blind. Cliff always had the big picture in mind, however, no matter how far-fetched that picture might be. He always worked toward a larger goal. Robin got mired in details. She was a wonderful technician, but she did not consider how each task might serve the lab's objectives. It galled Marion that Robin had been spinning her wheels for five years, and now because she'd fought with Cliff she refused to recognize the importance of his results for the lab. She was not thinking of the future at all. Marion sighed. "Why don't you sit down."

Robin hesitated. There was only one other chair, and it was Sandy's. The office was not set up for visitors.

Marion went around to Sandy's desk and dragged his chair out herself. "Sit down," she ordered, and Robin obeyed. "Now tell me what you want."

"I want my time back," Robin said. "I want to work on my own project without Cliff . . ."

"I imagine you can continue your bone tumor work," Marion allowed. "In the next few weeks there will be more time for that."

Robin sat back, thrilled with this promise, dazzled by the very thought of her own days and hours.

Marion was not done, however. "What do you want for yourself professionally, in the future?" she pressed. "How would you like your career to develop? What do you think would be your ideal situation?"

Robin's eyes widened. Was Marion actually planning to get rid of her? The development of her career? The future? What euphemisms were those?

"The thing about Cliff—" Robin began to explain.

"I don't want to hear about Cliff," Marion snapped.

Robin flinched.

"I want to hear about you."

Robin gazed into the air. "I would like," she said slowly, "to make some progress—and to feel as though my work actually made a difference. I would like to be part of a community where resources aren't so scarce, and it doesn't have to be a choice between my work or his, or now or later. I'd just like to be part of something where I don't always have to follow, I could also lead."

Marion nodded as she listened to all this; she listened carefully to every word. As a spelunker pokes gingerly into a dark underground passageway, Marion tried to think her way into Robin's narrow, self-pitying position: unpublished, unappreciated. Marion cared enormously about her postdocs; they were her academic children, and she only wanted to give the best advice. But she said something just then that devastated Robin. "It sounds as though what you'd really like to do is teach."

2

THERE WAS a hidden room at the Philpott. Newcomers walked right past the door where it stood, counterintuitively, kitty-corner to the stairs. The cleanup crew sometimes mistook it for a janitor's closet and unlocked the door, only to find a large room stuffed with scientific equipment instead of buckets and brooms. This was the institute's kitchen, where the scientists placed their orders for rich red media, chemical broth for growing cells.

The room had no windows. A large freezer and four refrigerators stood shoulder-to-shoulder against two walls. Thousands of dollars' worth of ingredients were kept in the refrigerators: liters of fetal calf serum the color of maple syrup; pen-strep (a solution of penicillin and streptomycin); Fungizone; and other antibiotics that the researchers mixed into media to fight off bugs and mold. A desk topped by a bookcase, the laminar flow hood, and two large carts on wheels took up the rest of the space. The room was packed to the ceiling with supplies: plastic funnels; cardboard cases of filters; test tubes with orange and white caps; dozens of foil-topped beakers standing up in rows, waiting to be filled. There were rolls of labeling tape—white, yellow, pale green, robin's egg blue—jars of powdered chemicals, and scores of books; fantasy and quilt-making books were shelved together with scientific catalogs: GIBCO BRL 1986, *The Quilter's Guide to Rotary Cutting*, VWR Scientific Products. The space was cluttered but entirely organized. This suited Nanette Klein, who ran the place.

Nanette was part tech, part cook, part witch, part dorm mother, certainly chief gossip at the institute. She might have been chief bottle washer, except she had other people to autoclave the glassware for her, thank *God*. She appreciated having the support staff, although she deemed them lazy. "They do *nothing*," she exclaimed. "I've seen them, and they spend half their time drinking tea!" Nanette herself was always busy, always scooting in her swivel chair. She was a kindly, scolding sort of person, unafraid to call a senior scientist a slob, happy to spend hours counseling a new postdoc from Pakistan, equally willing to scream at anyone who came in behind her back and left supplies and chemicals in disarray. She'd posted signs on her cupboards and refrigerators: CLOSE THE DOOR!!!! and DO NOT USE MY NaOH!! STOP!!!!

Despite her name, she was not French. As a girl in Wisconsin, she'd always dreamed of traveling to Paris and going to the Louvre, and sitting on wrought iron benches in the Tuileries. And when she finally arrived there as a young woman, the city was as cobbled and misty and elegantly stuffed with statuary and impressionists as she'd imagined. The city was magnificent, but the Parisians laughed when they heard Nanette's name. This was not a real name, they told her. This was, at best, a nickname, not a proper name at all. And Nanette laughed with them, although the laughter hurt. She still made light of her visit, and liked to tell the story. Her own mother had never been to France, of course. She'd loved the movie *No, No, Nanette* and thought the name was pretty. How could she have known?

Nanette shrugged and pursed her lips and leaned into her work at the hood. She was short and plump, pale from spending so many hours indoors. She had a large backside but tiny feet. She wore elaborate quilted vests she made herself—wearable art—and pinned her long, graying hair back with old combs. And always, she kept talking, but she kept her eye on the red media flowing from the white plastic carboy on the table, through clear tubing that ended in a protective glass bell, and then down into jar after sterile jar. She filtered the media and she dyed it red for pH testing. With her foot on a pedal, she meted out 450 milliliters into each jar, lifting her foot from the pedal and cutting off the remaining media in the tube at exactly the right moment with her scissors clamp. She knew the proper level in the glass by eye.

"So what brings *you* here on this nasty spring day?" Nanette asked

Robin, who sat in the smaller gray swivel chair Nanette kept for visitors. "Did you take my advice and kick him in the—"

"No!" protested Robin.

"Oh, well, that's a pity." Though Nanette's voice was sweet, her opinions were acidic. Legend had it that Nanette had been a researcher once herself, that she'd done brilliant work way back and then flamed out and given up on her doctorate. She certainly knew enough, and kept up with the journals. She was proudly overqualified.

"It's hard," Robin admitted.

"Only if you let him get to you."

"It's not just him," Robin said. "It's the whole situation."

"You mean, the whole situation around him," Nanette said with maddening authority. "But I'm not going to say I told you so. I wouldn't be so—"

"Marion says I should teach," Robin interrupted.

"Teach!" Nanette shrieked. "Is she out of her mind? What, stuffy little undergraduates, with their shitty little labs? I'd rather die."

"I know."

"She, of all people," said Nanette.

"I know."

"She only came to the Philpott to avoid teaching and to do her work in peace. I mean, why else would anybody come? God."

"I was so offended," Robin said. "And so . . . disappointed as a woman scientist, that she would say something like that to me."

"You mean you expected her to offer you support and mentorship and all that stuff?" asked Nanette. "Ha." She looked over her four dozen glass bottles filled with red media, pumped out all the media remaining in the carboy into one large bottle, then decanted from the large bottle into five small ones. She distributed the media evenly until those final bottles held the proper 450 ml amount. Now she'd used every drop of the precious liquid, and she turned and looked Robin in the face. "Don't you know," said Nanette, "that women are always meanest to other women? Especially women scientists."

"That's not really true," said Robin.

"It shouldn't be true, but it is." Nanette's caramel-colored eyes seemed to dilate slightly, magnified by indignation and her large tortoiseshell glasses. "They're always hardest on each other. It's because there're so few; they hate the young ones coming up. They're threatened."

"Marion Mendelssohn is not threatened by me," Robin said.

"She'd just rather see you off somewhere teaching. Off in some small school with no graduate program, no equipment, two courses a semester . . ."

"No!" Robin protested. "I know her. She would never want me to do that."

"Women *hate* each other in science," Nanette said. "You know why? Because the few that are around were trained by men. They survived by being twice as good and twice as competitive and twice as badass as the guys."

"You're so cynical," Robin said.

"Who, me?" Nanette protested girlishly. "*You* work here for fifteen years. I still remember when Mendelssohn got here. She barely looked at anyone. She wouldn't even say hello if you ran into her on the stairs. She's actually a lot better than she used to be."

"She thinks I should try out teaching part-time at Tufts," Robin said.

"Ooh, ooh, let me guess. She wants you to work for her husband as a teaching assistant for free!"

"No, she said he has funds to pay me," Robin said. "He hasn't been able to find a second teaching assistant and his class is bigger than he thought it would be."

"Oh!" Nanette was genuinely surprised. "Oh, well, that's different. That's not so bad."

"What do you mean? You just said she's telling me I should give up on research."

"So what?"

Robin blinked, shocked at how quickly Nanette had changed tack.

"TA for Jacob Mendelssohn? It's practically free money! And the semester's half over! Just grade a few problem sets . . ."

"But symbolically."

"Oh, so what about the symbolism. You could probably make twelve, fifteen hundred dollars! Take the money and run!"

Robin could use the money. Still, she was baffled by Nanette's advice. "And what about how women hate women in science?"

"That's exactly my point," Nanette told Robin. "Women scientists do hate each other. Mendelssohn's *never* gonna nurture you. Therefore, it is incumbent on you to take whatever shitty opportunity comes your way. It's a gift!" She loaded her jars of media onto the cart.

"You just said teaching is a fate worse than death."

"No, I didn't."

"Practically."

"Well, but working for Jacob isn't exactly teaching. He's so obsessive he wouldn't let you actually teach anything. You'll grade a little bit. That's it. A few problem sets. Lots of people have done it."

"Like who?" Robin asked.

"Lots of people . . ." Nanette said, searching her memory of postdocs in years past. "Akira."

"Akira?" Robin had never known Akira O'Keefe, although she'd heard about him. "Akira tried to commit suicide," Robin said.

"And others," said Nanette. "There were others too."

"I can't believe you'd use him as an example."

"Well, he suffered from depression," Nanette said. "And he had terrible luck with the mice—you know, the outbreak in the colony. He lost two years' work, and he was miserable. I mean, no one really understood how miserable he was. But it wasn't the *teaching* that got to him."

Slowly Robin took the stairs back to the third floor. She knew that in her own way, Nanette had tried to cheer her up. She'd tried all her best tricks—reminiscence, humor, sympathetic disgruntlement, even practical advice, but none of it helped.

In the incubator, Robin's cells were dividing wildly. She didn't care. They would not contribute in any way to her future. They were all part of the grand effort to reproduce Cliff's results. She hated working with those cells, but she hated it more that no one considered how she felt about the matter. The grant proposal was out, long gone to NIH, and Mendelssohn and Glass were pushing ahead. The two of them were preparing the R-7 paper to submit to *Nature,* and this was all they thought about. But now, undermining her very thoughts, Sandy Glass was rushing toward her in the hall.

"Robin! Robin! I've been looking all over for you," Glass exclaimed.

Startled, she wondered if he had some good news for her, or some idea. She hated herself for the way her heart pounded.

"You didn't buy your ticket to Aidan's concert." Glass shook his finger at her.

"Oh," she said.

"I've got the tickets in an envelope on the office door, and you can leave the—" He interrupted himself and looked at her. "You are coming, aren't you? You know he's singing Jesus. I've got us a block of seats, front and center of the mezzanine."

She'd been to Aidan's concerts before. All the lab went because, as Glass said, they were family, and because Glass happened to love early music. Aidan was terrific with the mice, but there was no doubt his singing had helped him get the lab tech position. While Mendelssohn didn't care about such extracurriculars, Glass was entranced by people who enriched the lab with music or photography or famous relatives, or at the very least, new languages: Tagalog, Burmese. When Aidan came along with his sweet, crisp baritone, Glass managed to get the lab to most of his performances. They'd sat through ballads and cantatas, and airs on period instruments: citterns and viols, lutes, krummhorns and sackbuts—or fat butts, as Cliff dubbed them. Robin liked classical music better than most, but she was hardly in the mood for a lab outing. "I'm going to try to be there," she said.

"Robin, you *will* be. This is Jesus in *St. Matthew's Passion*." Sandy rocked forward on his toes, as he always did when he was most excited. "This is a milestone in Aidan's career."

In addition to his love of music and pride in Aidan, Sandy had a political motive for the evening. The lab had fourteen tickets to the *Passion,* and Sandy had invited the Philpott's director and his wife along. Sandy needed support just now from the institute: publicity and as much internal money as the director could spare. As always, promotion was essential, but in this case, he and Marion had produced real, live results. Work in their own lab could bring heaps of attention to the Philpott from the outside world, showers of gold from the granting agencies in Washington.

Before the performance, as the audience swirled around under the vaulted ceiling of Harvard's Memorial Hall, Sandy stood as the evening's impresario, with the elderly and rather austere institute director, Peter Hawking, on one side, and Peter Hawking's plump, stentorian wife, Barbara, on the other. Marion and Jacob completed the inner quintet, beyond which floated Ann, shepherding Kate, the only daughter who'd agreed to come, Feng and Mei, and Cliff, Prithwish, Natalya, and her red-bearded cryptographer husband, Ivan—and where was Robin? At the moment Sandy was far too busy to think of looking for her. He was telling Hawking about the new paper for *Nature* and speculating on the chances it might be published sooner rather than later. Of course, Sandy had several ideas about facilitating this.

"Yes, I'm sure you do," murmured Peter Hawking.

Barbara put her hand on Peter's arm and laughed, as though he'd said something witty. But no one beyond Sandy's inner circle could hear the joke in the cathedral-like hall, with concertgoers and student ushers swarming all around. Laughter echoed against marble plaques cut with the names of Harvard's young Civil War dead: Nathaniel Saltonstall Barstow. Thomas Bayley Fox. Charles Redington Mudge. Name upon name and arch upon arch. All conversation was swallowed up in the vaulted space, its polished wood tracery, its stained glass allegory dark against the outside night.

Cliff strained to hear. He tried to move in closer. This was his research, after all. But the crowd was too thick, the lights already blinking. He followed the others up the carved staircase and into Sanders Theatre with its curtainless stage, the blond wood covered with risers and chairs for the choristers. Glass's party took two rows of seats, and unapologetically Sandy ushered Hawking and his wife into the front to sit between him and Marion. Kate and Ann took the seats to the left of Sandy, and Jacob took the seat to the right of Marion, and then the postdocs arrayed themselves in the row behind. The seats were on great wooden benches like pews in church, and when Robin rushed in, Natalya and Ivan scooted over for her. She'd arrived just in time.

Sandy was speaking earnestly to Hawking, and still Cliff couldn't hear. He longed to join the conversation himself. He was just one row back and two seats away from the great man, who had a Sputnik-era buzz cut, his bow tie, and a laconic, gentlemanly manner. If it were polite, Cliff might have reached out across Mei and Feng and tapped

Hawking on the shoulder, but instead he could only look on wistfully. He could not see Hawking's difficulties—his troubles trying to negotiate a future for the Philpott with its giant neighbor, Harvard. In these modern times, the Philpott was a poor principality ripe for annexation, and Peter Hawking had long realized that the question was not if, but on what terms, the institute would affiliate with the other schools and programs under Harvard's crimson umbrella. In Cliff's eyes, Hawking was all-powerful. He had achieved everything Cliff had ever dreamed of: the Nobel Prize, scores of patents, and membership in the National Academy of Science and every august organization you could name. Beyond all this, Hawking was famous for his witty presentations, his earnest delivery of sly jokes. He reminded Cliff of a biologist he'd admired at Stanford, the elderly Professor Carmichael, who taught Introduction to Microbiology. How funny he had been in lecture, and how good-humored about his fame. He'd written a textbook for his course, a classic in the field, and begun each chapter with an epigraph from Shakespeare, or Robert Browning, or Lewis Carroll. He would stand at the board and awe his students with every squeak of chalk. And how Cliff had wanted to be like him. How he wanted to hear the conversation now between Glass and Hawking. Wanted and wanted and wanted.

The lights dimmed, the small period orchestra finished tuning; conversation hushed. The double chorus took the stage in solemn black, and their conductor, Jim Marvin, was all business, with his game face on. At last the six soloists trooped to the front where they had chairs. The postdocs craned their necks. There was the alto, encased in crimson velvet; there, the soprano, draped in midnight silk with startling décolletage and a stole she shook out and straightened as she walked, as a white-breasted bird might settle her blue wings. The solo tenor and the baritone filed to the front, and then the Evangelist. And then at last, Aidan. Glass led the applause, but they all clapped with joy to see Aidan up there as Jesus, so clean and elegant, dressed in white tie instead of animal-facility lab coat, sparkling black dress shoes instead of blue booties.

They applauded until Jim Marvin silenced them. The hall was stacked to its carved rafters with students, friends, and parents. In the hush, as Sandy glanced behind him, he saw with satisfaction that the lab family's pews were full. He loved this sort of ceremonial event. He adored the prospect of sitting with a captive Hawking for three hours. Here was a man difficult to pin down for a ten-minute meeting. Now Glass had Hawking at his side for the entire concert—and the break. He had only begun to tell Hawking of his plans for R-7, and as the music rose, Sandy could not help but smile, imagining the seeds he was about to sow in Hawking's mind.

Jacob Mendelssohn followed the score on his lap, and for the most part, when Aidan sang, he approved. He thought Aidan was quite good, but the Evangelist was better; his enunciation was superb. Fortunately, the others could not read Jacob's mind, because he actually pitied Aidan a little for having to sing beside the Evangelist's pure, clean tenor.

Prithwish and Natalya and Cliff did not realize that the Evangelist had stolen the show from their own Aidan. He held the stage, feet planted, schoolboy solemn, blue eyes round, mouth stretching to shape the notes, all effort and sincerity. He was known in the lab for dumb practical jokes, for his terrible taste in boyfriends, for inventing obnoxious nicknames. Swish for Prithwish, Auntie Em for Marion, and If for Cliff. Onstage, however, Aidan was grand and stoic. They watched his every move, and waited impatiently for him to stand.

But Robin waited for the choruses. They were so simple and so chaste, like hymns, and then somehow, in their repetition, they began to fold themselves around her. The choir rose and fell in waves behind the soloists and the voices enveloped her with warmth. The soloists were bright, the Evangelist's recitative a tour de force, but the choristers stood for the community, and in their society of voices she began to feel the deepest consolation. She forgot the neglect she had been suffering, the lack of interest shown to her, the orders to devote her time to Cliff's project. She forgot how the lab's research was moving away from her. For a moment, she almost forgot her wrenching break with Cliff. Her resentment was so small in scale before the chorus; a shard of glass in an ocean of sound. And what did it matter that she'd practically been coerced to come? That she sat like a child behind her elders? She had entered a landscape where work and competition, and even heartbreak, seemed as small as a bridge or boat in a soaring ink-brushed Chinese painting.

Robin was not an enthusiast, but that night she jumped to her feet before the rest. She stood up in front, applauding, and hardly noticed what the others did or when they jumped up too, clapping, stamping, cheering, all around her.

Out in Memorial Hall, the undergraduate choristers raced through the audience with their black music folders, and laughed and flocked together, high on their success. Parents were taking pictures, boyfriends and girlfriends were embracing while the hired musicians made their way sedately through the crush, carrying their instruments in sensible brown cases. In one corner of the marble hall a young tenor stood sobbing, overcome by Bach. Tears streamed down his cheeks while his friends from the Collegium Musicum came to comfort him. Courage, Jacob told the young man silently. No need to cry; it wasn't *that* good. And he watched, amused, as girls rushed over to the boy, solicitously waving the flowers they'd been given, their single roses wrapped in cellophane.

Robin stood with the others, waiting for Aidan to reemerge. She watched Glass talk up Hawking, even while Hawking's wife held forth to Ann. Robin's feet tingled, as though they'd fallen asleep. Everyone was talking at once; Glass was still bubbling away, Cliff right at his side. For the moment none of it bothered her. In the din, with all her mind filled by the choir, she could hardly hear. And so she spoke to Jacob while the music still protected her. "I hear you might be interested in some help grading."

"Pardon me?" he asked, turning to her politely.

But as soon as she tried to speak again, Jim Marvin stepped into the hall to his choir's whoops and cheers.

"Oh, there he is," said Ann, pointing to Aidan trailing the conductor with the other soloists.

"Hey, Aidan! Over here!"

"Congratulations, man. We've been waiting for an hour!"

"Well done. Well done!"

"Aidan," said Sandy. "How we gonna keep you down on the farm?"

They surrounded him, while Ann took pictures. Long after that night, a photo from the concert stayed, taped up on a lab refrigerator. Everyone agreed it was the best group picture they'd ever had. Even Robin was smiling, practically laughing with pleasure. But it was late, and Barbara Hawking told the assembled she was getting tired. Sandy said he'd walk with Peter to get the cars. Ann suggested they should all start getting back, and so logistics cut the jubilation short. The group headed out the door into the chilly spring night. They ambled to the parking lot at the Philpott, just half a block away: first Sandy and Barbara and Peter, and then Jacob and Aidan, talking music, and finally Cliff, who found himself in step with Kate.

This was not an accident; Kate had meant for him to find her this way. All through the concert she'd sensed Cliff sitting in the row behind, and wondered if he remembered her. In the vast loneliness of the Hill School, she'd certainly remembered him: a biologist drawn to poetic tropes and puzzling conceits. She remembered how he'd listened. He'd found his way into Donne, even in the middle of her father's Christmas party, followed her inside through the metaphoric door. And then! He was like someone who'd never seen the ocean. He'd grown so quiet and thoughtful. She'd wished she could recite to him forever in the library. He'd sat with her and ignored everything and everybody else. When at last the party ended, and he'd stood up to go, she'd longed to run upstairs and get all her books and give them to him. She'd wanted more than anything to raid her mother's library and pull out every sixteenth- and seventeenth-century author on the shelves and give them to him like keys to great walled gardens. She'd seen he was a scientist who wanted to escape; she'd felt his need to travel somewhere new.

Now he noticed her walking next to him. "Hey, Kate," he said in mild surprise. "How's John Donne treating you?"

"He's okay," she murmured, studying the sidewalk. Then she looked up at Cliff and spoke directly. "Congratulations."

For a second Cliff was confused; they'd all been so busy congratulating Aidan.

"On your results," Kate amended. "My dad's excited."

Cliff flushed with pleasure; this was an ovation in itself. He wanted to take Kate's hand, she'd made him so happy; she looked so pretty with her delicate and earnest face, her light brown hair spilling over her sweater. *My dad's excited.* He could have kissed her. He loved her for those words—although instantly, greedily, he wanted to hear more.

She smiled back at him and wished he would take her hand. She wished he would kiss her. She wished, above all, that she were not fifteen.

They walked in silence for a moment, and he considered asking about the speech contest or school. Instead he said, "Could I ask you a favor?"

"Okay," she said.

"We're writing up the paper on my results, and I was thinking. . . . Do you think you could find me an epigraph?"

"An epigraph about what?"

"I don't know, something about mice, or viruses. I had a professor at Stanford who put epigraphs on all the chapters of his textbook—just these perfect literary quotes."

"I don't think I'll find anything about viruses," she said.

"No, you wouldn't." He brushed the idea away with his hand. "Never mind. I'm getting a little obsessive," he confided. "It's my first big paper."

"I know," she said.

They'd reached the Philpott. The Hawkingses had finally reached their car. Sandy and Ann hurried Kate away; Robin hitched a ride home with Natalya and Ivan while Prithwish and Cliff plotted to meet Aidan for drinks in Harvard Square. Only Aidan and Jacob, oblivious to everyone around them, were still deep in conversation, discussing instruments and tempi while Marion stood and listened. She was humble when it came to concerts, quite aware from living with her gifted husband that she herself was not musical at all.

There was one thing Marion had appreciated, although it seemed too small to mention. She had noticed the way Aidan closed his eyes after his last solo as Jesus. Once crucified, he'd kept them closed until the *Passion*'s end. Marion had watched him sitting in his chair, his eyes shut, with all the music storming around him, and he had never wavered. She had enjoyed Aidan's singing, of course, his voice like a turned wood spindle, warm, burnished, smooth, but she'd appreciated his silent performance as well. His stillness in the chair, his tranquil face, his eyes closed until the last note sounded and the conductor lowered his baton. Aidan was consistent to the end, and she admired that.

3

BACH HAD been good to the lab. No one knew exactly what Hawking said or whom he called, but within weeks of the concert, the journal article had jumped a long queue of more mundane submissions, and a glorious publication in *Nature* was planned for August.

The lab was entirely caught up in duplicating and developing Cliff's experiments, with Marion as field commander, spending every moment coordinating the effort. She was laying out the lab's claims, datum on top of datum, like tiny bricks. Still, every once in a while she looked up from this ambitious, intricate enterprise and marveled at Glass's virtuosity, selling their research to the world. After days on the road with his black garment bag, he arrived home fresh and full of energy. Bleachy hotel sheets did not bother him, nor did he care about noisy air-conditioner vents, slow room service, or bad food. He repeated himself a hundred times, but his message about R-7 never got old. Like many a troubadour before him, Sandy sustained himself with the great material he'd come to play.

He had devised two different talks: one twenty minutes, one forty; one popular, for the press; one technical, for conferences and workshops. Each culminated with a set of slides, his before-and-after mice shots, as he called them. The "before" pictures showed animals crippled with their tumors, their flanks swollen. Click! With a push of the button, Sandy transformed these images, advancing the slides to triumphant "after" pictures. Here were the very same mice, sleek, healthy, and, as Sandy told the press, full of piss and vinegar.

His talk was bold but never brash, his language unfailingly clear, on all points reassuringly scientific. He suggested wild, glorious conclusions, but he never spelled them out. He spoke of the promise of R-7, but never made promises himself. He allowed that one could imagine many applications of viral vectors in human cancer patients, and then left his audience to extrapolate further. This was Sandy's genius as a public speaker. He never let his own words run away with him, but invited every doctor and researcher in his audience to run away with his message, and discover its significance.

Glass knew publicity was a mixed blessing. Promising results meant pressure. He and his colleagues had all experienced this—the hunger for good news and new results, however slight. Patients would come to threaten, curse, cajole. They would arrive with copies of their records and films of their tumors. Sometimes they would cry; at other times they'd try calm persuasion, offer payments or private contributions to the Philpott or the hospital. Such encounters were almost unbearable. Still, Glass pursued publicity doggedly for the sake of funding and continuing the lab's work.

Glass knew that other scientists at the Philpott resented him; he did not pretend to be pure. He did pander to the media, and promote himself, but he treated real patients, and he intended to bring in funding of an entirely new order of magnitude. By the time the NIH reviewed and funded his grant proposal, he'd have his journal article *and* his profile in the national press, and perhaps some scientists would hate him, but the importance of his work would not be denied. There was a sense of manifest destiny in this, a touch of mythmaking. But Glass embraced mythology. He was an oncologist. He understood the uses of enchantment.

Sandy soft-shoed before the skeptics who sat sour-faced, preferring complex outcomes requiring subtle interpretation and probabilistic modeling. He understood their mistrust and jealousy, and graciously conceded all their objections. He agreed with their calls for larger samples, and more work. "Of course it is too early," he declared in hotel ballrooms at every conference. "We must not jump to conclusions."

And if he did not disarm his critics permanently, at least during his talks he took their weapons from them.

He handled patients and overeager journalists with equal aplomb, deflecting their excited question: "Are you saying your viral injections might cure cancer in humans?"

Sandy demurred, holding up his hand. "Oh, no, we have absolutely no evidence of that."

"But the results suggest—"

"The results with mice are remarkable, it's true. But extrapolating to human disease—that's a big leap."

"But you would admit that your work—"

"My lab's work—and, of course, the work of many others around the world—"

"The work might open up a whole new arena when it comes to cancer treatment."

"As a doctor, I can only say I pray that might be true. No one knows better than I do that we need some avenue of hope for the patients and their families, but today, as of this moment, all I can say to you with any accuracy is that if you're a mouse with cancer, I can give you a better prognosis than you had before."

He called Ann at odd moments from pay phones, and she'd hear his voice above the roar of thousands of physicians at a poster session, or the boom of jets taking off at the airport. "Ann!" he'd burst out, as if surprised. As if at midnight anyone else might possibly be home. "I'm in Cincinnati! . . . Going great! Going beautifully!"

She would try to keep him up to date, to tell him about the department meeting she'd just attended, and keep him posted on the girls— Louisa's cold, Kate's trouble with her chemistry teacher, Charlotte's disappointment that she hadn't gotten her summer travel grant. Sandy's responses were loud, enthusiastic. He was gloriously far away, and had not a minute to spare. His plane was leaving, the banquet was beginning, and he had to run. He spoke in old-fashioned telegrams. Couldn't wait to come home. Thrilled Charlotte wasn't going. Would be back Thursday. It was all good. Great. Fantastic!

His conversations with Marion were entirely different. Before dawn from the stillness of his hotel room in Los Angeles he called her at the lab, and the two talked and strategized for hours. He wanted to understand all the details of Cliff and Feng's work. He sat with a yellow legal pad and sharpened pencils and reviewed every detail of the newly accepted journal article. Then he discussed with Marion each interview and interchange he'd had the day before. While it was hard for Sandy to keep track of the details at home, he was attuned to the lab and everyone in it. He did not love the lab more than his family, but he thought about it more.

"We've got photographers coming," he told Marion joyously. Just a week after R-7's first mention in *The New York Times,* Sandy had landed an exclusive interview. Now, before the piece had even run, he was fielding phone calls from glossy magazines.

There was a long silence.

"Marion?"

"Yes," she said.

"They're coming Wednesday, just before I get back. And they're from *People.*"

"*People* magazine!" She was appalled.

"Marion." His voice was stern. "This is important."

"Why didn't you ask me first?"

"Ask you? This is a coup! A major coup."

"I don't want them here," she said.

"You just go about your business. Ignore them."

"No."

"They're coming anyway," he said.

Neither spoke. He sat, adamant, in a forest green wing chair in his hotel room, while she opposed him silently from her threadbare swivel chair at the institute.

"Marion," he tried again.

"I'm not going to be photographed by *People.*"

"Do you know what their circulation is?"

"I don't know, and I don't care."

"Yeah, but what do you read at the dentist?"

"*Nature,*" she said, without a moment's hesitation—and then, with the twist of lime that was her humor, she asked, "What do you read? *Scientific American?*"

He laughed. "You're a snob," he said. "Look, you don't have to be photographed. They can take pictures of Cliff and Feng."

"I don't want photographers in the lab."

"Too late. Too late," he said. "The genie's out. The results are in the journal article, signed, sealed, and delivered. Your name, Marion, is on the lips of every oncologist here. Don't you see?" he asked her tenderly. "We're famous."

But Marion was too busy to be famous. She was coordinating too many experiments at once. At night she closed her eyes and saw plate after plate of cancer cells, stacks of dirty cages, page after page of the copyedited journal article. She worked eighteen-hour days and still she was not finished. And there were the postdocs to consider, their tasks to direct, their complicated feelings to assuage. For several weeks now, Marion had struggled to keep Robin and Cliff apart, to allow them different schedules and separate jobs and keep them civil in too small a space. Still, they circled sullenly, only speaking to provoke each other. They were like beautiful fighting fish, exquisite with their jewellike colors. Put two in the same bowl and they lashed out, tearing fins and shredding gauzy tails.

Robin's two-day-a-week teaching assistantship at Tufts provided some respite. Marion was grateful to Jacob for thinking of that. And he was pleased with Robin. She was an accurate grader and a terrific lab supervisor. She seemed to enjoy the undergraduates. Marion wished that she could let Robin go entirely to teach at some small college, but she could not spare Robin's hands and time.

Robin looked almost cheerful when she came in that Tuesday after attending Jacob's lecture at Tufts. She walked briskly down the hall, cheeks rosy with the fresh spring air.

Once inside the lab, however, Robin's good mood evaporated. She stared and stared at her cells under the microscope. She'd had no luck using R-7 on the pancreatic cancer cells, and now she was failing with breast cancer cells as well. In every case, her cells remained clumped in their abnormal divisions; the genes carried by R-7 had done nothing to change them. She had taken every care, but Cliff's virus, so effective for him, seemed impotent in her hands.

She looked up from the microscope, recorded her findings, and put her cells away. Her throat tightened. What was wrong with her? Why did he get results where she had none? The gods of science had deserted her. Great, quarreling, choosing favorites, they'd chosen Cliff. Of course they would; they preferred young men.

He was at the other lab bench, grinning at one of Aidan's stupid jokes. He stood there laughing. Robin took a breath and came up behind him. "Cliff," she said.

"What?" Merrily, he wheeled around on his heels.

"Here." She ripped the pages on the cells out of her lab notebook and gave them to him. "They're yours."

He backed away, suddenly defensive. Cold. "What am I supposed to do with these?"

"Whatever you want," she said. "They're your cells. Take them."

He glanced down at Robin's neat notations. "You don't have much of anything here."

"That's your problem." She tried to stop her voice from trembling.

"Why is it my problem?"

"It's your virus. You figure out why it didn't work."

"It didn't work," he said, "because obviously you screwed up these experiments."

"I did these experiments perfectly. How dare you suggest I did them wrong?"

Aidan tried to intervene. "Why don't we take a break . . ."

Cliff looked only at Robin. "I'm not suggesting you did them wrong," he told her. "I'm *telling* you that—"

She slapped his face.

Prithwish, Feng, Aidan, Natalya all stood in stunned silence. Then they were all talking at once.

"Robin!"

"Are you okay?"

"Take it outside!"

"I told you we should all take a break. Let's all cool down now."

The lab telephone began to ring. Still Robin faced Cliff down, furious. His face was red where she had struck him, but she wasn't sorry.

"Don't take it out on me," Cliff said. His words taunted, but his voice was surprised. He was shocked by the force of Robin's jealousy. "It's not my fault you screwed up. It's not my fault you can't get the same results I did. Don't blame me for your mistakes."

"I didn't make mistakes," she countered desperately. And yet she had no evidence of that. She had nothing but her wretched notes to show him.

Still the phone rang. Prithwish finally picked up.

"*Thank* you," Aidan said.

"Mendelssohn-Glass lab." Prithwish spoke clearly into the black receiver. "Who is this? Who?" He strained to hear the little voice on the other end, a child's voice.

"May I speak to Cliff Bannaker?" the little voice inquired.

"Who is this?" Prithwish asked, confused.

"It's Kate."

Silently, Prithwish handed Cliff the receiver.

"Yeah," he snapped.

There was a long silence on the line, and then a timid "Hi, this is Kate Glass."

"Oh, Kate," he said, startled. "What's up?"

"Do you remember you asked me for a favor—to find you an epigraph for your paper?" She didn't wait for his response, but rushed on. "Well, I found one."

He took this in at the black wall telephone, with Robin seething at his back, and the centrifuge spinning, and the others considering what they'd just seen, watching silently. He'd long forgotten his idea about the epigraph. How could he have known that as soon as Kate received the commission she'd begun searching through her books? She'd hunted for hours in the wood-paneled Hill library. Alone in the afternoons at long trestle tables lit with green banker's lamps, she'd pored over possible texts on mice: Robert Burns's "Wee, sleeket, cowran, tim'rous beastie . . ." Roethke's "Meadow Mouse": "Do I imagine he no longer trembles / When I come close to him? / He seems no longer to tremble."

"Maybe you should get a pen," Kate suggested helpfully. "So you can write it down."

4

THERE WERE two of them, and they came with suitcases fitted for their camera lenses. They snapped together a tripod and planted it right in the center of the lab, so the researchers could barely get by. They wore light meters around their necks and unfurled white umbrellas to reflect the light. The one called Steve was the main photographer. He wore jeans and a plaid shirt open over a white T-shirt. His hair was long and blond, his gaze disconcerting because his eyes were two different shades of blue. The other one was Darius, Steve's assistant. He wore all black, from head to toe, even a black baseball cap, and he dashed around shaking yellow extension cords from a black bag, plugging in auxiliary lights, and holding up his meter like an indoor weatherman.

No one could concentrate. Equipment covered the floor. Robin was out, but Prithwish and Natalya turned and stared. Aidan stopped work altogether to admire Steve's cameras. Even Marion stood in the doorway, suspicious yet curious, impressed by what Sandy's PR had wrought.

"All right." Steve pulled out a small sheaf of papers and consulted with Darius a moment. "Which one of you is Cliff?"

"Over here," said Cliff, trying to look nonchalant.

"All right. Okay." Steve barely looked up. "Let me see . . . Who is Xiang Feng?"

Cliff scanned the room. "He was here a minute ago."

"He's downstairs," Prithwish volunteered.

"What's downstairs?" Steve asked.

"The animals," said Prithwish.

"Animals?" Steve brightened visibly.

"What kind?" Darius asked.

"Just mice," said Prithwish.

"Oh," said Steve.

"What did he *think*?" Aidan whispered to Natalya.

"Well, let's scope it out anyway," Steve told Darius.

"Couldn't hurt," Darius said.

But Marion folded her arms across her chest. "I'm sorry. We can't allow visitors in the animal facility."

There was a bit of confusion, some whispering back and forth between the photographers to the effect of who's she? The professor. The one you can't shoot.

"Excuse me, could we just look?" Steve asked Marion in obsequious tones.

"No," said Marion.

"Um, okay. Okay." Steve shook back his lanky blond hair in resignation. "Could we bring some mice out here?"

"No," said Marion.

Steve looked at Darius.

"I could bring them out here, but then I'd have to sacrifice them," Marion explained.

"You'd have to . . ."

"Kill them," said Marion. "If they come out, they can't go back."

"Well, um. Okay," Steve spluttered, reconciling himself to this bit of news. "Great," he said to Darius with mock self-pity, "the blood of these animals will be on my hands."

"Don't worry, I'm not bringing them out," Marion said.

Steve sighed. "Let me think. Cliff, could you come over here and look at something under the microscope?"

"Look at what?" Cliff asked.

"Doesn't matter. Just come over by the microscope and sort of adjust it."

Cliff came over.

"Just, you know, fiddle with the knobs. Pretend you're discovering something."

The others snickered as Cliff gazed down into the eyepiece.

"No, don't look straight down. Sort of look up from it. Just look up, say, forty-five degrees. No, that's too much. Move your chin about an inch. That's it. *Stop!* Don't move. How's the light?" Steve asked as Darius held his light meter right at Cliff's forehead.

Cliff's back was starting to hurt. The black and silver camera clicked and clicked and clicked.

"Could I have the green filter?" Steve asked Darius. "The one we used at MIT."

Cliff stared into the camera's dark glass eye. Millions of people would see his picture, read his name, learn about his results. He had never dreamed he could do anything in the lab to warrant this kind of attention. With a fleeting superiority, he sensed the others watching him, and then, just as quickly, he felt like an idiot. He dared not rub his itchy nose.

Then, suddenly, the photographers forgot about him. Steve tossed his film cartridges into a bag, and like a bored undergraduate began looking around the room. He walked over to Robin's lab bench, picked up some glassware, then put it down. He paced the tight space until, suddenly, his eye fell on Feng, who had just come upstairs and waited next to Marion in the doorway.

"Stop right there. You're Xiang Feng, right?"

"Yes. Right," Feng said. He had the abstracted, slightly stunned look that came of spending several hours with the mice. The photographers took him in. Cliff was handsome; he could have been an up-and-coming actor or lead singer in a minor band. But Feng's shoulders hunched, the expression on his face was altogether otherworldly as his glasses shone in the fluorescent light. Feng was a scientist to wake the dead!

Marion moved quickly from the line of fire, but Steve ordered Feng, "Just stay right there! Don't move."

At home Mei had teased Feng about the photographers. "You're going to have paparazzi now."

"Right, because we're all so famous."

"Maybe you can all advertise for different companies." She giggled. "You could endorse spectrometers."

They'd joked, but then he'd forgotten about the photo shoot. He stood perfectly still, watching as the two of them dragged over their tripod, umbrellas and extension cords, extra lenses, silver reflecting disks. Feng sighed. Publicity mattered a great deal to Mendelssohn and Glass. He knew that the institute was poor, and the lab poorer. He understood that knowledge might be parlayed into money, and so he played the game, observing the photographers as he stood still, posing for the lab's greater good.

When Feng was a child, he'd sometimes imagined that his own eyes were cameras. He'd played at remembering things that way, imagining that when he blinked, the shutters came down and he recorded what he saw forever. The light in the trees. His mother's face. The sun setting at home in reds and oranges, flamboyant in the silty air. He played that he might remember these things, but of course, over time, he could only remember pieces of them. He'd read a book once, in English, about a boy with a photographic memory. The boy could glance at a page and learn every word by heart. He could look at a table of numbers once and recall every digit perfectly. Feng had been much intrigued with this story, and yet he'd thought, how much more interesting it would be to have a photographic memory for faces or for landscapes. How much more valuable to possess perfect recall of the people that you loved, or the most beautiful places you had been. To lie in bed and watch them over and over in your mind, like a slide show before sleep. Memorizing digits was mundane; there were techniques for that. But what was the mnemonic for experience? Only art.

He would have loved a proper camera of his own. His hands itched to touch the black and silver equipment arrayed in front of him. He'd seen such lenses in the windows of Ferrante-Dege and wondered what pictures he might take with materials like these. Photographs of icicles melting drop by drop, precisely as liquid from pipettes. Pictures of a hundred yellow school buses, parked side by side by side in their school-bus parking lot near his apartment in Somerville. Bicycles in a blur of light. *Banal, banal,* he chided himself even as he conjured these images. He was romantic enough to fantasize about trying photography or painting, or even film, but not foolish enough, or self-indulgent enough, or perhaps American enough, to think that he'd be any good.

He was skilled at science, careful when he had to be, crafty when he had to be, but science did not move him. He was different in this way from Marion. She cared passionately about her work; she craved discovery. She tried to hide her feelings, and she succeeded with many people, but Feng knew better. He had worked long enough with her to see that research was her life. Experiments were beautiful to her; she lived for the chase. He could not live that way, pining for truth with an unrequited love. He was a little proud of his diffidence; he wore his nonchalance all the time, like safety glasses. He was imaginative, but at work he would not allow his imagination to seep out. Patience, diligence, sarcasm, pessimism, all protected him from failure and hurt. He was patient now, standing there, stock-still in the doorway.

A great relief came over Cliff as he watched Darius light Feng. He could go back to work. And yet he hovered at the periphery of Darius's umbrellas. Somehow, he could not stop watching the photographers. He could not entirely shake the experience, finding himself center stage, lit up like a movie star. He was one of the principals in the scene, and he half believed, half hoped that Steve would call him back again for more shots. It was ridiculous, but he couldn't help noticing how much time the photographers spent on Feng. Steve repeatedly called Darius to look through the viewfinder; he seemed so pleased with the startled Feng, hesitating there in a pool of light, his glasses shining with a kind of alien glow.

"Oh," Steve murmured, gazing through his viewfinder. "Oh, I think I love this picture."

The third-floor bulletin board began to fill with clippings, articles from *The Boston Globe* and *The New York Times*. There were interviews with Sandy, and even Marion. But the *People* magazine photograph of Feng took pride of place in the center of the board. There he stood, full length in glossy color, and alongside him ran a full column of print, headlined: "Can This Man Cure Cancer?" There was no mention of Marion or Cliff, and only the briefest reference to Sandy. The article spoke, instead, of Feng's childhood, his late-night discovery and long hours in the lab.

Raised in a remote northern village in China, Xiang Feng had little idea what a university was, let alone scientific research. He lived in a two-room apartment with his parents—Cheng, 58, a retired chemist, and An-Ling, 56, a school guidance counselor. Then, at 12, he aced a national exam to win a scholarship to a prestigious boarding school. "My mom and dad were sorry for me to leave home," he recalls. "However, they were happy for me to get an education."

A star student at Beijing University, Feng, now 28 and married to college sweetheart Mei, left China for the first time to work at the famed Philpott Institute in Cambridge, Mass. "Strange food," he says of his first days in the U.S. "I got a lot of stomachaches." However, his culture shock did not last long.

"Extraordinary," his boss, Sandy Glass, describes him. "Brilliant, and hardworking beyond anything I've ever seen."

The hard work paid off when Feng stayed late one night to care for the lab's many cancer-stricken mice. He realized then that a group of mice infected with the R-7 virus were actually getting *better*, not worse. Quickly he told others in the lab, and began to plan experiments to see if the virus might work as a natural cancer-killing drug. A second and third group of mice began to show the same amazing results after injection with R-7.

"Their tumors were actually melting away," says Glass. "We were astounded. Feng has made an extraordinary discovery that just might change the way we look at cancer and remission."

What does the future hold for this young researcher and his bold new approach?

"Sky's the limit," says Glass.

"Who knows?" Feng laughs.

"He is as modest now as when he got here," his colleague Prithwish Amirthanayagam comments. "He hasn't changed at all."

Except, perhaps, for one thing. Xiang Feng now counts falafel and hummus as his favorite American foods. Clearly, his stomachaches are a thing of the past.

The other postdocs teased Feng so much about this article that he took it down from the bulletin board several times. Still, despite his efforts, the article kept reappearing in the hall.

Techs from the second floor salaamed to him in the stairwell.

"Congrats," the postdocs from the lab next door called out.

"Disaster," he said, every time Prithwish or Aidan or Cliff mentioned his newfound celebrity.

"He hasn't changed at all," Aidan and Natalya would chorus sweetly.

"Oh, you guys," Feng muttered. "Will you please give it a rest?"

"I'm writing that down," Cliff said, opening his lab book to the lexicon of Fungi in the back. "Let's see. *Disaster:* noun meaning 'national celebrity in *People* magazine.'" And then: "*Give it a rest:* idiomatic phrase meaning 'I'm too busy curing cancer to listen to your bullshit now.'"

Cliff tried to hide his own disappointment that he did not appear in *People*. He was a coauthor on the journal article, but *People* made it seem as though R-7 came from nowhere. In the magazine, Feng's discovery was purely serendipitous, instead of something Cliff had been working toward for years. Feng was even more upset than Cliff. He made light of it, but he was horrified by his picture, and his dumb comments about food.

Glass was moved to address the issue at a lab meeting. "Ignore the media." He spoke to the group, but he looked at Feng in particular. "*People* is in the business of selling fairy tales, that's all. Bottom line is, you can't buy publicity like this. The first reporter who ever wrote about me got everything wrong. Every single thing, including my birthday."

Naturally, the more Feng ignored them, the more journalists loved him. They adored his shyness, his foreignness, his sudden seemingly inexplicable brilliance. They loved that he came out of nowhere—or nowhere they'd been. They loved Feng for being Chinese. And, of course, Cliff could never compete with that. There he was, the sandy-haired, freckled Californian, the Stanford grad, inescapably American.

This was success, but it wasn't sweet. Success made Cliff hungrier than before. He'd longed for results, and he had results. He'd craved respect from Glass and Mendelssohn; he had that too. He'd been vindicated in his approach. But what he really wished for was still the first thing, the only thing that mattered: ownership of his work. If there were photographs, he wanted to be in them. If there was a fairy tale to be sold, he wanted it to be his fairy tale. He wanted recognition for his own research. This was a quixotic hope within the great brick scientific factory of the Philpott, unrealistic in the collective context of the lab, selfish of him as a member of the Mendelssohn-Glass family. But there it was.

He knocked on Sandy and Marion's office door.

"Yes," Marion called.

"Could I show you something?" Cliff said, opening the door just enough to speak.

"All right," Marion said. "Come in."

"I've got something for the journal article."

"Cliff, the article is at the copy editor," Sandy reminded him.

"I know, but this would be easy to insert." He gave Marion a scrap of notebook paper.

"What's this for?" she asked.

"It's an epigraph," said Cliff.

"Why would we . . . ?"

"Let me see that," said Sandy, and he took the paper and laughed. " 'What's your dark meaning, mouse'? *Love's Labour's Lost,* Act 5, Scene 2, line 19."

"I thought we could use it," Cliff said. "You know, as a quote at the beginning of the paper. As sort of a lighter touch."

"A lighter touch?" Marion was genuinely puzzled.

Sandy snorted. "Cliff," he said, "this is a journal article."

"Professor Carmichael used to do it. Do you remember the epigraphs in his textbook?"

"No," said Sandy.

"I remember Carmichael," said Marion.

"Well, I just thought, his epigraphs were kind of . . . good. Witty."

"We don't use epigraphs," Marion said.

Cliff started to explain, and faltered. "Okay," he said, "I just thought—"

"It isn't done," she said simply.

"It's pretentious as hell," Sandy added.

"All right," Cliff said. Then he couldn't help himself. "Kate found it for me."

"Who's Kate?"

"Your daughter," Cliff told Sandy.

"She found this?" Sandy's voice softened as he picked up the lined paper.

"She thought it would speak to the fact that we're looking for meaning in mice, and the meaning is dark and elusive," Cliff said.

Sandy smiled gently as he looked at the words Cliff had taken down. *Dark mouse.* Sweet little Kate. Then the reverie was over. "We never use epigraphs," he said.

And Cliff backed off into the hall, embarrassed he'd even brought it up. The data in the paper were his, but his authorship did not extend to personal flourishes. He was just a journeyman, his contributions all subsidiary to Glass and Mendelssohn. Someday he would have a lab of his own; he would be the master and keep postdocs under him. He would have his own funding, equipment, lab space; he might eventually even cultivate his own quirky style. Someday he would achieve all this, and the time did not seem as far off as it had before, but he had not fully earned his independence. How he longed for some small detail just his own.

5

Passover was the only holiday Marion celebrated, but she observed it with characteristic rigor. Philomena cleaned the apartment from the tops of the kitchen cabinets to the baseboard in the hall closet. AAA Sparkling Windows came, as did the carpet cleaners. Sandy teased her about this, of course.

"You like Passover because it's hard," he accused her one day in the office. "Because it's got protocols and you have to organize for it, and turn your house upside down for it, and eat matzo and jam, and suffer for it."

There was some truth in this. There was a stringency about the holiday that Marion enjoyed. She liked the idea of cleansing body, house, and soul. Passover preparation appealed to her as a kind of cleaning of instruments, the periodic check and renewal of materials in order to get better results.

"You like everything to be difficult."

"No," Marion said with a hint of a smile. "That's not true."

She celebrated Passover in memory of her parents. She had her mother's furniture and silver; it seemed only right to clean it as her mother did. So Philomena polished the delicate secretary and rubbed the silver until it shone. Marion had her father's silver kiddush cup, and her mother's set of pale green Noritake dishes, service for fourteen. So Marion used the cup and set out the china once a year for her seder. She had been given these things to use.

Unusual for her, the morning before the seder, Marion stopped in at the lab briefly, and then took off the rest of the day to instruct Philomena in the kitchen, to set the table, and to buy another dozen eggs for her annual sponge cake. She wrote out place cards in her small, tight handwriting and arranged the names around the table, from Jacob at the head all the way down to Kate and Aaron at the other end. They were not small enough to share the piano bench anymore, but they were still the youngest and always sat together at the foot of the table. In addition to the Glasses, there were various acquaintances and hangers-on. There was, this year, a desiccated but important chemist named Helene Kaufman, and the Nobel Prize–winning biologist Mike Kalb, now gone to seed, in Marion's opinion, as a doomsday prophet on the environment. There was a young mathematician visiting Harvard—Laslo Boulibas, whose name sounded something like a stew. And the Mendelssohns' perennial last-minute guest, an English anthropologist named Jonathan Collins, who was in town for the holiday by way of Tunisia. An eclectic bunch, but this was always the case. People just seemed to turn up. The visiting scholars, Jacob called them. These mystery guests were sometimes brilliant scientists with fascinating research programs, and sometimes neurotic misfits, and sometimes both, but it seemed to Marion essential to include them at the seder table. Where else would they go? She did not entertain merely for pleasure, but with a sense of duty. With almost superstitious generosity, she and Jacob opened up their home each year, just as they set out a cup of wine and opened their door for the possible appearance of the prophet Elijah.

She lifted the white damask tablecloth and checked for dust on the table's claws, which were part cat, part birds' talons, curling around mahogany balls. Here was the sleeping dragon of Marion's childhood, now dusted and entirely in order. Raindrops trickled down the freshly washed windows, but she didn't mind. In the kitchen, the soup simmered in its stockpot on the stove. The front hall smelled of Murphy's oil soap.

When the Glasses burst through the door, Marion caught a pained look on Philomena's long, carefully made-up face—the look of a librarian who has just reshelved all her books, only to be besieged by hordes of noisy patrons. There were many Glasses, and they all talked over each other, especially Sandy. Their raincoats and umbrellas filled the entryway, along with numerous pocketbooks and flowers wrapped in rattling florist paper.

Sandy planted himself in the center of the living room and introduced himself to the other guests with such volubility and handshaking that he seemed in that diminutive space like a wonder of nature come indoors, some spreading tree, extending branches everywhere. "Mike!" he exclaimed to the biologist, and he clasped Mike Kalb's hand as if he knew him well. "Helene!" he cried with equal force, since the octogenarian chemist was quite deaf. "And Laslo, of course! Don't get up. Tell me, what have you proved?"

"Absolutely nothing," replied the twenty-six-year-old mathematician with a look of sleepy diffidence, as if, at six o'clock in the evening, he'd just got out of bed.

"Jacob. Aaron." Sandy shook hands with each. "Who are we missing?" Marion was amused to see that Sandy forgot to introduce the extra guest he'd brought, the boyfriend, Jeff, whom Charlotte had invited along. Marion looked the boyfriend over carefully when he came in. His hair was thick and curly, and he had a tanned face and eyes startlingly confident and blue. He was a handsome boy. He wore a shirt and tie like a little lawyer. So this was the infamous Yudelstein? He didn't look so terrible.

"May I help with anything?" Ann asked.

"Oh no, there's nothing to be done." Marion scanned the living room, counting heads. There were the scholars, and the boyfriend, and Sandy's daughters, all grown so tall, their hair long down their backs. Louisa, Charlotte, and Kate always seemed to Marion rather fanciful. Perhaps it was the blue transparency of their eyes. The girls looked thoughtful enough, but never seemed to be thinking anything in particular. The dark-eyed Mendelssohns were puzzlers and game players, scientific, mathematical in their thinking. Clearly the Glass daughters belonged to some other species.

"We're missing Jonathan Collins," Marion told Sandy. "But he's always late."

"Then we should start," said Jacob, and they all gathered at the table, which extended from the dining room into the adjoining living room.

Jacob cleared his throat, and waved at Kate and Aaron far down the length of the table. There was something so fond and proud in the gesture that they looked down at their plates and squirmed. Jacob didn't notice; he began to read "The Story of Passover" from the thirty-year-old New Revised Reform Haggadah, a well-worn book, published in Cincinnati and written by Rabbi Isidore Mendelssohn, PhD, Jacob's late father.

" 'Our forefathers were once slaves in Egypt,' " Jacob began. " 'Now we are free. At the dawn of our existence, we knew man's inhumanity to man, and yet we transcended the bleak conditions of our experience. We progressed toward spiritual liberation. In wilderness we labored toward a new covenant based on the social ideals of truth and justice for all. What great legal system, what constitution, what social norms, have not their foundation in the Mosaic covenant of our forefathers? The Passover story is not merely the epic history of one nation, but the universal story of Western civilization.' "

No one liked the Mendelssohn Haggadah, not even Jacob. He had never cared for his father's purple prose, his dogmatic universalism, his constant literary parallels between the Passover epic and Milton's *Paradise Lost*. In Isidore Mendelssohn's commentary, Pharaoh became a tragic figure much like Milton's Satan, and Pharaoh's soldiers were the rebellious angels, falling into the sea. For years, Marion had suggested that Jacob read a different Haggadah at the table, something more—or rather less self-consciously—modern. But Jacob could not bring himself to discard his father's work. He, who understood intuitively that old science must give way to new, could not condemn his father's commentary as dated. He heard his father's voice in every sententious sentence. Every line was freighted with the PhD in English literature for which Isidore had labored. The effort showed to Jacob, because he knew that his father's father had not finished college, and he knew how his father had worked and taught at the Hebrew Union College seminary, and written his dissertation over many years at night. He heard the pathos in his father's proud and grandiose Haggadah. The self-conscious dignity of the book, its very pedantry, signified to Jacob better than anything else on Passover what it meant to be newly free.

Lacking these insights, the others at the table endured the seder as best they could. Sandy began to amuse himself by playing with his silver dessert spoon—casting it at different angles to catch the small nodding reflection of the old chemist, Helene, who wore a cameo of a lady who was herself wearing a miniature necklace with a tiny diamond on a chain. Helene's sleepy face was now drooping so that her chin nearly touched that diamond. Soon she would graze her empty soup bowl. Charlotte was having a better time. She'd slipped off her shoes and was rubbing Jeff's leg under the table, while he tried to contain his laughter. Next to Jeff, Laslo tilted back in his chair and eyed the ceiling, doubtless contemplating all those theorems that had eluded him before. Only Mike Kalb listened intently as Jacob read. There was some important comment Mike wished to make, and he kept raising his index finger, and shaking his Nobel mane, but Jacob was reading as quickly as possible, and he didn't even look up. At the bottom of the table, far in the outfield, Aaron cast a furtive glance at Kate, a look both humble and curious.

When at last the reading was done, and the singing of songs, and the explanation of each item on the seder plate, Philomena ladled out the chicken soup with matzo balls, and the guests came back to life. Mike Kalb could now make his point that the ten plagues could be read as metaphors for environmental catastrophe. "The water turns to blood, right? The country is overrun with frogs. We've got sickness in the cattle. Boils. It's the whole ecosystem out of whack. And yet the pharaoh ignores each new problem that comes up. The whole order of nature is upended, and the government looks the other way. That's very powerful to me."

"I see," said Helene, gingerly sipping her soup, "or, more accurately, I feel, that you have sterling silver spoons, Marion."

"Yes? What is it, Helene?" Marion called back. Helene had a soft, quavery voice, difficult to hear above the others at the table.

"The sterling conducts the heat much better than plate," Helene murmured into her bowl. She was close to ninety, and so famous for her fifty-year-old discoveries in chemical thermodynamics that she was accustomed to people craning their necks to hear her speak. Over the years her modesty had grown, so that now she was as soft-spoken as she was deaf.

"I wanted to ask you about Robin's cells," Sandy told Marion.

"No shop talk," Marion told him.

"Why not?"

"Because this is a religious holiday," Marion said.

"Not to me," he shot back impishly. "I assure you none of this means anything to me."

"You sound like your father," Ann murmured.

"He sounds like *my* father," said Mike.

Sandy grinned. "No. My father was assimilationist. *I* am assimilated."

"Bravo!" cried Jonathan Collins, the wiry, bearded, tardy English anthropologist, who had just popped up suddenly, as he so often did, walking through the unlocked door. He was carrying a bottle of wine, and wore a clean but rather wrinkled white dress shirt. "Have you finished the seder already, Jacob?" he asked, rushing in and embracing each of his hosts.

"Oh, yes," said Jacob. "We like to start early and get through it as fast as possible."

"I see, I see," said Jonathan with professional interest. "Is that the assimilated tradition, as it were?"

"We don't just race to the end," Marion protested, a little embarrassed.

"Yes we do," said Jacob.

"I like the seder," Marion said.

"But which is more important?" Sandy asked. "The Haggadah or the dinner afterward?"

Much debate ensued as Philomena cleared away the soup bowls. Marion maintained that the religious ritual was more important, while Sandy teased her to admit that the whole point of the exercise was the food. Meanwhile, Jonathan Collins was asking if what he'd heard about the Pasteur Institute and the new AIDS drug was true, and Jacob was saying yes, and Sandy no—even while he tried to shoo off Jeff Yudelstein, who wondered if Sandy would be interested in being interviewed for the *Crimson* about his new work. "No, no, no," said Sandy, barely glancing Jeff's way. "No, I don't think I'll have time for that."

"We'd love to do a short piece on you guys," Jeff said.

Sandy shot him a look as cold as a blast of liquid nitrogen, a look that meant: Since when are you "we," and since when am I "you guys"?

Jeff did not wither, and Mike was about to divulge a scandalous bit of information, when Helene tipped a full glass of red wine onto the tablecloth and Marion jumped up to blot the stain. Still, Jeff persisted like an insinuating mosquito, until Sandy practically shouted, "Look, you can go speak to the postdocs, all right?" and had the satisfaction of catching the disappointment in Jeff's eyes.

Now the conversation hushed. Marion was carrying out a platter laden with stuffed breast of veal. Philomena followed with new potatoes, and in procession after her, Ann, along with her three daughters, all of whom had been commandeered, carried side dishes. "Exactly like the three graces," Jonathan quipped as Louisa, Charlotte, and Kate brought in their platters. "That is to say, the Jewish graces: Kugel, Farfel, and Tzimmes!"

"Oh, God," Charlotte said.

"Have another glass of wine," Louisa told her.

"I would, if it weren't so bad," said Charlotte.

"Was that an anti-Semitic comment?" Kate whispered in Louisa's ear.

For the girls, Passover was just the same as it was every year. Marion's dark, cluttered apartment, the long white table, the Miltonian Haggadah, the cut-glass salt dishes with their miniature silver spoons, the gossip about science and the jokes about religion, the pale green dessert plates with slices of Marion's own sponge cake teetering on top of them. The cake was what the girls always waited for, even now that they were practically grown up. Marion baked a Passover sponge cake that was exceedingly tall, fine, and dry, and when she spooned compote onto each plate, the cake sponged up the syrupy fruit, and as Helene said, the reaction between the two was sublime.

After dinner, Jacob made no move to conduct the other half of the seder service.

"We won't be plunging back in for the second round?" Jonathan asked him.

Jacob looked down the table at his sated guests and retorted, like the experienced lecturer he was, "Don't you think they've had enough?"

And so Jonathan read the concluding prayers alone at his place, while the others sat talking softly about Robert Gallo and sipping tea.

Only Sandy paced the room, still sprightly after the heavy meal. He waited for his chance, and then caught Marion as she went into the kitchen. There, like an incorrigible smoker sneaking a cigarette, he started to talk shop again.

"I'm worried Robin has been moving too slowly," he told Marion.

"I told you," Marion said. "I'm not discussing it at the seder."

"This isn't the seder, this is well after the seder." Sandy gestured at the kitchen table piled with platters and dirty dishes.

"You know what I mean."

"I think she might be dragging her feet," said Sandy.

"No, Robin would never do that," Marion protested, drawn in despite herself. "She's been having some trouble with her—"

"She's always having trouble."

"Yes, well, but I don't think it's for lack of trying." Marion was concerned, of course. She had stood at Robin's side, reviewed her data, observed her cells. She had encouraged Robin, motivating her by promising she could move on to her bone tumor work full-time once she was finished contributing to Cliff's work. By now Robin should have progressed to duplicating Cliff's work in vivo; she should have been injecting the mice themselves. But Robin was having every kind of trouble—equipment trouble with the incubator, trouble with her cell line. Bitterly, Robin had even accused Cliff of giving her tainted cells to work with. Marion had chastised her for making accusations like that. She'd taken an unhappy Robin aside in the storage room and said, "I realize you're frustrated."

"It's impossible for me to work like this," Robin burst out.

"You can't just blame Cliff," Marion reproved her. She was too delicate to add that blaming ex-boyfriends for one's failures was not the behavior of a scientist.

"My position is untenable," Robin said softly.

Silently, Marion had agreed. Robin was miserable; she was struggling, agonizing that she would never claw her way out of this experimental hole and back to her own research.

"In the long run," Sandy said now, "the delays with Robin won't really matter."

Marion considered this.

"We've got the paper fast-tracked. We'll have our names in *Nature*. And the results are fabulous." He looked into her eyes. "Admit it: they're fabulous."

Philomena had started washing the china. Jacob came in bearing the seder plate.

"Now we start collaborating in earnest. We'll get Stanford and

Cornell jumping on the bandwagon with more and more people. We'll get objective, external confirmation. Can you imagine?"

"I can, but I don't want to," Marion said.

Sandy smiled impishly. "Oh, you never want to imagine anything. But you're tempted. You're almost thinking about how it will be."

And he was right. She did nearly follow him into his castle in the air. She almost forgot she was standing in the kitchen. She hardly thought about the holiday, and the wine stain on the tablecloth, and Jacob, who was gazing at her with his clever eyes.

6

THERE WAS something wrong with Marion. Of course Jacob saw it at once. She was not herself. She worked as hard as always, did just as much, but she tore through her days with reckless speed. Her eyes were shadowed; her nights restless. She turned her pillow over and over in bed. Jacob hoped that this would pass, but he was afraid for her. She'd been infected by Sandy's hype.

He had believed that Marion would never succumb to Sandy's ideas. She would never imbibe—or if she sipped his enthusiasm on occasion, she carried her own skepticism with her at all times, like quinine. Now, however, with R-7 everything had changed. The strategy was all Sandy, all the time. The plan was to push forward with this research program, and to move fast. Jacob had observed this aggression in the journal article itself, even in the technical language there. The paper was streamlined, straightforward, bold in its claims, practically quotable. That was all Sandy.

"What's wrong with the paper, if it's well written?" Marion asked one morning at breakfast after Aaron had left for school.

"It's not just well written," Jacob said. "It's slick."

"I don't think so," she said. "Obviously, the referees didn't feel that way." She was completely irrational on the subject, so close to it all, she couldn't see. Sandy had that effect on people. He drew them in nearer and nearer, into his shining conjectural web, and then stung them with his enthusiasm.

"He's treating this publication like an advertising campaign," Jacob said.

She sighed. "I know you think it's brash to speak of the results."

"Brash? I think it's revolting." If Marion was leery of Sandy's efforts with the press, Jacob was absolutely appalled. "Don't you see? He's setting up expectations for R-7 that no one, not even you, Marion, can fulfill." The toast popped up too soon in the toaster, and Jacob impatiently slapped the two slices down again.

Marion had been the dominant partner in the lab. The lab was hers; had been hers to begin with. She had been the one who'd invited Sandy in. She had been the one who set the course, and decided on every word for publication. How insidiously Sandy had undermined her authority. He'd preyed upon her doubts when the research went poorly, magnifying the lab's shortcomings and her frustrations with his own impatience. Then, in an instant, with just the glimmer of possible success, Sandy had seized his opportunity, had charged forward, and Marion trailed in his wake.

Jacob rued the day he'd ever recommended Sandy as an expedient to Marion; he cursed himself for urging that Faustian bargain on his wife. She was the scientist, but suddenly she took the supporting role. She had a unique mind, but Sandy's language, Sandy's vision, and Sandy's presence went out into the world. Like a woman, she would stand in Sandy's shadow. Like a woman, she would listen quietly, and work behind the scenes on details, while Sandy appropriated the bigger picture. And Jacob was jealous—not jealous of Marion and her relationship with Glass, but jealous *for* her. He burned with the desire for her to proceed on her own terms. To develop her ideas at her own pace. To earn recognition without Sandy; to write her papers without Sandy. To succeed without leaning on Sandy to mediate and manage her success.

"He's rushing you," Jacob said.

"What do you mean?"

"You seem harried. He's pushing too hard."

"The results are public now," she said simply. "We have to rush."

"You didn't care so much before about what was public."

She looked at him strangely. "I always cared," she said. "The difference now is that we're first."

"It's dangerous to be first," Jacob pointed out. "It's not necessarily the best position to be first."

"Yes, it is."

The toast was ready, and he brought it to the table. Marion took her coffee black, and her toast burnt. She buttered her black toast and then glazed the butter with bitter orange marmalade. She loved to taste the bitter in food as much as other people loved the sweet. "In any case," she said, "we *are* first, so there's no point discussing whether or not it's a good position. We're first, and we need to use it."

"You sound just like him," Jacob said. "Just listen to yourself. That's Sandy's sport—thinking about science as a competition."

"It is a competition," she said.

"You never thought that before."

"But don't you see?" Marion said. "I was never in the running."

"Right, because you were working," Jacob said. "Why don't you let Sandy place his bets and go off to the races."

"Because it's my race."

Not yours, he thought. His. All his.

He brooded all day about this conversation, and then just when he was hoping to speak to her, she had to stay late at the lab and missed dinner. She came home past eleven, but he waited up for her, listening for her light, quick footstep on the stairs. It had been raining hard. Her hair was damp, as was her trench coat, but she didn't seem to notice. She just hung up her umbrella and wandered in, and he surprised her when he called to her from the kitchen. She'd thought he was asleep.

"You're soaked," he said when she came in.

"The mice are beautiful," she told him.

"Yes, well, I hear Robin's cells are not."

"I hope she isn't broadcasting her problems everywhere," said Marion, sitting down with him.

"She isn't broadcasting anything. I saw her today after class, and I spoke to her."

"That wasn't necessary," Marion said.

"What do you mean? Am I encouraging her to betray a confidence?"

"No, I mean, you can ask me about the lab. And you do ask me. You know everything already. You don't need to speak to her."

"Oh, well, I like external confirmation of what I already know," Jacob said mildly.

Something in that startled her, something sharp, and almost mocking. The suggestion that he spoke to Robin behind her back, the punning reference to the confirmation of Cliff's results that Robin had not been able to provide. "I know you don't like the paper," she told him, "but you have no right to stand around sniping from the sidelines. You have to stop."

"No right?" he asked.

"No."

"I have every right," he told her. "Because you can do better than this."

"I cannot do better than this," she burst out, exasperated. "This is the best work I've ever done."

"Shh. You'll wake Aaron."

"Why can't you see," she whispered to him, "that these are the best results we've ever had?"

"Because they're only potentially the best results. And you are getting carried away. You know better," he whispered back. "Think, Marion. You know better."

"I know these results are the real thing," she said. "I know I'm right."

"He knows you're right, and you believe him."

"No, he believes me, and you don't. I don't think you ever will," she added wonderingly.

They sat together in the yellow kitchen light, the table layered with scientific journals and student problem sets. Jacob took Marion's hands in his; he clasped her delicate fingers. "I won't just believe you," he said fiercely, "I love you. When you can reproduce Cliff's numbers, I'll believe your data."

In silence they undressed for bed. Marion slipped on her nightgown and Jacob watched her brush her teeth the full one and a half minutes the dentist recommended. She still fretted over particulars. She still thought like a perfectionist, but all her perfectionism served Sandy's ends. She had not entirely forgotten the pursuit of truth, but she had begun, like Sandy, to think that she possessed it. In silence Marion got in under the covers and curled up away from Jacob. He wanted to say something to her. He wanted to explain himself, and whisper in her ear, "Marion, I'm sorry." But he wasn't sorry, and in any case, the damage was done. He could expound on his position all night, but he knew she was too annoyed to listen.

He missed his wife. He wished she would turn to him and admit that she was rushing. He longed for her to confide in him and think her problems through with him, but she was sailing in a new direction, and nothing he could say would stop her. She'd tried the future on for size, tasted success. He wanted her to succeed—but to do it right. Not with press releases, and articles in the popular press, and photographs. Not with Glass. He thought and thought about Sandy Glass. He tried to trace exactly how and when Glass had begun to steer Marion's lab in his own direction. He lay awake and considered how the lab had changed under Glass's influence. He thought of Cliff. And he considered Robin.

She was floundering. She faithfully attended Jacob's lectures at Tufts and sat in the front row with a stack of graded labs or problem sets in her folder, but while her attendance never flagged, Robin's manner had changed as the weeks passed. She put up a good front when Jacob spoke to her, but in the lecture hall, when she, like so many of the undergraduates, assumed fallaciously that the professor could not see her, Robin slumped down in her seat and stared into the distance. She looked utterly dejected and distracted. Her experiments were still not working.

After finals, during the first week of June, Robin came in with a stack of exams and sat with Jacob to record her section's grades. They sat in his office on the nubby orange couch that Marion had banished there, and Jacob asked her how the work was going. He asked in the most casual way, just as he always did, but this time Robin's eyes welled up.

He was torn, then, about what to do. He dispensed tissues all the time to undergraduates, but they were children. He could not shame Robin by admitting he knew she was about to cry.

She surprised and impressed him. Somehow she willed her tears back; they did not flow onto her pale eyelashes. He gave her a moment, and she steadied her voice and answered clearly, "It's not going well. I'm not sure what I should do."

"Oh, you know, these things usually go badly," Jacob told her.

"They go badly for me," Robin confessed. "It's not just these experiments. My own aren't working either, and I've tried to be patient, and I've tried blaming people—and equipment—but I just can't seem to . . ."

"You've done well here," Jacob said.

"Thanks."

"And you can do well there too."

She looked at him then, and all her gathering doubts seemed to cave in upon her. Despair lodged in her throat; she could scarcely swallow.

Don't cry, he thought. He did not fully know why, but it was enormously important to him at that moment that she not cry.

She struggled with herself, but when she spoke, her voice again held steady. "Cliff's results are so good—so clear—but I can't get the experiments right. I don't know what's wrong with me."

Jacob thought carefully before he spoke. He looked at Robin as she sat before him in her short-sleeved summer shirt; he considered her bare arms, her fine open face, the humility and baffled sadness in her confession. He thought about the place, the time, and Robin's state of mind. Quite deliberately, Jacob considered what his words might mean to her—hesitated a moment—then shot his subtle arrow anyway. He said, "The results seem almost too good to be true."

Part IV
Intuition

1

JACOB'S WORDS slid in easily; they slipped under Robin's skin so fast, she scarcely felt them until several moments later, when she was practically out the door. Even then, the construction was so casual, "almost too good to be true . . . ," she might not have noticed anything, except for the decided coolness in his voice. His words were mild, but his voice was cold, and it was the cold that crept inside Robin after the first moment, startling and paining her. What was he really saying? What was he trying to tell her? Even as she left the office, she turned back in confusion. "Do you really think . . ." she said. "Do you think there's something wrong?"

Jacob looked up at her. "Something wrong with what?"

"About what you said before?" She couldn't spell it out: the denigration of his wife's own journal article; the terrifying, disorienting opening of a world of doubt.

"What was that?"

"Do you think there's something wrong with the data?" she whispered.

Jacob looked her in the face, and his eyes were so dark, and so lively, Robin felt for a moment that he was playing with her. She sensed, for an instant, that he could see right inside of her, and she drew back, horrified. There was a good five feet of empty space between them, but she felt as though Jacob had touched the inside of her thigh. Her heart was racing, but he'd already turned away as if nothing had happened.

"Something wrong with the data?" he repeated slowly, absentmindedly, as he shuffled the papers on his desk. "No, of course not."

She told herself nothing had happened. Later, she almost convinced herself she had imagined the whole conversation. Still, she could not shake his words; they persisted inside her, clinging tenaciously like seeds with hooks, like little burrs. He would deny it, but his words were meant for her. That was the frightening part. Anyone else would have written off his comment about the results as a sour joke or chance remark, but Robin saw the significance immediately. She was struggling in the lab; she was failing to duplicate Cliff's results. How could she possibly ignore Jacob's sly suggestion that the results were flawed? That perhaps the problems she was having in the lab were not of her own making? That there was something wrong with Cliff's experiments themselves? What did Jacob know? What did he suspect? Nothing. Nothing. Nothing. He would never question Marion's judgment. He deferred to his wife entirely when it came to science. He'd given up his career for her. Everybody knew that.

Why, then, had he spoken to her that way? Was he just tormenting her? Teasing her? Why would he toy with her like that?

He was strange. He had one of those odd, angular minds you ran into sometimes in science. He was brilliant and fastidious. He was known primarily as Marion's husband, but he was also highly opinionated. She thought of him at the Bach concert, sitting with his score, making some point about the music at intermission, shooting down Peter Hawking himself for offering a different opinion. Jacob was a force to be reckoned with. He was not what you might expect.

That weekend, she went to Plum Island with three friends from her building. Tomas drove. He was a two-hundred-fifty-pound, bushy-bearded watercolorist who lived alone on the third floor with his sweet-faced parakeet, Pippin. After matriculating at Harvard, he had run into trouble in his freshman year and taken a decade's leave of absence, financed by his parents and punctuated by a couple of nervous breakdowns, so that he could devote himself to art. Tomas's father was Jewish, his mother Cuban. He was bilingual, but he spoke English with a slight lisp, as though he had spent time in Spain. His gentle manner belied his burly exterior. It was he who planned the Plum Island expedition each year, just as it was he who invited his neighbors to his place for tea. He was a community builder, and a family man of sorts, devoted to his mother and his father in Georgetown, and his sisters in Potomac, Maryland. Shyly he'd approached Robin in the lobby two years earlier and said, "I was wondering if you would you like to share some champagne with me. I'm celebrating a new stage in my life. I've just become an uncle."

Larry and Wendy sat on the backseat. They worked at MIT in the computer science department. Larry had a pronounced New York accent, and wore a white cowboy hat and bolo tie, as if to show he came from a part of Brooklyn in the Southwest. He built harpsichords from kits in his spare time, although he played them badly. He and Wendy had lived together for seventeen years, sharing their love for programming and gaming, a taste for Indian food, a voracious appetite for science fiction, classical music, and Scottish country dancing. Harmonious in their enthusiasms, they abhorred together beautifully as well, detesting religions, superstitions, condominiums, and corporations. Larry and Wendy militated to keep software in the public domain and away from greedy profiteers like Lotus and WordPerfect, and their upstart rival, Microsoft. While other people wore FREE MANDELA T-shirts, Larry and Wendy donned shirts emblazoned FREE SOFTWARE. They wore their hair long, in ponytails, and their glasses large. Larry had the broader, beefier face, and when he grinned under his white hat, he looked strangely rabbinical. Wendy was long-faced and long-nosed, her blue eyes set close together. She dressed in denim skirts and, inexplicably, white kneesocks pulled up to her bony knees. She didn't mind looking like an elderly schoolgirl. She liked it. She and Larry each wore NERD PRIDE buttons. The term had been coined by Larry's mentor at MIT, and it suited Larry and Wendy perfectly. They had T-shirts with the slogan as well. NERD PRIDE on the front, and on the back, the legend: A WELL-ROUNDED PERSON IS POINTLESS.

One year, while hiking, Robin had ventured to Larry, "But you know, you and Wendy are actually *very* well rounded."

"No we're not," Larry and Wendy retorted instantly, almost in unison.

Neither Larry nor Wendy could drive, and so they sat in the back of Tomas's Volkswagen Rabbit. Blithely oblivious to Tomas's roaring accelerations and screeching turns, the two of them sat side by side, playing cribbage.

They parked at a distance from the sandy spit of land they'd come to walk, because the piping plovers were nesting and the beach roads were closed. On foot, Robin and Tomas, Larry and Wendy set out with binoculars and birding guides. Robin carried bottles of water, and Larry sprayed himself up and down with bug spray. He had a phobia of mosquitoes and ticks and convinced himself regularly that he had contracted Lyme disease. Larry sprayed so compulsively that the others didn't bother; they believed walking next to him was protection enough.

On boardwalks bleached gray they clomped across the beach. The sand rippled under the hot sky, and the scant grass fluttered in long ribbons.

"Bobolink," Larry said, and put up his binoculars at once. Wendy had her birding journal open and at the ready, and Tomas his sketchbook, but Robin hung back. She didn't feel like identifying anything.

"Yellowthroat," Wendy declared.

"Where?" Larry demanded.

Robin and Tomas pushed ahead where the boardwalk cut through bracken and trees twisted with the wind. The branches and tree trunks looked like driftwood, but they were alive, and they tangled together in a little copse. The boardwalk curved in here under the sheltering leaves, and the place was quiet, a dappled refuge from the sandy flats and dunes outside. Sweating and puffing, Tomas found his spot and unloaded his supplies, then unfolded his easel and took paint box, water jars, and brushes from his backpack. His hands were big. Even his fingers were chubby, but when he began to paint, every line on the page was delicate, every wash of color translucent. The branches above them emerged on the page; the rough, weathered bark of the trees. "Don't look," Tomas said, catching Robin.

He was shy about his work, and easily discouraged. He often told Robin he wasn't very good—that his painting was just therapy.

They couldn't see Larry and Wendy, but they heard them in the trees, whispering loudly, deep in conversation.

"Aren't you going to find some birds?" Tomas asked Robin. "Go. Go." He waved her off. "Find some birds."

"I don't really want to," Robin said. She wanted to tell him just then. She had to talk to somebody. Still, she could not speak. Her ideas were too confused. Was it her own problem she couldn't reproduce Cliff's results? Or was it, as Jacob hinted, something else? Since she'd spoken to Jacob, Robin's impatient mind had given her no rest. Why had reproducing Cliff's results been impossible for her? What was wrong? Problems with the data? Mistakes in Cliff's analysis? Something Marion might have missed? But Marion did not miss anything. Jacob knew that. He knew Marion best of all.

The four of them stayed out all afternoon, and followed the boardwalk its entire circuit through the dunes. Larry and Wendy became grumpy for lack of birds. There were supposed to be brown-headed cowbirds and willets and all kinds of warblers flying by, and they had seen only the bobolink and the yellowthroat.

"I think I've got a bite," Larry said dolefully, examining his arm.

"That's impossible with the amount of chemicals you've sprayed on yourself," said Wendy.

"Obviously, it *is* possible," he snapped. "I have a high susceptibility to insects." Out of sorts and out of patience with the others, the wounded Larry marched ahead down the boardwalk. Binoculars held high, he looked left and right and far in front of him.

"A little ice cream might cheer him up," Tomas mused.

But there was Larry just ahead, standing with binoculars fixed on a brown speck near the parking lot.

Wendy rushed forward. "What is it?"

"Shh. Shh." He waved her off.

The three of them put up their binoculars and peered out from behind Larry. Some sort of sandpiper was standing there in the distance, perched on a fence post. It was certainly a sandpiper with its long bill and wiry legs, its mottled brown feathers and small, neat head. But the bird didn't sound like a regular sandpiper at all. It sounded like a child learning to whistle.

For several long minutes, they stood mesmerized by the leggy bird. They didn't dare move or speak until the odd piper fluttered off its perch and flew away.

"That," said Larry, "was an upland sandpiper."

"No way," Wendy protested.

"It was, it was, it was!" Larry cried with childish glee.

"Upland sandpipers are very rare here," said Tomas, riffling through his bird book. "They don't live out here. . . ."

"It was rare," cried Larry, jubilant. "It was incredibly rare."

"But how do you know?" Robin asked.

"Didn't you hear it? Didn't you hear the whistle?"

"It wasn't supposed to be here," Wendy said in a reproving voice. Whether she was reproving Larry or the bird, Robin and Tomas couldn't tell.

"But we saw it anyway," Larry said, scribbling the entry in his book. "I pegged it!"

There was no arguing with him. Larry didn't know much about birds, but what he did know was indisputable. He'd forgotten his bug bite, and his bad mood, and he pranced away swinging his binoculars by their strap, and trying to whistle as the bird had. Robin trudged along, bemused. Such small things, such tiny victories—whether finding birds, or winning at cribbage—made Larry so enormously happy. He pitched his cowboy hat back off his sweaty face and took Wendy's hand in his, and he grinned until his eyes were slits of pleasure, and then he shouted into the big empty sky, "Ha!" Because he'd pulled a bird out of that long empty afternoon. Not just any bird, but a rare find.

And then Robin saw it; she saw the expression on Larry's face, and knew she'd seen that look before. That look of triumph, that giddy smile, silly with happiness. That was Cliff with the mice; that was the look she'd seen in Cliff's eyes when she'd watched him through the window. She shook herself and blinked, but all she saw was Cliff, holding a mouse up by the tail. Her nose brushed the red glass as she watched him moving busily about the room, carrying cages from rack to counter. He plucked a mouse out of its cage and put it in the isolator, and then turned the CO_2 spigot at the wall. That was odd. She'd thought so at the time. Marion did not allow her researchers to gas experimental mice. Why would he bend the protocol like that? She closed her eyes and tried to reconstruct what had happened next, but she could not. All she could remember was Cliff, and his face—lit up, jubilant, blissful, arrogant, all at once.

2

IN THE lab the next day, Robin realized, with some embarrassment, that she was the only one who'd gotten any sun over the weekend. Telltale freckles dotted her arms and face, while everyone else looked pale as before. She half expected the others to ask her where she'd been and tease her about slacking off, but they scarcely looked up. Cliff and Feng were working on Cliff's virus, preparing batches to ship to labs at Stanford and Cornell. They'd been freezing one-milliliter aliquots of virus in lysate solutions and filling out forms all weekend. She glanced at Cliff uneasily. He was completely absorbed in the paperwork in front of him.

He no longer worked to ignore her. He had actually turned his mind elsewhere. Over weeks and months, she had been the unforgiving one, the silent historian of their ruined friendship, and conservator of their heartbreak. He lacked her perfect recall of every argument. Nor did he possess her hair-trigger imagination, her ability to find a slight in every interaction. He was not unfeeling; he felt a great deal, but he rode emotions like horses until he wore them out. He accepted their breakup. He had stormed and grieved at the time, but he was only as lonely as he wanted to be, and, Robin observed, he was hardly alone for long. There was already someone new, a lab tech from the second floor named Nella. Catching them flirting by the bike racks, she'd turned away, hurt, and at the same time fiercely glad Cliff was as callow as she'd thought.

All that summer, Cliff labored steadily. Flare-ups over space or lab chores, or requests for information, were now increasingly rare. Robin kept to herself, and only seethed from a distance. In July, Marion began allowing her to work part-time on the bone tumor project, although, like everyone else, she was expected to continue supporting Cliff.

The days were stifling, but Cliff liked the suffocating afternoons and long, still sunsets. At last, in August, the journal article was published; his claim was made. His data flew into the world. Now all he had to do was work relentlessly to follow up. Natalya went to the Cape for a week, and Aidan spent ten days at a music festival in Maine, but Cliff didn't want to go away. The only breaks he took were to play volleyball at the Harvard bio labs. He'd go in the evenings with Prithwish, and they'd play pickup games against anyone they could find. They'd spike and set and dive for the ball until they dripped with sweat and dirt.

One August night after a game, Cliff sat on the steps with Jeff Yudelstein. A few months before, no one in the lab had had the time or patience for a student newspaper, but now that the initial media flurry was over, and the photo shoots and phone calls had died off, it was amusing to sit back and answer questions from the Harvard *Crimson* reporter, who happened to be Charlotte Glass's boyfriend. She was serving as photographer, and Cliff couldn't help wondering whether she was using her father's camera.

"Xiang Feng isn't here?" Jeff asked. He had a folder full of press clippings.

"Nope," said Cliff.

Jeff frowned and fussed with his tape recorder, consulted his notes, and then asked rather plaintively, "Were you there when Xiang Feng made the discovery?"

"The discovery?" said Cliff, slightly annoyed. "It was my discovery. They were my experiments."

"What do you mean?" Jeff asked.

"Well, let's start from the beginning," Cliff said coolly. "Let's start from the virus. Respiratory syncytial virus."

"Could you spell that?"

"Sure." Cliff began to tell Jeff about his work modifying the virus, and his application of the work to breast cancer tumors in mice. He did not leave out Feng's observations, but he did not begin there either. He told his story patiently, explaining the context of Feng's dramatic observation one weekend. It was just a student newspaper, but Jeff was eager enough, and quick enough to take everything down.

"Is this too much detail for you?"

"No, not at all," said Jeff. The *Crimson* came out only once a week in the summer; campus news was slow, and Jeff had plenty of space for a feature article.

Of course, Cliff didn't bring up everything. He did not confide in Jeff about his long walk that night in December, or his sudden rehabilitation in the lab. He did not mention that he'd despaired of science, or talk about the way the work consumed him in the winter. He spoke instead of the years he'd spent on the work, and his hopes for the research now that it was public.

Listening to all this, Charlotte lolled on the steps, slightly disaffected, waiting for the interview to end. She wore small squinty glasses and a halter dress from Oona's in the Square. She was not as tall as Louisa, or as pretty as Kate, but she was more audacious than either. She was long past hating that, like her sisters, she was named after a Great Nineteenth-Century Woman Writer. She wore her ruffled peony of a name with flair, as she might pin a large silk flower onto a vintage black overcoat. She had style, and she could barely bring herself to watch as Jeff grubbed and snuffed, scribbling in his steno notebook. Jeff was funny and even lighthearted when he forgot that he wanted to be editor of the *Crimson* and get a Rhodes scholarship, and go to law school, and clerk for the Supreme Court. He was witty among friends, but right now Jeff sounded both obsequious and aggressive, and she couldn't wait to get him out of there.

She was bored, Cliff assumed, looking at her. She'd done Jeff a favor by coming along with the camera, and maybe by convincing her dad to arrange the interview. This was going on too long; Cliff was growing a bit tired of Jeff as well. He was glad when the hour was done and he could say good-bye. He shook hands with both Jeff and Charlotte and sauntered up the steps into the grand old building as casually as if the institute were his own house, then ran up the flights of stairs to the third floor. The empty lab no longer seemed a prison, but his own sanctuary. In the past, he'd hated to work late, alone, but now he loved evenings here. He had all the equipment to himself.

Without looking, he reached for his lab book. Twice he ran his fingers along the empty metal shelf above his bench before he realized his book was missing. Where was it? He always put it there. He scanned the cluttered bench tops and then padded into the stockroom. Swinging open the door, he heard a gasp.

"You scared me," Robin accused him, and clutched a stack of books and papers to her chest.

"Sorry. I didn't know you were here. What's going on?"

"Nothing," she said. "I was just looking up some stuff." She wanted to get by. She was in a terrible hurry to leave.

"Why were you looking up stuff in here?" he asked, puzzled. And then he saw his lab book in her arms. "What are you doing with that?"

She handed it to him.

"Why did you take my lab book in here?"

He was much bigger than Robin. Fleetingly she remembered the way he had once stood in a doorway, barring the way until she tried to duck under his arm and he caught and kissed her. That had been more than a year ago. Cliff stood before her now, indignant, blocking the only way out.

"I'm doing bookkeeping for the colony. I needed your tag numbers," she lied.

"Why didn't you ask?"

She couldn't look him in the face.

"Robin?"

"Could you just let me by?"

"You were sneaking around behind my back." He was amazed that she would pry into his lab book and then try to cover it up like a kid shoplifting. He was shocked she might be that petty, and that dishonest.

"I'm sorry." Somehow she squeezed past him and escaped into the hall. She could not explain. She just couldn't. She couldn't say, even to herself, what she was doing with Cliff's lab book, or what she was searching for. She ran down the hall to the stairwell, then, closing the fire door behind her, ran down a flight of stairs for good measure and sank down on the bottom step. What had she been after? There was nothing wrong with Cliff's lab book, at least not in any of the entries she'd had time to read. There was no smoking gun in his notes.

She leaned over, resting her head on her knees. She hated herself for looking at what wasn't hers; she despised her own suspicions because they were secretive and speculative. There was nothing wrong with Cliff's work—except that it was so much better than hers. Wasn't that the problem? She closed her eyes and forced herself to face the question. Where did these doubts come from, if not from her jealous imagination? No, she protested within herself, she had reason for skepticism. Her efforts to reproduce Cliff's results had been meticulous; in fact, she was far more conscientious in the lab than he. Her work with R-7 had been more than competent. Jacob himself had suggested she was not the problem. She reminded herself of all this. Still, her conscience pricked her and provoked her, and she was ashamed.

She forced herself upstairs again and back into the lab, where Cliff perched on a stool, his lab book in front of him.

"What the hell is going on with you?" Cliff demanded.

"I was out of line."

"Look," he told her. "If you have a question about my numbers, ask, okay? Come to me, and I'll give them to you."

"Okay," she said. "I will."

"I'll give you the tag numbers now." He dragged over a stool. "Just sit down and look at them. Can we do this? Can we have a truce here?" He put his arm around her shoulders. He didn't mean anything by it, just an attempt at normalcy. He was a tactile person, as quick to hug his women friends as he was to smile. He gave away glances and gestures, and he was charming that way, or incorrigible, depending on how you looked at it.

Robin flinched, and he let go. "I know it's been bad between us, but I can't take this animosity."

"I'm sorry," she said as Cliff opened up his lab book for her. Still, despite her apology, despite all her resolutions, curiosity drew her further. She had been struggling with her doubts for so many days, she thirsted for answers. Almost inaudibly, she asked, "Why didn't you break your animals' necks?"

Now he flinched. "What are you talking about?"

"I saw you sac your mice," she said.

"When?"

"I watched you in March. I saw you do it through the window, and you gassed them. You didn't break their necks."

"Jesus, Robin, what is going on?"

"I don't know," she said. "You tell me."

He sprang up. "You were spying on me."

The words hurt, but for the first time Robin saw fear in his eyes. She'd pressed and pressed, and now, for the first time, she'd drawn blood. He'd bent the rules, and when she called him on it, she'd scared him. She was so startled that for a moment she didn't know what to do. "I thought there was something wrong," she murmured. "I thought it was me, and I thought it was the equipment, and I thought it was the cell line, but it wasn't. It was you."

He was indignant again, filled with righteous anger. "What are you trying to say? That I screwed up my own experiments? What are you doing—coming in here, taking my lab book, checking on my data? Why can't you just be honest with me, and come to me openly?"

"I'm being honest now," Robin said. "I'm coming to you now. Why didn't you break your animals' necks? Why didn't you sac them properly?"

He might have admitted then that he didn't always decapitate the animals, or argued that Marion's strictures weren't necessary, but he panicked instead. "I did sacrifice them properly," he burst out.

"All of them?"

"Look." He turned to the page in his lab notebook where he'd recorded the deaths. There was the date in March, and all the data she was looking for in neat columns. He had sacrificed twenty-three animals, then dissected them. There were the tag numbers on the ruled page, printed boldly in black ink. The numbers made sense. She'd shaken him, but only for a moment, and now he was himself again, his new, confident self.

3

THE PICNIC was sacred. Every August at Walden Pond, the lab celebrated its successes and mourned the grants that got away. The picnic was a celebration and a wake, a feast and a swim fest. Mendelssohn and Glass each spoke, and typically said a few words of encouragement and thanks to each researcher, a subtle but public form of evaluation.

No one missed the picnic without good cause: a bout with stomach flu, a death in the family. Robin could hardly have skipped the eleventh annual picnic just to attend a friend's wedding. She missed the gathering because she was a cousin of the bride, and had a part in the ceremony as bridesmaid.

"She's the only one who couldn't come," Marion told Jacob as they unloaded the car. Brandishing two beach umbrellas, Aaron had gone ahead to stake the lab's claim on the scratchy sand.

The Mendelssohns were the advance team. Marion had brought a folding camping table and aluminum lawn chairs, old, clean blankets to spread upon the ground, and two coolers filled with individually wrapped sandwiches and desserts: brownies, lemon squares, and cookies from Rosie's Bakery. There were extra condiments, bowls of chips, potato salad, green salad topped with large croutons, quarts of prewashed blueberries, and packages of paper plates, plasticware, and napkins. Jacob and Aaron dragged all these things down from the parking lot in Aaron's old Radio Flyer wagon.

Although Sandy was bringing drinks, Marion heaved a container of spring water with a spigot onto the table. As usual, she'd planned for every contingency. She carried extra garbage bags and sunscreen, and even a first aid kit. The others used to laugh at her for this, but the year before, when Aidan spiked his foot on a rock, Marion had been prepared.

Sandy and Ann and the girls arrived next with the cider and sodas, and Feng and Mei pulled up with Natalya and Ivan. Prithwish had hitched a ride with Aidan and his new boyfriend, Tim. Cliff came with Nella. Marion and Jacob waved each of the newcomers down, flapping towels from their relatively secluded spot. Then Marion settled back in her lawn chair, satisfied. Aaron had found a good place close to the trees and far from the crowds, though the beach tapered out here, and the sand was coarse and sparse.

"You know, it's so rocky here," Sandy began from his lawn chair next to Marion.

"Don't start," she told him. He brought this up every year, insisting they should have gone to Crane Beach or Horseneck Beach, or even to the Cape, but Marion wouldn't think of driving so far just for a picnic. She was not a sun lover, and she liked her beaches to come with trees. She was dressed in blue linen pants and a white linen top and wore a large straw hat. She could swim, but no one had ever seen her do it. She preferred to watch the others from under her umbrella, to take in the scene: the noisy clamor in the distance; the green pond's graceful curve, fringed thick with oak and pine.

There were the sunbathers and then there were the swimmers. Aidan and Tim, Louisa, Charlotte, and Natalya all arranged themselves in various states of undress on the sand. Cliff rubbed Nella thoroughly with sunscreen. But Feng and Mei and Prithwish ran down to the water and waded in. Shivering in her black tank suit, Mei inched her way along. She was small and fair, with a dark birthmark on her thigh; her hair was cut like a boy's, severely short, a jagged frame for her large eyes and faint eyebrows. Feng splashed her on the backs of her knees, and she screamed and splashed him back.

"Hey, what are you doing?" Prithwish protested, caught in the cross fire.

"I'm getting out," Mei said to Feng in Chinese.

"Why?"

"Because I'm freezing!"

"Keep moving and you'll stay warm. Come on, swim."

"No. I'm frozen."

"Come on."

The three of them swam out a bit deeper, and then deeper still, until they could no longer touch the bottom of the pond, where mud oozed and sucked every footstep. They treaded water now, and spoke in bursts, out of breath from the cold and the effort.

"Isn't it odd this is Thoreau's pond?" Feng said in English for Prithwish's benefit. "Don't you think it's ironic there is an ice cream truck?"

"What's wrong with that?" Prithwish asked.

"And parking lots and restrooms?"

"I thought that's why we come here," Prithwish said.

"Ah." Feng flipped over on his back. He filled his lungs with air and floated, gazing up at the sky. Where Walden had once been crystalline and still, the water was choppy with kayaks, the air filled with talk and children wailing. In China, of course, the great sites were always packed. He could not even imagine the Forbidden City without crowds of sightseers. There was justice in that—the imperial palaces thrown open to the people. Walden, however, had been only a little pond, a place for meditation. And now, where Thoreau had contemplated self-reliance, you could buy Popsicles.

He missed his anonymity. He rued the way he had become the name and face associated with the lab's hot new work. The attention had distorted his role in the lab and damaged his friendship with Cliff. Where once they had joked constantly and teased each other, now relations were guarded and polite between them. Glass had taken Feng aside and spoken to him, tried to encourage him during the media barrage. He'd insisted in the long run that all this would help Feng find a good position, start a lab of his own, and establish himself at a biotech company or university. "You're a known quantity now. You have a name," Glass said. "Do you know how valuable that is? It's terrific. You'll be able to write your own ticket."

But writing your own ticket and being written on were two different things. After all his press Feng wondered what kind of worth he could accrue, celebrated for the wrong reasons, lionized as the key figure in someone else's research program. "Look, it's just a matter of emphasis," Glass explained. "The articles aren't wrong. Face it. They like you. You make good copy. Roll with it."

"I'm not some kind of hero, just for—" Feng protested.

"Roll with it," said Glass again.

"It'll blow over," Mendelssohn predicted.

Feng was not comforted by this. He wanted to succeed; he and Mei looked forward to earning at least one living wage. They wanted to have a child, but they scarcely spoke of that, a baby was so far beyond their means. He hoped to do well, but he wanted to succeed scientifically. This media success was only rhetoric and hearsay, the opposite of science.

Onshore, Kate sat cross-legged in cutoff shorts over her bathing suit. She was trying not to stare at long-legged Nella, who must have been six feet tall. Cliff's new girlfriend seemed a feminine Gulliver arrayed there on her towel, her slender fingers just brushing the sand.

"What's up?" Cliff asked, friendly as ever. He sat down next to Kate with his sandwich in hand.

"Not much." She was slightly miffed, and at the same time she knew she had no right to be. She viewed him with a mix of offended pride and sixteen-year-old humility.

"How's John Donne?"

"Dead."

She hadn't meant to sound quite so perfunctory, but Cliff laughed and laughed. "I guess that's the problem with the seventeenth century," he said. "It's kind of over, isn't it?"

"Kind of," she said. Her heart was pounding, her mind confused. Were he and Nella serious? Had she told a joke just then? "So you're famous now," she said.

"Not really."

"Charlotte brought Jeff's article." She picked up the copy of the *Crimson* lying on the sand. There was Cliff's picture on the front page and the headline "Postdoc Wants to Make Cancer History."

"Here's hoping no one reads it," Cliff murmured as he skimmed the first two columns.

"Well, it's just a student paper," Kate reasoned. "And it's the summer."

"Could we sort of . . . hide this?" Cliff slipped the folded pages under Kate's beach blanket. He had just begun to understand Feng's frustration with the press.

"Is it that embarrassing?"

"I come across like a total jerk trying to steal credit."

"I think it was meant to be flattering," Kate ventured.

"Yeah, well, it isn't."

"It's not really about you, anyway," she said philosophically.

"Who else could this article be about?"

"It's all about Jeff," said Kate. "It's about how he wants to be editor of the newspaper. It's him showing off, not you."

"Hmm."

"Hmm, what?"

"You're very . . ."

She held still, waiting. She was very what? Smart? Small? Perceptive? Persuasive? Pretty?

The word remained unspoken. He picked up her paperback and read the cover out loud: "*She Stoops to Conquer* by Oliver Goldsmith."

"We're doing it in the fall at school," Kate said.

"Oh, you're going to be in it?"

"I'll probably write the program notes. But I'd like to . . . I wish I could . . ."

"Who would you be?"

"Kate," she said. "Kate Hardcastle."

"Since you *are* Kate, they should give it to you," Cliff said, turning the slim book in his hands. "What's it about?"

"Well . . ." Kate began.

But just then her father announced, "All right, enough of this eating and lazing around. Who's swimming across the pond? Natalya? Aidan?" He sized up Aidan's boyfriend, who lay face down, working on his tan. "Tim?"

"God, no," said Tim, voice muffled in his towel.

"Where's Robin when I need her?" Sandy growled. "Cliff? You coming?"

"Yeah, I guess so." Cliff smiled at Kate apologetically, then stood up and stretched. "Here." He returned the book, then dumped his keys and wallet and T-shirt in a heap at her feet.

The four men marched down to the water, Glass first—short, wiry, and intrepid, with zinc oxide on his nose—then Aidan, blond and European in his monokini. Prithwish wore swimming trunks in a blue-and-white hibiscus pattern, and his belly hung over the top. He'd grown stout, but he was a fast and fluid swimmer. "Hurry up," he called to Cliff, who much preferred the warm Pacific to this frigid water. Cliff's red bathing trunks had faded to a dull rust color, and his skin was pale for lack of sun, but Kate thought he had a beautiful back, broad and bony. She imagined Cliff would outswim them all.

They glided off, kicking fiercely. Glass and Prithwish swam in front; Aidan and Cliff followed. Competitive and quick as ever, Glass set a punishing pace. Prithwish and Aidan slowed a little, but Cliff found, to his surprise, that he had no trouble keeping up. His body relaxed into each stroke, and his muscles seemed to curl and stretch with joy just to move again in water.

When the four were no more than specks heading to the opposite shore, Kate wandered over to the table and picked out a chocolate chip cookie. Next to the drinks cooler, Jacob and Aaron sat playing Go on towels in the sand.

"Do you know how to play?" Aaron asked politely.

"No."

"We could teach you," he offered.

"No thanks."

He was hurt, but said nothing. She was just a year older than he. As grade-schoolers he and Kate had played for hours at these picnics, digging moats and mounding up castles of wet sand, but that had been a long time ago. Now she hurried away to her sisters and her mother.

Charlotte was in a funk. Jeff was busy traveling in Brazil because he'd gotten his summer travel grant. She wished she'd gotten hers, but she never spoke of her disappointment. She didn't want to give her father the satisfaction. Disaffected, she viewed the pond through dark sunglasses and listened to the Talking Heads through earphones until she was almost someplace else. Louisa, however, had brought a folder full of photocopied journal articles and was highlighting them industriously.

"I might not work on Robert Hooke," she informed her mother.

"Might not work on him!" Ann exclaimed. "I thought you loved him."

"I loved *Micrographia*," Louisa said grimly. "Hooke was an ass-hole."

"Oh, really."

"He slept with his sixteen-year-old niece."

"Well," Ann began. "In those—"

"I just can't write my dissertation on somebody like that."

"I thought he was the most important, most neglected English scientist."

"And he discovered the great red spot on Jupiter," Kate chimed in.

"Well, he was a great scientist, and he is neglected," said Louisa, "but he's also a slime bag."

"He may have had his problems," Ann conceded, "but presumably the work is more important to you than the life."

Louisa thought for a moment. "No," she said.

Ann smiled at that.

"What?" Louisa asked, irritated.

"Nothing." Ann wasn't going to call Louisa naïve and stand accused of condescension. She wasn't going to fall into that trap. Still, she knew something about the interplay of selfishness and creativity. Her own unfinished book examined three eminent Victorians: Thomas Carlyle, Charles Darwin, and Elizabeth Barrett Browning. Each had been hampered by a mysterious psychosomatic ailment, each freed by sickness and neurosis to pursue the life of the mind, even while their families sacrificed for them and their servants catered to them. For years Ann had contemplated the way that weakness became strength. More than once as she ran her busy household, and organized her husband's and children's lives, she'd wished that she, too, could come down with some mysterious but non-life-threatening ailment; that she, too, could be delivered from the ordinary realm of errands and appointments, college teaching, and schedule keeping into the rarefied realm of art, or medicine, or science. She had come to envy, and even admire, Browning's reclusiveness, Darwin's delicate stomach, and Carlyle's acute hypochondria. In her professional as well as her personal life, Ann had come not only to forgive but to find the creative power in willfulness and human frailty. And so when Louisa fell out of love with Robert Hooke for being a sexual predator, as were so many men of his class in his day, as well as a genius, as so many men were not, Ann thought her daughter a bit shortsighted.

"If I'm going to devote years of my life to studying a scientist, it's going to be somebody I respect," said Louisa.

"You have high standards," murmured Ann.

"You mean ruling out incestuous relations? How is that such a high standard?"

"I just meant it might be difficult to find a great neglected early modern scientist who was also an entirely good man. You might find someone great and good, but I doubt in that case he'd also be neglected."

Louisa stuffed her journal articles and highlighter into her beach bag and flopped down on her towel. "I'd compromise on the neglected part," she said. "If he—or she—has to be famous, so be it."

"That's very generous of you," Ann said.

"Oh, stop it, Mom."

"Stop what?"

"Just stop making fun of me. You sound like Dad."

"I'm not making fun of you, sweetie," Ann said. And, in fact, her heart broke a little at the thought of Louisa struggling like a latter-day Diogenes, searching through history for an honest man.

Cliff was warm now from swimming. They were at least halfway to the other bank, and the trees rose up in front of them, lush and green. But Aidan was lagging far behind, and called out, "Hey! Hey, you guys!" Glass didn't hear Aidan at first, and kept on swimming, but Cliff stopped, treading water.

"Are you okay?"

"I'm getting tired," Aidan called. "I think I want to head back."

"I'll go with you," Prithwish offered.

"It's okay, I'll be all right."

"You shouldn't swim alone," said Prithwish.

"I'm really fine."

Prithwish and Cliff hesitated a moment, their heads bobbing in the green and silver water. The pond was deep, and it was a good twenty-minute swim to either shore.

"I'll go with you," Prithwish decided, and swam back toward Aidan.

"Come on, Cliff," Glass sang out. Cliff was getting a bit tired himself. Still, he felt he had no choice but to follow. He put his head down and paced himself, swimming in Glass's wake. Not for nothing did Glass jog every morning. Not for nothing did he train and run the Boston Marathon each year. He was scarcely out of breath when they finally made it to dry land.

There was no beach on the far shore of Walden Pond. No one had trucked in sand here. Cliff pulled himself up onto the rocks.

"Hey, don't stop now," Glass complained, and Cliff remembered Glass liked to turn around and swim back without any rest at all.

"Just let me catch my breath," said Cliff.

"You'll only get cold," Glass warned him, but then he climbed up out of the water as well. "Stand over here in the sun. My God, this lab could use some exercise." He looked at his Rolex Oyster watch and shook his head. "You guys are atrophying." Then, without missing a beat, "I wanted to talk to you about the *Crimson* article."

Tired as he was, Cliff wished he were back in the water. He should have known not to ask Glass for rest.

"This is not how we want to present ourselves."

"I know," said Cliff, "I didn't think—"

"Well, you should have thought about it."

"It's just a student paper," said Cliff. "And it's the summer weekly issue. Nobody's going to read it."

"Your interview is in the public record now," Glass snapped.

"You told me to meet with him!" Cliff burst out. "You asked me to speak with him."

"I assumed that while speaking to Jeff, you'd use your common sense."

"Look, he asked me about my role in the work. I just answered his questions."

"Your answers," said Glass, "do not match any of the other stories out there."

"You mean the stories about Feng. Well, Feng didn't want to talk to Jeff. Nobody wanted to talk to him, so I'm sorry, but I had to do it. Jeff asked what I did, and I told the truth."

"Journalism has nothing to do with the truth," Glass snapped. "There is a time and place for the truth, but journalism is very simple: one interview, one story. Just that one story, and then the other side of that story. There isn't time for your alternative version, and my commentary, and everyone's two cents. There just isn't time. We are selling exactly one thing here. We are selling R-7. Not you. Not your career."

"I wasn't trying to sell myself in the Harvard *Crimson*," Cliff said softly.

"That's how it reads." Glass slipped back into the water. "That's how it comes across. And it's bad for the lab. It just makes it that much harder for us to do what we need to do."

Cliff caught himself as he was about to speak. He choked back angry words, but then he couldn't help himself and blurted them out anyway. "If you were so worried about keeping the lab on message, then you should have done the interview yourself."

Glass said nothing. He pushed off from the bank and didn't even look at Cliff.

"The article wasn't really about me, anyway," Cliff called as he scrambled in after Glass. "It wasn't about the lab, or me, it was all about Jeff. It was really just about how he wants to become editor of the paper."

Otterlike, Glass glided out on his back, head up, looking over at Cliff. Steely-eyed, but with just a hint of humor, he said, "Now, that is certainly true."

Crouched at her sisters' feet, Kate was playing with Aaron's magnetic chess pieces in the sand.

"I was wondering where those went," said Aaron. He dusted off the pieces and set them up on the little board. "White or black?"

"I don't want to."

"Look, I'm just using these." He pointed to the skeleton crew of men he'd set up on his side. "You can be white."

"Go, Kate," Louisa cheered.

"Oh, God," she muttered.

"You used to play very well," Ann reminded her.

"In sixth grade." She studied the board and tried to remember the opening her father once taught her.

"That's not bad," said Aaron, countering immediately.

She tried to ignore him as he knelt across from her in the sand. She'd always liked the game, but, perfectionist that she was, she hated struggling at it. After some thought, she ventured forward with her knight.

"Are you sure you want to do that?" Aaron asked.

"Oh."

"Try something else."

"No, I already moved it."

"It doesn't matter. That's better," he said. Then, two moves later: "Have you thought about your bishop? Good."

He was coaching her, guiding her into position. Gradually, her many white pieces and his few black gridlocked in a draw.

"Good game," he said.

She looked up at him. "No, it wasn't."

"Why not?"

"Because you were giving me the answers. You were practically forcing me to win!"

"I wasn't forcing you, I was teaching you," Aaron said.

"That's how your dad taught you?" Kate asked skeptically.

"Yeah." Aaron glanced toward his father. "Sort of."

Jacob snorted with laughter from his chair.

"There they are." Ann pointed to Cliff and Sandy in the water. The two of them were swimming more slowly now, steadily stroking toward shore. "I was getting worried about you," she chided Sandy when he finally arrived.

"Why?" he asked, drying himself off with his towel.

Disgruntled, and more than a little out of breath, Cliff paced the sand. He would have liked to walk down the beach, follow the trail under the trees and take a few minutes by himself, but it was time for the toast. Marion was distributing plastic champagne flutes. Prithwish and Aidan were popping corks on the green bottles of Martinelli's sparkling cider.

"Did you swim all that way?" Nella asked Cliff in her South African accent. "We'll have to get you a real drink, then."

"All right, everybody, gather round. Gather round," Sandy ordered in his jovial, commanding tones as he and Aidan and Prithwish poured. And everyone did gather, cups overflowing. Even the kids, tall as they were nowadays. Louisa and Charlotte stood at Ann's side, and Kate and Aaron took glasses. The sunbathers roused themselves.

Natalya and Tim crowded in. "We have a lot to celebrate this year," said Sandy. "Some great results, some great follow-up. Our *Nature* paper." The researchers whooped and Aidan whistled as Sandy held the fresh black-and-white offprint high in the air, a small stiff banner in the breeze. "And last but not least the new grant from NIH, funding to commence in September."

"Phew," said Prithwish amid applause and laughter. They could joke now. Funding after such a long drought was like coming back from the dead.

"We have a lot of work ahead of us," said Marion.

"Believe it or not, we're just laying the foundations," Sandy said. "Aidan and Natalya, I've said it before, and I'll say it again. We've got the best lab techs in the institute. Not to mention the best baritone!"

"And with the new funding, we're hoping to hire a third tech to take some of the load off of you," Marion announced.

Cliff glanced at Nella and smiled, imagining she might be the one invited upstairs. She rolled her eyes and snorted comically. "Yeah, right, you *wish*," she whispered.

Aidan and Natalya knew better and exchanged nervous looks. They dreaded the arrival of an entirely different tech from the second floor—a woman highly competent, but kooky as well, whining, droning, mirthless, braless. "Please God, not Billie," Aidan murmured under his breath while Natalya whispered furiously in Russian to her husband.

"Prithwish," said Sandy, "your teamwork on R-7 has been outstanding. Time and again, you've done everything we've asked, and more. Feng, what can I say? We're blessed. Who am I leaving out?" He made a show of looking behind him, and then grinned. "Oh, yes, Cliff."

Cliff looked down at the sand unhappily, even as Marion praised him, in what were, for her, superlatives. "You've done very well."

"You've shocked the world," added Sandy, whose superlatives were just that. "And your work is gonna turn the cancer community upside down." Cliff glanced up. As always, he was amazed at how fast Sandy's mood changed. Then Sandy looked Cliff full in the eye and added joshingly, "All you need is a little humility and patience."

This coda confused and hushed the group. For just a moment no one spoke or even moved. Then the cool breeze off the pond ruffled Marion's stacks of white paper napkins and the toast went on merrily. "To R-7! To the lab!"

Only later, in the parking lot, did Marion take Sandy to task. "That was unnecessary."

"What do you mean?"

"Criticizing Cliff like that, in public."

"I didn't criticize him publicly. I talked to him about the interview in private. All the way on the other side of the lake."

Jacob and Aaron were coming up the path with the loaded red wagon in time to hear Marion tell Sandy, "I didn't ask you to be my enforcer."

"Oh, come on, Marion," Glass wheedled.

"I'll speak for myself, thank you very much," she snapped, and Jacob cheered silently to hear his wife talk like this. He loved to see her stand her ground before Glass, as of old.

4

As THE last cars were loaded and the coolers drained of melted ice, Robin was marching down the aisle in Phillips Congregational Church in Watertown on the arm of a groomsman named Tom. At the altar, as rehearsed, she and Tom separated, and Robin took her place in line with the five other bridesmaids. Like them, she carried a white nosegay, and like them wore a sea-foam green taffeta dress with a tight bodice and full skirt, a sash tied in an oversize bow at the back, and puffed sleeves the size of giant melons. She tried to think happy thoughts.

She thought about how beautiful the church looked in the late afternoon light, with its white walls and dark wood pews. She considered how lovely her auburn-haired cousin looked walking up the white cloth runner. Carolyn's train streamed and rippled over the steps to the altar, and as she stood there with the groom she seemed to glow to her fingertips. Robin thought how glad she was that her father and her uncle had started speaking to each other once again, and that there was peace in the family, at least for a while. And then, inexorably, her mind turned to Cliff. She could not stop questioning his data in her mind. There had been a time she'd searched his face to judge his moods. She'd watched him watch other friends, or even women he hardly knew, and wondered constantly what he felt and thought. Now, however, she was consumed with curiosity about what he'd done.

She had her own offprint of the journal article, and she must have read it twenty times. She knew by heart the shape of every column on the page, and the placement of each figure. His data in the article looked fine. But the data were more than fine; they were spectacular. Too good to be true? She was horrified at herself—that just a granule of skepticism and resentment could swell like this inside of her. Even now, in church, at her cousin's wedding, her imagination raced ahead: no one was at the lab. Everyone was driving back from Walden Pond. Mendelssohn and Glass would head home, and the researchers would meet for burgers at Elsie's, as they always did. The lab was empty, and Cliff's paperwork was there to read.

What a strange fever had taken hold of her. At the reception, with the band playing and the family all around her, even then, in every lull, suspicion washed back over her. She stood apart.

She was the only scientist in the family, famously erudite and famously single. Her interminable postgraduate studies were a source of bemused pride to her dad, who often wondered aloud when she would get a "real job." Her life in Cambridge was the subject of much talk among her cousins, who had just about given up trying to fix Robin up with friends. Even now, in the white reception tent, the cousins urged her on and pressed her forward in the crush as Carolyn prepared to throw her bouquet. But Robin did not want the flowers, and stayed diffidently on the fringes of the crowd. Carolyn turned her back on the girls and threw her bouquet over her head, and the bridesmaids screamed and the flower girls shrieked and jumped up the way Robin had seen dogs on the Common jump up to catch tennis balls in their mouths. One of the little girls caught the beribboned prize, and the bridesmaids turned away, smiling but slightly disappointed, toward their boyfriends.

"I didn't see you trying very hard over there," her father teased.

"Sorry, Dad," she told him. "I guess I'll just have to be an old maid."

"Don't say that." He dabbed his perspiring face with his handkerchief. He was flushed and overweight, hot in his suit. She worried about her father, and pestered him often about going on a diet, and quitting smoking, and getting a stress test. She was afraid he would get lung cancer or emphysema, and more immediately that he had hypertension, but he never listened to her when she went on about these matters. Maddeningly, he always said, "You can start giving me medical advice when you have a medical degree." And then Robin's stepmother, Lynn, would jump to his defense.

"I like your style," Robin had told Lynn once. "I like the way you stand up for Dad and defend his right to die."

Robin despaired for her father, but she loved him. She had no patience for her stepmother.

When all the toasts were said and the dancing done, Tom drove Robin back to Cambridge. "Just tell me where," he said. And she guided him through Harvard Square, up Broadway to Felton Street.

"This is it?" he asked uncertainly, as he gazed at the Philpott Institute.

"Thanks, this is perfect," she told him, and hurried out. "I just have to check some stuff at the lab."

"Nice outfit," the guard told Robin as she sprinted past in her bouffant dress. She flushed, but didn't stop. She pushed open the heavy doors that led to the back passageway, and ran up the stairs to the second floor, with its peculiar smell of ammonia and pencil shavings, its linoleum tiles checked black and green like the mottled covers of composition books. Up again on the black iron stairs, her heels clanged on the metal treads and her nosegay of white roses flopped and drooped. She threw it down on the table in the lounge.

Darting inside the lab, she flicked on the fluorescent undercabinet lights, and found her copy of the journal article on her desk. Then she reached for Cliff's lab book and riffled through its alternating white and yellow pages, devouring the numbers there.

She had looked at most of this before, but now she compared his notes to the printed data in the article. Her heart was galloping; her lungs cramped and strained at the tight bodice of her dress. There is nothing here, she told herself. Still, she checked the numbers in each table. Meticulous as a scientific bookkeeper, she combed through the raw data and final draft. Line by line she audited Cliff's accounts. She took a deep breath and closed the book. There were no discrepancies.

She turned the lights off and stood uncertainly for a moment in the darkened lab. Her trepidation faded; her huge anticipation sank away. She walked deliberately down the hall, and then she walked a little faster. Her shoes clicked on the hard floor, faster and faster. Her heels ticked down the stairs to the first-floor exit as she ran to the animal facility.

As Robin unlocked each door downstairs, her dress billowed about her knees, the synthetic fabric rustling around her like a shower curtain. Frantic though she felt, she paused at the lockers and donned lab coat and hairnet. She peeled disposable booties from the stack and slipped one over each pump. She was not afraid of the eerie light or squirming animals, the faint smell, the kitchen refrigerator that served as morgue—all the more gruesome for its ordinary white and chrome, its butter compartment and crisper drawers, and even the snack drawer meant for cheeses, stuffed with stiff mouse bodies in their body bags. She was not afraid of the scuffling mice, the wounded animals staining each other as they fought. She feared none of this. She was afraid of herself for rushing down so desperately, in search of . . . what? Evidence Cliff was not as lucky or as talented as everybody thought.

In the animal room she turned on the examining light and took down the clipboards that hung from the cage racks. She pored over the registry of births and deaths and procedures in between. The notations were all routine, whether in Cliff's scrawl or Feng's firm block letters. She peered at the nude mice in their cages. Generations had come and gone since March, and any surviving animals from then were old and blind. She would go home. She would forget all this. Still, she slipped into one last room.

The dissection room was unusually neat, the table clear except for its polystyrene dissecting pad. The drawers underneath were locked, but Robin knew where the key was kept, and opened them one by one. Trays of rusty pins emerged, boxes of extra gloves and black plastic bags, and there, in the bottom drawer, a messy pile of papers, mostly scratch, along with a couple of thin-line permanent markers. Robin's fingers trembled as she held up the pages to the examining light. There was Cliff's handwriting, sloping, spiky, unmistakable on three pages ripped from a spiral notebook. She could not tell if these were just draft notes for his experiments in the journal article, or for some other set. Then on the second page she saw a notation for injection with R-7, and the date, March 21.

She began to run down the hall, her heels sliding in the slippery booties. She pulled them off, tossed her hairnet. She dumped her lab coat in an open laundry bin. Then she pulled her shoes off altogether and began racing up the stairs in her stocking feet. Carrying keys, journal article, three pages of data, and her dyed satin shoes, she sprinted for the first-floor photocopier.

CLIFF AND Feng spent Monday morning mocking up their poster for a conference at MIT. They stood at a table in the third-floor lounge with flowcharts detailing how R-7 entered and subverted cancer cells. The process was both simple and elegant in theory: the virus with covert forces in tow approaching, parachuting in behind enemy lines, and knocking off the cancerous sentinel, then donning the enemy uniform and proceeding to destroy the enemy infrastructure. Illustrating these war games accurately on paper was not easy, however. Cliff had prepared elaborate diagrams showing the genetic structure of R-7 and the genetic structure of the target cancer cell. Feng had typed up several pages of exposition explaining exactly how virus and cancer cell fit together. The two men now stood arranging and rearranging diagrams and notes on their foam core board.

"It's too cluttered," Cliff said after some thought. "We should take these out." He discarded two pages of Feng's description.

"I think we need those," Feng said.

"They're too wordy."

"I think," said Feng, "the diagrams need a key."

"They shouldn't need a . . ." Cliff caught his breath and sneezed. "What is that?" He rubbed his eyes. "I'm allergic to something in this room." A bunch of flowers lay half dead on the side table near the couch. "Who left these here? God." He tossed the wilted blossoms in the trash. "The diagrams should speak for themselves," he said, quoting Sandy Glass.

"Accuracy is more important than elegance," Feng retorted, quoting Marion Mendelssohn.

The two of them faced off for a moment, tense and almost rivalrous, like brothers, opposites in the same family, one taking after the father and one after the mother, neither willing to give way. Feng made his point, but Cliff knew that he was right. The poster was supposed to advertise, not explain. How many times had he been told that in grad school? The poster was a storyboard; the cartoon version. And so, with some authority, he set Feng's wordy pages off to the side.

Cliff was exerting control as he never had before, and control was his prerogative. Feng did not dispute that. Characteristically, he did not debate the issue further, but in that moment Feng resolved to work on something else. He needed something of his own, even if it was on the most trivial problem. In the lab, solitude had always been his friend, and obscurity meant freedom. Cliff's lexicon of Fungi made Feng seem merely cynical. The scrawled definitions: "axiom = assumption; assumption = confusion; confusion = status quo"—all those transcriptions of Feng's sayings hardly captured the contradictions in his character: his reticent imagination; the sublimation of self, masking independence. He was tired of Cliff and his famous discovery.

Restless, Cliff propped his poster on the couch, then on a chair, and finally on the counter against the microwave. He backed into the doorway to look at the result, considered his composition, and then paced a little in the hall. He just wanted to get the presentation right. All his thoughts and actions served R-7. Cliff saw now that you could not become possessive of this kind of research. Instead, he, the researcher, had become possessed by his creation. Was there some way to simplify the diagrams? He wanted graphics bold enough to stop people from across the room.

Pacing in the hall, Cliff nearly collided with Robin. "Oh, sorry," he said.

She stared at him hard. She couldn't help herself; it was as if she saw him for the first time.

"I said I was sorry," he told her, irritated by her piercing look, and he kept walking.

She ducked into the cold room with its cluttered shelves of old equipment, its defunct Beckman centrifuges. Shivering, she tried to compose herself.

She'd spent half the night poring over her photocopies. The notes included the numbers for several experimental mice, along with the outcome of injection with R-7. This material was familiar to Robin. There was nothing wrong with the data—except for one thing. There was too much.

Robin had stared at the columns in Cliff's sloping handwriting. He'd recorded the ear-tag numbers of each mouse sacrificed; the record continued from one page to the next, spilling over messily. Had he repeated himself? Written down the same data twice? No. Each mouse number was unique. But there were too many mice. The total number dissected in the notes was thirty-three, ten more than what Cliff had recorded in his journal article.

Robin checked and rechecked. Had Cliff forgotten to include some mice in his final results, or had he intentionally excluded them? Why would he publish his results with some animals and not with others? Was there something wrong with the missing ones? Had they been contaminated?

Sleepless then, Robin sat up in her apartment with Cliff's flimsy draft notes on one side of the couch and the stiff journal offprint on the other. The notes and article would not reconcile.

Resentment had pushed her to this point, a shameful desire to pull and pick at his results, even hurt herself a little, as one might feel picking the scab off a wound. She'd hoped to find something wrong, but now that she had, she did not know what to do. Suspicion had brought her strength, but the evidence justifying her suspicion terrified her. Searching for mistakes, she had not expected anything but relief. She hadn't considered what would happen if she succeeded. She might have been jubilant, but jealousy did not carry her that far and led, instead, to darker emotions. She had never felt so angry in all her life. She was angry about the journal article, which was surely nothing more than a house of cards. She was angry at Sandy and Marion for betting everything upon this work. Most of all, she was angry at herself. She felt the irony acutely, that this was the one discovery she'd made in almost six years at the Philpott, and the finding was purely negative. She had uncovered not truth, but falsehood. How despicable she would seem to the others; how hateful she seemed to herself for even contemplating crying foul.

That evening the sky was gray and sullen, the August air so heavy she felt she was pushing aside curtains as she walked home. She was wearing a shirtwaist dress—comfortable in the air-conditioned lab, unbearable outside. She wiped the sweat from her eyes as she cut through Harvard's quadrangle of redbrick laboratories. In the grassy courtyard the scientists were warming up, shirtless, batting the ball back and forth over the volleyball net despite the heat. Prithwish and Cliff and a couple of people from the second floor were there, warming up to play some plant biologists from Harvard. She stood and watched for a few minutes as the men set and spiked the ball. The courtyard rang with shouting; the men fought hard for every point. Cliff jumped up at the net, stretched his long arm, and slammed the ball down at a wicked angle. Then he turned back to Prithwish, bowed, and grinned. His grin faded only ever so slightly as he saw Robin standing on the sidelines.

A drop of rain pelted her face, then another. It began to pour. Robin took cover in the doorway of the bio labs where the bronze rhinos stood guard. Even in the cloudburst, the guys whooped and jumped with the ball. Cliff dove to make a save and skinned his knees and elbows. He was wet and bloody and dog-happy. The rain delighted him, even as it brought him down.

"Water polo!" he called out, palming the ball with one hand and heaving it into the net.

Robin had never seen anyone look less guilty. But how did guilty people look? Was he really so deluded? Had he deceived himself so well? Why not? He charmed everyone; he spoke and smiled and had you like the ball in the palm of his hand. She'd known he was a charmer, but she hadn't understood the half of it.

That night she padded up to the fifth floor of her apartment building and knocked softly on Larry and Wendy's door.

There was no answer. Of course she should have called first. She shrank away, embarrassed, when Larry finally came to the door.

"I was wondering . . ." Robin began.

"Do you want to go to the Toshiro Mifune Festival?" Wendy interrupted at Larry's shoulder. She was holding the Brattle Theater schedule.

"Actually," Robin said, "I was wondering if I could ask your advice about some weird stuff going on in the lab."

"Weird stuff in the lab. Come in, come in, that sounds like fun," said Larry, ushering Robin inside.

The apartment was at least three times the size of hers, and overlooked the Common. The place was painted white and had an airy, albeit slightly cluttered, feeling. There was a real entrance hall, and a formal dining room, which Larry used as his wood shop. The built-in china cabinet displayed Larry's tools behind its glass doors, and a sawhorse stood in place of a table. In the living room, several harpsichords in varying degrees of completion stood on spindly legs or lay prostrate on the floor. Bookcases were piled high with computer-science texts and board games in their boxes. The walls were adorned with completed jigsaw puzzles sprayed with fixative, mounted, and framed. Renoir's *Dance at Bougival* hung in the apartment, as well as Van Gogh's *Starry Night*.

Robin took a seat on the futon that served as couch and guest bed. Wendy poured her a glass of seltzer and placed it on the coffee table next to the one thousand pieces of Vermeer's *The Lacemaker* while Larry asked cheerfully, "What's the dirt?"

And so Robin told them about the journal article, and her apprehensions. She told them how she'd come across the three pages of data stuffed in the drawer. She told them what she'd seen, and what she had concluded. "I saw him sacrifice his mice on March twenty-first," she said, "and that was the same day he recorded here." She offered the three photocopied pages to Wendy.

"How do you remember what day it was?" Wendy asked.

Robin flushed. "My diary," she said. "I wrote it down."

She took out the journal article, creased and worn with reading, and began to push aside the pieces of Vermeer so she could spread the pages on the table. "Ah, ah, ah," warned Wendy as Robin mussed the edge of the puzzle. Robin stopped and simply handed the pages to Larry, who nodded as he followed her finger from one data set to the other.

She was amazed at how much better she felt disburdening herself. Her terrible thoughts took rational form. Her doubts changed from secret monsters to cogent questions. In the telling, all her ideas and her actions were beyond suspicion; they were entirely justifiable.

She was unprepared for Larry's response. "Well, what are you suggesting? You're telling us Cliff is actually hiding data?"

"Why would he try to hide his data?" asked Wendy.

"I think he was . . . I think the data didn't conform to his ideas," Robin spluttered, "and so he suppressed the results that didn't fit."

"No scientist would do something like that," Larry declared.

"Never," said Wendy. "And besides, if he was so anxious to suppress his data, why would he leave his notes in the dissection room for you to find them?"

"I think, possibly, he made a mistake, or forgot . . ."

"He may have left some kind of draft notes around, but lie in a publication?" Wendy turned to Larry. "Have you ever heard of something like that?"

Larry squinted thoughtfully, as if he were scanning every scientific field. "There are instances. I mean, there have been scandals in the past, but they're rare. And they're almost always disputed. There's almost always some explanation. Look," he said to Robin, "people just don't come out in refereed journals and lie about their work. It's crazy. First of all, they'd never get away with it. There are too many safeguards. They'd get caught by their principal investigator. Or the referees would find something fishy in the article. And then, even if the thing did get published, no one would be able to reproduce the work later on, and the scientific community would catch them. Think about it logically. Once your paper is published, everyone else is going to try to follow in your experimental footsteps, and they'll get bad data of their own. It's unavoidable. Six months later or six years later, the truth will out. You suppress bad data—it's going to cost you your career."

"No one would do it? Or no one should do it?" Robin asked.

"Both," said Larry.

"What put this idea in your head?" asked Wendy.

Robin could see they thought the worse of her for speaking up. She'd offended them, blaspheming their ideas of what a researcher always did and said and meant. Larry and Wendy were both atheists, of course, but they kept the scientific faith, hallowing intellectual honesty, and technology, and the pursuit of progress. Though they were nerdy, they were pure of heart. Larry had devised all sorts of programming solutions, and Wendy was famous for her ingenious methods for testing and debugging code. She was known at MIT as the Queen of Bugs. They were frighteningly skilled and devilishly imaginative, but neither could conceive of such dishonesty as Robin proposed.

"So you're alleging some of this data isn't in his paper," Wendy said. "How about his lab book?"

"I'm not sure," Robin confessed, "but I don't think it's all in there either."

Larry raised an eyebrow. "What are you trying to say?"

Robin stared down at the murky-colored puzzle pieces in front of her.

"His record keeping is shitty," said Wendy. "I'll give you that."

"Even if it is," Robin said, "you don't just lose ten animals in the publication process."

Larry and Wendy looked at each other, and Robin was embarrassed to see herself through their eyes, desperately collecting Cliff's discarded draft notes, hunting spitefully for some weapon against him. Even so, her neighbors had no explanation for the raw data she had found. "I think there's a problem here," she insisted.

"Highly unlikely," said Larry.

Robin flinched, but then she countered. "Highly unlikely isn't the same as impossible."

"No, no, no," Larry began again.

She listened to his argument. Still she was unconvinced. Her intuition told her Cliff had cheated.

On the ground, in the lab, intuition was a restricted substance. Like imagination and emotion, intuition misled researchers, leading to willful interpretations. While scientists like Mendelssohn knew how to wield it properly, young researchers had their intuition tamped down lest, like the sorcerer's apprentice, they flood the lab with their conceits. Plodding forward in the daily grind, Robin had not conceived a scientific intuition in years. She'd learned from hard experience not to trust her inner convictions lest they betray her. Now, however, her intuition was quite clear. "I can't keep this to myself," she said.

"Well, of course you can't," said Wendy.

"Once you go over all this with Cliff, you'll straighten everything out," said Larry.

Robin looked uneasily at her neighbors. They really believed this was all some kind of misunderstanding.

"You're going to talk to him, aren't you?" Wendy asked.

Robin didn't answer.

"You have to talk to him," Larry told her.

"I know," Robin said, "but I can't."

"Why not?"

She'd given Cliff her word that she wouldn't sneak around behind his back; she'd agreed to come to him first. How could she admit she'd broken those promises? To his credit, he'd managed to put aside his animosity and carry on calmly. If she confronted him with these notes, there would be no more keeping up appearances. It would mean war.

6

CLIFF WAS not an entirely unsuspecting adversary. He had suffered Robin's hostility for weeks, enduring her suspicion and prying eyes. Still, he was horrified by her new campaign against him. She had dug up some draft notes of his, and come to Mendelssohn with them, waving what was essentially scratch paper, as though she'd found a smoking gun. Sandy was out of town. Naturally, Robin had picked a time he was away. She knew Sandy had little patience for postdocs' complaints.

"This is unbelievable," Cliff protested to Marion. "She's stealing my notes."

"I didn't steal them," said Robin. "They were right there in the dissecting room for anyone to find."

"And photocopy behind my back? I can't—"

"Stop it," snapped Mendelssohn, and the two of them hushed and stood before her like a pair of misbehaving children, shamed but unrepentant. "Robin," Marion said, "you asked for time for your own work. In June we agreed you would begin your bone tumor project. You insisted Cliff stop making demands on you, and from what I understand, he has stopped. Why, then, have you been devoting yourself to second-guessing his results? Why have you been spending so much time studying his data? Is your own work no longer pressing?"

Cliff snuck a look at Robin and saw her redden. He was glad to see her get her dressing-down, and then again, he almost pitied her. She had always been slender, but suddenly she looked too thin. Her features seemed sharp, her expression miserable. She was such a thorny person, so consumed with doubt.

"What do you want?" she'd asked him once as they lay together, spent.

"Nothing," he said, and he meant it.

She propped herself up on her elbow, facing him. "I meant, what do you want in science?"

He traced his finger down her neck and over her collarbone. "Oh, fame and fortune. What else?"

She'd studied him then, searching his face. He saw the flecks of sun in her brown eyes, golden specks.

"What is it?" he asked her.

"I decided to be a biologist when I was sixteen," she said.

He'd laughed ruefully. "Didn't we all?"

Her eyes darkened; the gold was gone. She rolled over, turning her back on him.

"Hey, where are you going?" he protested. "Don't hide."

"I don't think," Marion continued, "that anyone should examine Cliff's private notes without his permission, and I don't want to reward this kind of behavior on your part, Robin, by passing judgment. Do you understand me?"

Robin nodded.

"Our work requires a certain amount of trust and, failing that, a modicum of respect." Marion handed Robin back her photocopied evidence and Robin took the pages, humbled, mute. Again Cliff was glad, relieved Robin would stop spying. Then Mendelssohn spoke again. "However, I have looked at these notes, Cliff, and I'm a little puzzled by the data here. There are numbers here I haven't seen before."

Now it was Cliff's turn to endure Mendelssohn's sharp questions and Robin's furtive glances. While Robin had been downcast seconds before, now she was alert. He had to explain that he'd used these three pages simply for jotting down notes, and that, in fact, they contained numbers from more than one data set. He'd scrawled his notes on the same pages he'd used for earlier experiments. He pointed to where one column of mice ended and the new column of mice began.

"What about the date?" Robin interrupted. "Why are they all dated March twenty-first?"

And he had to explain the date was only on the second page, and referred only to those mice, not the others.

"So those other mice were from last winter?" Robin demanded. "When? November? December? Why are their numbers all three hundreds?"

"You know all the mice in that line are three hundreds," Cliff told her.

"Why did you use the same pen, months apart?"

"Robin!" Marion shook her head in amazement.

"You still had the same ballpoint pen for three months?" Robin pressed.

Even Marion winced at Robin's pettiness. Confronted with his sloppy notes, Cliff had been defensive; he'd scrambled to explain the sloping ballpoint columns and decipher his own scrawl. He'd been ambushed and forced to interpret records he'd never meant for anyone to see. But his poor records and quick talking could hardly match the desperation, almost the hysteria, in Robin's questions. Dredging up his papers, Robin was so far out of line as to be unreasonable. How could anyone answer them? Cliff could only be grateful Mendelssohn understood that.

The others were turning away from her. They were sorry for her, but also wary; she seemed so obsessed, her behavior so erratic. Robin came in less now, and at odd hours. The others understood that sooner or later she would leave the lab altogether. Instinctively they avoided confronting her, or even discussing research with her anymore. She had talked to Feng and Prithwish, and tried to mine Aidan for information about Cliff's animals. She was spinning an intricate theory about Cliff and R-7, and all the strands came from her own mind.

One afternoon that fall Prithwish discovered Robin in the animal facility studying the log. He shook his head at her. "What are you looking for?" he asked gently.

"Nothing," she said.

He didn't question her further, but she knew what he was thinking: Then why are you down here? Why don't you just get on with your own work? She knew exactly what the others thought, and it hurt to be treated like a hazardous material, to be isolated and manipulated with gloved hands.

At times she felt the others must be right about her. She was obsessive. She must be mad. Cliff's evidence was all there to see, published
as hard fact, and she was only hurting herself by trying to chip away at
what was demonstrably true. Then, strangely, the unpopularity of her
position seemed to her the mark of truth, and a sign of disinterested
authenticity. She had no allies; her assertions were unprofitable, detri-
mental to her career. Her own work was submerged in her suspicions;
her days in the lab were numbered. She had already begun conversations with Mendelssohn and Glass about where she might go, or what
she might do next. On the other hand, Cliff had everybody on his side.
The others wanted to believe him, needed to believe him; he himself,
like a scientific pilgrim, had approached his experiments desperate for
a miracle, and for that very reason she was sure he'd selected data that
told the story he wanted to publish.

One person in the lab still spoke to Robin freely, and that was
Billie, the new lab tech. Tall, wispy, dolorous, Billie was always snif-
fling and gently, sadly grieved. After ten years at the Philpott, she suffered from asthma and sinus problems, which she attributed to fungus
in the institute's walls. The building was indeed old, and badly venti-
lated, but Billie also believed that the metal wire in women's bras conducted electricity from computers and other lab equipment and caused
breast cancer. Over the years her concerns had blossomed into a fanciful worldview in which the physical plant strangled its own denizens,
seeding fungal parasites into researchers' bodies so that gradually the
Philpott's scientists became susceptible to the very diseases they were
studying. She ruminated constantly about leaving the institute, but she
lingered on, a blessing and a curse, endowing the Philpott with her
skills and her neuroses.

Unfortunately, the other techs were tied up with the R-7 work,
and Robin needed Billie. Robin had scraped together some modest
leads with her bone tumor project, and Mendelssohn and Glass were
pushing her to submit a research note before she left in the spring. The
lab didn't need the publication. Marion had pressed Billie on Robin
with the purest intentions—to save Robin time and help her move
along. But Billie needed direction, she needed guidance; and so Robin
began a new phase of her exile: she and Billie working together, the
lab's least wanted.

"I think I know why they attack each other," Billie confided to Robin one afternoon as they were tagging young mice. With an instrument the size of a single-hole punch, Billie pierced each animal's ear, affixing a numbered metal tag, her movements deft and gentle as if she were fixing price stickers onto peaches at the grocery store. "You know why?"

"Why?" Robin asked stoically.

"Because the chi in the facility is weak," Billie told her. "See how cold it is and clinical? How there's metal everywhere? On the bench top. On the cage racks. The walls."

Robin looked warily at the windowless white walls.

"There's no earth energy here, no water energy. Just metal," Billie said.

"Metal is easy to clean," Robin pointed out.

"I believe this facility is a breeding ground for conflict." Billie plopped a newly tagged mouse into its cage. "Just imagine if we brought fresh flowers into this room, and painted the walls pink." She glanced down at the pink mice. "Or lavender. And if we changed the lighting and gave the mice little climbing structures and nests made out of natural materials."

"Climbing structures?" Robin asked in disbelief.

"For a long while I've been looking for other people with SBS— Sick Building Syndrome," Billie explained. "Now I see hundreds of animals are affected as well." She tagged another mouse. "The animals are stressed. The environment is making them ill. They have no privacy. There's nowhere for them to hide."

"Um, Billie," said Robin. "Could you just . . . put it . . ."

Billie put the animal back in the cage, and picked up yet another. "I see myself in them," she confessed. "They're suffering from this place. Look at this little guy." Billie held the animal right up to Robin's face.

"I'd like to finish up here." Robin stepped back from the busy mouse marooned on Billie's fingertips. Curious, the animal explored the edges of Billie's hand, and then dashed up her arm. Billie plucked up the mouse and replaced it in her palm. "They fight because this place makes them fight," Billie said. "That's why they bite each other. I'm not saying set them free. I'm not saying give up experimenting. I'm just starting to wonder what we can do to change the feng shui in here and give some thought to the imbalances—"

"Billie," Robin interrupted in exasperation. "Could we get on with it?"

"In these rooms," Billie continued.

At that moment the mouse in her palm leapt onto Robin.

She screamed. Robin was not afraid of mice, but she was so startled she shrieked. The wizened nudes hardly ever leapt like that, so high, so far. They scarcely ever acted so alive during procedures. Hearing her scream, the red-eyed mouse froze, clinging to her lab coat like a tiny monster come to life. "Get it off," she shrieked at Billie. "Get it off!"

"Hold on." Carefully, stealthily, Billie reached for the mouse, but it ran up the lapel of Robin's lab coat. She felt its little body through the thin material. Sickeningly, she imagined the animal was going to climb inside her collar. She thrashed and tore at her lab coat in panic.

"If you'd just stand still," Billie suggested, but Robin ripped her coat off and threw it on the bench top. She ran out of the room to the end of the hall, and then she cried as she had not cried since she was a very little girl. She cried because she had lost control, because her situation was absurd. She wept for loneliness.

But she forced herself to stop. She knew Billie would come looking for her; at any moment someone from upstairs could come walking by. She choked back her tears, took off her gloves, and dried her cheeks as best she could with a clean tissue she found in her skirt pocket. Her face felt swollen; she knew her eyes were red. Still, she donned a fresh lab coat and walked back into the animal room, where Billie was still bustling around with the mice as if nothing had happened.

"He's all right," Billie reassured her immediately. "I picked him up and he's in there." She pointed to the little daredevil, now tagged and caged. "And I tagged these guys. Numbers 603, 604 . . ."

"Just a sec," said Robin, picking up her logbook.

"You see what it does to them," Billie said. "You saw how that poor animal flew off the handle. I'm really starting to believe that they're unbalanced. They express the disequilibrium in their environment."

That evening Robin went to find Nanette downstairs where she taught Beginning Quilting in the first-floor lunchroom. The dozen or so students were all women, some postdocs, some secretaries, along with several institute wives. They were from Pakistan, Japan, Brazil, and South Africa.

As Robin slipped inside the door, Nanette brandished a small orange-handled tool.

"Ladies," she said, "take out your rotary cutters. Hold them gently but firmly in your favored hand. You will be drawing them across the fabric with your straightedge as your guide. Watch as I demonstrate." Nanette adored teaching women from other countries. With their exotic color choices, they made the craft their own, piecing a magenta medallion against a background of palest green, placing bloodred triangles like origami cranes in a sea of gray. "Your rotary cutter is like a pizza wheel. It is very, very sharp. What do we do if we cut ourselves with our rotary cutter?" She paused for effect and then cried out: "For God's sake, get out of the way so the blood won't ruin the fabric."

Nanette had always told Robin that she'd taken up quilting because her job mixing media was not geometrically challenging enough. Robin knew, however, that it wasn't just shapes and edges Nanette wanted in her life, but people.

"All right, let's take our scraps and begin." Nodding at this one, correcting that one, Nanette walked from table to table as the women bent over their work.

"You look terrible," Nanette whispered to Robin when she finally made her way to the back of the room.

"Thanks a lot."

"What's wrong? What happened?" Then she took on her teacher's voice. "If you'll excuse me for a moment, ladies." She ushered Robin out into the corridor.

"I've had a bad day," Robin admitted.

"You look exhausted. You're still not sleeping?"

"Not too well," said Robin.

"You know what you are?" Nanette began.

"Frustrated," said Robin.

"Depressed," said Nanette. "Did you know insomnia is a sign of clinical depression?"

"I'm stuck working with Billie on a dead-end paper; the lab is moving ahead with Cliff's results . . ."

"Sleep with 'em and forget 'em," Nanette said. "Move on."

"But I have moved on."

"I'm getting worried that—" Nanette began.

"So am I," Robin interrupted. "I've been thinking about going over to see Uppington."

"Your advisor?"

"Is that wrong? I've got to get some outside advice. I just don't know whether he screwed up his record keeping by mistake or on purpose. . . ."

"I'm not worried about Cliff's results; I couldn't care less about his results," Nanette said, touching Robin's shoulder. "I'm worried about you. This place gets to people after a while. It's poisonous."

Robin laughed shakily. "Oh, please don't tell me about the toxins at the institute. I've been listening to Billie all day."

Nanette peered at her. "You know you can call me anytime—day or night," she said.

"Are you putting me on a suicide watch already?" Robin asked.

"This is not a joke, young lady."

"You should get back to your class," Robin said.

"They're fine," Nanette said. "Can I tell you a secret about this place? The institute is not worth diddly-squat. Can I tell you about the research that goes on here? People are saving lives every day in theory, in the future. They think their work is the most important thing in the world, and they don't have a clue about what really matters. And you know what matters? The here and now. That's all. The rest is zilch, but scientists can't see it. Their own postdocs call for help, and they don't care."

"I'm not calling for help," Robin said, offended.

"Yes you are," Nanette told her.

"No, I'm pointing out problems in Cliff's data."

"Robin, Cliff's problems don't matter," said Nanette. "Compared to your mental health, this research really doesn't matter."

"I disagree," Robin said simply.

"Be careful," Nanette warned her.

"I have been careful," Robin said, "and it doesn't work."

7

JOHN UPPINGTON was English, and overstretched. He had many students to support and futures to settle. When Robin finished her degree, Uppington had suggested that she go to work with Mendelssohn at the Philpott, because Mendelssohn's lab was so small. "I think you might be less neglected there," he'd told her in his self-deprecating way. He was a short, stocky, slightly deaf advisor, close to seventy. His black hair had almost disappeared, and then sprung up again hopefully in little tufts in his ears and nose, and especially atop his eyebrows. The peak of his career long past, Uppington had settled on a medium-size eminence from which he viewed the field and pronounced upon the future of biological research. He was a member of every academy and society devoted to the national welfare and the greater good. His lab was always bustling, although, like Uppington himself, the place was not what it had been twenty years before.

As he listened to Robin in his office, Uppington was surprised by her story and, although he didn't say so, shocked by Robin's account of Marion's cool response. He had sent Robin to Marion precisely because he'd felt they had so much in common. There was a purity about them, a desire for truth as an end in itself. They were both perfectionists, exacting and patient. It distressed him to discover the two were out of sympathy. Marion, who worked with such care and concentration, should have given more time to Robin. She, of all people, should have respected Robin's opinions.

"Well, Robin," he said when she had finished. "I don't like to interfere where it's not my business."

She studied his desk.

"This is really a matter for Marion and Sandy to discuss together. I shouldn't like to interpose my own opinions. However . . ."

She looked up in an agony of suspense.

"The data do seem odd," he conceded.

She breathed again. "You don't think I was wrong to point it out?"

"No, not at all," he said. "I would certainly have pointed out the discrepancies myself, although I'm sure there's a very good reason for them. Generally, in cases like this—and they do come up—I would suggest a meeting with the principals, as it were, and one or two scientists outside the institute, for the general purpose of untangling what may be tangled, and clarifying what might be muddled. A great many difficulties can be avoided with the infusion of a little fresh air. I chaired a little committee like this just the other day at MIT, where we mediated some internal differences, and by the end, everyone was smiling, and everyone shook hands. It's really quite remarkable what a quiet conference room and a box of pastries can accomplish."

Sandy rejected Uppington's idea outright. "Don't you see what she's doing?" he said to Marion. "She's sneaking around behind our backs, slandering us to anyone who'll listen." It was a brilliant October day, and after finishing their lunches the two of them had stepped out to stroll down Oxford Street, past Harvard's brick Peabody and Semitic Museums, their stately maples green and crimson. "She's trying to undermine the integrity of the lab."

"Possibly," said Marion calmly.

"Do you think it's any accident that just as our new paper goes out for review, she's wangled this public interrogation?"

"Private seminar," corrected Marion.

"You don't mind, do you?" He stopped walking for a moment and viewed her in amazement.

"Of course I mind," she told him. "But I have confidence in our work. I have nothing to hide."

"You know that this is all about her obsession with Cliff."

"You mean their falling-out."

"Of course."

Marion thought for a moment, then said, "I think her motives are confused."

"God, Marion, stop acting so high and mighty."

"Stop panicking," she said. "It serves no purpose."

"I warned you they'd be trouble."

"Yes, and you seemed to be looking forward to it," she said drily.

"I don't think you understand how much she hates him."

Marion refused to let this ruffle her. "We'll sit down together and separate her legitimate concerns from her private grievances. I think it will be a useful exercise."

"Therapy session, you mean," Sandy grumbled.

"And if in fact Robin has found some errors worth correcting, so much the better."

"It's not good, Marion."

"No, it's very good for the work," she contradicted. "Maybe it's not good for the marketing of the work."

Hurt, Sandy turned away. There was an inequality in their partnership, and he felt it keenly just then, the assumption that Marion was the true scientist and he only the workaday clinician.

"You always overstate your case," she told him earnestly. "Why not accept criticism, whatever the source? Why should we always rush to dismiss any opposition to our ideas? Take the objections seriously and use them to make the work stronger."

"So you want to reward Robin's behavior."

"I want to engage her in a proper forum."

"Give her ammunition."

"No, diffuse her anger."

"It's going to be a disaster—you know that," he grumbled.

"No, it won't," she said.

He shook his head at her faith in criticism and academic rigor. She was imperious, but also innocent, and he knew he must protect her.

"Sandy doesn't want to sit down with Robin," Marion told Jacob that night at dinner.

"Really."

"What do you mean, 'really'?"

"Nothing," Jacob said.

She and Aaron looked at him across the kitchen table. It was just that Jacob never spoke without meaning something by it.

"He's worried about what Robin might say, given an opening."

"Are you worried about her?" Jacob asked.

"I'm worried for her," Marion said.

"Ah, that's something different," said Jacob.

"She's become very . . ."

"Depressed?" said Jacob.

"I was going to say desperate."

"She's never struck me as the desperate type," he said.

"How does she strike you?"

He didn't answer immediately. He was remembering the afternoon Robin came into his office. He had given her a gift that day. He'd had no idea how she would use it, but he'd given it to her anyway—a bit of knowledge; not a fact, but a piece of his own perspective. Cliff's results were too good to be true. She might have thrown away the offhand remark, small and cutting as a piece of glass. And yet he'd known she would not discard his idea. She had been prepared to hear it, and understood its significance. She'd picked up the broken shard he'd offered her and she'd begun to use it as the lens it really was. She'd begun to question Cliff's rushed data collection, to challenge the procedures, if not the results in the great R-7 paper.

In his gentler moments, Jacob felt a twinge of guilt for arming Robin in this way. He did not care about Cliff, or Sandy, but he did fear he'd opened Marion to attack. He had given Robin a dangerous gift; he had given her his own skepticism. He had not known how far she would carry his point of view. But he did know that Marion would purge herself of anything or anyone interfering with her work. Ultimately, Marion's research was far more important than R-7 or Sandy's claptrap about someday curing cancer. As far as Jacob was concerned, his wife's work was basic science. Cancer was her instrument, not her enemy. The disease was her reveal, framing and displaying the workings of the cell.

"How did Robin strike me?" Jacob mused. "I would say . . . disciplined. The opposite of Cliff."

"Why do you say Cliff isn't disciplined?" Marion asked sharply.

"It's just my impression," said Jacob. "Do you disagree?"

She cleared her place unhappily and took Aaron's empty plate with her.

"Hey, wait, I wasn't done. I wanted seconds," Aaron protested, and with baffled affection Marion forgot Cliff and looked at her little boy, her chess champion, now almost six feet tall, ready to wolf down another helping of chicken.

"Here. I'll get it for you." Jacob retrieved the plate from Marion.

His hopes for his wife were even more audacious than her own. He had a tendency to wish his own fierce brilliance upon her, and to foresee her unconditional success in his imagination. Such brilliance and success had been wished on him when he was a boy, and in his heart he knew the vanity of such wishes, but he couldn't help himself. He loved Marion selflessly, and demandingly, and not quite fairly. At times, as he had behaved with Robin, he took advantage of Marion for her own good. And yet his actions were so subtle, there was no way Marion would have guessed. He loved his wife, not merely with all his heart, but with all his mind. Marion accepted his sacrifices for her, had come to expect them as her due, but fortunately for her, she could not read minds, not even Jacob's. She would have been frightened by the devotion to be found there.

Overruling Sandy's objections, Marion calmly marked her calendar for Uppington's meeting. Despite Cliff's shoddy record keeping, she'd bolstered her confidence in him by speaking to Feng privately.

"Feng," she'd begun as she sat with him in the office. "I want you to know that I will hold anything you say here in the strictest confidence. But I wanted to ask you, because you have worked so closely with Cliff, whether you've sensed anything not quite . . . anything even slightly out of the ordinary in his work."

Feng started back in alarm, and with some remorse Marion saw the position in which she'd placed him: possible informant on his colleague and friend.

"I only ask," she said, "because I want to understand how the data got muddled and the numbers transposed. Good practices in the lab are my responsibility. If there was a lapse, I blame myself. I suspect the pressure to get our grant submitted had a great deal to do with it. Did you feel rushed? Did you feel that the experiments could have gone . . . better?"

He watched as she took up her knitting, an elaborately textured sweater of ecru wool. "They could always go better," he said.

"Well, yes, of course, but there comes a point when the outcome is endangered," Marion pressed him. "From your own experience with Cliff—did you ever find yourself uncomfortable with his practices?"

A great many thoughts and images flashed through Feng's mind: Cliff's tense behavior in the animal facility, his late hours, and particularly his insistence on injecting the animals himself. Feng remembered the morning he had arrived to find Cliff had already finished the injections. He had resented Cliff's proprietary behavior, although he understood it. However, he dared not confess this to Mendelssohn, even as he deigned not show Cliff his true feelings. Mendelssohn had given him an opening to air his grievances, but he was not Robin.

He had a well-earned abhorrence of this scenario—one researcher pulled out to inform on another. His father had been denounced in this way by his own colleagues, and forced to wear a dunce cap painted with his crimes. His father had been paraded up and down and forced to recapitulate the errors of his ways. At that time, Feng's mother had taught him to lie. She'd brought down the family photos and taught him to lie about each person in them. The two of them practiced until the lies were second nature. All this because they were the wrong sort of people—wealthy, intellectual, and landowning. His father's disgrace had nothing to do with science. The colleagues who had betrayed his father had been coerced themselves, and in the course of time, the betrayers were themselves betrayed. The whole charade had ended years before, but no one in Feng's family had ever been the same.

"He was pushing hard toward the end," Mendelssohn suggested.

"He worked very hard," Feng conceded.

"I'm afraid he may have done his work too fast," she said.

Feng nodded but said nothing, and his silence steadied Marion. There was no one in the lab she respected more than Feng. His integrity seemed to her unimpeachable, and just now his deep involvement with Cliff's work comforted her more than she could say. With her knitting gathered in one hand, she stood to see him out, and she thanked Feng for meeting with her, which he had never known her to do before. She didn't seem herself. She was thanking him and apologizing all at once.

8

THE MEETING took place in a borrowed Harvard seminar room both airy and dusty, painted ivory from its cornices to its radiators. Cliff came in with a pile of notes, and Feng followed after him, and they sat next to Mendelssohn and Glass on the far side of the dark wood conference table.

Robin could barely keep her hands from trembling as she sat there, nor could she look at Cliff. Art Ginsburg, once Marion's nemesis, now a Harvard professor, came in and shook Sandy's hand, greeted Uppington as an old friend, and kissed Marion on the cheek. Robin knew Professor Ginsburg had stolen Marion's ideas in the past. Years ago, hearing of her metabolic work with mice, he'd pursued a similar line himself and then presented his results first at a major conference, effectively stealing her thunder. Robin couldn't help shuddering to see him. Working for Marion, she had been brought up to distrust him. He was arrogant and lanky, with curly gray hair, a haughty nose, and deep brown eyes that ranged in their expression from bemused to pitiless. He wore a tweed jacket over corduroys and had a habit of opening his mouth wide and then shutting it again, as if he were trying to clear his ears after a long flight. He took out a sheaf of papers and busied himself with a red pen, even as Uppington called the meeting to order and Jeremy Choi burst through the door.

"I'm terribly sorry!" Choi was a young professor at BU and a protégé of Uppington's, which meant he was bound to come to the meeting even though he was busier than Ginsburg. He had been raised in Hong Kong and trained at Cambridge, and his English accent was far more pronounced than Uppington's, whose words and tones had flattened and smoothed like river stones from his long years in America. Choi's accent had not had time to mellow like that; he had no time for anything. "Have you already begun?"

"Not at all," said Uppington.

Ginsburg announced, "I'll have to leave at eleven."

"Well, let's get started, then," said Uppington, and he nodded at Robin. "Let's begin with just a brief outline of your observations and your concerns about the *Nature* paper."

He gave Robin the floor, and smiled encouragingly. Still, in the long, sickening moment before she began to speak, she felt all eyes on her, and heard Ginsburg's watch ticking. How odd she must seem, unruly and quixotic, tilting at errors no one else could see. She had been granted a hearing, but she was nothing to these men; she had no rights or reputation, no useful results to offer, only her critique, her niggling doubts about a fine research paper, her failure to reproduce what Cliff had done so well.

Choi produced a yellow legal pad and printed the date in the top right corner, and Ginsburg opened and shut his mouth. She was sure if she'd been a fly he'd have swallowed her on the spot. She wished she could have flown away; she devoutly wished to disappear, but she began to speak instead, and she spoke brilliantly.

She spoke of her high regard for Cliff's paper and her desire to see his experiments reproduced in her own lab and elsewhere. She spoke of her difficulties duplicating Cliff's work, first with pancreatic cancer cells and then with breast cancer cells from his own cell line. Was the problem her equipment? The cell lines she was using? Her own technique? She had eliminated each of these factors in turn, when suddenly, accidentally, she stumbled on three pages of notes. "I think perhaps the data in these pages was not accurately transcribed in the final drafts of the paper," she told the group. "The raw data conforms better to my poor results than to the excellent results the lab has published." And she passed around photocopies of Cliff's notes along with annotated copies of the journal article. "The discrepancies are highlighted in yellow," she explained as the scientists studied the evidence in front of them. Column by column, line by line, point by point, she referenced the data missing from the paper. "The data from Cliff's draft notes suggest a different outcome from the one published in the article," she said.

"How different?" asked Ginsburg.

"I've drawn two graphs illustrating the differences," said Robin, passing them around.

Uppington harrumphed at this approvingly. Choi leaned forward and took the two graphs Robin offered him. Even Ginsburg unfolded his reading glasses.

"The first graph displays the published results from R-7, and the second shows what the curve would look like if all the results from the raw data were included. As you can see, the published results cluster beautifully. However, when we take the published and unpublished data points together, they . . . scatter. In the published results nearly sixty percent of the mice are cancer free. When we take the published and unpublished results together, we find only thirty percent of the animals are cancer free, and almost seventy percent still have cancer after treatment with R-7."

Her manner was controlled, her arguments rigorous. The care she'd taken with her evidence, the graphs she'd drawn, the clear expression of her ideas—this was Robin at her best. No one heard the beating of her heart. Only Cliff noticed the slight tremor in her fingers.

He nearly shook with anger. Robin was accusing him of cheating—and how artfully she made her case. Not a word betrayed her jealousy; every phrase supported her claim to dispassionate judgment. By her account, she did not seek out his notes, but found them by accident! She did not directly accuse him of misrepresenting his results, but suggested he had transcribed them incorrectly. Naturally, she did not mention spying on him in the animal facility or prying into his lab book. She did not bring up the fact that she had taken notes that belonged to him, and photocopied and distributed them without his permission. She was the model of restraint. He wanted to jump up and set the record straight. But he saw how well Robin's calm manner served her; how acute her observations seemed, refined with understatement. How would he look if he attacked her? Cliff held still and scribbled down her points so that he could reply to each in turn.

"I don't have any charts or graphs," he began. "Just a simple apology and an explanation. The apology is for the notes that Robin found, which include data from several different sets of experiments. I jotted numbers on scratch paper in the dissecting room, and then as soon as my hands were free I copied them over into my lab book. My scratch paper has been lying around in disarray for far too long, and I recognize that this was both messy and misleading. In writing up my results, I never referred back to those scraps, but only worked from my lab notebook, which I've brought with me today. It's an open book for anyone to see. Now, to begin with Robin's first . . . her first concern . . ."

One by one he took on Robin's assertions and, it seemed to her, sidestepped each in turn. He confessed he had been careless. He had been rushed. Marion Mendelssohn nodded here. He had been sloppy because he'd tried to do too much himself. He turned to Feng, as if to say he could attest to that. Then he opened up his lab book on the table, and there the dates and data matched up precisely. As he showed his lab book and interpreted the numbers there, his voice was lively, his enthusiasm infectious. The tortuous connections Robin had attempted gave way to a scientific argument so natural, so compelling and intuitive, that everyone in the room seemed to relax. Choi leaned back and took a handkerchief from his pocket to clean his glasses. Sandy Glass knit his fingers together with bemused pride. Even Ginsburg twisted his mouth into a wry semblance of a smile.

And Robin watched the meeting slip away. Her graphs lay forgotten on the table. She had spoken well, but Cliff spoke better. He had the more compelling argument, because his results were beautiful. Her results were negative, her argument distasteful. He worked in the bright empirical realm, and she had mucked about with dark, dubious, moral forebodings. Perhaps Cliff's record keeping had been poor, but his achievement was tangible; his mice had been sick and now they were well. Even as he spoke about his work, Robin felt the mood shift. With a flick of the wrist, the meeting became a research seminar. Ginsburg and Choi and even Uppington looked at Cliff with true interest, as if to say "Now, here's the real thing; here's matter for discussion." How delighted they were to return to science.

Marion delivered her admonitions about observing the proper forms in future, and Uppington thanked Robin for speaking up about possible confusions. Ginsburg suggested imperiously that the minutes of the meeting should be written up and distributed. Cliff whispered something to Feng, who smiled and shrugged. They all preached about rigor, Robin thought, but they based their work on trust. Cliff was so intelligent, so winning—he would be a star. And why did she mind so much that he was messy going about it? Many, many researchers were messy. Lab directors could not put their fingers on every scrap of paper in their labs at every minute of the day. There was the book way of working, and then there was the reality. There was the presumption that everything that touched the nudes was sterile, and the reality that equipment was often only fairly clean. There were the rules and regulations posted in the lab and animal facility, and then the general standards of the community. Robin's case against Cliff might as well have been a case against the status quo, an argument against the natural bumps and jolts of the creative process. If only she could pin him down, hang him by the thumbs until he told the truth. Even as she held still at the table, all her rage welled up inside of her and she wanted to lunge at him and seize him by the throat until he cried out and confessed. But what weapons did she have? What recourse was left to her? She would always be the diligent little malcontent, while he was the creative one. Feng was the favorite in magazines for his immigrant success, but in the scientific community, Cliff's story of perseverance was the one everybody loved to hear. Poor record keeping in the past actually made Cliff's triumph brighter. He was the postdoc who finally made good, Prince Hal throwing off his shoddy workmanship and showing his true colors, coming of age at last.

Heartsick, she gathered her papers together.

"I thought you handled yourself very well," said Uppington.

That afternoon in the lab, Robin knew she could not stay until the spring. She could not continue across the room from Cliff, swallowing everything she knew and felt.

Through the windows the October light seemed hooded; the sun shone furtively. Deciding to leave, she began to feel a measure of peace. She had that power, at least—to turn away and go. Still, even in that moment of release a flood of regret rushed over her. She was going to have to leave the institute with her bone tumor project unfinished. Her work belonged to the lab. The cell lines and the equipment and the animals she'd used could not be moved.

She would probably give up any hope of a first-tier academic job. She was sorry about that—although she knew that after all these years and all this meandering, such a position would have been a long shot, anyway. She was sorry that the others were going to perceive her leaving as mostly personal, the outcome of her breakup with Cliff. She winced at that, but she could not stay.

She didn't say good-bye that evening, nor did she take anything from her lab bench but her purse. Still, she looked once around the room quickly, shyly, in a kind of farewell. Then she walked out into the hallway and down the stairs.

Someone was coming up as she descended; someone puffing, a little out of breath. "Robin," said Nanette. "I was looking for you. I have something for you."

Robin stood still. She had lasted to the end of the day; she would endure this.

"Here's the phone number," Nanette said, "of someone who found out some things about this institute he shouldn't have. It's a guy who uncovered a lot of crap and suffered for it. He knows what's gone on here—and he's had to deal with people trying to silence him. I want you to have this." She held out a little sheet of notepaper—pink paper, Robin noticed, bordered with purple hearts. There was a phone number and address printed in black pen, below the name Akira.

Part V
Inquiry

1

THE WORLD outside was wet. The morning's rain had stopped, and bright autumn leaves lay in tatters on the ground, shellacked to streets and sidewalks. Cliff and Prithwish were spearheading the effort with R-7 and everyone was pitching in, except for Feng. He had taken up a small project on the side, just a little thing, modest in scope, but entirely his. The project was Robin's bone tumor study. With her blessing, Feng had taken over the work and was trying to complete it.

"I don't want you to spread yourself too thin," Marion had warned him.

"It's okay," he said.

She frowned. "I don't want this to be a boondoggle for you." She couldn't help feeling superstitious about the unfinished work Robin had left behind. She knew it was irrational, but everything Robin had touched seemed unlucky to Marion. Doomed to disappointment.

Feng looked at Marion searchingly. She wondered if he understood how she had tried with Robin; how she'd argued with her, urging her not to give up, not to succumb to bitterness and isolation. She saw now she should have given Robin more guidance; she should have tended to Robin's wounded pride. She had been too caught up in the work and managed her academic children badly. She judged herself for this, and as usual, she judged harshly. She had tried for a better ending. She deplored the way Robin had left so suddenly, her work undone; it was a kind of suicide—at least professionally—a destructive, vindictive, frightening act. Marion saw the troubled look in Feng's eyes, a silent reproach.

But she misread Feng's expression. He was not thinking about Robin, but about the language Marion had used. His English was superb. He scarcely ever came across a term he didn't know, but for once she'd stumped him. He had never heard the word *boondoggle* before.

The lab was different now, the atmosphere so much lighter. Cliff hadn't realized until Robin left just how tense he'd been. He'd felt her staring at him, her look so penetrating, he'd thought at times she wanted to pry him open, the way he'd seen jewelers pry off the back of a watch. Then there were his papers, his notes and lab book. He had no longer felt safe leaving his notes strewn about, but gathered them up at the end of the day and locked them in the file drawer under his bench top. He'd never even thought to use the key to that drawer before Robin began prying. He'd had to ask Marion for it.

He'd come to think Robin had suffered a breakdown. People did crack in the sterile, claustrophobic quarters of the lab. The researchers were like miners or submariners, and inevitably some foundered. It was a confining life. He'd known someone in grad school who'd had a nervous breakdown and been hospitalized. He'd known others whose marriages broke apart—one friend in particular had had a disastrous affair with a professor. It was hard to tell how much trouble came into the lab with people and how much was caused by the work. In Robin's case, all he knew was that something had snapped, and she'd transferred all the frustration from her own failures onto him. It had been a horrifying transformation. She, who had always been so self-possessed, abandoned herself to accusations and conspiracy theories. What could she possibly have gained from it? Absolutely nothing. She seemed to have lost any hope of professional advancement. Furiously, irrationally, she'd simply tried to bring him down, and so he had begun to think that she was sick. The others thought so too.

Prithwish said, "I think something was wrong with her."

Billie overheard his remark as she came into the lab. "I could see she was out of balance; the environment was poisonous to her. That was why she fell apart in the animal facility."

"Fell apart?" Cliff turned to Billie.

"She went to pieces," Billie said.

"When was this?"

"Two, three weeks ago."

Cliff and Feng looked at each other. That would have been just before Uppington's meeting.

"She didn't get help," Billie said. "It makes me very sad."

"Of course it's sad," said Prithwish.

"I wish I could have done something for her," said Billie. "I had a book I was going to lend her, but now she's gone."

"She's not dead, you know," Aidan broke in. "She just left the lab."

"Well, I miss her," Billie said.

"You didn't know her," Natalya retorted, and Billie shrank back, rebuffed. She couldn't help it; the others didn't like her. And she was new in the lab. She would always be new.

"It's for the best," Aidan said of Robin. "She was in a bad way."

"She changed," said Prithwish simply.

"Now she can move on," Aidan declared.

"But where?" Natalya asked.

Nobody knew. Billie had heard she'd gone up to New Hampshire for a few days, and there was a rumor she was going to move back there. Prithwish had it on good authority from Nanette that she was tech-ing for Uppington at BU, at least for the short term, just to make ends meet.

In fact, Robin was just a few blocks away, across Mass Ave. Under scant gold leaves she made her way up Avon Street until she came to a house on the corner surrounded by a pale green fence. The fence was six feet tall, and she had to walk all around the periphery until she found the gate.

Stepping inside, she found herself in the autumn ruins of a rose garden. Thorny canes and withered leaves surrounded a Victorian house with a great barnlike gambrel roof and peeling brown paint.

A gardener was raking leaves from under some hydrangea bushes, and she marveled at the deep pink blossoms still clinging to the stems.

"Excuse me," Robin said. "I'm looking for Akira O'Keefe."

"You're looking at him," the gardener shot back. He seemed pleased at her surprise.

She hadn't expected him to have reddish brown hair. He was not what she'd imagined. Ignorantly she'd assumed he would look much more Japanese. He was extremely tall and slender. His nose was freckled, his eyes quick and black behind gold-rimmed aviator glasses. He seemed to have trouble with his sight; he blinked continually, eyes darting everywhere, from her to his growing leaf pile to his stack of folded leaf bags.

"Nanette suggested I come see you." She stood at a little distance, trying not to step in the mud.

"I've already read a copy of Cliff's paper," Akira said.

"I guess Nanette's told you all about me," Robin said, feeling a bit exposed.

"I know everything." His rake was metal, with quivering bent prongs. "I hope before you left the lab you made copies of all the materials you found there. Have you been keeping a journal?"

"Well . . ." Robin began.

"You'll need all that."

"I wasn't exactly sure . . ."

"Mendelssohn and Glass are very good at instilling self-doubt," said Akira, "because they have none. They transfer it into their postdocs."

Robin flinched. She had tasted bitterness, but never in such strong concentration.

"You'll have noticed by now," Akira said, "that people at the institute have a tendency to lie."

"People in general? No," Robin said.

"Yes, people in general."

"And who would they be lying to?"

"To themselves," Akira said. "Marion killed my work because she didn't like where it was going. She saw where I was heading, and she sacrificed my mice."

Robin stuck her hands in her jacket pockets unhappily. He was a kook. "You're talking about the outbreak in the colony."

"They *say* there was an outbreak in the colony," Akira told her. "The truth is they didn't like my results. I had negative results."

She shook her head, indignant. Marion would never have sacrificed an entire colony of mice without evidence of contamination.

"They hate me," he told her. "Marion had me barred from the institute. Did you know that?"

"No."

"Yeah, she didn't like me coming around after I'd officially left." He flipped his rake over and cleaned out the prongs. "She didn't want me talking to people and that kind of thing, so at one point she called security and got my name listed as Do Not Allow Upstairs. I think I may be the only person officially barred from the Philpott. There may be others, but I believe I'm the only one. She hates me. They both do. My last year, the two of them turned against me big-time. They didn't like me; they didn't like my work; they wanted me gone, and they killed my mice for it. They almost killed me, but Nanette came over and took me to the hospital. Unfortunately," he said, "people get sacrificed quite often in science. Could you hold that bag for me? You can't see it so clearly when you're inside," he told her. "You always think it's you, but it's not. The system favors them. It's feudal, actually. There are the lords and ladies like Glass and Mendelssohn, and then the postdocs are the vassals paying tribute every year in the form of publications, blood, sweat, tears, et cetera. If there's a conflict, they call the shots, and there's really nothing you can do about it. Lord Glass and Lady Mendelssohn know the truth. If you cry foul, they break you."

"We had a seminar about my concerns," said Robin.

"Yeah, you had your little show trial. That's just cronyism. You've got evidence of foul play—"

"Well . . ." Robin hedged.

"Either you're making the claim or not." He took the heavy leaf bag from her and crimped the top. "You're dealing with investigators who believe what they want to believe. Look, lying is a human trait, and it works well in religions and philosophies, but in science it's a recipe for disaster. There's just too much money involved. Drug money—and I don't mean the guys in Harvard Square. I'm talking about the pharmaceutical companies. Don't you think academics are all tangled up with corporations? Don't you think Sandy Glass is in the pocket of a drug company—or would be, if he could? There's big bucks out there, and where there's money like that there is no such thing as academic freedom, or independent inquiry."

"The Philpott is independent," Robin said.

"Yeah, right. It's a principality of Harvard. The Philpott is like Vichy France. Let me ask you a question."

He was too tight, his motions quick with pent-up energy. He spoke too fast, as if he were afraid she'd interrupt or leave too soon. He sounded as though he hadn't talked to anyone in weeks.

"Do you want justice?"

"Of course," she said.

"Are you willing to suffer for it?"

She wished she could just turn away and laugh, make a joke—anything to break the tension. But he was not joking; he was looking her over with his darting eyes.

"Are you?" he asked.

"Maybe," she said.

He snorted, unimpressed. "Wrong answer."

"Look, I didn't come here to be interrogated," Robin said. "I just wanted to talk to you about your experience and maybe discuss . . ." She trailed off. There didn't seem to be much she could discuss with Akira. He might be good at delivering manifestos, or rallying troops for guerrilla warfare, but he was clearly not the sort of person who talked things over. "I came here for advice," she said.

"All right," he said. "Here it is. I've read everything Nanette gave me; I've looked at the data and I think your case is exactly what we've been looking for. I've spoken to Hackett and Schneiderman at ORIS and they're willing to meet with you."

"What? ORIS?"

"Yes, *the* ORIS, at the NIH. The Office for Research Integrity in Science."

Robin spluttered, "I—I never gave anyone permission to . . ."

"I've worked closely with Alan Hackett and Jonathan Schneiderman in the past. I didn't mention your name to them—only the outlines of your case. I made no promises; I did not reveal your identity; I'm only conveying their interest. Whether you meet with them is up to you."

"I'm not meeting anybody," Robin protested furiously. "I don't know them. I don't even know you—and I never authorized you to be my spokesman to the NIH!"

"Well, that was my mistake, then," said Akira, "because I thought your allegations of fraud were a serious matter. . . ."

"There are no allegations of fraud," said Robin. "My only claims were about possible error."

A slight smile played about Akira's lips. "Either you're making a charge or you're not," he said again. "If you're going to pursue this, you'll have to decide what exactly you are pursuing."

"I'm pursuing the truth," said Robin.

"And would that be a gentle, conciliatory truth, or the real deal?" Akira asked her. "Because there's no point working on this if you don't know where you stand. Naturally, you aren't used to making judgments," he allowed. "In the lab it wasn't your place to think about what was right and what was wrong."

She was amazed. Where he should have been apologizing to her for presenting her case to ORIS—albeit anonymously—he was apologizing *for* her instead, excusing her ignorance and timidity. He spoke with such a strange mixture of intelligence and paranoia that she scarcely knew how to listen.

"You were just a servant," he told her. "It takes a while to stop thinking like one. Grab that, will you?"

She gave him such a look, he picked up the folded leaf bag himself.

"I've got to get going," she told him.

"I want to show you something," he said.

"I really have to go."

"No, wait," he said. "Look at these first."

They were the biggest dahlias she had ever seen. They bloomed high above her head, each blossom honeycombed in deepest purple.

"They're gorgeous," she said.

"They're Art's favorite."

"This is Art Ginsburg's house?" She glanced with new respect at the massive brown building.

"He was on my committee at Harvard, and he took me in. He hired me a couple of years ago."

She was shocked. She had never imagined Marion's nemesis capable of helping anybody. He of the reptilian smiles at the seminar table.

"He's a good guy," said Akira. "He got me working here as horticultural therapy. He was the one who turned me on to dahlias. I didn't know anything about plants when I was inside. They were too busy killing me."

How quickly, Robin thought, she'd moved from dedicated research to the muddy land of malcontents. Just weeks before, she'd been a scholar, and now she was listening to a vindictive gardener. If science was cruel and feudal, still she had enjoyed the privileges of the court, the instruments and time there, the great storerooms of materials, the labyrinthine passageways of discovery leading mostly to dead ends, but always promising more, a glimpse of greatness from far off, the glow of success just around the corner. She was still new enough to the outside world to see those who had cast science off as the impoverished ones, and to hope that she would not remain among them. She felt for Akira, but he also frightened her. She did not want to be used by him, or become like him. She did not want to curse the kingdom from afar, but to vindicate herself and find her way back.

2

THE RUMORS about her weren't unfounded. She'd cobbled together some part-time tech work in Uppington's lab during the week, and on weekends she took the bus to Portsmouth and helped her father with odd jobs around the house. Her dad didn't climb ladders anymore, so she did a bit of roof work. She cleaned the gutters, although she wasn't quite as dexterous as she had been when she was a little girl. Her arms had been so thin then and her hands so small that she could snake in and out, cleaning debris from the tightest places. She patched slate, as well. She knew how to angle a hatchet to cut the edge accurately, and how to bore a hole in the stone with a punch and hammer. She liked it on the roof, even as the days grew colder. She liked balancing there, close to the November sky. She had worked too long with the animals underground. The views from the roof surprised and delighted her. How colorful and crisp the world looked from above, the gnarled crab apples with their shriveled fruit, the overgrown rhododendrons, the crumpled rivers of dead leaves. On top of the house she allowed herself to think Nanette was right. How little science seemed outside. How paltry the future looked next to the here and now.

"How's it going up there?" her father called from the ground.

"It's great," she called back. "I've found my true calling. I'm going to be a roofer."

She thought her father would laugh, but he surprised her with his strong words when she came down. "You aren't going to give up your research after all this time! Not after all the years that you've put in."

She stood before him in her jeans and dirty sweater, and she shrugged. Her face was windburned and her lips were chapped. "I didn't know you cared so much about my work," she said.

"All that time," he reproached her, "all your training. You don't just throw all that away." His admonition reminded her of the night she and Cliff, Feng and Mei, and Aidan and Aidan's old boyfriend Russell had gone to the Brattle Theater to see *Gone With the Wind.* They sat in the dark theater, nibbling malted milk balls and passing tubs of popcorn between them. She and Cliff had been a little irreverent and snickered at some of the melodramatic parts while Aidan and Feng hushed them. At the moment Scarlett cried to Ashley, "Take me away—there's nothing to keep us here!" Cliff and Robin shook with laughter.

"Shh!" Feng told them.

"Nothing?" Ashley chided Scarlett, up on screen. "Nothing except honor."

Cliff's soda went up his nose, and Robin buried her face in his sweater.

"This is the best part!" Aidan whispered furiously, whacking them.

"The best part or the worst part?" Cliff asked.

"Get ahold of yourself," Aidan demanded, and he was only half kidding. "You're ruining it for me."

"Don't you think this movie is just a tiny bit stupid?" Cliff asked, and that set Robin off again. There was no way around it; the two of them had the giggles and could not control themselves. Cliff grabbed Robin and they stumbled toward the exit even as Leslie Howard and Vivien Leigh locked lips. People started hissing at them. They were blocking the view of Ashley's fey blond head bent over Scarlett's dark hair.

"Help. Wait," Robin yelped to Cliff.

Once through the door, they found themselves outside—not just out in the lobby, but outside the theater altogether. They'd ducked through the emergency exit and ended up on the street, clutching their coats in the cold.

"Damn," said Cliff as they realized they'd left all their candy in the theater. There was nothing for it but to get ice cream. Ever after, whenever someone complained in the lab or made noises about leaving, Cliff and Robin would cry out, "'There's nothing to keep me here!'" and then Feng and even Aidan would chime in: "'Nothing? Nothing except honor.'"

Robin's father sounded like that now, carrying on about the time she'd spent, and what a shame it would be for her to quit—as if she'd trained to be a knight, and might now bring shame upon herself. Or would she be dishonoring him? He had always complained about her training because it took so long and paid so little and because no one in the family really understood what she did. On the other hand, he'd boasted, too. He was shocked she might even consider quitting.

But she had not given up. She joked during the day about chucking it all, but she woke up in the night. Like an alarm clock, her imagination rang and rang with possibilities.

In Cambridge, Larry and Wendy told her to be patient, to trust the slow accretion of scientific progress, the natural selection of ideas by which the false and unsupported fell away. "Look, if there's a problem, it'll come to the fore. It's inevitable," Larry told her as they sipped tea in Tomas's apartment.

"You can only hide it for so long if your work is buggy," Wendy said.

Tomas looked up from his sketch pad. "All things come to those who wait?" he ventured.

How long? Robin wondered. Eighteen months? Three years? How long before further experiments did not pan out and eager imitators re-examined Cliff's premises and faulty methods? Could Larry and Wendy really expect her to know the truth and suffer in silence?

Robin looked at her friends with some trepidation, then made her announcement. "I've called the Office for Research Integrity at NIH."

"Good grief!" Larry yelled.

"Oh, please," said Wendy.

"You called ORIS?" Larry asked as if he loathed the very word.

"Why? What's wrong with that?" asked Robin. "I spoke to Alan Hackett and sent them copies of my stuff."

"You spoke to Hackett?" Larry exclaimed. "Robin, you have no idea what you're getting into."

"Why didn't you come to us?" Wendy demanded.

"I hope you didn't tell him anything," said Larry.

"Why would I speak to him if I didn't want to tell him anything?"

"You are very, very naïve," Wendy reproved Robin.

"He's an ambulance chaser," Larry said, "and an extremely dubious character."

"He's a respected scholar."

"A respected scholar twenty years ago."

"He's testified before Congress . . ."

"Ha," said Larry. "He's a professional ruiner of reputations and of lives."

"Haven't you read his paper on Dillmore?" Wendy asked.

"No."

"He spent a year dissecting Richard Dillmore's paper in *Science* so that he could publish a detailed attack on Dillmore's methods, his data analysis, his supervision of students, and his character."

"He did one piece of good work," allowed Wendy. "The exposé of the Fienberg affair . . ."

"Excuse me, what is the Fienberg affair?" Tomas asked.

Wendy turned to him. "You haven't heard of Leonard Fienberg?"

"Actually, you of all people will appreciate this, since you're an artist," Larry told Tomas. "Leonard Fienberg was a researcher who faked his results by painting his mice. He wanted to show he could graft white skin onto brown mice and brown skin onto white mice, so he painted the animals the appropriate colors."

"He actually painted the tummies of the mice," said Wendy.

"Paint-by-numbers science," Tomas said.

"Exactly, and Hackett exposed him, back in eighty, and he's been living off the glory ever since. They gave him a desk at the NIH, and a phone. He's not a researcher, Robin. You know that, right? He's not a thinker. He's just a . . . a . . ."

"A hack," said Wendy.

"He's like an undertaker. He has no interest in constructive work; he just sits there looking for weaknesses, dissecting journal articles for his postmortems. He sees fraud everywhere. Fraud is his obsession. He actually feeds off the public mistrust of science."

"He's more like a vampire," said Wendy.

"Does he sleep in a coffin?" Tomas asked. "Does he wake the dead?" Almost unconsciously he had begun sketching a cadaverous figure, long toothed, with claws for hands, a caped man rising from a tomb, his lips dripping with blood.

"He's not creative," Wendy declared.

"I disagree," said Larry. "He's extremely creative. How else could he and Schneiderman come up with all this stuff? I'm telling you, the two of them sit around all day handpicking journal articles so that they can bring the authors down."

"They sounded completely professional on the phone," said Robin, "and knowledgeable."

"Of course they sound professional and knowledgeable," said Larry. "That's their job. Listen, take my advice. Do not get started with them."

"But why shouldn't I get started with them?" Robin blurted out. "They aren't some kind of crackpots. They're officials of the NIH."

"No, no, no," said Larry. "You don't understand. They are the official crackpots of the NIH. Everybody hates them."

"Loathes them," added Wendy.

"They look at you," said Larry, "and they smell blood."

"Mendelssohn and Glass?"

"No, *you*. See, you don't get the politics of the situation here. You would be the sacrificial lamb."

Robin bristled. So Larry was an expert about this, too. He could see dark doings at NIH, even though he'd never done biological research in his life. "How is it you know so much about ORIS?"

"Richard Dillmore is a very close friend of mine," Larry said. "And unfortunately I have an excellent understanding of what they did to him."

"It's really Orwellian over there," said Wendy.

"That isn't my impression," said Robin.

"Robin, you've been living in a lab for ten years," Larry admonished her. "You play with mice all day. You know nothing about the politics of science in this country."

"It's really all about Big Brother watching you," Wendy said.

"Excuse me." Robin's cheeks burned with indignation. "If there were no ORIS, what recourse would I have? What could anyone ever do?"

"I'm sorry, but clearly you have no understanding of how ORIS works," Larry said.

"Stop it, you guys. Stop!" Tomas cried out. "Stop picking on Robin. If she wants to bust someone for cheating, then let her!"

For a moment the other three sat in stunned silence. They had never heard Tomas raise his voice before. Even Tomas seemed surprised. "She can do what she wants."

"We aren't picking on Robin," Wendy said.

"We're trying to protect you," Larry told her.

"Thank you, but I think I can take care of myself," Robin said.

"Have you met with them face-to-face?" Larry asked. "Do you have a lawyer? Do you really have advisors? Have you done your homework?"

She'd known Larry and Wendy would disapprove, but she was shaken by their vehemence. How could she have known the two of them were experts on ORIS and its doings? Robin looked away, and caught the expression on Tomas's face—at once tender and frustrated. He wished he could help her, but he knew nothing about the NIH or scientific fraud. It was for Robin to defend her decision to Larry and Wendy, and especially to herself.

Larry and Wendy knew everything, but they did not understand her position. She had no money, no savings, scarcely any way to make her rent and keep her apartment. She had no standing in the scientific world, not even a proper affiliation anymore. She had only her discovery, her sole piece of intellectual property, the gap between Cliff's raw data and his published work. This was not jealousy, or falling out of love. This was knowledge of Cliff and what he'd done. They could warn her all they wanted; she'd broken through to her own chamber of discovery; she knew what she knew. She was no longer suffocating, weak and anguished with his success, but moving freely, beyond his gravitational field, fired by convictions of greater force. She knew he had misrepresented his findings, and even if that knowledge was awkward and inelegant, unacceptable, she would still trust and use her intuition.

She listened to her neighbors' dire warnings, and tried to remember Hackett's telephone voice: slightly metallic and precise, nerdy, much like Larry's own voice, in fact. He'd spoken to her with slight self-mockery.

"Well," he'd told Robin after he'd received the photocopies she'd sent him, "this is all very interesting, of course. And I guess the best thing I can tell you is that we'll just have to wait and see what Jonathan says when he comes back to the office next week."

"Jonathan Schneiderman," she said.

"Yeah, that's right, Schneiderman. He tends to have a good nose for these things."

"Akira probably mentioned me to him."

"Ah, yes, Akira." Hackett sighed.

Robin listened intently. She cared a great deal about what that sigh meant.

"He was a sad case," said Hackett.

"He felt that Glass and Mendelssohn were trying to destroy him," Robin said cautiously.

"Mmm, that's right. He did. But they weren't. He's a lovely guy, and we still talk now and again. Unfortunately, his view of the world is so conspiratorial, you have to take him with a grain of salt. To tell the truth, I didn't pay any attention when he called us about you."

Robin's confidence in Hackett rose tenfold. "Do you have a sense of what might be going on in my case?" she asked.

"Yeah," he said laconically. "I mean, I have a *sense*, but you learn pretty early on in this business to look before you leap."

Schneiderman was the forthcoming one. He had a deep, burly voice and a direct, pugnacious manner, magnified by the fact that he and Hackett used a speakerphone. Schneiderman sounded like a big bear at the bottom of a deep pit. "We'd like to meet with you," he told Robin when he called the following week. "We'd like to set a date."

"Do you ever come to Boston?" she asked.

"Do we ever come to Boston? We should. We should be traveling to Boston all the time. And to New York, and Pasadena, and everywhere in between. Unfortunately, we don't have the funds."

"Ha." That was Hackett in the background. "Just to be clear: this is a shoestring operation. We are engaging in ethics on a budget."

"Is that possible?" Robin asked. "To do what you need to do?"

"It's necessary," Schneiderman said firmly.

"If you'd asked me ten years ago whether this office was probable I would have said no," said Hackett. "Now it turns out the improbable has become our area of expertise."

"Because you study improbable results," Robin said, catching on.

"No," Hackett demurred. "We're anthropologists, really. We study people, is all."

"We study data," Schneiderman told Robin, and his voice rumbled reassuringly like the idling motor of a car.

"But in fact, it comes down to human error," Hackett said drily. "Human error, human intentions."

"Our job," said Schneiderman, "is to investigate possible misconduct, misrepresentations, and data manipulations, and this is where I think it would be extremely valuable for us to sit down with you, Robin, and really take apart your data."

Your data, she thought. How strange that now Cliff's data was in some respect hers.

Schneiderman continued, "I think that a face-to-face meeting on this could be of real value."

There. He'd said it, and she held the word close. There was value in this enterprise. Her cause was not hopeless, or ill-founded, or imaginary. Hackett and Schneiderman were willing to meet with her—even they, who'd seen it all. She did not deceive herself that working with them would be easy, and yet she was hopeful at the prospect. She might gain a correction to the published journal article, or even an apology from Mendelssohn and Glass. There would be some value in saving time for other scientists who tried to reproduce Cliff's results. Saving them time, she might make a small contribution of her own. She could not be angry and alone forever. She would not let Marion write her off as incompetent even as Cliff fabricated his success. No, she would justify herself. And if she was naïve and foolish, if her actions were irresponsible, she would fight anyway.

"You have no idea what you're in for," Larry warned her now, in Tomas's apartment. "They're just looking for new troublemakers, and if they take you on, you'll never be anything else. They'll ruin your life."

Well, what if they did? Robin asked herself defiantly. Even then, she felt she could do worse than championing the truth.

3

As THE weather grew colder, jollification in the lab increased. After Thanksgiving, Aidan and Natalya found a box of old pipettes and strung them up for the holidays. Blue, green, red, and orange, the pipettes dangled festively from the ceiling. Prithwish was going home to Sri Lanka in December to get married, and the others teased him mercilessly about it. They teased him about the girl, whom he scarcely seemed to know, about his telephone bills, about his journey home, even about the date set for the wedding. "How do we know you didn't pick the date to get out of work?" Cliff asked him.

"I told you I had nothing to say on the matter," Prithwish replied airily. "Our parents chose the date and there was nothing we could do about it."

"Yeah, but how did *they* pick the date?" Cliff asked with mock suspicion.

"Actually, it was our grandparents," Prithwish corrected himself. "They chose the date according to our horoscopes."

"You don't believe in horoscopes, do you?"

"No, of course not," said Prithwish. "My parents don't either. They're both physicists, and they find horoscopes quite inconvenient."

"So why use them, man?" Aidan burst out.

"My mom thinks that we should use the horoscopes just in case," Prithwish said. "She thinks they are highly unlikely to be true, but she follows them on the off chance that they are."

"You make no sense whatsoever," said Cliff. "One day you're single, and then you come in with no warning, announce that you're engaged and I have to look for a new roommate."

"Now you admit this is what you really care about," Natalya told Cliff waspishly from the doorway. "You will have to look for someone else to share your rent. Selfish."

"Thanks a lot," Cliff retorted easily. He hadn't been thinking of his rent. He and Prithwish had lived together in cheerful squalor for three years, and Cliff really was going to miss his roommate. He had offered to share the apartment with Prithwish and his bride when she arrived—at least until the couple found a place of their own, but Prithwish didn't seem too eager, and continued to pore over rental ads in the newspapers spread across his bench top. "You'll leave me recipes, right?" Cliff asked plaintively.

The others laughed. Everyone knew Prithwish couldn't cook.

"What is it?" Feng asked as he came up from the animal facility.

Cliff and Prithwish laughed harder. Aidan wiped his eyes. It was so easy to laugh when the work was going well. A second major article on R-7 was well under way, a new expanded experimental group of mice had been injected in the facility below. Cliff was their leader now, and a tireless, gracious leader at that. He pitched in on all the scut work himself, and volunteered for the most tedious tasks. He stayed late to finish paperwork and came in early for procedures with the mice. His enthusiasm was infectious. Prithwish and Aidan and Natalya shared Cliff's jubilant spirits, just as each shared in his results. Even Feng seemed gently optimistic. The media flurry had passed, and Feng was making headway with the bone tumor project. He and Cliff were working happily in parallel.

Where the lab had once reflected the somber, earnest caution Marion cultivated, the place was now attuned to Sandy's vivacious imagination. Always, before, the future had seemed dreadful, cold and steep, almost impossible to summit. Now the view was dazzling.

"Where's Billie?" Aidan asked Feng.

"Downstairs," said Feng.

"You got her to stay down there?"

"Sure," said Feng.

"You really are a genius," said Cliff.

Feng grinned. He had no trouble working with Billie. She thought him rude and taciturn, and he did not disabuse her of that notion. He'd explained that he had no interest in feng shui, trained her to do exactly what he wanted, and then left her to it.

"I just have one question for you," Aidan told Feng. "How's your chi?"

"Who knows?" Feng said.

"How are your mice?" Cliff asked.

"Not great," Feng said.

"Which means . . ." Cliff looked up at the ceiling for inspiration. "The mice are dying because their bone tumors are so big, because you've actually gotten Robin's tumor promoter to work. Which means you've got a publication! Ergo, 'not great' is yet another synonym for 'breakthrough'! Am I good or what?" He reached up and swatted the dangling pipettes with his hand.

"Ah, there you are," said Marion from the doorway. "Cliff and Feng, may I see you for a minute?"

Sandy Glass was in the office, but that didn't surprise Cliff, because it was almost lunchtime. The two of them often called him in these days. They had begun to treat him more like a junior colleague, and less like a glorified student.

"What's up?" Cliff swung himself up and took a seat on the end of Marion's desk, while Feng politely took as little space as possible by the door.

Marion swept the two of them with one of her critical glances. She looked pale, Cliff noticed suddenly, and sad, and fierce. "We've received a request for information from ORIS," she told him, and passed him a piece of NIH letterhead. "They're auditing the lab."

Cliff stared at the letter in confusion. The words were right there in front of him, but he could not comprehend them. He passed the letter to Feng. "What do you mean?"

"See, they've named you and Feng specifically," said Sandy, pointing to the place, "in a complaint brought by Robin Decker, for investigation of possible fraud."

Feng did not look up. He was devouring the paragraphs before him.

"This is unreal," Cliff whispered. "Robin did this? I can't believe she'd do something like this."

"Yeah, good for her," Sandy said darkly. "I always said she was a go-getter."

"But what does it mean?" asked Cliff.

"Ha. What does it mean?" Sandy asked with rhetorical flair. "It means that when Robin left the lab she didn't really go away. It means she's fallen in with vicious characters who will use every opportunity to exploit her and her so-called cause."

"Vicious!" Cliff exploded. "It's a violation. I can't believe she'd do something like this. It's such a violation of trust."

"And what it means," Sandy continued, "is that Marion and I are going to have to divert our time to mounting a defense of everything we've done with R-7, during which we'll lose ground on all the progress we've made. It means a public inquest at the NIH and a shadow of guilt on all our work, even while we prove our integrity to our own colleagues in the field."

Cliff looked at Feng. "Why did she name you?" he asked. Robin had never before directed her suspicions toward Feng.

"That's something I'm curious to find out," said Sandy. "I suspect it's something Alan Hackett and Jonathan Schneiderman contributed. A general broadening of the complaint to make it appear less like a personal vendetta."

"Will I be sent home?" Feng asked. His voice was so calm, and in contrast to Cliff's horrified exclamations, the question was so practical, that Sandy and Marion didn't even register it at first.

"Pardon me?" said Marion.

"Could I be sent home?" Feng asked.

"You mean deported? No, of course not," Marion declared. She spoke with complete conviction, although she knew nothing about deportation, green cards, or student visas.

"Look, enough of the doomsday prophecies," Sandy said. "Will the audit be unpleasant? Yes. Will an investigation hamper our research? Undoubtedly. But the question is who will prevail, and there is no doubt of that at all. We'll crush them, because we have the results and the documentation to do so, and that's all there is to it. Marion and I have spoken to Peter Hawking and we have his assurance that every resource at the institute will be available to us. Peter is well aware of the situation with Robin. He is very adept with these sorts of claims, and he knows how to fight them." Sandy wasn't just speaking figuratively here. Hawking knew how to marshal institute funds to fight necessary battles. He was a master of the art of indirect cost, managing and channeling expenditures, even billing grants for legal fees. "He did a terrific job with Akira O'Keefe, for example," Sandy said. "Peter has, unfortunately, dealt with things like this before."

Magically, before their eyes, Sandy took up his spear and cudgel and sat before them at his desk in full battle mode. His voice seemed to expand until it squeezed out any doubt or fear in that little room. And it was extraordinary how cheerful he sounded, how his blue eyes sparkled. They'd known his temper and his infectious optimism, but they had never experienced Sandy managing a major crisis. They had not seen him with his patients in the hospital. For a moment, even in their confusion and distress, Marion and Cliff and Feng looked at him in awe. For a fleeting instant they almost relished the thought of following Sandy Glass into battle against the disbelievers and vengeance seekers, the barbarians at the scientific gate.

Still, the shock was terrible. Within the hour, the others in the lab all knew; in half a day, the rest of the institute knew as well. Peter Hawking was said to be drafting a secret memo to ORIS on the subject. Sandy was supposed to have retained the services of Leo Sonenberg, defense attorney to the stars, counsel to indignant politicos and the embattled rich, as well as sometime Harvard law professor. Neighboring researchers on the third floor declared the Mendelssohn-Glass lab in crisis, and techs from other labs came through regularly on little errands upstairs. Aidan, Natalya, and Billie were accosted for information. "No comment," Aidan tossed over his shoulder as he ascended the stairs. "I know nothing about this," said Natalya. But Billie described Robin's breakdown in the animal facility to anyone who would listen.

"She started screaming," Billie told a bunch of researchers in the lounge, "and then I tried to calm her down and she ran away." Billie sighed. She was only a little pleased by the attention she was getting talking about the situation. Her eyes widened behind her glasses, and her soft graying hair fluttered around her shoulders like a half-blown dandelion puff. Softly, earnestly, Billie let the seeds of new rumors fly. "I think she was really suffering here. It was the animal facility, and especially the mice. She couldn't take it anymore."

There were those who imagined Robin had grown hysterical, or even suicidal. There were those who began to think Robin had joined forces with Billie to demand an investigation of work conditions in the Mendelssohn-Glass lab. And there were even some who had heard Robin was in the early stages of some kind of class action suit against the institute. There was no evidence for this, except that Glass and Mendelssohn were closeted together in Peter Hawking's office. Successive new speculations chased each other down the corridors and into every stairwell. The Philpott was aflutter with diagnoses, dismay, and glee.

Inside the windowless media room, with the door locked, a breathless Nanette phoned Robin, but only reached her answering machine.

"Call me!" Nanette whispered. "All hell is breaking loose, and I'm convinced you're going to bring the lab down! You sneaky, sneaky girl—why didn't you tell me you were starting an investigation? Call me please and tell me everything!"

But there was no word from Robin all that day, and no explanation was forthcoming.

At lunchtime, Feng walked over to the Harvard bio labs. Softly, he opened the door to the huge, high-ceilinged Krakauer lab, where six postdocs and four graduate students were studying algae. "What's wrong?" Mei called out in Chinese, as soon as she saw him. He never came over so early in the day.

Feng hurried over to her lab bench and answered in Chinese as well. "The government's Office of Research Integrity is auditing our lab. They're investigating me and Cliff."

Mei gasped. "But why?" Her colleagues were working all around them, but by speaking their own language they were entirely alone, their conversation nothing more than background music or birdsong to the others.

He told her everything that had happened, but he was just as confused as he had been before. He could not quite believe Glass when he said the lab would prevail. Nor did he entirely trust Marion's assurances that he would not be penalized because he was foreign, and a

Chinese citizen, at that. And yet, even in his anxiety, the violence of Robin's action overshadowed everything else. To go to the highest authorities and press charges on Cliff's data! She might as well have come into the lab with a knife and ripped Cliff's notes to shreds, and smashed the glassware, and seized the poor mice and thrown them against the wall. She sought to destroy her own colleagues' work, their word, their reputation. To do all that, and to spit in the face of her own mentors. What had influenced her to act this way? Whose spell had she come under? "Glass and Mendelssohn think they just added my name to mask the fact she's really after Cliff," Feng told Mei.

"She must have felt he stole her position from her," Mei said, thinking aloud. "When Cliff had his success, she must have felt that he humiliated her somehow—because she had been the most senior postdoc."

"Maybe," Feng said. "Who knows why she did it?"

Mei frowned. "I'm sure he does."

Cliff was numb. That strangling paralysis was setting in, the desperation Cliff had vanquished just a year before. His luck had changed again, and despite all his accomplishments, and all Marion's and Sandy's protestations of support, he could not shake the melancholy that crept inside him. He could already sense the fates turning against him, and his good fortune withering away.

Robin had set her dogs on him, and Cliff knew they would not rest until they found some fault. His work had been brilliant, but already he knew the inquiry would tarnish his results. ORIS would broadcast Robin's suspicions publicly. He might dart to left or right. He might escape their grasp, but he would be marked. Already he could hear the world whispering around him. In that respect he was helpless. He was doomed.

At the end of the day, a scant handful of snowflakes floated in the air like dust motes. He thought for a moment of walking down to the river, but this time he didn't want to be alone. He unlocked his bike and began riding home to Somerville, back to his brick building with its ugly wrought iron balconies. The neighbors had strung up Christmas lights, red, green, and gold, spelling JOY, PEACE, and LOVE. He hoisted his bike and carried it up the stairs to the apartment.

"Hey, man," Prithwish called out, poking his head into the

pass-through from the kitchen to the dining area. Cliff's heart sank. Prithwish was on the phone again.

"I'm just ordering pizza," said Prithwish.

"Oh, good," he called out, for he'd just that moment realized he was famished. "Thank you!"

"Half pepperoni?"

"Yeah." Cliff swung his backpack onto the floor and stretched out full length on the futon. "God, I'm so tired. What's to become of me?"

"What was that? Anchovy?"

"No. I said, what's to become of me?" Cliff bellowed, with self-mocking drama.

"Oh, is that all? I thought you were changing the order." Business concluded, Prithwish came around with a couple of beers, tossed one to Cliff, and sank down into the creaky papasan chair.

"Stop being so damn cheerful," Cliff said, but he appreciated Prithwish's cheerful manner. "Just because you're getting married and moving out—you don't have to gloat."

"All right." Prithwish pulled a long face. "What's to become of you?"

"It wasn't a rhetorical question."

"Well, I don't really think anything terrible is going to become of you," Prithwish told Cliff more seriously. "Work like yours is going to stand up."

"I know, I know—if I ever get to finish it."

"Oh, come on, we'll keep at it."

"I feel like we had this one perfect, shining paper, and now all that is going to be tarnished."

"How can it really be tarnished if it's true?" Prithwish asked.

"Jealousy. Politics."

"Those are always going to be there," Prithwish said philosophically. "Those are just part of the game."

"They shouldn't be," said Cliff.

"But they are, so you have to get used to it," said Prithwish. "You can't let it get to you."

"I just want to keep working." For the first time, Cliff's voice trembled. He hadn't articulated until that moment how desperate he was to keep moving on the project. R-7 was everything he had, and everything he'd ever dreamed: his life, his future, his contribution.

"You can keep working," said Prithwish. "You will! We won't stop."

Cliff rolled over and looked at Prithwish. He loved his roommate. He loved Prithwish's loyalty and his trust in R-7. Prithwish had never been jealous of Cliff's success, or if he had been jealous, he'd never let it show. He'd never begrudged Cliff anything. Someday, Cliff thought, he would repay Prithwish. Someday, when Prithwish needed a good word, or a helping hand, or an antibody shipped, Cliff would jump at the chance to help his old friend. Already his imagination was reviving, and he glimpsed himself, as through a doorway, in a senior position capable of largesse. His mind was still limber, flexible enough that he might be doomed one instant and famous the next. First melancholy, and then sentimental, emotion after idea tumbled over Cliff, because he felt so grateful he was not alone. It was not Cliff alone against ORIS, but the whole lab together, and they would keep the faith. They would prevail.

Marion was sure of this as well. Devout pessimist that she was, she knew her own lab and the results in it. She had only to walk into the animal facility to see R-7 in action. A full sixty-five percent of Cliff's experimental mice were responding to the virus. Their tumors had withered away, and in many animals had disappeared entirely. These were tangible, unambiguous results, and she would defend them against all comers. If only Cliff had kept better records.

Meticulous as always, Marion had set about the task of collating and copying all the R-7 materials for ORIS. She had prepared labeled binders full of notes, and zealously annotated pages of raw data.

Sandy was elated by the reams of evidence Marion had compiled. He saw the papers as munitions piles, neatly stacked as sticks of dynamite. "It's like setting a fuse," he told Marion in the office. "I just can't wait to fire this stuff off."

"Hmm." She frowned as she studied the notes in front of her.

"Why so gloomy?"

"If Cliff's notes had been in order, we would never have had this problem. Aidan's records are a mess as well." She leaned down on her three-hole punch with all her weight, but she'd jammed too much paper into it. She could hardly make a dent.

"Here, let me." Sandy cracked the hole punch altogether as he tried to do the job.

"Now you've broken it!" Marion cried, aghast.

"So what? Really, Marion, you're blowing everything all out of proportion."

"I don't think you realize how bad this is going to be."

"For us or for them?" Sandy asked.

He won a faint smile for this bravado, but Marion was chastened by the tangled mess of notes she had uncovered. All the paperwork relating to R-7 was rushed, disorganized, and sometimes even fragmentary. She'd spent days piecing scraps together. She had become an archeologist of the recent past.

"Oh, come on, no lab is going to have totally transparent records," Sandy said. "No one is going to be coherent in the middle of making groundbreaking discoveries. These are private notes here!" He picked up a sheaf of papers in Cliff's handwriting. "They weren't written for submission to some kind of trumped-up interrogation. And you should be careful, Marion, not to organize them so well. You rearrange and annotate them too much, and ORIS will hold that against you."

She looked up, startled, because Jacob had made exactly the same point a few nights before. He'd added, "Cliff should be the one pulling together his notes, not you."

"No, ultimately, they're my responsibility," Marion had told him stoically.

"I disagree," said Jacob. "You're losing too much sleep over this. You're trying to cover for Cliff when you should be moving ahead."

"I can't move ahead without defending the work we've done," Marion retorted, and she said as much to Sandy now, adding, "I have to pull the record together and make it coherent."

"Just don't make it too pretty," said Sandy.

"Pretty? There's no danger of that." She sighed and went back to work, sorting photocopies into one set of binders, and original notes into another.

"Everything's going to be all right," Sandy told her softly. "You'll see."

She looked at him with a mixture of irritation and affection.

"I know you just want to get this over with," he said.

"Do you know what I want?" she said. "I want the originals of the three pages Robin found."

"Doesn't Cliff have those?"

"He thought he did, but somehow they've disappeared. We have several sets of photocopies and no originals. This is what I'm dealing with, Sandy, so don't tell me everything's all right."

"*Going* to be all right."

"Ah, so you admit things are not exactly going well right now."

"I admit nothing. I have nothing to hide, and nothing to declare," said Sandy, "and neither should you. Stop acting guilty when you're not. Stop dreading everything when you have nothing to fear." He took Marion gently by the shoulders, as if to shake the self-criticism and second-guessing right out of her. "Buck up."

Despite herself, she felt a little better to hear Sandy speak this way. He had such complete faith in their work and in her that she might have given up her own agnosticism if he could have produced the originals of those three pages. She had hunted for them, and Feng had searched. Cliff had spent the greater part of a day looking for them, but they were nowhere to be found.

4

THEY DIDN'T look like monsters. Their whiteboard was covered with jottings and sketches, their office filled with academic journals and squat computer monitors and dead plants, just as if Hackett and Schneiderman were really scientists, and not creatures gone over to the dark side, as Larry and Wendy had suggested. They were big men, but big in different ways. Alan Hackett was in his sixties, well over six feet tall, but baby-faced and gangly. His brown hair was cut boyishly and his ears stuck out. His blue eyes were oversize as well, as if to make him extra-alert. He chewed gum constantly, working his bony jaw as he talked so that he chewed his words, and then slowly drew them out again to examine and even laugh at, as if his ideas were half-ridiculous, ripe for cracking. Jonathan Schneiderman, on the other hand, was perhaps fifty, barrel-chested, entirely bald, with a full beard. His arguments were detailed and rapid, and all his sentences punctuated with an earnest resonance.

"Well, you know," Hackett began with his usual diffidence, "we can never predict how these will play out . . ."

"You have one of the strongest cases we've seen," finished Schneiderman. "We've read the paper closely, reviewed your materials, begun to analyze theirs. The discrepancies between the raw data and the published work are staggering. As you might imagine, the interviews have not shed light on this at all."

"More heat than light," drawled Hackett.

"You've interviewed Cliff?"

Hackett stared at her in mock surprise, and she was mortified. She hadn't meant to sound so eager, yet her overriding concern slipped out. How would he try to cover now? Could ORIS pin him down even a little?

"We're in the process of interviewing everyone by phone," said Schneiderman.

"But the documents are the core of the investigation," said Hackett. "We start from the published work and then trace our way backward. It's a kind of reverse engineering, if you see what I mean. But you'll be pleased to know that just as you suggested, the data gets more and more spotty as we proceed."

"Well, I'm not *pleased* to know it," said Robin.

Hackett grinned.

"You've brought the three pages with you?" Schneiderman asked.

She hesitated, her hand on the handle of her briefcase. It was a slim maroon leather briefcase in perfect condition. Her father and stepmother had bought it for her when she got her doctorate, imagining she'd need it for job interviews or formal presentations. She felt the irony that until now the briefcase had never been used.

"It's very important that we have the originals," Schneiderman said.

"The materials your former colleagues sent were rather misleading, to say the least," said Hackett.

"What do you mean?" Robin lifted her briefcase onto her lap.

"They were put together in the most artful way. I think it was Marion Mendelssohn who wrote the notes and constructed the binders." Hackett gestured to a low bookcase stacked with huge three-ring binders. With a pang Robin recognized Marion's neat print labeling the spines. "They're very well done," said Hackett. "Particularly the notes intended to fill in lacunae in the data sets."

Schneiderman leaned in toward Robin. "We've got an extensive pattern of deception here."

"Marion would never try to deceive anyone," said Robin. "I want to be clear about that. I've made a very specific complaint about a very specific line of inquiry."

"Understood," said Schneiderman firmly. "Unfortunately, these complaints sometimes lead us to larger problems, further questions that result in greater implications for the lab as a whole."

"Narrow inquiries will broaden over time," said Hackett. "Despite our best efforts, they will do that. It seems to be the nature of the beast."

"It's the nature of all research," said Schneiderman. "And in this case, what we have is a careful collaboration to cover up some initial interpolations and data manipulations, or in layman's terms, lies."

Robin's hand brushed the clasp of her briefcase. She hugged the smooth leather to her with its precious contents, the original three pages of Cliff's notes.

"May we have them?" Hackett asked.

She shook her head slightly.

"Our methods are forensic," Schneiderman explained. "Our objective is to find out exactly what happened to this data, but at this point we're working from dim photocopies arranged and edited by the very people we're investigating, and introduced by the director of the institute himself." He handed Robin a formal letter from Peter Hawking on institute stationery. "I'm sure you'll understand our desire to get our hands on original notes—the raw data, if you will."

The investigators were dizzying her with layers and connections she had never considered. Marion covering up problems. Feng colluding to manipulate the data. She had come forward with a simple complaint against Cliff—an accusation of dishonesty. Hackett and Schneiderman seemed intent on finding a web of deceit throughout the lab, extending outward through the institute. Was one small set of untruths really so telling? Did the fault lines in Cliff's work really extend so far? She did not want to think that way. But then how else could scientific liars prosper, except with the tacit consent of the community around them—a heedless will to believe, on the part of peers, collaborators, and mentors alike? The scope of this speculation fascinated and repulsed her. She looked hard at the ethics watchdogs before her, no longer truly scientists, but anti-scientific sentries. She had no trouble imagining them demolishing years of work.

"We should have the original materials you found," Hackett insisted. "We need our 'primary sources,' if you know what I mean."

"I know what you mean," said Robin, "but I'm not sure I'm going to give them to you."

Schneiderman looked disappointed, and Hackett seemed genuinely surprised to be denied like this.

"I'm just not sure that when we're talking about the possibility of fraud, we're talking about the same thing," said Robin.

"Generally, if you want answers, you don't limit your questions," Hackett said testily. "We'll need the originals."

Robin flushed at this presumption. "I'm not giving them to you."

"All right," said Schneiderman.

But Hackett smiled at her and said, "You will."

The offices of Paul Redfield (D-Ill.), were spacious but plain, the furniture square, sharp cornered, and heavy. The receptionist herself seemed like a period piece, with her contralto smoker's voice and glasses on a chain.

"You're here to see Ian Morgenstern?"

"Yes."

"One moment and I'll let him know that you've arrived."

Robin sat down and waited for several minutes, and the receptionist smiled beneficently. "These are all Illinois artists," she explained as Robin glanced nervously at the art on the walls. "They are from the Depression era, and most of them were created under the auspices of the Federal Art Project. This bridge here is by Emil Armin. This woodcut is by Todros Geller."

Robin stood and examined the woodcut of two men laboring in the shadows of looming smokestacks. The image looked as though it had been drawn in soot and sweat and tears. But the cheerful assistant who came to get her didn't give the artwork a second glance as he ushered Robin into an interior office.

"Here you are," he said, delivering Robin to an office with no art or Craftsman-style furniture, just piles and piles of papers and a television and a computer and a dot-matrix printer spewing a daisy chain of pages onto the floor.

"Welcome." Ian Morgenstern stood up and leaned over his desk to shake her hand.

He seemed even younger than he'd sounded in their conversations on the phone. Morgenstern was strong nosed and slight in build, with sandy blond hair curling up over his forehead in a near pompadour. His eyes were steely blue, his tie hung loose around his neck. His white shirtsleeves were rolled up, but his suit jacket was placed carefully over the back of his chair. She took a seat and watched him. She would be careful.

"I'm sure you know how grateful we are that you were willing to come," he told Robin. "As you know, science and scientific conduct are two areas upon which Representative Redfield has focused over the past several years—"

"Why?" Robin asked.

"What was that?" Startled by the interruption, he nearly lost his train of thought.

"Why is he interested in science?" Robin tested him.

"Ah. Why science? Why scientific misconduct? Why do they come under the purview of the House Committee on Energy and Commerce? Very simply: tax dollars. The National Institutes of Health received six *billion* dollars last year. That was not money pouring into our primary schools, or for the homeless, et cetera, but money spent entirely on research. There are people in the scientific community who take that appropriation as their divine right. Representative Redfield begs to differ. In a year when every national program—from services for the aged to support for the arts—is under scrutiny, if not constant attack, he feels that someone has got to step up to the plate and say: 'Just where is that six billion dollars going?' " As he grew excited, Morgenstern's speech accelerated and his voice pitched higher. "Here we are, sacrificing scarce resources to fund research that we hope will better our lives. Does this mean we give the NIH carte blanche? For three years now, we have been publishing an annual list of awards designed to spotlight waste in government-funded science. Have you seen it? Here's a copy. It's called the Redfield List of Wasteful and Decadent Research Appropriations, or the Red List, for short. Every month, we choose a grant or project for red-listing, as a way of spotlighting where exactly our federal research funds are going."

Robin had hoped to probe Redfield's motivation, to qualify his in-

terest, but now she sat back with the Red List in her hands, stunned by
this barrage of words. Clearly, Morgenstern was no mere staff member,
but Redfield's speechwriter, aide-de-camp, and cavalry all in one. Even
later that night as she slept on the train, Robin heard Morgenstern's
quick, high-pitched voice, his words pinging in her mind relentlessly,
like the hoofbeats of a thousand tiny horses.

He pointed to an entry on the Red List. "Here, you see, we have a
study of obesity in urban pigeons. That's one of my favorites. And this
one: a grant to teach children to watch television better. Isn't that great?
We're going to teach kids to watch TV! And here's one I love: a grant to
conduct a comparative ethnography of UFO sightings in immigrant
communities. This is a federally funded study of how we feel about phe-
nomena that do not exist! But this isn't why we've asked you here today.
In the past year, Representative Redfield has grown increasingly concerned about the specter of fraud in the scientific community—incidents that highlight a culture of deception in many federally funded
projects. Your own experience as a whistle-blower at a prestigious institute, your observations, and particularly the evidence you have compiled, lead us to believe you would be a compelling witness." Ian
Morgenstern's face glowed with pleasure as though he were congratulating Robin, indeed offering her a crown of laurels. "We would like to invite you to testify before the Subcommittee on Science and Technology."

Calm descended on the office. Robin realized with some surprise
that it was her turn to speak. "This is interesting," she said. "But as I've
said before, my complaint is very limited, and I think you'll find it very
technical. I'm not sure it's really appropriate for this sort of testimony."

"Oh, I very much disagree," Morgenstern said.

"As for my observations and my documentation, I want to make it
clear that they were planned for a limited audience of scholars and
ORIS investigators only. I never intended to display them in such a
public forum . . . and I don't think it's necessary to—"

"Ah, but a public forum is necessary, if we are talking about the
public good," parried Morgenstern.

"I am not talking about the public good," Robin replied deliberately.

Morgenstern frowned. She'd silenced him, and she enjoyed the sensation. He was far too smooth, too quick, much too eager to enlist her in his master's political cause. "I know myself," she said, "and I am not at all sure I want to testify."

"But you should," said Morgenstern encouragingly, as if she were simply shy. "And we can subpoena you, in any case."

Her heart jumped. The sober distance she thought she'd achieved was gone. She'd thought she'd been so careful coming here. She'd told herself she would test the waters, and suddenly she was flailing and thrashing, and she had no idea where the bottom was. She burned with anger and dismay. Pride alone compelled her to speak. She said, "I can't continue this conversation without representation."

5

"I assume that I'll go back," Feng told his lawyer.

"What do you mean, go back?"

"To China."

"What are you talking about?" Byron Zouzoua demanded. He was an arresting-looking advocate of Cameroonian descent, New Jersey raised, Harvard and Oxford educated, just a few years out of Yale Law School and keen to make his name. His complexion was black as obsidian, his hair close cropped, his voice deep, and his fingers long and delicate. His suits were crisp, beautifully cut, his shirts perfect, to Feng's eye. "You're not going anywhere, man. You're not seceding from this controversy."

Feng did not argue, but looked at Zouzoua with a mixture of skepticism and misery, and just a touch of amusement at the stern reprimand. His dark humor had not deserted him.

"You will not go back anywhere. This media frenzy is not about you, and it's not about science. Do you think these people have a clue about science?" Zouzoua scoffed at the folders of newspaper clippings on his desk.

The file was now voluminous indeed. Feng had been elevated, lionized, adored as the young Chinese researcher who had stumbled upon a possible cure for cancer. He had been the soft-spoken genius, unaware of his own powers, realizing for the first time that R-7 diminished tumors in experimental mice. Always, in the stories, he was in the dark, toiling silently, far from home. Always, he had sacrificed his homeland and his native food, his family, his childhood (his boyhood journey far away to school was epic)—all for science. He had been a Horatio Alger for the scientific age, working his way from peasant rags to intellectual riches; from poverty and village ignorance in China to a world of possibility in America.

And now the dream was falling apart in all the newspapers. The work with R-7 was suspect. An inquiry at the highest levels was under way, and Feng's very integrity questioned. Great wondering articles appeared in *The Boston Globe;* a critical analysis was published in the Science section of *The New York Times.* Feng's picture flashed on television newscasts, reporters had begun to call the lab, and even Feng's apartment. As quickly as he'd embodied hope, he now became the target of suspicion. As intriguing and delightful as his shy, mysti-fied face had been, his was now the face of doubt.

Zouzoua scowled at the old profile of Feng torn from *People* maga-zine. "What you are experiencing is the xenophobia of this country. That's the first thing you've got to understand and the first statement we have to make. There is no area of inquiry in the United States un-tainted by politics, and, unfortunately, there is no political arena un-touched by the specter of race." Zouzoua spread his open hands before him as if to say "Need I say more?" and Feng marveled at his perfect white cuffs, the glint of his cuff links, the pinkness of his palms.

"These fascinate me," Zouzoua said of the clippings on his desk. "They're all the same. Every article, every venue, from *People* to the *Times;* every byline and every date. They all tell the same story—and it's about how we see difference. If we can expose that, if we can really open people's eyes to the prejudices and racial politics underpinning this investigation, that would mean something."

"Would it mean something for me, too?" asked Feng. While he ap-preciated Zouzoua's broad vision of the situation, he could not really believe that such visions or bold statements would be of any help. Since when did reporters retract their articles because they had come to understand their own subtle racism? He'd thought he had inured him-self in the lab to forces beyond his control, but all the mysteries and difficulties there appeared small and manageable compared to the storm raging outside, the blizzard of articles driven by—what? ORIS?

Public interest? Xenophobia? Or were the new articles spawned by the ones that came before?

No one teased Feng about the attention now. There were no more postings on the bulletin board. One day, in fact, the old clipping from *People* disappeared.

Lab meetings were fraught. Marion knitted furiously, bent over the fisherman's sweater she was making for Jacob. As she grew more anxious, her pattern seemed to grow more elaborate. She knitted cables and honeycombs, double zigzags, basket weaves, diamond and trellis patterns, and the stitches were perfect, tight and even. She held her yarn taut against her index finger, even as she studied documents on the table. No matter what was happening, she kept the tension of her wool consistent.

Cliff was ashamed to think that once he'd been even a little jealous of Feng for getting so much press. He had been afraid before that Feng would get the credit for R-7; he'd never imagined Feng would take the blame as well. What a lot of time he'd spent fretting that Feng would get all the glory. How foolish he had been. These days, envying Feng could not have been further from Cliff's mind. He had no envy left, and he had no time.

Feng's story had been cruelly publicized in the popular press, but everyone in the scientific community knew that Cliff was the driving force behind R-7. Feng had tapered off his contributions even as Cliff stepped up his efforts. Researchers in the field were keenly aware of this. They calibrated the reputations of their colleagues and competitors with precision, and had awarded Cliff the lion's share of credit for R-7. In their eyes, the full weight of the ORIS investigation fell on him as well.

Nothing had prepared Cliff for this constant battering. He felt that every time he paused in answering Hackett and Schneiderman's questions on the phone, they took his silence as an admission of guilt. He was sure every detail he could not recall would be held against him. Cliff's earnest, bespectacled attorney, Tim Borland, talked about a vigorous defense; he used the words *outrage, disbelief,* and *travesty.* Sandy Glass scoffed at ORIS, and mocked what he called their fishing expedition. Brave words, but they were only words. The investigation persisted, shadowing days and weeks, and Cliff's inner certainty could hardly shelter him from the accusations and suppositions raining down upon his head.

The day Prithwish left for Sri Lanka, Cliff took refuge in the animal facility. He scanned the cage racks for his experimental mice, and tried to comfort himself with their good health. Marion and Sandy had decided to delay submitting the new journal article. "This is not a reflection on you," Sandy had reassured Cliff.

"We want the paper to get a fair hearing, that's all," said Marion.

Cliff understood their logic, but he was miserable all the same. He was losing time, missing the chance to publish when his work was freshest. ORIS could deliberate for months. They would announce their findings at their leisure, and his new work would remain under wraps, smothered with innuendo.

He knew now that he and Feng and Marion and Sandy would all be testifying before Representative Redfield's Subcommittee on Science and Technology. They had not been asked to testify, but commanded to appear. The documents and data ORIS had collected—even Cliff's personal notes—would be presented and entered into the *Congressional Record*. He perched on a stool in the room where most of his mice lived, and he tried to take this in. What chance could he have in front of Redfield? His work was beautiful, but the world was arbitrary and unfair. His methods were elegant; his work, this last year, the deepest joy he'd ever known. And now, just as he'd found his scientific way, ORIS blocked his path. He stood on the threshold and ORIS locked the door. He told himself he would not panic, he would not give up; but he would be testifying before politicians whose views were preordained. He had as little hope of escaping summary judgment as the animals scuffling in their cages.

There was so little he could control. Labs at Stanford and Cornell were working to reproduce his results. Once, those researchers had been the competition. Now they couldn't work fast enough to satisfy Cliff; he prayed for Hughes's and Agarwal's success as a hostage prays for family to redeem him. If only he could give up this waiting and go to Ithaca or Palo Alto and advise the scientists there. Of course he could not interfere; those trials had to proceed independently. Still, he longed to guide them.

How beautiful it must be at Stanford now, the great avenue lined with palms, the red-tiled central court soaking up the sun. But then, even Cornell sounded lovely to his ears, the campus split with gorges, boulders sheathed in ice, and all the fields knee-deep in snow. He wanted to run away, but he could not go. He was not a coward; he would not allow Robin to defeat him. Nor did he take his stand alone; his friends stayed with him, talking and teasing as they had always done.

"You aren't bringing Nella?" Feng asked one wet December day as they divided colonies of cells into new dishes. Glass's Christmas party was that night.

Cliff frowned, concentrating. "I haven't seen Nella in a while."

"And would that be because you're seeing Beth?" Aidan asked him.

The others suppressed muffled laughter. They all knew Beth Leibowitz, the secretary downstairs.

"Do not talk about Beth," Cliff said with mock severity.

"Why not?" asked Natalya.

"Beth is a delicate flower," Aidan said.

Natalya snorted. "A delicate—?"

"She's *shy*," Cliff interrupted.

"Oh really?" Aidan said. "We'll have to do something about that."

"No, you don't." Cliff turned to him. "She's scared enough of you already."

"Of me?" asked Aidan, flattered.

"All of you, so don't start," he warned, but it felt good to bicker and banter in that way. Even petty disputes amused him now. Such was the gravity of his situation.

"It's almost like a death sentence," he told Beth that evening as they drove to the party in her Volkswagen Rabbit.

"Oh, don't say that."

"I mean, it makes you understand."

She looked at him with tender concern. She was soft and gentle and utterly unscientific. "What do you understand?"

"I see now that science is what I love. It's my life and they're trying to take it away from me. I never appreciated research before, and now I see it's my—"

He stopped short; he couldn't say the word. These were Robin's sentiments. Unconsciously, he'd followed her turn of phrase, her anguished declaration.

"I hate it here," she'd confided once at the end of a particularly horrible day.

"Then do something else," he said. "Go to business school or New Guinea or something; climb around in the rain forest canopy. You like heights, right?"

She laughed, but then she was serious again. "I want to give up, but I can't."

"You can't do what you want?"

"No. I realize you always do what you want, so it's not such an issue for you."

"Mmm."

"But I can't give up research, because it's my vocation."

The scientists drank more than usual that year. Ann noticed right away. They laughed louder, talked faster than the other guests. Even Marion drank almost a whole glass of sherry, and Sandy teased her mercilessly.

"Let's see if you can hold your liquor. You're looking a little red in the face."

"I doubt that very much," Marion retorted, and took another sip. She sipped with great deliberation, as though she were courting mortal danger. Her pinched, concerted face sent everyone around her into peals of laughter.

The merriment seemed to Ann a little forced. Now Marion and Sandy both had representation. Marion employed Sybil Halbfinger, famous for her early work in civil rights, her arguments before the Supreme Court, her seminal articles on jurisprudence, her white pageboy haircut and girlish voice and frilled collars. Contrary to expectation. Sandy had not chosen Leo Sonenberg, attorney to the stars, but the understated Thayer Houghton-Smith, who litigated high above the Boston skyline from offices fitted out with wing chairs and nautical paintings, grandfather clocks and china urns—antique ballast to counteract the vertiginous view. These lawyers were necessary now, each serving as a *masque de guerre,* projecting a grimace of formality.

"Who wants another glass?" asked Sandy, scanning the room.

Cliff and Beth slipped away to sit on the stairs. Kate just happened to be walking by, and came upon them there.

"Hey, Kate," said Cliff.

She noticed the way their fingers entwined. "How do you do?" She held out her hand to Beth.

Surprised by this formality, Beth roused herself to shake Kate's hand. Beth wasn't tall as Nella had been, or pre-Raphaelite like Robin. She had a small face, deep-set brown eyes, a tiny nose, tender mouth, weak chin, and a great deal of rough brown hair tied back. When she smiled, Beth seemed to shrink into herself, her eyes crinkling smaller, her mouth and chin receding with self-effacing pleasure. Surprised, almost offended, Kate could only think: *She isn't pretty!*

"What's going on?" Cliff asked.

"I don't know," she said. Of course she knew all about the investigation.

"Don't you have anything to rehearse?" He turned to Beth. "Kate is educating me in English literature and drama."

Beth laughed softly, and leaned against him.

"Yes, well, I'm not competing on the speech team anymore," Kate said.

"What? You gave it up?" Elbows on the stair runner, he sat back in mock surprise.

"I wasn't very good," she said.

"I thought you were," he insisted. "Don't you have anything to read us?"

"No," she said, and then instantly regretted her curt tone. She knew he must be suffering; he must be exhausted, beset as he was on all sides. "Well, I don't know." She relented, and disappeared in some confusion into the library.

Beth had gone off to the dessert table when Kate came back carrying a worn copy of essays by Francis Bacon.

Undistracted now, Cliff turned to her, and she felt his smile brush over her, as if they were standing quite close together and his eyelashes and his nose and his lips were brushing hers. She wanted to sit next to him, but she was too shy.

"I found this," she said, and sat as near as she dared—just one stair down. "This is the essay on truth."

"Excellent." He leaned over her shoulder to see the page.

"'What is truth? said jesting Pilate, and would not stay for an answer . . .'" Her voice trembled a little as she read. She hoped he'd see why she had chosen the essay—that he would understand all she meant by it: all the lies and doubts and ugliness of the investigation would come to nothing; in the end the truth of what he'd done and what her father and Marion and the whole lab had achieved would come out. "'Truth is a naked, and open day-light,'" she read, "'that doth not show the masks, and mummeries, and triumphs, of the world, half so stately and daintily as candle-lights. Truth may perhaps come to the price of a pearl, that showeth best by day, but it will not rise to the price of a diamond, or carbuncle, that showeth best in varied lights . . .'"

"Hold on. Slow down," he said.

"Do you want to read it yourself?"

"I'm a bit . . . I just need to follow a little more slowly," he said. "So the truth is a pearl—and what was the diamond again?"

"He doesn't say, exactly. Maybe half-truths are the diamonds and carbuncles, because they're faceted. They're more complicated, so they look better in candlelight."

"Oh, yeah, of course." He looked through the archway in the entrance hall to the dining room table, which flickered with the soft light of Ann's Hanukkah candles. "What does a carbuncle look like, anyway? I thought a carbuncle was a big, ugly, festering sore."

"It's a jewel," she said.

"I don't think so."

"It is."

"How much do you want to bet?" he asked her.

She picked at the hem of her new black dress. "Nothing," she said.

"You'll bet me nothing. You don't seem very confident."

"I know I'm right," she said. "You can look it up."

"All right, let's look it up, then. Where's the dictionary?"

She led him into the library, and then into her mother's office, beyond. She turned on the desk lamp in the little room, which had once been a screened-in porch and then was converted into Ann's writing space. The battered wood desk was covered with stacks of graded papers. A well-thumbed volume of Darwin's letters lay open near the computer, along with credit card bills and shopping lists, and paperweights of clay and painted wood, framed pictures, a miniature Kate, and a shockingly young and bearded Sandy, clasping a baby and two little girls. Cliff hesitated in the doorway. Guests weren't meant to come inside Ann's office.

But Kate was already opening the *American Heritage Dictionary* right on top of her mother's papers on the desk. Briskly she was flipping through the Cs. "Come, look," she said. "Carbuncle."

"Ha!" said Cliff. "'A painful localized bacterial infection of the skin through which pus is discharged.'"

"Okay, fine," she conceded, sounding a little like her father. "But look at definition two: 'A deep red garnet.' And in this case, Bacon was talking about precious gems. So I'm right." She shut the book.

"I think you're just half right," said Cliff.

"Well, in the context of the essay I'm completely right."

"So truth depends on context?"

"It shouldn't," Kate said.

"But sometimes it does," he said.

"I'm not going to let you get away with that."

"No?" He reached past her to turn off the light so they could go. "What would you say then?"

"Lots of things." But she was far too flustered by his presence in the sudden darkness to argue.

6

Wedding of Angeli and Nate was 100 in the shade. I walked home
barefoot from the T. My heel was bleeding. C. carried my shoes and a
goldfish even though I said . . .

ROBIN SHUT the diary on her lawyer's desk. The very sight of the open
pages made her cringe.

"Can they really do this?" Robin asked her lawyer.

"Yes, they really can subpoena your notes, and your lab books, and
your personal diary. They can indeed," her lawyer told her. She was a
scrappy attorney named Laura Sabbatini: wiry, with small glasses, a
freckled face, and short, spiky brown hair. When she spoke, Sabbatini
spoke with emphasis, as one accustomed to instructing small children,
or to explaining the world to those less brilliant, or more naïve, than
she. She did both frequently, for she was the mother of two small boys,
and by far the brightest associate at Brooks, Weinbach, McCabe. She
was a little tornado of activity, and she had what people variously called
a killer instinct, a cutthroat mentality, or a mean streak. As she understood it, she'd earned her moniker as a killer simply because she liked
to work.

"Not my journal," Robin said. She'd already acceded to Hackett's
arguments that her case was better served with primary documents and
sent him Cliff's original notes by registered mail. Giving in to ORIS
had been bad enough.

"Your journal is some of the best evidence we have," said Sabbatini.

"They'll try to use it against me."

"Oh, two can play that game," Sabbatini told her. "Where was that section?" She leafed through the bound composition book. "Yeah, I like this part." She adjusted her glasses.

> *I said I didn't want to and he said why not. I told*
> *him it was too soon but he said he didn't think so. Accused*
> *him of not listening, but. . . .*

"Stop. Stop!" cried Robin, covering her ears.

Sabbatini looked up, amused. "When it comes to relationships in the workplace, it's a very, very thin line between consensual sex and sexual harassment. So if Cliff and company want to use your diary, they'd better watch their backs."

Robin took a moment to assimilate this. Six months after she'd left the lab, her questions were not hers anymore; her doubts had grown into weather systems of their own, her single intuition now transformed into a conspiracy theory implicating not only Cliff but nearly everyone who worked around him. After working so closely with him for so long, why hadn't Feng spoken up about Cliff's unorthodox record keeping? How could Marion, famous for overseeing every detail, have allowed Cliff to work virtually unsupervised? Had they not seized rapaciously on the promise of Cliff's work? Starved for results, they'd conjured up a banquet. Cliff had begun, and then the others followed, and the entire scientific community began to partake. Weren't they all, then, eating air?

"I don't want to use my diary as a weapon," she told Sabbatini.

"But it is a weapon," Sabbatini shot back, as if she relished the thought.

At times like this, Robin felt as if she'd stepped through the looking glass into another world, where lawyers and politicians were the true investigators and scientists the pawns. Here, evidence was personal, not chemical or biological. She looked around her in this alien landscape and she understood that she was being used.

Nevertheless, she had information that deserved publicity; she had rescued data that deserved a hearing, and the inquiry had provided

Robin with an audience. In the land of ORIS, Robin's suspicion was praised as insight; her frustration called prescience; her skepticism no longer deemed self-destructive jealousy, but valuable, honest, and rare. Publicity had its price, but so did silence. She'd had no choice but to let her doubts loose, and watch and worry as the lawyers on the other side gave chase.

"I don't want you to twist my words around," she warned Sabbatini.

"I'm just saying—they start twisting, and we'll twist back," said Sabbatini. "Hey, listen to me. The nastier this gets, the better off we'll be. The more personal and ad hominem they are, the better. Bring it on! The more mud the merrier. You know why, don't you? Because they're desperate. They are so desperate." Sabbatini bounced a little in her chair. "You still don't believe me, do you? Let's draw up a little balance sheet, okay? Let me see. What have you got? You've got ORIS seriously questioning the lab's integrity, you've got Redfield on the warpath, you've got the press smelling blood, you've got an incipient scandal and cover-up going on at the institute. You've got the truth. Not to mention—me! And I've told you about the Secret Service. They've started their ink analysis on Cliff's notes. They're going to do the forensics to find out exactly how many pens Cliff really used there, and whether some of that data is really much older, or whether it was all from the same set and he really just left some of it out. You thought those questions that you asked would never get a real answer, but they will be answered. You've got the Secret Service on your side. You've got cutting-edge technology. Now, what do they have? Hmm. They have their prevarications; they have their pride; they have your diary."

"But I don't want them to have my diary," Robin said, fretting.

Laura Sabbatini knit her fingers together and rested her chin on her hands. "Oh, come on, Robin," she chided, as though Robin were afraid of spiders. "You have practically the entire government working on your case."

"That's an exaggeration," Robin said.

"And the whole world ready to take up pitchforks for your cause."

"It was just one op/ed piece," said Robin.

"All right. So almost the whole world. We're going in there and shooting down the liars and the cheats and blowing the cover off an entire culture of scientific finessing and fraud. Don't tell me you're expecting this thing to be pretty, too."

The inquiry wasn't pretty, and that was just what Nanette liked about it. She phoned Robin regularly and left messages in a breathless Mata Hari voice. The two of them met for coffee at Café Algiers, surrounded by its red walls and polished brass samovars. They sat at the back where the kitchen door swung open to reveal Yasser Arafat's picture pasted on the wall, and Nanette predicted the downfall of the institute. She was sure the ORIS inquiry was going to bring the Philpott crashing to earth, and Robin thought she seemed strangely eager for this catastrophe, considering the institute was Nanette's employer.

"Doesn't matter," Nanette said blithely. "I could get a job at MIT in a minute. I'm good."

"True," said Robin.

"The only question," said Nanette, "is whether Harvard dismantles us, or we implode from scandal and misspending first. You saw the article in the *Globe,* didn't you? 'Philpott Near Empty: Hard Choices at the Cambridge Institute'? Actually, that was just Part I."

"I know," said Robin, who had been contacted for an interview for Part II.

"Everybody's running scared. I can't tell you. People are starting to hoard media," Nanette declared, exaggerating just a little. "They're coming in with double orders, upping the amounts so they can run more trials at once. It's a psychological thing, like the way people act before a blizzard, or a war. With the audit and Redfield's shit list and all, people aren't even sure where their next grant is coming from." Nanette stretched out her legs and rotated her tiny feet slowly. "I'm working ten-hour days. Do you see the swelling in my ankles? My doctor says my job is exacerbating my edema."

Robin looked down with some concern. Nanette's ankles were in fact puffing out over her shoes.

"I'm supposed to keep them elevated, but I have to use the foot pedal." Nanette shrugged and smiled. "See, I can't wait for the committee hearings. It would really be better for me if the institute went belly-up."

"You don't mean that."

"Oh, it would be so fascinating. I love to watch chronic over-achieving SOBs scramble. The people who never give their underlings the time of day. Little words like *please* or *thank you*. All the type As killing their postdocs and ignoring their wives for the sake of science; fighting tooth and nail to get ahead. Everybody and their neuroses just running for cover. I love comeuppance." She clasped her hands to-gether. "Comeuppance is such a beautiful thing. I just adore it."

"But where would I work, then?" Robin asked.

"Work!" Nanette shrieked. "You'd be writing your tell-all book. You wouldn't ever need to work again."

"But I don't want to tell all: Who would hire me? That's the last thing I would ever do," said Robin. "I love research." She said it so softly, Nanette had to lean in to hear the words.

"You what?" Nanette took Robin's hand in hers. "You love what?" She shook her head, mystified. "You poor, poor girl." Nanette threw up her hands. "She loves research."

7

THE FESTIVITIES in the lounge were for Prithwish and his bride, Sarojini, who had finally returned from Sri Lanka and set up house in an apartment on Elmer Street. There was wine and cheese and there were blue tins of Danish butter cookies. Aidan had rigged up the slide projector to display pictures of the wedding on the wall so that the beige room filled with silk and gold and sun. There was laughter and teasing, and ogling of the banquet, but the party was subdued. Outside, the dirty snow had begun to melt, and each pale evening was strengthening and growing longer. The hearing was twelve days away.

"It's been a good week," Sandy insisted to Marion after the others had gone.

"Good for what?" she asked. "We got almost nothing done." The pressure of the hearings, the dread of them, had built until the most mundane tasks required almost superhuman concentration.

"Nothing done? We've got letters of support from the Chinese Consulate, and the Asian Law Caucus, and the ACLU. We've got Houghton-Smith's protest against journalists for colluding in a case against academic freedom. Then there's my letter, of course. Did you see the new draft?"

He took her hand and pulled her down the hall and into the office. "Sit down. Now, take a look at this."

" 'In Defense of Science,' " she murmured. " 'An open letter.' "

"Read it aloud," he urged her.

" 'When the NIH feeds unproved accusations to Congress; when scientific disputes are judged by the representatives of government agencies . . .' " she intoned.

"No, not like that, Marion. Can't you hear? There's a rhythm to it. Let me." He snatched the page from her hands. " 'When scientific data are subpoenaed at the will and whim of Congress; when the Secret Service is employed to analyze personal papers; when characters and careers are shattered, and vital publications suspended purely by suspicion; when scientists are attacked, intimidated, and assumed guilty until proven innocent; when the public discourse about science is polluted by assertions of negligence and fraud; when the scientific community is maligned as weak, corrupt, and incapable of regulating itself independent of government interference, *then we believe* science itself is under siege. The intellectual freedoms we cherish in America are at stake.' " He looked up at her.

"Was that the preamble?"

"Exactly." He was as proud of that letter as he'd been of anything in his life. "But look at the end. Look at the signature."

"Peter Hawking."

"You can say it," he told her. "I'm brilliant."

She shook her head at him. The signature was a stroke of genius. He'd crafted a Jeffersonian defense of science that the director of an embattled institute could champion with dignity—and disseminate among his colleagues.

"We've got the signatures of eleven Nobel laureates, counting Peter," he told her. "I'm shooting for twenty. Then we start publishing in the major newspapers."

"Sometimes I think you're actually enjoying this," she said.

"False accusations? Attempts to bring us down?" he shot back. "Absolutely not. But if you're talking about fighting the good fight, and tackling the other side—then, yes, I admit I do enjoy that. I *will* enjoy it." He placed his manifesto on her desk. "And I'm sure," he said softly, "you worry enough for both of us."

Cliff was the last one in the lab that night. Sometime after midnight he began packing up. He perched on his stool and rummaged through the papers on his bench top until he turned up the book that had arrived that day. The volume was a paperback copy of *Bleak House,* which had come with a message: "Dear Cliff: If any novel reflects the times we live in, this is it." Kate had sent the book and the brief note—the drafts had been much longer. She'd thought and thought about what she could do, and then settled on the book because he'd always asked her for some piece of literature. Cliff smiled faintly and opened the little paperback to Chapter One. "London. Michaelmas Term lately over, and the Lord Chancellor sitting in Lincoln's Inn Hall. Implacable November weather. As much mud in the streets . . ." His eye skipped down. "Fog everywhere. Fog up the river, where it flows among green aits and meadows; fog down the river, where it rolls deified among the tiers of shipping and the waterside pollutions of a great (and dirty) city. Fog on the Essex marshes, fog on the Kentish heights. Fog creeping . . ."

Kate had begun to write: "I hadn't understood before that American bureaucracy could act in such Dickensian ways, crushing innocent people in its path." And then she'd crumpled up the paper and written: "The machinery of government and its self-serving ends, added to the ignorance of bureaucrats swayed by irresponsible accusations, make Charles Dickens seem prescient, to say the least." But that managed to sound stentorian and prissy at the same time. She had wanted to say that she trusted and believed everything would be all right—without sounding Pollyannaish. She'd wanted to tell him what she knew about her father, but it was hard to put into words. She knew that, difficult as he could be, her father was just too clever to lose a battle like this one. She knew that he would protect Cliff in the pinch, that in the end her father was the one you wanted on your side.

Sandy Glass was much on his daughters' minds. The girls had often fretted about his sharp words and demanding expectations, but they had never felt protective of him before. Now, as the time came for Sandy to travel down to Washington, his daughters began to worry. Louisa made her way down MIT's Infinite Corridor, lined with club posters and classrooms and computer labs, and office doors windowed with old-fashioned white glass, and she imagined him coming under fire, attacked for supporting his young postdocs' work. She had often been annoyed by her father, and frustrated by him, but she was surprised now by how proud she was of him. He could have distanced himself from his postdocs' work. Instead, he chose to champion Cliff and Feng and rally other scientists around their cause.

Her father was loyal. Marion was loyal, too, of course, but as always, Sandy was the active, vocal one. He was the one on the front lines, championing his postdocs' work—defending Marion, as well. What would she have done without him?

Louisa longed to go to the hearing, to sit in her father's corner. Characteristically, however, Sandy dismissed the idea. "I've never heard anything so ridiculous in my life. You will not be missing classes for this particular exercise in futility, and I am not going to have this whole family at the beck and call of Mr. Redfield."

He was so brave. Would he go to the Capitol and get ambushed there? Would he say something impolitic? He was fond of the beau geste and, Louisa fretted, more of a debater than a strategist. She did not speak of her concern, however. If Louisa had her mother's tender nature, she had her father's impenetrably cheerful manner, as well. She deflected any questions from friends with a laugh and a wave of the hand.

Louisa could avoid the subject, but up the river at Harvard, Charlotte did not have the luxury. Just days before her father flew to Washington, she sat down for dinner with Jeff in the dark-paneled Dunster House dining hall, and he said, "We got a pass to attend the hearings."

"What?" She drew back.

"We got a press pass at the *Crimson*," he told her.

They were sitting at a long trestle table, their green cafeteria trays resting on polished wood. Portraits of former house masters lined the vaulted hall, along with the stuffed head of an unfortunate moose.

"I want to go," he said.

"No you don't," she told him.

"I really do," he confessed. Ever since he'd interviewed Cliff, he'd followed the story of R-7. He'd read all the articles about Feng, and gazed, fascinated, as one might ponder the portrait of a serial killer, at the black-and-white photo of Robin in *The Boston Globe*.

"You do not want to go," Charlotte said, aghast. "It's a conflict of interest, for one thing, and you know it."

"I wouldn't write the story," he said, hedging. "It's just that I have all the background on the research. Actually, it turns out I did practically the only extensive interview of Cliff Bannaker before the inquiry. My story is pretty much the only record of his side of—"

"What are you *thinking*?" Charlotte demanded. "It would be totally unethical for you to go to the hearing. I can't believe you're even suggesting it. No journalist would do something like that."

"Well . . ." he began, but the conversation was going badly, and he didn't want to upset her more. He refrained from telling her he had been contacted by several publications interested in his perspective, his insights about where the ORIS investigation might lead.

"This is my father we're talking about," said Charlotte, half rising in her seat.

"I know," said Jeff. "I know it's your father."

"Right, of course you know. How else would you have gotten the interview with Cliff in the first place?"

"I only said I wished I could go," he said. "I didn't say I was going."

"I can't believe you would even suggest going down there to DC—to watch."

"I'm sorry," he told her, and he meant it, but the undergraduate in him, a little too young, a little too eager, couldn't help adding, "It's just . . . it's going to be a great story."

"I'm sure you'd love it," Charlotte burst out. "I'm sure you'd love a ringside seat. What is wrong with you?"

"I'm not going," he said. "I am absolutely not going, and I apologize."

But it was too late. Self-promotion had yielded to self-preservation too late. Charlotte sprang up in a fury, tray in hand. Her uneaten Salisbury steak, twice-baked potatoes, and green beans sloshed together on her plate. Astonished and aggravated at her father's prescience about her boyfriend, she slammed her tray onto the table and tossed her cranberry juice straight into Jeff's face.

Loud cheers from a table of rugby players followed Charlotte as she left the dining hall, and the hapless Jeff Yudelstein behind.

Of course, he understood her point of view much better in retrospect, and regretted every word he'd said. But Jeff had not yet learned to feign sensitivity before he felt any, nor did he know how to pretend diffidence. He couldn't help looking forward to the subcommittee hearings. He had worked and slept in the little brick *Crimson* building for nights on end, and he'd been bitten by the bug, the intense desire to divulge, to tap and crack the events of the day. As young scientists thrill at possible discoveries, and young painters open their eyes to the infinite shades and colors of light, so Jeff had awakened to the world of politics and public affairs. That world was so complex and new to him, its power struggles, its adjudications, its dissemblings so enticing, how could he not want to go to Washington, to attend the hearings there?

All the rest of that week he walked through the Yard hating himself, cursing his stupidity. He sat in darkened lecture halls composing apologies, utterly distracted by regret for what had passed, and yet, even then, he could not stop thinking about the hearings. Heartsick though he was, he could not suppress his curiosity.

8

THEY SAT in silence in the back of their taxi. The traffic ebbed and flowed around them as they inched past fountains bordered with spring pansies, statues, limestone edifices, the national associations of nearly everything.

"What is it, Sandy?" Ann asked at last.

"Nothing," he said.

"Are you nervous?"

"Of course not," he snapped. Still, he looked strangely subdued, almost defeated in his dark suit and yellow tie.

"What is it, then?" she pressed him.

"It's not what I envisioned," he murmured.

"What? Washington?"

They had been to DC a hundred times before, but she didn't understand. This was not how he had envisioned his congressional debut. Secretly he'd always meant to arrive in the Capitol a conquering hero, or rather a co-hero with Marion. He'd planned for ribbons and ceremonial picture taking, festive garden parties at the National Academy of Sciences, where he and Marion would nibble strawberries dipped in chocolate and hobnob with their senators under white tents. He'd intended formal dinners and testimonials, certificates calligraphed in vermilion, lapis blue, and gold. He'd imagined entering the city in its grandest, most expansive form. Instead he'd been summoned to an anthill of bureaucrats and bean counters. He'd arrived shackled with prohibitions from his lawyer. Reduced to defending the lab, he'd fanta-sized about leading thousands of scientists marching on the Hill. But the reality was different. He carried in his briefcase a written statement defanged by Houghton-Smith. His hands were tied.

Ann gazed at her husband. He looked almost ill in the lurching cab. His shoulders slumped, his eyes were pained and tired. She could see he had a headache, although she knew he would deny it. She wanted to reassure him, but what could she say? He knew every trick; he was the master at restoring confidence in friends and patients. What could she possibly say, now that it was finally time to reassure him?

"We'll get through this," she said.

Turning to the half-open window, he murmured, "This is not how it was meant to be."

The hearing room was cheap and small, a shoe box stuffed with slick tables, angular chairs, video equipment, and clunky microphones trail-ing thick black cords. A handful of reporters crouched between the sec-ond row of chairs and the back wall. Scruffy and eager, they rustled in the back. Yudelstein! With a little shock of surprise and hatred, Sandy saw Yudelstein among the rodents. The jolt was painful, but it shook Sandy alert. Animosity surged through his melancholy body as he whipped around and faced forward. Bristling, he took his seat and looked straight ahead into the face of Representative Redfield.

Paul Redfield was nearly seventy years old. His eyes were pale, keen, and blue. He had a sharp nose and thin, smooth-shaven cheeks. He was in the pink of health; the kind of man who outlived all his doc-tors. He had served in the navy in the Second World War, supported his family as a newspaperman and then a trial lawyer. After five terms in the House, two children, and five grandchildren, and forty-nine years of marriage to Mrs. Redfield (Shirley), he was known in his dis-trict as the Rock. He was steadfast, and as his opponents pointed out, he was hard. When he spoke—and he spoke at length—he hammered out opinions set in stone.

"At its best," Redfield read from his typed opening statement, "the scientific community in America dedicates itself to the health and well-being of the populace, the prosperity and security of the nation. We, the taxpayers, entrust the NIH and the research programs it funds to address the medical problems plaguing our society: heart disease, cancer, diabetes, and other ailments that tear apart so many families and destroy so many lives. We, the family members, the caregivers, and the patients suffering, have waited patiently for progress, and new hope where there has been none. We, the taxpayers, foot the six-billion-dollar bill. How distressing—how appalling, then, to find, in recent years, a growing number of scientific scandals violating the trust of the community. How shocking to uncover a culture of deception corrupting the very research programs to which we have entrusted our tax dollars and our hopes." Redfield looked up from his text and gazed across the narrow chasm between the congressional table and the table of researchers called to testify.

They were all quite still, Cliff and Tim Borland, Feng and Byron Zouzoua, and, of course, Marion, who was listening with idle hands, her half-knit fisherman's sweater stored safely at the hotel. Meek, and mute, Sandy took his medicine as Ann watched, along with Jacob and Mei in the second row of chairs. Everyone was there except the instigator. Ann was relieved she didn't have to look Robin in the face. Her ingratitude, her lack of common decency! She was nothing less than an arsonist, setting her own lab on fire with furious sparks, then watching the conflagration spread throughout the institute—in fact, fanning the flames. Thankfully, Robin was absent, having finished her testimony the day before, detailing what Redfield termed her ordeal.

The congressman had a term for everything. He used his opening statement as a battering ram, expatiating on the trust of the taxpayers, and his personal belief in accountability. He declared that those funded by the public were, in fact, public servants, not scientific grandees, not princes of the realm, not prospectors, but public servants, as he himself was, and all his colleagues on the subcommittee as well. Several aides nodded. Redfield's logic was unassailable; his dogmatic public servitude irreproachable; above all, his oratory was uninterruptible.

A C-SPAN video camera recorded on its tripod, and the print journalists took notes until Redfield spoke so long that even they began to scribble less. Redfield had refined the art of circling back upon his arguments and restating them with ever-greater strength. If he bored his listeners, then that was his venomous intent. He spoke until his opponents lost their concentration, anesthetized by his rhetoric. He seemed, Ann thought, to hold even Sandy in his thrall. Like a python, Redfield would squeeze the life and very air out of the room.

His arguments were entirely simpleminded, concluded Jacob, at Ann's side. But then, Jacob was hard put to look upon a politician as anything other than a moron. While Ann fretted that Sandy would not have time or spirit left to defend himself, Jacob looked at Redfield and saw only pompous ignorance. He seriously underestimated Marion's opponent.

When questioning finally commenced, the ranking Republican on the committee, Brock Lindell, took his turn, and mildly asked Feng how long he had worked at the lab, how long he'd worked with Cliff, how many projects he'd been working on, and whether he thought it was possible to pursue so many projects at once without ever misplacing paperwork. Lindell sent his queries out with parachutes, and Feng or Cliff had only to pull the string provided for their answers to float pillowed to the ground. But Redfield gave no quarter. He leaned forward in his chair and shot out questions like the trial lawyer he'd been thirty-five years before. "I would like to enter this document into the record," he told the clerk. "A document entitled Fungi. Mr. Xiang, do you recognize this as your work?" He passed a photocopied page over to Feng.

"This is Cliff's handwriting," said Feng.

"Granted. However, it is my understanding that these are transcriptions of sayings and definitions that you invented in the lab. For example: 'Government Appropriations for Cancer Research: GAC (acronym): "sick tax." Conference (noun): "cancer junket."'"

"Well, they were definitions attributed to me," Feng said nervously. "They were meant to be facetious."

"Were they?"

"Of course."

Redfield scanned his copy. "'Research (verb): "To search again." Research initiative (verb): "To search again for the next five years of funding."'" The congressman whipped off his reading glasses. "Perhaps these definitions were meant to be facetious; they are also quite revealing."

"I must interject here," said Byron Zouzoua. "This is an extraordinary line of questioning, which does not focus on experiments or data, but on the culture of the laboratory."

"In my opinion, that culture is highly relevant," said Redfield, "particularly when it's a culture that scoffs at the economic realities of medical research."

Zouzoua lobbed back, "I worry about focusing on ephemera like private jokes. You are trying to characterize a scientific culture that is, in fact, complicated by the diverse national cultures involved. You're shifting this inquiry away from cold, hard fact into a realm of cultural and character analysis. And how quickly we find, sir, that character analysis devolves into character assassination."

"I see your point," said Redfield, but he did not apologize for making his, and as he continued, no detail was too small, no connection too tangential, to pursue. "We have received the ink analysis of your three pages of notes," he told Cliff, "and the findings are unequivocal. You used one pen to record the data on these mice. One pen to record the identification numbers of these mice, their date of dissection, and the outcome of injection with the R-7 virus. One pen was used here, and one pen only, suggesting that in fact these notes were all made on the same day—they were not, as you stated earlier, jottings made at different times, over different months. These notes refer to the one group of mice, and record one set of data. You published some of that data, but you withheld the rest. I would—"

Tim Borland half rose from his seat. "I would like to record my strong objection to this implication of my client. Despite repeated requests, we have not been able to review this so-called ink analysis. We have not been privy to the methods by which the Secret Service studied the ink on the page. We have not been allowed to contact the agents who conducted the analysis, nor have we received copies of their report. We have been blindfolded and blindsided by a process that seems designed to intimidate my client and obfuscate the evidence at hand. Until we receive these materials, my client cannot answer questions on the matter."

This was a stout defense. Still, Sandy stared down at the table, disheartened to sit with the others, who were cowering beneath the procedural arguments of the attorneys. Cliff and Feng spoke gingerly. They were circumspect and fearful, coached by their attorneys to talk little, and answer to the point, or not at all. Where was the outrage that Sandy knew they must feel?

Marion had never been a great public speaker. She read her prepared statement without once looking up from the page. When Redfield questioned her about exactly what kind of supervision she had provided Cliff and Feng, she answered haltingly.

"Do you think you could have done more to watch the postdoctoral researchers in your lab?" Redfield demanded.

"Yes," she told him.

Sandy gazed at her, urging silently: Oh, Marion, look him in the eye, at least. Tell him: Yes, of course I could have done more, but in a lab a certain amount of delegation is necessary. I wasn't there at every moment while these experiments were conducted, but the methods, the results, and the underlying strategy here were always in my purview.

"Presumably you are responsible for those postdoctoral students who work in your lab," said Redfield.

Not students, Sandy corrected silently. Remind him they aren't students. But Marion didn't correct Redfield.

"Presumably you work in a supervisory role," Redfield said.

Marion nodded.

"Then where were you when these experiments were going on? Where were you when your students recorded their results?"

She flinched, visibly shaken. Sybil Halbfinger tried to interject on Marion's behalf, but Redfield pressed on.

"Here is my question for you: have you done *anything at all* to safeguard the scientific process?"

Ann watched Sandy's neck and shoulders tense, his fingers clench. He was angry, and as Redfield questioned Marion, his anger grew. He had entered the room obediently, listened quietly, submitting to the terms and restrictions of this hearing. But how could Redfield interrogate Marion like that? How could he treat her with such disrespect? She knew more than ten Redfields; her tiniest conjecture was worth a thousand of his nostrums. Marion, he pleaded inwardly, speak up.

Heart beating faster, Sandy curbed his impulse to interrupt. He bit his lip, waiting for his turn to speak. The session was long, and threatened to go overtime, and still Sandy waited furiously at the table. The reporters were sidling off, shuffling out the door to other rooms. The congressmen who had already spoken had excused themselves as well.

Each had said his piece and then ducked out. The little room, so crowded before, was emptying. When his turn came at last, Sandy scarcely had an audience. There was no crowd to absorb his rage, nor did his prepared statement come close to expressing his indignation. "A manifesto is unnecessary here," Thayer had informed him when they prepared Sandy's statement in Boston. "A recapitulation of your letter in defense of science is exactly what we don't need."

Sandy glared at the text before him. Thayer's language was well considered, bristling with refined contempt toward ORIS and its inquiry. But contempt was not what Sandy wanted here. His lawyer had advised him to fight this battle with thistles, and Sandy needed spears and sabers. He glanced up from his typed statement and saw Redfield looking at his watch and then conferring with an aide behind him.

He'd witnessed a one-man tribunal masquerading as a House hearing. He had watched Redfield interrogate Cliff and Feng and even Marion. His throat tightened as he read. He'd seen Redfield batter and bruise his own partner and collaborator, the best scientist he knew— and by far the most principled. How could he let this pass? How could he allow this hack to brutalize her?

He put down his prepared remarks. "What I've seen here today has shocked and disgusted me," he burst out, ignoring the pressure of Houghton-Smith's hand on his arm. "What I've witnessed today has no place in what we call a democratic country."

How well Louisa knew her father. He did like a beau geste, and he did love to launch himself forward, alone on his horse, into fiery debate. He was wily and pragmatic, but his blood was up, and he forgot himself.

"I came here to participate in an open, honest inquiry," said Sandy, "and what I've found is nothing more than a show trial, a witch hunt in which a few unlucky researchers are held up on display—hostages to Representative Redfield's assault on scientific research in America. We have come here, American citizens and one Chinese national, seeking a chance to prove our innocence and clear our names. Instead, we've suffered hostile questioning, an outrageous Secret Service inquiry, and repeated attempts to turn our personal papers, and even our private jokes, against us. All this in the name of public accountability. Mr. Redfield, you have talked a great deal about a culture of deception in scientific research today. With all due respect, sir, I feel compelled to question the culture at this hearing: a culture of governmental interference and intimidation, a culture of hatred, ignorance, paranoia, and suspicion I can only liken to McCarthyism."

Redfield was listening now. Everyone in the room was listening. In vain, Houghton-Smith whispered in Sandy's ear. In vain, Ann prayed silently for her husband to collect himself, but Sandy had not finished. He was violating protocol, almost certainly damaging his own cause, but he would not stop speaking; indeed, he could not.

"Is it any accident you keep a list of scientific projects you dislike?" he asked Redfield. "Or am I the only one who looks at the Red List and sees the specter of those creative men and women who were blacklisted? Is it any accident—"

But Redfield did not let Sandy finish. Leaving aside his own closing statement, he answered Sandy's fire with his own. "We have a fine tradition in America of taking the part of the victim when we are called to account," he said, "and I see you play the victim well. But let's remember who the victims truly are when it comes to scientific fraud: not you, Dr. Glass, not I, not any of my colleagues here. The victims are the taxpayers. The victims are the hopeful and deluded public. I see that you're offended. It offends you as a physician and a scientist that a governmental committee might call you to account. It offends you deeply that we might question your work, your methods, and your results, or probe into information that you insist is of a private nature. Let me ask you this: if your research process is private, then why do you accept public funding for it?

"You have professed surprise and shock at the questioning here. Do you know what shocks me? I am shocked by the aura of entitlement among American scientists. I am shocked by the expectation of public trust. Well, where I come from trust is earned. What have you done here to earn my trust?

"There is another victim in this matter," said Redfield. "And her name is Robin Decker. You knew her well, but you chose not to listen to her. She came to you and Marion Mendelssohn to speak up about the irregularities she'd seen and the fraudulent claims she'd witnessed. She went to other scientists and pleaded for a full hearing. However, her findings received only a cursory review. Since that time, in pursuit of the truth, she has given up years of research to start over in a menial technical position. She has given up her postdoctoral salary and her benefits. When she arrived in Washington to testify this week, she stayed in the home of a friend's parents, because she could not afford the cost of a hotel. Let's remember who the real victims are."

Downcast, almost sorrowful, Marion listened to this description of Robin's struggle. But Sandy shook his head defiantly.

"Robin had a full hearing," Sandy declared. "Don't try to pretend otherwise. We have statements from every scientist there."

"Yes, let's talk about *your* show trial, your so-called seminar," Redfield snapped. "Your laboratory is the oppressive regime. You are the dictator there in a totalitarian system. Yours is a culture of accepted truths corrupted by your desire for more and still more funding, and a lust for quick results. Your lab is but one example in a long line ORIS is just now bringing to light. Exaggeration is rewarded. Lies are justified."

Redfield was living up to his name, for his face was reddening. "I fault the senior scientists in each case. I fault the principal investigators who nurture quick fixes and engineer the fast track from a whiff of success to pharmaceutical riches or academic glory. I fault the principals who should know better," he said, nearly spitting out the words. "You are collaborators in the true sense of the word. You reward intellectual dishonesty. In the face of good publicity you sacrifice good practices. In the face of possible results you stifle all dissent. Your rationalizations are no better than those of the Germans who collaborated with the Nazis."

Redfield's staffers cringed. Reflexively, Ian Morgenstern ducked his head as if to avoid a blow. In the passion of the moment, Redfield didn't notice. He spoke only to Glass. At Sandy's side, Houghton-Smith stared in amazement. Sandy had spoken recklessly; he'd forgotten everything, and yet he'd provoked the congressman to even more treacherous rhetorical heights. Redfield had invoked the Nazis. As in tennis, Sandy had drawn the error, and scored a victory.

But Sandy was no tennis player. The day was won, but he did not retire from the court. Even as Houghton-Smith gestured for his client to desist, Sandy leaned into his microphone and said, "I insist on responding to Mr. Redfield's last statement."

The clerk announced that time was up. The representative from Tennessee suggested that they all adjourn.

"I'm sorry," Sandy said. "I cannot let this pass."

The floor was his again; every man and woman remaining shocked awake.

"Sir," Sandy said, "I take exception to your remarks as a scientist, as an American, but above all, as a Jew. Six million of my people perished in the Holocaust, among them members of my own extended family. To compare my conduct to that of Nazi collaborators is an insult to me and to the entire Jewish community. Such a statement is beyond tasteless; it is deeply anti-Semitic, and I demand an apology."

For a moment the room was silent. Well played, Jacob thought. And in the back row, Jeff Yudelstein watched in wonder. Even he, the newest of reporters, saw what Sandy Glass had achieved. Redfield was on the defensive. Still testy, Redfield was now the one explaining himself. His analogy was not meant as an insult to American Jews, but as an indictment of corruption in the scientific community, a culture of falsehood in which compliance was rewarded and truth tellers shot down. His analogy, perhaps unfortunate, perhaps misleading, was not at all meant as a slight to the sacred memory of those who perished. He was clarifying mightily, but he was too late. The words had sprung from his mouth and flown into every notebook and tape recorder, to multiply in print and on the radio, and on every public access cable station.

This would be huge for Feng. Byron Zouzoua realized it instantly. The Holocaust trumped everything. The accusation of anti-Semitism lifted the discourse to an entirely new level. Media attention on Feng, the brilliant, inscrutable Chinese, could hardly compete with this, the representative's anti-Semitic faux pas.

Thayer Houghton-Smith felt his stomach lurch again from despair to hope. He had nearly given up on his bull-in-the-china-shop client, and then Glass invoked the Holocaust. He had dropped the H-bomb. What more could anybody say? Was Sandy actually a genius?

Was he insane? Marion wondered, half in awe at this oratorical excess.

Ann bent her head to hide her astonished face. She was sure Sandy had never uttered words like these in his life. Her husband had never used the term *my people,* except perhaps in the punch line of some Jewish joke. Instinctively she understood he spoke metonymically: by *people* he meant Marion. When he demanded an apology, what he wanted was an apology to Marion, whose rough handling enraged him. Even now, after all these years, Sandy's deep attachment, his love for Marion, still took Ann by surprise. To see him defend Marion so recklessly, to watch him throw himself in front of her, hurt, even though Ann felt, high-mindedly and politically, that his behavior should make her proud.

9

As REDFIELD swept out of the hearing room with his staff surrounding him, rebuffing journalists in a rear-guard maneuver, Charlotte and Louisa Glass were riding a tall bus an hour north of Boston to visit Kate at Hill. Parents' Weekend at the Hill Academy was scheduled to begin that evening, and Ann, with her usual care, had asked that one of them go up for the first night to keep Kate company until her parents arrived the next morning. Both sisters had volunteered. It wasn't just a matter of taking care of Kate; it seemed a point of family pride as well, to go out to Hill, hold up the flag, and guard the home front.

The sisters were the only two passengers on the bus, and the driver seemed to have forgotten them as he picked up speed through the dun-colored farms. The John Parrish Hill Academy had not a single hill to its name, and Charlotte could see the church steeple from far off. "Excuse me? Excuse me!" she called to the bus driver. Swaying, she and Louisa made their way to the front.

"Oh, there you are," the driver said.

"This is our stop," Charlotte snapped.

"Relax," Louisa murmured, and Charlotte shot her a look, because her sister sounded so much like Ann.

They tumbled out the doors, narrowly avoiding a slush puddle, and carried their bags across the two-lane highway that cut through the campus. They had both attended Hill themselves, and they felt almost old and wise as they trudged across the vast and muddy fields toward the main quad. Parrish Hill had an ethereal, storybook quality, as if it had been fixed in time one hundred years before. To the south, the ground sloped quietly down to the great pond. In the west, a bunch of students trundled off, like farm girls in a John Everett Millais painting, cheeks glowing in the rosy afternoon light, lacrosse sticks pitched over their shoulders.

Louisa took a deep breath. How sweet the air was after the stale city. She had forgotten.

A small figure was running toward them. They could see her from far off. Eventually Kate dashed up, breathing hard.

"Have you heard anything?" she asked.

Charlotte shook her head. "We were probably on the bus already if Mom tried to call."

"Oh." Kate took one of Louisa's bags.

"It's light," Louisa said. "I can carry it myself."

"No, I will. You're the guest," said Kate.

Louisa looked at Charlotte, amused and touched by how happy Kate was to see them. Hill was such a beautiful, desolate place.

"Are you hungry?" Kate asked. "There's an opening reception in the old gym, but it's not till eight. We can have an early dinner." She was wearing a brown corduroy skirt and there was a run in her tights. Her parka was ancient, faded, and green.

"You should really hit up Mom for some new clothes," said Charlotte.

"Well, it's not like she has time to go shopping this week," Kate replied in the reproachful tones that had earned her the family nickname Kate the Saint.

The three of them walked directly into the Commons, picked up cafeteria trays, and stood in line. Out of habit, Charlotte reached for her Harvard ID card, and then remembered that no cards were required. Guests came and went freely for dinner. There were no security guards or keys. The school was simply too remote to make such precautions necessary.

Dinner in hand, the three cast about for a few moments. "Where do you want to sit?" Louisa asked.

"I don't know," said Kate.

"Well, where are your friends?" asked Charlotte.

Stricken, Kate scanned the dining hall. She wasn't sure she could scare up enough people at any given table to qualify.

"Your pseudofriends? Your imaginary friends?" Charlotte pressed.

"All right, fine." Kate led her sisters to the far edge of a rather literary-looking group, where she introduced them to a French girl named Sylvie, who wore a Hermès scarf; a spectacled young fogy named Stephen; a jolly, pudgy type named Monty; a sophisticate named Nick; and a small kid named Matthew, who was clearly the Jewish one. Each of them said hello graciously. Then they continued talking among themselves about the spring production of *Equus*.

As usual, Kate was left to contemplate her dinner. She began to pick at her ravioli swimming in tomato sauce, her dish of chocolate pudding, her two slices of garlic bread. She was almost accepted by the others, certainly tolerated, but she was not one of them. She worked with them on the literary magazine, but her poetry was never picked. She was secretary of the drama club, but no one considered her an actor; she'd never had a part on stage. Sad to say, she was rather common at Hill. She was not African, or even African-American. She had no uncles in the Senate. Her father was not a Wall Street wizard. Her mother was not a famous activist, nor did her family attend the season in New York. Hill prided itself on its diversity. Students came from every sort of privileged background. They overcame stunning deprivations, as well. Here again, Kate fell short. She had not escaped the killing fields of Cambodia or been plucked like a rose from inner-city Baltimore by the scholarship committee. The Hill literati were fond of her, but she could not claim them as close friends.

Stephen was a little different. He was charming, even chummy when he chose to be. People said his grandfather was rich, but his parents had raised him on a commune in Oregon. He loved arcane bits of information, rare books, antiques. He'd bought a Victorian-era walking stick at a shop in Boston and been suspended for it, under the stricture that no weapons were permitted on school grounds. He claimed his middle name was Daedalus. This seemed fanciful and pretentious—but you never knew with him. It might have been true.

"Hey, Kate," he called from across the table. Louisa stared at him; he looked so familiar. "Can I borrow your *Tristram Shandy*?"

"Where's yours?"

"Lost."

"Well, where did you lose it?"

"My dear," he said professorially, "if I knew where I'd lost it, obviously it wouldn't be lost."

"Don't lend him anything," said Monty.

"Yeah, I wouldn't," Matthew told her.

"Please. I beg of you," Stephen said, and came around and knelt before Kate on bended knee.

"I'm sure it's on reserve in the library," she told him.

"Malignant thing," he said.

Then Louisa remembered where she had seen Stephen.

"He was Prospero," she whispered to Charlotte.

He'd played Prospero in the school's *Tempest* the year before. Louisa recognized the whimsical expression on his face, the round glasses, the way he spoke: formal, and at the same time flip. He had been such an odd image with those glasses and his wooden staff. Such a mix of innocence and sophistication, part Phileas Fogg at the Reform Club, part Saint-Exupéry's Little Prince. And now he must have been at least six inches taller, so lanky, and carelessly bemused. And trying to borrow books from Kate!

Charlotte viewed Stephen with a gimlet eye. After all, she knew something about callow youths.

That night Charlotte and Louisa curled up in sleeping bags in Kate's attic room. Years before, some girl had stuck glow-in-the-dark stickers on the overhanging eaves. Galaxies of tiny stars and planets filled the room as soon as Kate turned out the light.

"It's like a planetarium." Louisa lay on her back, admiring the view.

But Charlotte got straight to the point. "You should watch out for Stephen," she told Kate.

"Why?" asked Kate.

"Because he's trouble," Charlotte said.

"What do you mean?"

"You know what I mean."

"She thinks he likes you," Louisa said, amused.

Kate sat up in bed, genuinely surprised. "He does not."

"Definitely stay away from him," Charlotte warned.

"Really?" Kate was piqued by the suggestion. She'd always assumed Stephen liked boys better than girls, but then she wasn't sure. Maybe he wasn't sure either.

"He's bad news."

"Why?"

"Don't listen to her," Louisa counseled. "She's grumpy, and she's off men."

"You are? Even Jeff?"

"Who?"

"You broke up with Jeff?"

"Dumped him," said Charlotte.

"Dumped cranberry juice on top of him," amended Louisa.

"Well, Dad will be—"

"I'm not discussing it with Dad," snapped Charlotte.

"She's afraid of making him too happy," Louisa told Kate.

"Very funny," Charlotte said.

"He'll find out, anyway," said Louisa, who hadn't been nearly so philosophical when she broke up with her own boyfriend the year before.

"I just wish—" Kate began.

Charlotte interrupted, "Oh, don't say you like Stephen."

"No, I just wish Mom would call from DC. It isn't like her not to call."

"They'll be here tomorrow," said Louisa, "and then she'll give you the blow-by-blow."

"I hope Dad didn't lose his temper," Kate said in a small voice.

"Of course he didn't lose his temper," Charlotte said. "That's what lawyers are for."

"To stop you from losing it?"

"To lose your temper for you."

"I'd kind of thought they'd make it up here after all and surprise me," said Kate.

"Come on," Louisa told her gently. "You knew it would be us."

"In loco parentis," Kate murmured.

"By the time they flew to Boston, and got the car, and drove out here . . ."

"I know, but I sort of thought your coming was just one of Mom's contingency plans," Kate said. "Do you think if the hearings are running late, that's a bad sign?"

"No! Why are you always so alarmist?" Charlotte asked, although that was exactly what she'd been thinking.

The glowing stars faded, and the sisters lay in silence as they thought about their father. Unjustly accused, would he lose his position at the institute? Would he have to resign from Harvard Medical School? These questions did not spring from material concerns—losing their house, or dropping out of school, never occurred to them; they were too tough-minded, and at the same time, too sheltered for such ideas. Their worries were all for their father. Their identities were still tied to his, wrapped up in his cause and his career. His brilliance was the centerpiece of their family. His impossible hours, his weekends on call, his absences had structured their lives. His work as a healer, his research, his arrogant benevolence all comprised the central myth of their childhood, and they half dreaded the demolition of that myth, the smashing of their household god. What would become of the family then? What new religion would guide them?

What would become of him? Sandy Glass had never felt better in his life. He'd turned the tables on his accusers and he was jubilant. As Zouzoua had predicted, the media stampede had turned from Feng. Redfield, with his choice of words, by turns shocking, racist, and unfortunate, had raised the red flag and drawn public fury on himself.

The uproar over Redfield's comments swirled in all the newspapers, and privately, Sandy's own lawyer called him brilliant as the articles on Redfield's faux pas poured in: opinion pieces chastising the congressman, official statements from the American Jewish Committee, the Anti-Defamation League, and the presidents of major Jewish organizations. There were requests for Sandy to speak to the medical chapter of Boston's Combined Jewish Philanthropies, and calls for Redfield to resign as chair of the Committee on Energy and Commerce. What a delightful pickle! What a savory stew!

Few enjoyed the brouhaha more than Sandy's own patients. They embraced him at office visits, and hailed him as a returning champion in their rooms.

"Redfield really put his foot in it," said Mary Stoughton. She had a breathing tube in her nose for extra oxygen, and spoke in wheezy bursts, but she was planning to make it to her ninetieth birthday.

"He did, indeed," said Sandy.

"It's the most absurd thing I've heard in my life," Mary said to the elderly daughter keeping watch by her bed. "He called Dr. Glass a Nazi. I said to the nurse this morning—'They've called Dr. *Glass* a Nazi!' Of course, Redfield must resign his post."

"We'll see," said Sandy, grinning.

"Mother is drafting a letter to Mr. Redfield," said Helen Stoughton, who had been taking dictation on a yellow legal pad.

"That's what I like," said Sandy, pressing Mary's hand in his. Her skin was white and papery, and the blue veins showed through. Old age had overtaken her, and cancer was wasting her, but she clung tenaciously to each day. She still knew the time, and followed the fortunes of her associates. She'd always enjoyed her lively Jewish doctor, but never more than when he was in the news. He was on her team. Indeed, he *was* her team, battling in the papers mightily, fighting Redfield and the whole House of Representatives. Mary never doubted that he did all this on her behalf.

"The next thing is, we ramp up our work here on the home front," Sandy told Marion at lunch.

"I wish we could," Marion said.

"And why can't we? What's the problem now?"

"Well," said Marion, "we've got a lot to finish with Feng and Prithwish on the bone cancer paper."

"That little thing?" Sandy scoffed. "I thought you'd knocked that one off weeks ago."

He snatched up the draft from her desk. "You've still got Robin on there as a coauthor?"

"It was her project before she left," Marion said simply.

He practically laughed with exasperation, she was so scrupulous.

"She made a contribution," Marion said, "however small."

"And this would be the same Robin who is attempting to destroy our careers?"

"We've already had this discussion."

"It's like including Benedict Arnold on the list of Founding Fathers. You know—for his early contributions to the American Revolution." He skimmed the first couple of pages, heavily annotated with Marion's red pen. "You are spending an inordinate amount of time on this. It's hardly worth your attention."

She didn't answer. He was right; the results were modest, but she couldn't help herself. Relieved as she was to be done with subcommittee hearings, impressed as she had been with Sandy's performance, her anxiety was such that she could not let any ambiguity in Feng's paper pass.

"And Cliff?" Sandy asked her.

"He's struggling a little," she said.

"Why?"

"Why do you think? He's overwhelmed, and he's distracted by lawyers and reporters, preparation for the hearings—"

"Oh, please." Sandy cut her off. "Let's snap out of it, shall we? I am so goddamn tired of these excuses. This is exactly the time when he should be doing his best work. We should be cracking the whip so Cliff gets the job done. Show ORIS what kind of stuff his results are made of."

"It's easy for you to say," Marion said reprovingly. She was feeling overwhelmed herself. On the one hand, she wanted to burrow into editorial work, revising the bone tumor paper until the storm outside blew over. On the other, it was maddening to hone these minor contributions while the great thrust of the lab's efforts remained in abeyance. Cliff's new article, unpublishable until the inquiry was over, remained in escrow.

She had begun to feel like a woman with a bag of gold hidden in her house. She longed to secure her treasure in an academic journal, but she had to wait at least another month for the results of the ORIS inquiry. She'd had such plans for Cliff's work, such schemes for new experiments. She'd scarcely told Sandy the half of them, and now she despaired lest thieves carry her ideas off or, more likely, forge their own versions independently. She wondered if circumstances were distorting her perspective. The inquiry that kept her from publishing, the scrutiny that hampered all their work, the defense that took up so much of her time, only seemed to magnify the potential of R-7. Paradoxically, in her mind, Cliff's results seemed better and better the

longer ORIS questioned them. She, who had always practiced diffidence, now suffered from the suspicion that she'd touched something
great.

"The inquiry takes its toll," she said quietly.

"Look, the inquiry is something we can beat. Scientifically it's ir-
relevant. It's pure politics; it has no merit. Have you seen the paper?
We've made the point abundantly clear. Letting ORIS get to us is the
big mistake. Cliff should be working harder than ever."

"I don't think you realize—"

"I realize everything," Sandy cut her off.

He had just that morning seen Kristen Braverman, a breast cancer
patient a lifetime younger than Mary Stoughton. Kristen's children
were still in grade school. Sandy was treating her aggressively. Her face
was gaunt, her skin had a gray tinge, poisoned as she was from chemo
and her even more virulent disease. She wasn't doing as well as he had
hoped, but there were other drugs. Sandy had tried to impress this
upon her.

Her eyes were pure blue, fear blue. But he never looked too long
into his patients' eyes. Far safer to take their hands, and laugh, and
joke. He had taken Kristen's hand firmly in his and told her, "If you
think you feel bad, imagine how your tumors feel."

She had smiled wanly at her husband, as if to say "This is what I have
to put up with from my doctor." But Mike Braverman was not yet ready
to make jokes with an oncologist. He was still reeling from his wife's diagnosis, still growing accustomed to the idea that his wife could die. He
was just a greenhorn searching for the words, the funds, the winter
clothes for life in this new country of disease.

"What other options do we have?" Mike asked Sandy Glass continually. That morning he followed Sandy down the hall and past the
nurses' station, and into the pastel lounge, and still, somehow, he
pressed for a better forecast of what lay ahead.

Sandy might have paused to commiserate with Braverman; he
might have let the tears fall, but he did not believe in mourning prematurely. Conversely, he might have brushed off the grieving husband
and moved on to his next appointment, but he was never so overtly
brusque, even when he was out of time. A few words about the spirit?
A little prayer? Advice on the healing powers of meditation? Sandy left

that to the chaplains. He stood, instead, with his patient's husband by the floor-to-ceiling window in the lounge, and gazed out at the city with its row houses and greening parks, its labyrinthine streets turning and feinting and doubling back upon themselves. He gazed out across the Charles to Cambridge, and he said, "We're working on what can be done." He spoke with the scientist's version of the royal *we,* which he knew families found most comforting. "We're working on new treatments even now."

"Why don't you stop making excuses for Cliff and send him on rounds with me?" Sandy told Marion. "That would light a fire under his—sorry, imbue him with a sense of urgency."

Cliff did have a sense of urgency, and still he struggled. Downstairs, he scanned each cage, looking in on his pink wriggling charges. He gazed at his newly healthy mice, the latest group he'd identified as in remission. Quickly, he inspected the troops row by row. One cage caught his eye. Were some mice missing? There were supposed to be four inside.

He pulled the cage out and held it up to see. Two animals were busy. The other two were lying still and small at the back of the cage. They were alive, but barely moving. They weren't bloody; there were no signs of fighting, but even when he prodded them with his gloved finger, they didn't run about.

What was this? Were they dying? Were the tumors back? Or was there an outbreak in the colony? His heart heaved inside of him, even as he isolated the two limp animals. This wasn't good; this wasn't good. An outbreak, just when he needed his animals most. He would euthanize the afflicted ones, of course. Dissect them and try to understand. He would go to Marion. They would contact the veterinary staff immediately. He closed his eyes for a long moment even as he stood there before the cage racks. He was jumping to conclusions. Two infected mice didn't necessarily spell disaster. Still, he felt a sick foreboding.

He went to see Beth at her desk on the first floor and tried to tell her what he'd seen.

"If they begin dying now, then that's the end. I won't get a second chance."

Her eyes crinkled with concern as she picked up the ringing phone and said, "Philpott Institute."

He began shaking her Lucite box of paper clips, dumping the clips into his palm and then pouring them back into the box again.

"One moment," Beth said, "and I'll connect you." All the while her eyes were fixed on him, worrying, wondering to see him in such a state.

"I'm afraid things will start going wrong," he confessed when Beth hung up.

"But I'm sure you'll figure out exactly what's happened." She tried to reassure him.

He shook his head. Everything had to be perfect; this was the moment for reinforcing his earlier work. The mere premonition of a problem would fuel doubt, and inflame ORIS.

"It's just two sick mice, right?"

"No, no," he said impatiently. "It's the others that I'm worried about." She had no idea what he meant.

All the rest of that day he and Marion worked together. They euthanized the sick mice and the other animals in their cage and sent off all four bodies for analysis. They examined the other mice in the colony and found no evidence of illness. Marion was quick and calm.

"We won't know anything until we get the autopsy results," she told Cliff as they took off their disposable booties.

"And what if . . . ?"

"We won't borrow trouble just now," she said. Of course she knew exactly what he feared. Like him, she dreaded an outbreak in the colony, but to her rational mind, the risk at this point was only theoretical. Cliff, and Cliff alone, was seized with premonitions that all his mice would die. His imagination raced forward and he envisioned Marion's hard decision to exterminate his animals. He'd lose his new work, the crucial evidence for his ideas and his innocence. He tried to dwell on better possibilities, but he could only consider this terrible end.

That night he lay on his unmade bed and drifted in and out of sleep. He dreamed of his animals stiff and dead, half buried in their bedding. He dreamed of cages and cage racks, huge pieces of equipment, centrifuges, spectrometers crashing down out of the clear sky. They were beautiful colors, the deepest inky blues and blacks, so that even as they fell he couldn't help but look. The machines were upon him, crushing him, and he was reaching out to shield himself, and then reaching desperately for Robin, pulling off the thick bathrobe in which she'd wrapped herself, stroking her pale freckled shoulders, loosening her long fine hair. He wrapped his legs around her and pulled her tight on top of him, and he had never felt so warm as when he held her there in his arms, except she wouldn't let him kiss her.

He woke up hot, throbbing, and confused. He washed his face and paced his room, trying to calm himself. Still, he was horrified for dreaming of her, and wanting her, and most of all for being possessed by her like that, for sensing her inside of him. He felt in some terrible way he was becoming like her, assuming the worst. Attacking him from without, she'd found a way under his skin, so that suddenly, unexpectedly, he began to see the world through her eyes. Research, which had once been dreary, and then addictive, now seemed a tragic enterprise, one false hope yielding to another, progress shattered by bad luck, and the greatest expectations doomed to disappointment.

10

SHE THOUGHT about him constantly, about what he'd done, and what he'd said, but above all what he'd do when he heard the inquiry's findings. She wondered how Uppington and Marion and Sandy would respond, but she thought especially of Cliff, because, secretly, she knew the inquiry's conclusion. She'd been contacted by Morgenstern, and she knew at least part of what ORIS planned to report. In just days the inquiry's conclusions would come out. Would he admit the truth at last? Or would he strike back harder? Suddenly, she was half afraid he'd hurt her in some way. She stayed up late, and sometimes left the lights on at night. Once, she heard a great boom, and jumped up terrified in bed. She crept out to the living room and saw that an overloaded bookshelf had crashed to the floor. There was no risk he'd come near her. She told herself this all the time. Still, she could not shake her fear, the guilty price she paid for her own long struggle to hurt him.

One May night she and Nanette were leaving the Harvard Square Nickelodeon. They were picking their way through the onslaught of incoming moviegoers, and caught in this stream, Robin looked up into Cliff's face. He was with Beth, and he saw her instantly. Her cheeks burned, and she felt herself blushing to the tops of her ears. With a glance he pierced her offended sense of justice and cut her to her resentful core. She turned away, repelled, humiliated. For what could she uncover in his expression? No guilt, no confusion, no fear at all. Only disdain.

All that week she felt the hard accusation in his eyes. She felt his hatred everywhere, even in Uppington's lab, where the other researchers tacitly sided with him. They were coldly civil, but spoke to her only when necessary.

There were myriad ways to fail honorably. You could fail to get a job; you could experience equipment failure, a failure of communication, a failure of nerves; you could fail to get funding. You could get scooped. Your advisor could be stolen by another university and you could be orphaned, displaced, and dispossessed. Your lab could move and your animals could die, or refuse to breed, or suffer post-traumatic stress. You could pick the wrong project in the wrong place, or the right project at the wrong time. All these were acceptable ways to fail, established ruts. Robin, however, insisted she'd failed because other people in her lab were cheating. That was unheard of. She was "the whistle-blower" in all the papers, famous as an accuser, but in Uppington's lab she was a turncoat. Uppington had taken her in, and his students accepted that, but they didn't have to approve of what she had done.

Only one postdoc spoke kindly to Robin. She was overweight and English, and she was new to the lab. She wore running shoes and black polyester pants and lumpy sweaters, and she tied her thick hair back in flyaway ponytails. Her name was Simone, and she had trained in Israel.

The first time Simone sparked a conversation, Robin assumed it was just because she was new, and the others hadn't informed her yet of Robin's status as political pariah. But Simone spoke to Robin more than once about her roommate troubles.

"I'd like to find my own flat," she told Robin, "but the rents here are outrageous!"

They were standing in the cold room, where Robin was looking for a batch of cells. "Did you go to the housing office?" Robin asked.

"Of course. Where do you think I got those outrageous quotes?" Simone said.

Robin opened a great vat of liquid nitrogen and pulled out a long metal rack crusted with ice.

"It's ridiculous to live here," said Simone as one of Uppington's graduate students rushed in. He was big and clumsy, and he bumped Robin hard as he squeezed by.

"Hey!" Simone barked at him.

"Oh, sorry," he said.

Robin closed the vat. White vapors curled into the air theatrically. "Thank you," she whispered to Simone as she escaped into the lab.

The telephone was ringing and ringing there on the wall, and Uppington's students bent over their work with amazing indifference. Robin could not help thinking they expected her, the refugee, to answer the phone for them. She waited, but the phone kept ringing. She waited, and no one budged.

"Hello," she said at last, as she picked up the old-fashioned black receiver from the wall.

"Yes. Robin Decker, please." It was a man's voice, high-pitched and self-assured.

She was so startled to hear her own name that she didn't respond at first. Then she said softly, "This is she."

"Oh, hi, Robin," said the man, as airily as if they spoke all the time. "This is Art Ginsburg."

Ginsburg! Her eyes darted over the lab equipment and the other postdocs.

"I wanted to congratulate you," he told her.

"Why?" she asked, and suddenly she sensed the others weren't concentrating so hard; they no longer turned entirely away from her. "What do you mean?" She held the receiver tightly to her ear.

"Good news, of course." He was trying to be collegial, even avuncular. Immediately, she feared something had gone wrong with the report, with ORIS, with the journalist's article. She strained to hear more, but either Ginsburg did not want to betray a confidence, or he was enjoying his inside knowledge far too much. Even his congratulations were a kind of one-upmanship. He just said, "You'll see tomorrow in the *Times*."

Grim-faced, Sandy Glass jogged the streets of Chestnut Hill. His newspaper had not yet arrived. Still, he steeled himself for what was to come. He took a turn around the lower drive of an old run-down estate. The trees were flowering now, the grass and street sprinkled with white petals. He hardly noticed. He'd lain awake thinking the night before, then drifted off in early morning and nearly overslept. He'd pushed himself out of bed and out the door.

He did not know exactly what the *Times* would print, or the extent of the damage he'd see that day, but there was no question in his mind he would overcome every obstacle and untruth ORIS threw before him. He had no doubts at all; he was entirely unafraid. He saw himself alone in battle, surrounded but undaunted, like a firefighter engulfed in flames. He gave no thought to Robin. His only concern was for the people in his lab. Getting them out safely was all that mattered to him. He was determined to carry Marion safely to the ground.

Usually so careful about pacing himself, he ran too hard and came home winded. He bent over at his own gate, cramping, gasping for air and scanning the bluestone walk for the newspaper. The lights were on and Ann was waiting for him in the kitchen with the *Times* open. He felt a prick of annoyance that she had seen the article first.

"Sandy." She was searching for the words. "It seems as if . . . Well, you should . . ."

He snatched the front section, saw his name, and inhaled the entire article in a moment. He sucked it all in from first to last. *The New York Times* had "obtained" a copy of ORIS's draft report on the lab. The report's official release was weeks away, but here it was in black-and-white, for everyone to read. ORIS had found evidence of fraud.

"Thayer called while you were running," Ann said.

Of course there was no question how the *Times* had obtained the copy of the ORIS report. This was Redfield's work. Redfield had lost his temper, and he'd paid for that, but then he'd got his temper back again. He'd waited for his moment and sprung the ORIS findings on an unsuspecting public, ambushing his enemy like a master predator.

Ann spoke again. "I'm so sorry," she said, "but I'm sure—"

He didn't hear her; he was already diving for the phone.

"He left his home number," she told Sandy, still assuming he was going to call Houghton-Smith.

"No," he said, dialing impatiently, stretching the long telephone cord away from her, into the dining room. "I have to talk to Marion."

The news shocked and spread through the family. The injustice of the findings, their surprising, vengeful publication—all strained belief. Louisa was on her way out the door when Charlotte phoned her.

"It's so unethical," she said to Charlotte. "How can the press just jump on something like that—preliminary findings! They're being published as an indictment! And their so-called interview of Dad is just three lines of comments, and he says everything he told them is quoted wrong."

"Journalists just want to be first," Charlotte said. "It's just a race to them. They don't actually care about accuracy."

"Where are their standards?" Louisa asked, and she flopped down on her bed with the phone in hand. "They have no interest in the truth!"

"Journalism isn't about the truth. You know that," said Charlotte. She was calm and self-assured, quite confident in her hatred of Jeff and journalism and all journalists. It was Louisa, the older sister, who shook with disbelief. To see her father humiliated this way! To see him presented by ORIS as the willing dupe of an ambitious postdoc. She understood that there would be no quick comeback from this, no easy recovery. This was such an assault on her father's reputation that she suffered the blow herself; she trembled for him.

"What will he do?" she asked as soon as she could reach her mother. She was pacing now with the phone, up and down her apartment's narrow living room.

"Well," her mother said, in the confident, reassuring tones Louisa hated most. "Of course, we'll be talking to our lawyer about the next step. Marion is speaking to her attorney as well. We will need to see the full text of the ORIS report, and of course we'll file an appeal."

"When can I talk to Dad?"

"He's just left for the institute," Ann said, and then she added soothingly, maddeningly, "He's going to be fine."

Louisa couldn't believe her mother was still using that voice on her. The "it's perfectly normal" voice their mother put on to confront puberty and other crises. Ann couldn't win, of course. She understood her daughters' fears so well, they felt they had no privacy. Sandy was never empathetic; the girls could count on that.

"Don't worry, sweetie," said Ann.

Oh, save it for Kate, Louisa thought as she hung up.

But away at Hill, Kate had already heard from her mother. She'd crouched down next to the pay phone in the stairwell, and Ann's warm, familiar tone was sorely needed. Kate dreaded going to the

Commons for breakfast all alone with this news—her father's work and good name savaged. And what of Cliff? How would he survive this report and keep on working? She felt even worse for him—and then guilty for it.

Hunger alone compelled Kate to leave her room and go to breakfast. In the Commons, she picked up her tray and walked past the table where the dining hall staff laid out newspapers for those students who subscribed. There lay stacks of *The Boston Globe* and *The Wall Street Journal,* and of course piles of *The New York Times*. She tried not to look. She turned away, and then her father's name on a loose paper caught her eye anyway. The article was boxed, below the fold. Her stomach pitched as she saw the word *Glass* and the headline "Of Mice and Men." She took two small boxes of cereal, a bowl, a glass of milk, and a banana, and fought the impulse to turn back to her room. She had never felt so conspicuous as she forced herself inside the dining room.

"Hey, Kate," Nick said, and Stephen pushed his own newspaper onto the floor to make room for Kate's tray.

She slipped into a chair and studiously began peeling her banana.

"Oh, God," Monty said companionably, and yawned and stretched.

"Shall I get you some coffee?" Sylvie asked.

"Thanks," said Kate, although she never drank it.

When Sylvie returned from the coffeemaker the Europeans frequented, Kate tried to take a sip from the cup offered her. How cold the world seemed. The bitter coffee lingered, terrible on her tongue.

The others hovered at the table, saying little. The dining room began to empty, and Kate gathered her books for Latin. "I don't really feel like going," she confessed.

"Then go somewhere else," said Stephen.

She looked skeptically at him.

"It's only a half day today," Monty pointed out. They had school on Saturdays, and half days on Wednesdays.

"I'd go with you," Stephen added carelessly.

"I can't cut class," she said.

"Then skip out in the afternoon."

Faintly, she remembered Charlotte's warning about Stephen. Much stronger at that moment was the fellowship she felt from her pseudo-friends. Her cheeks stung as she realized the others were ministering to her in their own way, clustering around her in solidarity. They were aristocrats, and said nothing about it. However, there had been other occasions when each of them had needed lifting up. There had been the day Matthew's father was profiled in *The Wall Street Journal*, his face crosshatched in pen and ink, although the text of the article was far less delicate, with its references to "the man known as the junk-bond king." There had been the dustup between Sylvie's mother and her art dealer, less commonly reported, but painful nonetheless. There had been Stephen's parents' divorce, and Monty's brother's expulsion. They knew a little about public humiliation in the Hill Literary Society. Kate hadn't understood that before. Now she looked at the others with surprise and gratitude, and some embarrassment. Suddenly, however briefly, she had become one of them.

Sandy would have been touched by his daughters' concern if he'd had time, but he was at the institute, taking on all comers. He'd rushed to Peter Hawking first to gauge Hawking's reaction to the news.

"Well, it isn't *good*," Hawking told Sandy as they sat together in the director's office.

"Of course it isn't good," Sandy said, "but it's an opportunity to take a stand."

"I think we've taken the stand," said Hawking drily. "We've fought our little battle here for academic freedom."

"But it's not a little battle," Sandy said. "It's a war, and ORIS is just one part of it. Don't you see—they're in Redfield's pocket. This isn't just about us, it's about controlling scientific research through government funding. First he slanders us, and then he'll slash our funding. Don't you see? He wants to legislate our research programs. And that's got to stop."

"Well, I do see," said Hawking. "I can see that quite clearly. The question is whether the battle is winnable right here, right now, at an institute that has run a deficit for the past three years. The question is whether we have the resources and the time to wage such a war."

Sandy leaned over the desk and assessed the distinguished, gentlemanly scientist across from him. He had been a wonderful researcher in his day. Now the stubble on his head was white. Hawking was well-spoken, sometimes even wise, but he lacked imagination.

"It's a question of balance," Hawking said. "It's a matter of considering the other projects and the other grants pursued here. We don't want to find ourselves besieged."

"But we are besieged. That's just my point," said Sandy. "A policy of appeasement will never work, because all the projects in this institute, all the grants in the nation, are linked together. Where they question us, they will question other researchers as well. Where they mistrust one result, they'll call other scientists liars too. The whole scientific enterprise is suspect to Redfield and his people. You said it yourself in your open letter," Sandy added, shrewdly forgetting that he had written the letter himself. "All of science is on trial."

And Hawking sat back and thought of the institute trustees' meeting later that month, and the negotiations with Harvard, which had stretched on far too long and threatened to break down. He thought of the two senior scientists who were being wooed by pharmaceutical companies, and he could not deny that the Philpott was besieged.

"We have no choice but to fight this battle," Sandy told him, "and we can absolutely win. They want to talk about ethics? Let's talk ethics. How ethical is ORIS? They want to talk about evidence? They want to talk about suppressing data? They've pursued a hypothesis of guilt based on three scraps of paper. ORIS selects a tiny fraction of R-7 data to use in their own report and they entirely ignore the rest. They take the claims of one disaffected former postdoc and amplify them into a cause célèbre. Where's Hackett and Schneiderman's discussion of Robin's motivations? Where's the disclosure of their political goals?"

"Easy, Sandy, easy," murmured Hawking.

"Look, I'm just saying what we all know," Sandy declared. "NIH *established* ORIS to appease the Committee on Energy and Commerce. Redfield holds the NIH budget in his hands. You and I both know ORIS was built specifically for ritual sacrifices before Congress. It's a forum for public executions. Redfield sits in state and watches ORIS pit the word of one researcher against another. They're brilliant little circuses, aren't they? You've got your young gladiators tearing each

other to pieces, titillating the public, terrorizing the scientific community. You've got your senior scientists thrown to the lions. If we don't
question this system, then no one is safe. This is *not* a little battle. "

"No, no. Of course not," Hawking said.

"It's a huge fight. And we have no choice but to win."

"Look," Sandy told Cliff and Marion later that morning in the privacy
of the office. "It's better to know exactly where the enemy stands. It's
better to know what they think and what they want to do."

And Cliff had nodded, pale as he stood before the two of them.

"This inquiry has been a farce," said Sandy. "The House subcommittee was like something from the nineteen fifties. The article leaking
the findings—beyond words. It's sad. It's tragic, actually, that the public mistrust of scientists should come to this. It's painful to see journalists and politicians play like this on people's fears. But I can promise
you our appeal will get equal press, and our exposé of ORIS will get
equal time."

Unconsciously, Cliff began clicking the button on the pipette he
was holding. Click, click, click, he clicked the instrument, as one
might click the top of a retractable ballpoint pen.

"I know it's a lot to take in," said Sandy, looking keenly at Cliff. "I
know you just want to be done . . ."

"I just want to keep working," Cliff said. He didn't realize it, but
he'd passed Sandy's test. The determination was still there.

"There is something else," Marion said.

"The autopsy results." The words seemed to swell and lodge in
Cliff's throat.

"There is no sign of infection," she told him.

He could breathe again. The colony was safe.

"But there were signs of recurrence," she said. "Small tumors near
the mammary glands and elsewhere."

That can't be, he protested inwardly. Those mice were in remission. He had treated them with R-7 and they had been healthy. Why
were they relapsing? "God, why now?" he murmured.

"Why not now?" she snapped, and he flinched at her sudden
anger. This had not been the considered response she was looking for.

A thousand apologies sprang to his lips and died there. He was sorry if he'd sounded so childish. He was sorry for speaking without thinking, for thinking aloud, for the inferior quality of his thoughts. Glass began talking again, but Cliff hardly heard. Sandy's voice seemed small and tinny in the silent snowstorm of Marion's displeasure.

She was the difficult one. She was the one quailing in the office, knitting furiously, consumed with doubt. "I think maybe we should publish a note in *Nature,* just to speak to some of the issues raised about our paper," she told Sandy after Cliff had gone.

"We will not!" he said, aghast. "We will do nothing of the kind."

"I don't mean a retraction," she told him. "Just an explanation of the data—to address the objections made in the inquiry."

"We will not retract our paper, and we won't partially retract our paper either," Sandy said. "We're not going to indulge in any half-assed apologies. We are not going to be cowed by a concerted campaign against us."

"I think we should clarify our work," said Marion.

"Our work is perfectly clear," said Sandy. "Three independent referees and the editors of an academic journal found it perfectly clear and compelling. If it's not clear enough for Redfield, that's a function of his own ignorance and prejudice."

She pursed her lips and bent over her tight stitches.

"Marion," he said. "If you know the truth, you have to fight for it."

"I just don't want there to be any doubt about our research," she said.

"But you know what we've done," he told her. "This is just politics. You can't lose sight of that." He shook his head. "I think sometimes I trust you more than you trust yourself. Listen to me. We know what we've done; we know our results. Nothing can change that."

Gratefully, she allowed his resolve to calm her. After the shock of the news, after the long, wearying morning in which nothing had been right, she began to feel herself again.

"I'm glad I have him," she told Jacob on the phone.

Jacob could have reminded her that Sandy had gotten her into this mess, rushing the grant proposal out. He could have pointed out that Sandy had opened the door to ORIS, when he urged Marion to let Cliff run wild with his R-7 experiments. There were many things Jacob

might have told her, but he was quiet. He would not risk sounding su-
percilious about Marion's troubles, or resentful of Sandy. He would
not wound Marion at a time like this.

"He's been extraordinary," she told Jacob, and her praise was heart-
felt, for the way Sandy buoyed her. He was an evangelist, she thought.
An evangelist of the most remarkable sort, for he could bring you all
the way around to your original position. What was the name for an
evangelist like that? Someone who could convert you to yourself.
Someone who would not let you waver, who brooked no doubts, but
held fast to your first idea.

Kate was not herself at all. She was irresponsible and self-indulgent. She
and Stephen had skipped out for the afternoon. She, who had practically
never broken a school rule, was wandering the city streets and wasting
time. How wonderfully delinquent; they could go anywhere. The Public
Garden, or Chinatown, or the shops on Newberry Street. She felt out of
place. They both did, away from Hill, with its geometry exams and Tac-
itus translations, its prim steepled church crowned by a gold rooster
weather vane. Kate nearly jumped whenever anybody glanced their way.
She'd almost expected to be arrested for truancy when she and Stephen
stepped off their bus. She was sure now that Charlotte was right about
Stephen. He was bad news, but then, Kate was bad too. She'd just never
realized it before.

They took the Green Line out to Huntington Avenue. If they were
caught, they'd probably be suspended, and then they'd be wasting
thousands of dollars of tuition, missing school.

"But they won't catch us," Stephen said with an experienced air,
and she wondered if he did this kind of thing all the time. She hoped
he couldn't tell her heart was pounding. She had never acted so sixteen,
so melodramatically disenchanted. She clutched her newfound anomie
as tightly as her purse. And yet she felt intensely happy; she could
scarcely remember her conversation with her mother and her anguish
for her father; she'd nearly frightened herself out of her own feelings.
She had not known this calculus before, combating great troubles with
small. With a sense of serious decadence, she followed Stephen inside
the Isabella Stewart Gardner Museum.

They checked their coats and left the cool spring day behind. Tree ferns and potted lilies, orchids, ginger, and flowering trees filled the glass-roofed court. The inner walls were pink as the interior of a seashell, and rose up four stories on marble pillars and Moorish arches. As they walked along the edges of the courtyard, Kate and Stephen passed stone chairs and friezes, metalwork from churches and from royal beds in France. Tapestries of noble ladies hung in colonnaded hallways, and the staircases were adorned with Japanese panels of inlaid wood.

"I'd like to have a house like this," Stephen said, as they walked into a room hung with vestments and solemn-faced Madonnas.

Kate almost laughed.

"The problem is, you can't get paintings like this anymore." He spoke earnestly, as if he had actually considered acquiring some. They passed into a red room with full-length portraits of young men in armor, and then into a pale green salon adorned with tapestries and silver mirrors partly tarnished. There were collections of lace and rosaries, and an enameled litter fit for a princess.

"This place is such a fairy tale," said Kate.

They'd come to a great coffered hall, the walls lined with forbidding Dutch oils. A young Rembrandt stood there in his self-portrait, and he seemed utterly bored by the dour, ruffed gentlemen and iron-faced women all around him. Kate stopped to look at him with his plumed hat, and faint mustache, and small, insouciant eyes. But Stephen walked right up to the Vermeer, *The Concert*, propped on a low table.

"This is the one I love," he told Kate. "Look at that composition on the diagonal."

She was conscious he was showing off for her, and she was flattered, and then dismayed. Was this how she had sounded when she'd read Donne to Cliff—so academic and so eager?

She gazed deep into the Vermeer, with its black-and-white tile floor, its three figures at the clavier, playing and singing before its painted lid. "It looks so peaceful and so far away, and harmonious," she said. "It's all about balance."

"No it's not. It's all about sex," said Stephen. "See the painting on the wall above their heads? That's *The Procuress*. And see how the man and the woman on the right are joined by that black shadow? And look at that cello in the foreground, lying there on the floor like the naked body of a woman."

Kate tried to make out the shadowy figures of *The Procuress;* she stared at the curving form of the cello on the floor. "You have a dirty mind," she said.

"It's not me, it's the painting."

"You make Vermeer seem so devious."

"That's what I like about him," said Stephen impishly, and he took off his gold-rimmed glasses and cleaned them on the bottom of his sweater. "It's all there—sex, deception, betrayal—hidden in plain sight."

"Do you think his sitters had any idea?" asked Kate.

"I'm sure they did afterward."

"But that would be defamation of character."

"Maybe they enjoyed it," said Stephen.

Angry tears started in Kate's eyes. "They did not enjoy it," she said.

"They were probably just hired models," he told her, stricken to see her so upset.

She glared at him.

"All right, no more Vermeer for you." He steered her by the shoulders into the pale green salon, with its carved wooden chests the size of coffins, and its altarpieces, its flat processions of robed figures. Kate stared at a pair of angels on a wood panel. The gold around them was crazed and worn and reddish like old cracked leather.

"I'm sorry," Stephen whispered.

She didn't answer.

"Did you see the Titian?"

"Shh," she said.

And then he stopped talking. They stood together before the angels and the saints, and they just looked.

To be believed; to see her knowledge public, her understanding ratified! Robin practically danced into work that afternoon. She would have a life again, and a chance for a scientific future. Cliff's lies had been exposed, and she was no longer incompetent, or hysterical with jealousy, but vindicated by ORIS itself.

In the hallway, Uppington bustled up to her and stammered with surprise. "It's a most . . . most . . . very impressive finding," he said to

Robin privately, "but I do hope for your—for everyone—for all of us, that we can—that we *will*—arrive at an end to this . . . if you know what I mean."

This was not exactly a ringing endorsement, and she heard him out with secret indignation. Uppington had treated her benevolently when she was in need, but even he found her victory difficult to swallow. She had attacked when she might have been demure; she had not only doubted, but advertised her doubts. She had involved herself with people of whom few scientists could approve, consorted with the enemy and scored points out of bounds.

Who had really cheated, then? Not Cliff, but Robin. Cheater. Cheater. She entered the lab and not one of Uppington's students deigned to look at her. Proudly, she kept on working, held her head up, recalled all the telephone calls she'd fielded that morning, the requests for interviews. Outside this building, in public, in DC, and surely in some other laboratories, there were people who read the newspapers and applauded her. She told herself that she had worked alone before and she was strong enough to keep on that way. Still, she hungered for some word of validation, some small sign from Uppington's grim graduate students and wary postdocs. She caught Simone's eye at the next lab bench, but Simone was suddenly engrossed in the cells before her, and she turned away.

Part VI
Open Questions

1

ROBIN SAT in the blue-carpeted hearing room of the NIH Appeal Board, and she saw that amateur night was over. The floor belonged to Houghton-Smith, and Borland, and Halbfinger, and Zouzoua. Philosophical declarations about truth and evidence, and political stands on public accountability, had all yielded to procedural arguments. The fact that the Secret Service analysts had no real scientific background, the fact that copies of their findings were withheld from the researchers' lawyers but freely given to Redfield's staff, the fact that ORIS's findings were leaked to *The New York Times* but mysteriously delayed from arriving in Boston, the fact that several pages of those findings were missing from the copies when they were finally mailed to Boston, due to what was termed a "clerical oversight"—these facts were the building blocks of Cliff's appeal. But, of course, there was more, as well. For Cliff's appeal hinged on discovery of Robin's character, Robin's motives. In the spring, the pressure had been on Cliff, but now the August heat had returned, and Robin was the one on trial.

How naïve and reckless she had been, trying to call Cliff to account. Hadn't Larry and Wendy warned her months ago not to get involved with ORIS? Hadn't they told her she would be the sacrificial lamb? ORIS had published its findings, but the conclusion of fraud was like a message scribed in sand. No final judgment, but an opening, instead, for resounding action, vicious attacks on Cliff's behalf. She watched the three distinguished scientists of the appeals board as they sat in patient judgment. They were an eminent physicist, an infectious disease specialist, and a high-ranking NIH administrator, a woman of color, with a degree in public health. All took notes, all listened intently to Tim Borland's slick, sophomoric voice.

"'Probably a bad idea,'" Borland read aloud from his photocopy of Robin's diary. "'But I let him—'"

"I'm sorry," Robin's lawyer interrupted. "You've just asserted that your main concern is the course of events from January through May. This is an entry from the previous summer."

"I think the background here is essential," Borland countered, "if we are to understand exactly when and how Robin Decker turned against my client."

"I disagree," Laura Sabbatini shot back. "And I think you should reconsider what I believe is an extremely dangerous approach."

"Dangerous for whom?" Borland asked.

But I let him kiss me, Robin remembered, as the two lawyers argued, and the chair of the appeals board, the lively, balding, physicist, tried to mediate. Cliff would have a separate hearing. There was no one in the room but Robin and the two lawyers and the three distinguished scientists. That was quite enough. Together, they made up a quorum for humiliation. Even through all the arguments and interruptions, Robin heard her words exposed. She tried not to hear them, but she heard anyway. She knew exactly what she had written, and she could see precisely where Borland was going. He was following her up the stairs to her apartment.

"'Let him kiss me and come up. We burnt the toast this morning and ran out of bread. Then we tried cereal and ran out of milk but he said he didn't really want to eat. . . . '"

Of course, she had always known this was coming. Of course, Laura was fighting Borland every step of the way. Robin had tried to steel herself, but in the end, there was really no way to prepare. And it was curious how sharp the pain was, how her own words cut. Who had she been then, when she'd let Cliff wrap himself around her? Who in the world had she been?

As whistle-blower, she had received her rewards, such as they were. She'd been asked to come to a major biology conference to participate in a panel on research ethics. She had been interviewed by *The Boston*

Globe and photographed, standing rather nervously, on the brick steps in front of the Philpott Institute.

Tomas had clasped both her hands in his and congratulated her. "I knew you'd win," he said. "And you know why? Because I never trusted Cliff, but I never said anything because you were together, you know? But the truth will set you free, right? I knew exactly how this would all turn out!"

"I've got the *Times* clipping plastered all over my refrigerator," Nanette told Robin, and she wasn't talking about her fridge at home: she meant her great silver refrigerator at work—the one all the lab techs saw when they came to pick up media.

Billie had called Robin at home. In her breathy voice she told Robin she was finally leaving the institute to try to cleanse herself of the contaminants in the building, to devote more hours to the Cambridge Task Force on Sick Building Syndrome, and, most urgently, to pursue her claims against the Philpott full-time. "The fact that someone I know has succeeded in the face of all this corruption is very moving to me," she told Robin. "I want you to know that. I realize we didn't work together very long, but you have been a major influence on me."

"Really?" Robin asked. She hadn't meant to be impolite. The slightly horrified question just slipped out.

"Major," Billie said. "In fact, when I wrote my letter of resignation, I cited you and your struggles as one of my primary inspirations."

How strange the way success and failure contained each other. How close vindication and humiliation had proved. There had been a time when telling the truth seemed necessary, a drastic measure to survive in science. But her ideas and her understanding had been appropriated by others; her notion of professional survival, sadly misplaced. How could she have imagined herself free of Cliff? She was sure now the two of them would drown together. She had overcome him during the inquiry, but during this appeal she felt him pulling her under with even greater force.

Now she did her penance. Now she began to pay for what she'd done and said. Shouldn't she have considered the price of a scientific war such as she had waged? Shouldn't she have allowed for the fact that words were fungible?

She had insisted on questioning Cliff's character, and so, in some sense, despite all Laura's objections, it was natural for Cliff's lawyer to turn and question hers as well. She had begun exploring murky moral questions; should she have been surprised at the creatures that lashed out at her in the mud? At her own sharp sentences biting her back?

"'Sometimes I wish him harm—physical harm,'" Borland read aloud.

And, of course, Laura Sabbatini objected again. She asked the distinguished panel to consider what was relevant to the appeal and what was not. She insisted that Borland confine himself to the scientific data. She noted that Borland had argued ORIS invaded his client's privacy, took notes out of context, and defamed his client's name, even while Borland indulged in exactly those tactics in his client's defense. Robin's lawyer objected and insisted, and succeeded in engaging the panel in a full discussion of the acceptable parameters of evidence in such a case. And Robin tried to sit up straight. She tried to look ahead at the appeal board, to study their professorial, kindly faces. "Do you want justice?" Akira had challenged her.

"Of course," she'd said.

"Are you willing to suffer for it?"

What was justice? An official NIH report? An article in the newspaper? An ethics panel? That kind of justice seemed fleeting, vindication that went quickly out of date. She hardly knew what justice was anymore, but she was suffering.

Even as his lawyer sparred with Robin's in DC, Cliff was working in the animal facility, dissecting mice. He had sacrificed a new batch, and the rate of remission was still over sixty percent. Still, he was finding more and more recurrences. He stood before the dissecting table and studied the corpses before him and the numbers in his lab book. Hours slipped away and he kept working, plucking up loose skin with his tweezers, examining emerging tumors and then normal mammary glands.

Recurrence was an intriguing finding in itself. What did it mean about the interplay of virus and immune system and cancerous cells? How were cancer cells cropping up again? How might they regenerate after wholesale extermination? On the one hand, he was fascinated by the phenomenon. And on the other, he was almost out of his mind with anxiety. He had feared a viral outbreak in the colony. That would have been a terrible setback, but this was devastating. This wasn't just bad luck; this was the failure of R-7 itself.

He had been a talented but sloppy student. He'd excelled in high school, and even in college, relying more on memory and wit than understanding. It wasn't until graduate school that he began to dedicate himself fully to his work, and even then, he'd been flippant, taken each publication as his due, his beginner's luck as his just reward. Only with R-7 had he begun to learn what work was. He was careful now, dedicated almost to the exclusion of all else. How, then, could these experiments and these animals fail him when he had learned so much?

One by one, he opened up his animals and gazed inside. There were the mammary glands, the first pair almost up at the neck of each mouse. There were the red blood vessels threading through pink skin. A good many animals were still cancer free. He told himself the healthy ones were still in the majority. He had teased this pattern out himself until the results made sense and random observations resolved themselves into a profound design. But scientific designs were unforgiving; such schemes as his were hungry for more and yet more evidence, ravenous for facts. And what if his results were only temporary? He shuddered at the question. He had not appreciated research before, its value or its real heartbreak. How strange that even with all his animal work, and all the sacrifices, he'd never understood that this was life and death.

"Don't desert me now," he whispered to the tiny corpses on the table.

On a crisp October afternoon, Sandy bounded into the office, fresh off the shuttle from DC, and declared, "We're winning."

"Really?" Marion asked drily.

He waved her off. The lab was no longer on the defensive. The lawyers were prosecuting the appeal brilliantly. And so, naturally, Marion was unhappy.

"But you're *never* happy," he pointed out.

She was complaining about the research time she'd lost to the appeal. She bemoaned every hour and every day away from the lab.

"But you always do," he said.

"Sandy." She spoke in such a voice that he stopped teasing, at least temporarily.

Chagrined, he saw how pale and tired she'd become. The inquiry and controversy had worn away at her. He had not shielded her well enough from the petty world outside.

"You're right," he said. "You've lost too much time. You should be working. Let's not waste any more thought on this."

"That's easy for you to say," she murmured as she rose to walk down the hall.

"I mean it." He opened the office door for her. "Go on." He gave her a little push, as though to shoo her back into the lab. "Go back in there. I promise you, we won't even speak of the appeal again."

"Don't make promises you can't keep," she told him.

"How do you know whether or not I can keep my promises?"

"I think I know you pretty well," she said.

"So don't always assume the worst."

Then she kidded him, with a straight face. "The worst is usually a safe assumption."

"Don't be safe," he said, and he was perfectly serious, even though he was smiling. He spoke entirely from his heart. "Don't let all this political nonsense frighten you away."

Still, she worried. The labs at Stanford and Cornell were not getting the results they'd been looking for with R-7. At Cornell, P. K. Agarwal had had some initial success, but nothing on the scale of Cliff's results. At Stanford, Richard Hughes had run into numerous technical problems with the virus, and concluded that the sample Cliff had sent had partly thawed in shipping. Cliff was preparing new samples for Hughes, and had spoken extensively to Agarwal on the phone about the correct methods and conditions for replicating the R-7 experiments. Of course, repeating experiments in different labs could not happen overnight. Marion had no right to hope for results just to assuage her own anxiety or impress the appeals board at NIH. She knew better than anyone that scientific results did not pop up on demand, and so she tried to suppress her longing for confirmation of Cliff's work.

But what if the troubles at Stanford and Cornell were not easily solved? These were not, in fact, the first attempts to reproduce his work, and the thought of Robin's failure haunted her. Of course, there had been extenuating circumstances. Robin had never been an impartial judge of Cliff's results. Marion deeply regretted setting Robin the task of replicating them. But how embarrassing, how potentially devastating, if two respected investigators at other institutions could not replicate Cliff's work either.

And then there were the recurrences. Ordinarily, she would have looked into a phenomenon like this with intense curiosity and undiluted pleasure. But now? Why now? Cliff had asked, and she had jumped on him for reacting so childishly. Still, privately, as more animals grew sick, she began to echo his foolish question. Why now, indeed? She could not help dreading another public disaster.

But Sandy was right; this was no way to think. She was a researcher, not a politician or a press agent. She could not allow the ORIS inquiry to creep further inside her. She walked down the corridor and looked into the lab where Prithwish was working with the two new postdocs, Mikiko and Nir. She peeked into the cold room and the lounge, and finally discovered Feng in the stockroom.

"I've got a job for you," she told him.

He turned to her, surprised she'd go to the trouble of buttonholing him among the shelves of clear glassware.

"I want you to look into the new recurrences with Cliff," she said. He scarcely blinked.

"We need to understand what's going on with the recurring tumors," she told him. "He's begun; he's working around the clock, but he's got his hands full. He's going to need help."

"I'm sorry," Feng said.

He'd answered so quietly that for several moments she didn't realize that he had refused her.

"I wish I could," he told her, turning away.

She studied him. In all his time at the lab, Feng had never refused to do what she asked. Certainly he'd never denied a direct request.

"I'm beginning new experiments with the bone tumors," he told her apologetically. "And I'm training Miki."

Coming from Feng, this was practically insolent. She was growing angry, but she tried not to let it show.

"I think this is vitally important for Cliff—and for the lab," she said. "We need your help."

"I don't think I'd be any help to Cliff," Feng demurred. "I've been away from his work too long. I'm sure I would ruin his experiments, because it's been so many months since I helped him with his project."

This was not insubordination, or laziness. This was Feng distancing himself from Cliff's work. Feng was making it clear he had severed his connection to R-7 entirely. All through the R-7 publicity, and then during the inquiry, he'd tried to keep his head down. He'd done his part; and when necessary, he'd played along. But she felt now the way Feng used his silences as weapons, how he wielded diffidence in his own defense. He was not going to work on R-7 again. She could order him as much as she wanted, and he would not change his mind. He would never speak against Cliff as a collaborator, or voice doubts if he had any. He was too doubtful of himself, and too private. Still, he wouldn't touch Cliff's work. There was something wrong.

She did not speak of it to Sandy. She did not want him to cheer her, or to soothe her, or to bully Feng. Nor did she unburden herself to Jacob. She needed to think alone. What did Feng know about Cliff? What had he been concealing from her? To hide his doubts about Cliff's work would have been just as bad as lying. To conceal his lack of confidence until now! The very idea infuriated her. Hadn't she approached Feng at the very beginning? Hadn't she asked him to tell her candidly if he felt anything was amiss? Why would he have kept the truth from her? If he'd wanted to distance himself from Cliff, that would have been the time to do it. That would have been his chance. No, he couldn't have known anything then. But did he surmise something now? Over time, had he come to think that Cliff's work was simply too complex, too fraught with difficulties? Had ORIS succeeded in undermining his confidence entirely? This seemed more plausible. As Sandy might have put it, the politics of the situation had frightened Feng away.

The situation *was* frightening. The idea that Cliff might have cheated was foreign to her; the idea that any scientist might cheat, improbable. And yet, at times Cliff's results themselves seemed improbable as well, and fleeting. When she and Sandy stood up together to defend their work, their arguments were adamant, their purpose fixed, the corrupt motives of their enemies quite clear. But when she reflected alone on all that had passed, the lab's success seemed like a brief dream. The way forward scientifically was far from obvious. As for enemies— the lab seemed to be its own worst enemy now, and Cliff's would-be collaborators at Stanford and Cornell were strewing more obstacles in the path for R-7 than anyone on Redfield's subcommittee.

Still, she would not succumb to doubt. She had honed her doubtful instincts once. Doubt had been her scientific ally, the whetstone for her sharpest questions. Now she struggled against doubt as if it were merely an emotion, and not also a kind of intelligence. She fought off doubt as another person might have wrestled with self-pity. As she went about her work, she tried to think as Sandy did, and dismiss the fear and lack of confidence that plagued her. In the animal facility she took out Cliff's animals and held them under the light. Palpating them one by one, she examined those with no tumors left, and those with almost none, and then the few whose tumors had recurred. She held the animals' pink, wriggling bodies and checked their ear tags against the logbook. The records were clear and accurate, Cliff's notations up to date. But then, how would she know if he adjusted or revised the numbers, or sacrificed mice without telling anyone? He could easily have killed those animals that did not conform to the story he wanted told. The postdocs answered to Marion, but she depended on them for the truth of their answers. She could not monitor them every minute of the day.

Jacob was practicing in the back of the apartment when she came home. She heard his weaving melodies and double-stops, but she couldn't face him. Instead, she slipped into Aaron's little room off the hall.

"Hi," he said as she came in.

Too big for his old desk, Aaron sat hunched over, working out chess problems on paper. His desk light was a translucent world globe, which cast a blue glow over his homework folders and his notebooks. His bunk bed stood against the wall. He'd insisted on getting the bed when he was four years old. Marion had hinted to him then that she didn't think a bunk bed would be necessary, but Aaron wouldn't hear of anything else, arguing, "It'll be useful when I have guests." Now the lower bed had become a storage area. Gradually Aaron's teddy bears and plush frog had migrated down there, along with his old school notebooks, his Rubik's cubes and spheres and polyhedrons.

"How are you?" Marion asked Aaron.

"Good."

"And how was school?"

"Fine," he said.

"What did you do today?"

"Nothing much."

She looked over his shoulder at the printed chess diagram on the desk. Only six weeks into the new school year, he did not find eleventh grade terribly interesting.

"Does Dad know you're home?" he asked.

She shook her head.

"Could you tell him? He's been working on that piece a *very* long time."

"All right," she said, but she didn't go, and he looked up at her briefly, owlish but unsuspecting.

"What would you do if someone cheated while you were playing chess?" she asked him.

"No one would do that," he said with rational innocence.

"But just suppose someone did."

"No one I know would do that." He knit his brow and squinted, trying to wrap his head around such a counterintuitive idea—someone playing chess, where the rules were absolutely the pleasure of the game, and then breaking them.

"What would you do?"

"I guess I'd have to ask him why."

2

"WHAT DO you care what your neighbors think?" Nanette asked Robin as they stood in line at the Janus Cinema.

Robin ducked her head down. "I see them all the time at the mailboxes, or even in the elevator. As soon as Larry or Wendy comes near me, it's as though I don't exist. I disappear."

"Please," said Nanette. "I had a *boss* who didn't talk to me for three years. We hated each other so much we communicated solely through graduate students."

"For three years?"

"Well, maybe it wasn't three years. I guess it was more like three months."

"How did you keep your job?"

"Oh, he fired me. But the point is, I didn't let it get to me."

"But I have to live with these people," said Robin, stuffing her hands deep into her jacket pockets.

"So, I had to live with my boss, too. It's the same thing," said Nanette.

"Maybe I should move," Robin said.

Nanette dismissed this. "Your problem is you have a thin skin. You're overly sensitive. I've always said that. You've got to be tough. Do your thing and ignore everyone else. You're good at the first part, but then you still want everyone to like you. Give it up."

"I don't need everyone to like me," Robin retorted. "I just miss my friends."

"They couldn't have been real friends," said Nanette.

"They were," Robin said sadly. They had been real friends, but she had offended their deepest beliefs. She was a heretic, for she'd lost her faith in the natural selection of ideas.

"Two for *The Witches of Eastwick,*" said Nanette, and then, to Robin, "Who are you kidding? You can't move; you've got a rent-controlled apartment."

"I don't know if I'm going to have a job much longer, either."

"What, Uppington's firing you?"

"No, but I don't think he can come up with a full-time position for me."

"Didn't he promise?"

She shook her head. He'd hinted, he'd suggested—he'd apologized, of course. "I'm terribly sorry, Robin," he'd told her. "But I just don't have the funding for you right now." And she was beginning to understand that he never would.

"Stop moping," Nanette ordered. "One large popcorn," she told the kid at the candy counter. "Of *course* with topping. Do you want a drink?" she asked Robin, and then, "Do you have any cash?"

Carrying their popcorn, icy drinks, and straws, they padded down red-carpeted passageways into the underground theater and found two seats close to the screen.

"Why don't you just wear glasses?" Robin grumbled as they sank down into their chairs.

"Why don't you just apply for a new position and get it over with?" Nanette retorted. "And by the way," she added, "I don't need glasses. I prefer to sit close so that I will be enveloped by the picture."

"Yeah, right," said Robin.

"Ginsburg has a job opening," Nanette said. "Akira told me he's looking for a new postdoc."

"Do you get all your information from Akira?"

"Well, he should know," said Nanette, eyes on the screen as she watched the trailer for *Raising Arizona.* "Let's go see that."

"What do you mean, he should know?"

"Well, he lives with the man. He should know if he's hiring."

"He lives with him? He lives with Ginsburg?"

"Shh! You didn't know that?"

"No, you never told me that."

"Oh, Robin." Nanette sighed. "Do I have to spell it all out for you?"

"I'm sorry, I thought he was just—"

"Hey, keep your voice down," whispered Nanette, who had great reverence for the movies. "It's starting."

"He is so creepy," Robin whispered back. "I could never work for him."

Nanette shook her head and reached for more popcorn. She adored Robin, but her friend had a deficiency—she lacked a certain cynical gene. She couldn't just laugh or excuse people for what they'd done. Of course, this cynical deficiency had enabled Robin to bring an entire laboratory to its knees. Nanette highly respected and enjoyed her for that. Robin's judicial experiments were brilliant, and they wouldn't have worked for a normal person. A researcher with an ordinary tolerance for absurdity, injustice, and dissembling never could have pushed her case so far. But how Nanette wished she could supply Robin with some cynicism, how she wished she could just help Robin lighten up and laugh.

"Oh, don't be ridiculous," she told Robin now. "No one ever said you had to live with him too."

That fall, whispering ruffled Cliff everywhere he went. Of course, there had been whispering before, but the jealous talk was latent. Now, in the aftermath of the ORIS inquiry, without confirmation of his findings in other labs, dry rumors and withered expectations brushed him at every turn. There was trouble with R-7 at Stanford and Cornell. In other labs, in other hands, his glorious results were just not panning out. Surely there was something wrong. Weren't his results supposed to be the next big thing? Or had there been a grain of truth in Robin's accusations? Beth had heard some people speaking snidely about his work. Prithwish nearly came to blows defending him against a couple of guys from the second floor.

"How's the paper coming?" sniped one of the postdocs as they unlocked their bikes from the racks in front of the building.

"Just wait," Prithwish shot back.

"Don't answer them," Cliff warned.

"Wait for what?"

"How long?"

"You'll see," Prithwish shouted, and got a little tangled in his tenses, as he did when he was angriest. "And we will see who will be laughing now."

If only "now" would finally arrive. Cliff longed to silence all his critics with some new success. He was miserable with his need for new results, but he could not produce them from thin air; he could not solve every problem instantaneously.

He willed himself success even greater than he'd had before, but suddenly every aspect of his work was problematic, from the new cell line he was using to the size of his needles. The woman who had replaced Billie was young and inexperienced, and he continually did her work over again. When he complained of Francesca's incompetence, however, Marion responded with stony silence.

She and Sandy no longer treated him like a junior colleague. They rarely called him into their office to discuss R-7 anymore. Their public loyalty had been unflagging, but the two of them were weary now, and far less generous in private than they had been during the hearings. Marion was particularly cold, and he suffered from her terse commands. She asked him to do myriad small tasks, even while she expected him to continue and somehow solve all the open questions raised by his past research.

"If the mice are relapsing," she snapped, "it's up to you to find out why."

"I realize that," he told her, "but it's going to take time. My cells aren't ready, I've had almost no support for the past six weeks—"

"I don't care," she said. They were standing together next to a microscope and she spoke in a low voice so that Francesca couldn't hear. "I don't want to hear excuses."

"You told me Feng was going to help me," Cliff protested. "Where is he?"

He hadn't meant to anger her, only to defend himself, but when he mentioned Feng she turned on him. "This is your work," she hissed. "This is your project, and you had no trouble acknowledging that when the work was going well. This is your discovery, and your career."

"I realize that."

"And therefore . . ."

He stood before her in confusion. Did she mean for him to finish her sentence? She left him hanging, but he dared not speak.

"Therefore," she said, *"you are responsible."*

"He has not been all he could have been," Marion told Sandy. They were walking again, up and down Oxford Street. The sky was overcast on that November day, and Marion had insisted on bringing her umbrella, which, as Sandy said, never failed to ward off showers. "He has not done everything I might have hoped."

Sandy shrugged. "Well, could have been, should have been—it's no use wasting time on that."

"No, I don't think you understand," she said slowly. "I've given this a lot of thought. I've considered all the problems and confusions and ambiguities in his work. I've gone over everything in my mind—and I think Cliff's results were rushed, and that our conclusions were aggressive. We published too soon; there wasn't enough there. His findings were too thin to support such an ambitious research program."

"His findings got us major funding," Sandy reminded her.

"And given the current situation, I'm not sure they deserved a federal research grant."

"Well, the NIH thought otherwise," Sandy said. "Even if they'd like that money back again."

"Maybe we should give them the money back," said Marion.

"What are you talking about? This is a research grant for open-ended work, not a government contract for manufacturing widgets. Research means risk; it means exploration, not delivery of specified results. We presented Cliff's work as an example of the kind of thing we might achieve."

"But we didn't know enough—he didn't know himself how much R-7 could do. There were too many questions."

"Marion, I've said it before, and I'll say it again: If you try to answer every question before presenting your work or publishing or applying for funding, you will get absolutely nothing done."

She prodded the sidewalk with the tip of her umbrella. "This was too quick, Sandy. We were opportunistic in our approach."

"Marion."

"I blame myself for putting so much pressure on Cliff to produce."

"He put pressure on himself," Sandy countered.

"He lied."

At last she'd said it. She'd said the words aloud. She and Sandy stood face-to-face with the accusation between them. She knew he would object and chide her for losing faith. She knew he'd think she was a coward, and dreaded his reproach for caving to the forces arrayed against them. She hated to leave him standing alone in support of a research program increasingly unpopular and unworkable. Still, she had to speak. He was her closest friend, her partner, and if they were to work together, she could not keep ideas from him. They could not strategize or collaborate at all if she did not confess her change of heart. "I think he may in fact have suppressed some data," she said, "and exaggerated in other cases. He may have cut corners in his procedures, and particularly his dissections. I think his record keeping might have been poor because at times there was nothing there to record."

"It's all possible," Sandy conceded coolly.

She studied his face. She imagined this was one of his rhetorical gambits, and waited for him to continue and tell her how in fact this could not have been the case. But he paused, and she realized to her surprise that he was not far from agreeing with her. "We have to let him go," she said.

He nodded, and she sighed with relief. He was with her, then. The tension left her face as she allowed herself her beautiful, rare smile.

"But," he added, "he will not leave until we win our appeal."

"You aren't serious," she said.

"I'm completely serious. How do you think it would look if we let him go now? We'd be conceding everything to ORIS—allowing them to ride roughshod over our good name, and those of any other researchers that take their fancy."

"No," she said.

"Marion, Redfield doesn't care for subtleties. He doesn't make distinctions between one misleading postdoc and wholesale fraud. He wants us as his test case for scientific corruption in America, and he won't have us. We don't deserve it. We won't be punished for being lied to."

"We are responsible for what happens in our own lab," said Marion.

"Maybe our postdoc was unworthy of our trust. Maybe he didn't deserve our defense," Sandy told her. "Those are still open questions. The point is, he stays until the end of the inquiry. After that, the decisions we make about him are our business."

How cold he was. His pragmatism stunned her. Had he always been so single-minded and calculating? She could not help thinking less of Sandy to hear him talk this way. But then she thought less of herself, as well, for engaging in such a conversation, for listening to him and scarcely arguing. She wondered how much she'd ever truly argued with him. She'd always enjoyed their debates, but in the end, who dominated their decisions? Hadn't he used her all these years? Hadn't he appropriated her research program? If that was true, she confessed to herself that she had used him as well. She'd depended on him to do the dirty work she wouldn't deign to touch herself: the politics, the scientific skirmishing, and ultimately, the ambitious overreaching for hot topics and newsworthy results. Agnostic that she was, she'd leaned on him for his scientific faith. She had never considered how pure that faith had been, flaming so strong with such scant data to support him.

"Don't look at me like that," he said.

He knew she disapproved of him for speaking frankly, and he was sorry, but abandoning ship was not an option. He simply could not allow Marion an admission of defeat. She was impractical—and this was both her strength and her weakness. She never considered appearances. She was angry at him, but he was the one who had to make the best of the situation. He was the one who would salvage what they had and prepare the lab for future work.

All that cold, drizzling month Sandy went about his business, meeting with Houghton-Smith, soothing Peter Hawking, waiting busily for the results of the appeal. He was good at shielding himself from unpleasant emotions, but not from Marion. They'd been too close, and he admired her too much; he was devastated to lose her good opinion.

A chill came over them. When they were alone, they had trouble speaking to each other. They had worked together so long and survived so much, that they had never imagined anything would change. Now this conflict over Cliff finally estranged them. Silently they opposed each other: Marion insisting they confront Cliff, Sandy insisting that they wait. Their partnership was such that neither openly struck out at the other. Sandy never chastised Marion publicly, and Marion did not castigate Cliff in private. Their position was already precarious, and Sandy and Marion knew their strength as a united front. They would not betray the rift between them. They were so careful with each other that their new postdocs scarcely noticed anything was wrong. Only the old hands, Cliff and Feng and Prithwish, Aidan and Natalya, felt the stiffness and the strain.

At home, their families sensed a sea change. Marion spoke bitterly to Jacob of Sandy's admonitions, his Machiavellian approach to science, his pettiness, his constant focus on funding and politics and presentation. "He's never considered content important," she told Jacob. "He's never valued research for its own sake—only for the publicity the lab can get. It's a game for him. Science is just his game—and I was a fool not to understand that."

And Jacob listened to her rant, and shook his head, and poured her coffee, but never smiled or said I told you so.

Ann noticed the estrangement too, because Sandy would not talk about Marion at all. He refused to speak of her, or even to hear her name. When Ann asked how Marion was, he ignored the question, or answered pettishly, "She's just the same as she's always been."

At Thanksgiving, Kate was surprised to see there were no places set for Marion, Jacob, and Aaron.

"They've gone to Florida," Louisa said.

"To Florida? Why?"

"Cousins," said Louisa.

"They never went to see cousins before," said Kate.

"She and Dad had a falling-out," Louisa told her.

"She and Dad?" Kate asked.

"I know," said Charlotte mischievously. "How could they ever have a falling-out?"

The table was set, the butter melting on their squares of corn bread, and Sandy had just finished carving the turkey, when his beeper went off and he was called to the hospital for an emergency. Then they'd helped their mother put away the perishables and wrapped the platter of turkey in foil. He was supposed to be back in an hour, and it would probably be longer, but the food would keep. They were all used to such delays.

The afternoon was long and quiet. Ann retreated to her study, desperate to get a little work done. In the living room, the girls spoke softly so she wouldn't overhear.

"They might lose the appeal," Louisa told Kate. "It's not going well. That's why the two of them aren't getting along."

"But they won't lose," said Kate.

"It's possible," Charlotte said. "Cliff's work isn't standing up."

"Who told you that?" Kate challenged Charlotte.

"Mom," said Charlotte.

"I don't believe it."

Charlotte stretched out on the couch. "So now Dad thinks Cliff probably did do some things wrong."

Kate shook her head. "But that's not true," she said.

"Why? Because you have such a crush on him?" Charlotte teased.

"I do not have a crush on him! I never did. I never liked him," Kate lied, but to no avail. They were both laughing at her, throwing pillows at her from the couch and leather reading chair, and Kate could only cover her head with her arms and plead with them to stop. Ducking down, she closed her eyes in embarrassment and confusion. She had never imagined Cliff as anything but innocent, and certainly never dreamed he'd do anything to deceive. She remembered the first time she'd met him—how charming he had been, and how miserable. How he'd said he really, really liked research. She remembered his eager interest in John Donne's poetry, and his request for a literary quotation for his paper. She remembered every word he'd ever said to her, and every smile he'd bestowed. But particularly she remembered his quiet desperation. He'd been like a soldier that way—a handsome soldier of the First World War, desperate to escape the trenches, questioning the very meaning of the conflict. She was abashed to think how she had enjoyed him for that, for his pain, for the agonizing drudgery of his work, for suffering in the lab under her father. And suddenly, to her horror, she could imagine him cheating his way to great results. He'd wanted to escape and to transform himself; he hated his work; he'd hated the sameness of it all and had come to think there was never any end. He'd despaired of succeeding the hard way, been bored to death by the realities of his position. Always, he'd been flirting with giving science up and choosing art.

Marion could not work like this. She'd held her fire for two weeks, thought carefully about everything Sandy had said, and considered every cost. She could not continue to work with someone dishonest, nor could she let her suspicions build without allowing Cliff an opportunity to defend himself. She knew that confronting Cliff would further damage her partnership with Sandy, and she knew that any actions she took against Cliff now could damage the appeal irreparably. Even so, she would test her hypothesis. She would speak to him alone.

She plucked him out of the lab one morning long before Sandy was due in, and she sat him down in her office and said, "I want to know what happened."

"What do you mean?" he asked her.

"You know what I mean." She waited across the desk.

Still, he did not wither under her glare. He did not turn away or look furtively at the floor.

"I want to know exactly what you did with R-7. I want to understand exactly why two major laboratories cannot reproduce your results."

"If I knew why, I'd tell you. If I understood the problem, I'd be on the phone to Agarwal and Hughes right now."

She knit her fingers together. "I'll tell you what I think," she said. "I think your claims are unfounded—or at the very least, exaggerated. I think your record keeping, your—"

He threw up his hands and said, "I've had every accusation thrown at me, and now this new theory that because two labs haven't yet reproduced my results, I'm guilty in retrospect. But I've answered every question about my procedure and my experiments, I've discussed every scrap of paper with ORIS. I don't know what else I can do. Either you believe me or you don't."

"We have believed you, and we've defended you," Marion said. "We've staked our reputations on you. Why didn't you show us all your data?"

"You saw everything."

She looked him in the face. "No, I don't think so."

He was pale, frustrated, indignant. "I don't know what else I can say to you; you'll think whatever you want to think."

"I do not think whatever I want to think," she countered, "and that's the difference between us. Why didn't you publish all your data?"

"I did."

"Everything."

He practically shouted, "Yes. Yes! Every single scrap of relevant data."

"Ah." She sat back sharply in her chair.

"No, I misspoke."

She caught her breath. She had him. Not in the angry outburst, as he thought, but in the wavering afterward. She gazed at him as though she'd just made a bloody discovery.

He was floundering. He heard his own voice, and the words spilled out in his defense, but for a moment even he heard his sentences as hollow formulas. His credo was rehearsed; his passion credible, but a performance all the same. "When I said relevant, I meant relevant to those particular experiments on that date."

She fixed her eyes on him in chilling fascination. "No. Relevant to the results you wanted."

"Not true. Not true at all," he protested.

But she'd found the equivocation she had been listening for, the willful confusion in his mind, the root of so many beautiful unfounded ideas. There it was; she'd caught him out. "Don't you see?" she told him. "Can't you see? The work isn't good. It isn't right."

He didn't see. His guard was up again. Once more he maintained he had done nothing wrong. She wanted a confession, but he had nothing to confess. After all, he could not confess to Marion what he would not confess to himself. What he told himself about his work was not exactly what he had done. What he had done, not exactly what it should have been. Still, Cliff's own perceptions of his actions were coherent, internally consistent. He clung to his defense for safety.

Perhaps his work with R-7 had been more about ideas than concrete facts; perhaps his findings had been intuitive rather than entirely empirical. He had not followed every rule. Strictly speaking, he had not broken the necks of all his mice, but gassed them, instead. He had not dissected every animal. He had not chosen to discuss every piece of data, but had run ahead with the smaller set of startling results he'd found. Still, aspects of his data were so compelling that in his mind they outweighed everything else. He had sifted out what was significant, and the rest had floated off like chaff.

"I never thought you would allow public opinion to influence you," he said.

"Not opinion," she told him. "Reality."

"I thought you were patient," he countered.

"You don't know what patience is," she said.

His voice trembled with frustration. "How can you say that? I've been working night and day. . . ."

"Doesn't matter," she told him almost tauntingly. "Doesn't matter if it isn't right. We're going to retract the *Nature* paper."

He started, aghast. He had never dreamed Marion could be so fickle—especially after defending him so staunchly before. He could certainly imagine Sandy lashing out at him in anger, or turning against him, but not Marion. She had been both employer and teacher, unwavering in her support. "You're going to let them win. You're going to let Redfield make the calls for you," he said.

"No, I make my own calls. And I don't think your results are sound, or your conclusions true."

"You can't retract my work," he burst out, but of course his work belonged to her and Sandy. The paper was the property of the lab, and they could do exactly what they wanted with it.

"I don't publish flawed results," she said.

"They aren't flawed."

"I don't believe that anymore."

"Do you really think I based all this work on lies?" he asked desperately. "Can you really sit there and . . ."

"It's bad science," she said. "I can't support it, and I cannot continue working with you."

"You mean you can't be *seen* working with me," he retorted.

She didn't deign to answer that. In the fluorescent office light, her dark eyes took him in with such ferocity, he could scarcely breathe.

Then, suddenly, she dropped him. She turned back to the paperwork on her desk.

"What about the work I'm doing now?" he asked.

She didn't answer.

"What about my funding?"

"That money's already spent," she murmured.

"Are you asking me to leave today?"

She shrugged. "It doesn't matter." She didn't bother to look up. "You can come in or not. You can finish out the year or not. It makes no difference to me. I will not be working with you."

Her disavowal echoed in his ears. She'd cut him off. In his worst moments, he felt that she—not ORIS, not Representative Redfield, not Robin, but Marion herself—had stolen his future. How could he possibly become a scientist now? How would he even have the heart?

He went in every day. Silently he went through the motions, culturing cells from the new tumors on his mice. As they had long before, the other postdocs watched him, and worked silently around him. He told himself that Marion didn't matter, but he knew that wasn't true.

When the mail arrived, he scarcely noticed the small brown package addressed to him. Then he saw the return address and slit the packing tape.

Kate had sent him a new book, a paperback copy of *The Picture of Dorian Gray*. He flipped through the pages, but there was no note. Gently he put the book down and threw away the cardboard wrapping. Wilde's tale of the beautiful young Dorian and his dissembling might have been the last stake through Cliff's heart, except that, fortunately, he was unfamiliar with the novel.

3

MARION PUSHED the bedcovers off, and then pulled them on again. She flipped her pillow over to no avail. Despite Sandy, she had let Cliff go. She'd spoken to him so directly even he would find no hope or ambiguity in her words. She had no idea what he would do, and she didn't care. In a few months he would be gone and she would be starting over. She'd already begun with Nir and Miki, and they were promising. Nir came highly recommended from the Weitzman Institute, and was already a presence in the lab with his big opinions and big hands. Miki was from UCLA, and a little dynamo. But, of course, who knew how these two would turn out? Miki could be brilliant, or just as easily turn out pedestrian results. Nir could be a breath of fresh air, or he might become a bully. It would take months and years to know; it took that long to find out about people.

The time was what she regretted most, for she looked back at all of Cliff's work as lost time. Amazingly, Sandy did not see this yet. When Marion spoke of retracting Cliff's paper, he still talked about waiting for the results of the appeal, and then suggested simply writing a note about the ambiguities in the paper. He refused to face the fact that there was nothing salvageable in this situation. She could scarcely face the idea herself, but there it was. They would have to start over. And there was something else. She had come to see that starting over meant letting go of Sandy himself. He was completely tangled in Cliff's faulty work. Sandy's name, his face, his every interview was tied to R-7. He had been the prime spokesman for the research, Cliff's most vocal defender, and now he was utterly unapologetic, unconscionably optimistic, even in defeat. To begin again would mean to divorce herself from everything Sandy had worked for, and every Pyrrhic victory Sandy had won. To begin again would mean asserting her own voice, and her own name, to devise a new research program, and a new approach. It would mean rebuilding her reputation for consistency and care, and slow, meticulous lab work. It would mean working again without any thought of glory, following small observations instead of imposing grand ideas. It would mean thinking small.

This was the long route, and it was the way forward; the only way for her. She knew she must give up Sandy and all his schemes for shortcuts, his visions of a northwest passage, his dreams of flight. But she had no words to tell him. She could not find the time or place.

The day came in February; the city was piled in ashen snow. Feng and Nir and Miki and Prithwish were all at work in the lab, and Nir was asking why he and Miki had to maintain the colony records downstairs.

"We are not slaves," he declared. "This is the work of lab techs. This is absurd."

"Oh, stop complaining," Prithwish said. He spoke playfully, but Nir was not amused. Nir wasn't tall, but somehow he took up a huge amount of lab space. He looked like a wrestler, with his broad shoulders and thick, muscular neck. He had served in the Israeli army, and couldn't talk about what he'd done there.

"I want to understand why this job is given to us," Nir insisted.

"Actually, it doesn't bother me all that much," piped up Miki.

Nir glared at the tiny traitor next to him.

"I could tell you the truth, but you won't like it," Prithwish said.

"Well . . ."

"It's just because you're new. That's all."

"In other words, a lab tech is more senior than me," said Nir.

Feng suppressed a smile as he stood waiting for the centrifuge, reading the book he'd found. " 'Out of the unreal shadows of the night comes back the real life that we had known,' " he read. " 'We have to resume it where we had left off, and there steals over us a terrible sense of the necessity for the continuance of energy in the same wearisome round of stereotyped habits, or a wild longing, it may be, that our eyelids might open some morning upon a world that had been refashioned anew in the darkness for our pleasure, a world in which things would have fresh shapes and colours, and be changed . . .'" He snapped shut *The Picture of Dorian Gray*, opened the centrifuge, and took out his colored tubes. How odd to tire of the world because it did not change. Feng himself had always appreciated waking up in the morning to find everything just as he had left it. He had always particularly enjoyed the fact that no matter how frantic you were looking for something, objects could not get up and move on their own from place to place. There was such satisfaction that your books or keys were often exactly where you'd put them. He wondered, in his self-satirizing way, if he was stuck with bench work because he enjoyed that sort of mundane order. He would never find research enchanting. Cliff had once recorded in his lab book Feng's definition of *experiment* as "a series of humiliations." Everyone laughed at that, because it was true. Science was all about failure, and bench work consisted primarily of setbacks. Conducting biological research was like climbing up a downward-moving escalator that then multiplied and divided and unzipped itself into a thousand new mutating walkways. The challenge was not to move upward or forward, but often only to stay upright. How satisfying, then, and how amusing when objects stayed in the same place, and forms and colors suddenly behaved predictably. These were the unexpected rewards of scientific life, the odd consistencies.

He was preparing a job talk for an interview at Rice University. There was an opening at Columbia as well, but the head of biology at Rice was pursuing Feng and hinting strongly that he would also find a position for Mei. Feng was wistful at the thought of New York. When he'd gone to Manhattan to speak and seen the trains and the museums and the restaurants, when he'd rushed through the streets with the assistant department head whistling for a yellow cab, he'd longed to move to that great city. But Marion said accepting the position at Rice, particularly if there was a job for Mei, would be the prudent thing to do. Of course, he agreed with her. He and Mei had no money at all, and as Marion pointed out, Rice would help them obtain their green cards. Two tenure-track jobs, and the university's legal department might make permanent residency in the States possible.

Still, Feng wondered, if circumstances had been different, would Marion have pushed him to go to Columbia? She was certainly eager to see him settled, but she might have been more ambitious for him if he hadn't angered her with his silence about Cliff's work. She had asked his opinion, demanded he take sides, and he'd abstained. She'd insisted he help her investigate what was going wrong, and he'd refused. He did not regret opposing her. Perhaps his thinking had been isolationist. How could he help it? She had power, and he had none. He told himself, defensively, the lab was hers, not his. It was up to Marion to decide what she believed and what to do. If she had a fault, it was this—her uncertainty about her own judgments, her need to lean on other people to ratify her own conclusions. Always she pretended she didn't care, but the pretense didn't hold. She cared too much. For her the lab was life and death, every decision fraught, every disappointment a personal betrayal. She was a romantic, always striving; she had no sense of humor when it came to her work, no sense of the cosmic joke.

She was sitting in the office, editing her formal retraction of the R-7 paper, when Sandy bounded in, his face flushed with pleasure. He was grinning, practically laughing. She hadn't seen him look so happy in months. "We creamed 'em," he told her. "Thayer called me, and we've won the appeal. We got the judgment against ORIS, a rebuke to Redfield's subcommittee, a call to reform ethics oversight at NIH. We got everything!"

Sybil Halbfinger had already called. Marion turned to him gravely and said, "I know."

This time no findings had been leaked to the press. Mysteriously, the conclusions of the appeals board had not reached the public at all—but Sandy would take care of that. The statement by the distinguished panel could not have been stronger. The poorly handled inquiry, the invasion of privacy, the intimidation that Sandy, Marion, and Cliff had suffered, the troubling use of Secret Service agents, the leaking of documents, and ORIS's willful, at times entirely fanciful, extrapolation from problematic evidence—all these aspects were detailed in the appeal board's forty-seven-page statement. The board's conclusions were unequivocal. Despite irregularities in the R-7 data, there was no clear evidence of fraud.

"'Poor record keeping does not necessarily indicate a desire to mislead,'" Cliff read as he sat with Tim Borland at their celebratory lunch in Romagnoli's. "'Inconsistent scientific results are not necessarily commensurate with data manipulation. Faulty or even false conclusions do not necessarily connote fraudulent claims.'"

"But this is the best part." Borland leaned across the table and flipped several pages. "Did you see? 'This panel recommends an immediate external review of the structures and processes used for ethical oversight at the NIH, with particular emphasis on the relationship between ORIS and the House Committee on Energy and Commerce.'"

Cliff shook his head.

"How does it feel?" Borland asked him.

"I don't know," Cliff said truthfully. "It hasn't hit me yet."

Borland laughed. "It will. It will."

Still, Cliff felt slightly dazed as he left Romagnoli's. He wandered toward the Park Street Station and then through the Public Garden, with its bare twisting trees, its swan boats in storage, its flower beds covered with mulch and a dusting of snow. On the frozen Frog Pond, skaters whirled and lumbered, slid and spun, and fell on the white ice. He could take the T back to Cambridge, or he could rent skates for the afternoon. He was free, no longer encumbered with accusations from ORIS or from Marion. Free of blame, and free of Robin. With a rush of joy, he realized that he could work again with a clear name.

He had been spared, and he was chastened, humbled by the victory. As one who survives a shipwreck, or a terrible disease, he asked God for strength and wisdom, and resolved to make a better start. He had made serious mistakes; he acknowledged that much to himself. There had been missteps. He had lost years of work; he would have to begin again on some fresh project. He had been battered and abused, and yet he was not disillusioned, even now. Not sorry, or sad, but eager to begin again. Out of this experience he'd discovered what he'd never fully known before: he loved science, the slow, exhausting work, the rush of discovery. He could never give that up.

And so he walked along, his shoes squeaking on the snowy path, and after long months of torment he felt his spirit revive. He had a great gift—this talent for restoration, this ability to see himself as a character in a bildungsroman. With just a little encouragement, Cliff's doubt and confusion melted away. Given grounds for hope, he saw the future stretching out before him, no obstacles to block his way, but glorious possibilities at every turn.

Now Robin saw that her own work had been in vain. Despite ORIS, despite the failure to reproduce Cliff's work in other labs, he'd won. She spoke to her own lawyer and heard the appeals board's decree. "Their attorneys turned this into a referendum on procedures and practices," Laura Sabbatini told Robin that morning on the phone. "Unfortunately, we were unable to move the appeals board to consider the merits of the case."

Robin listened carefully, but she said nothing. What was there to say? This was how the matter stood, and there was nothing she could do. There was no way for her to appeal the appeals board's decision.

"Do you see what I mean?" Sabbatini asked her.

And Robin said yes. She wasn't stunned, as Cliff had been. She did not have to wait for the news to hit her. She hung up the telephone in Ginsburg's lab, where she had been working since January second, and tried to lose herself in the bustle around her. She tried to forget everything but the tasks of the morning, extracting DNA from tissue samples, plating new cells and splitting older colonies.

Few events or emotions escaped Ginsburg's notice, however. He was an investigator who loved to prowl his spacious laboratories, to pace and measure his domain. When he was in town, he walked among his students and his postdocs and made chance remarks and daunting suggestions. He'd seemed to Robin, when she arrived, to be everywhere at once.

"What is it?" he asked her now as she stood at the microscope. "Is something wrong?"

Once again her flushed face betrayed her as she realized Ginsburg must have heard about the appeals board's findings. That was his way—to know all the news, and know it early.

"Step outside a minute," he told her, and she followed him into the hall.

"I'm sorry about the appeal," he said, "and I'm sure you are too."

She tried to speak then. She wanted to say something stoic and off-hand. *Oh, well.* Or *That's just the way things go.* Or *That's life.* But the clichés were difficult.

He was looking at her keenly, choosing his words. "You did very well," he said at last.

"Thank you," she said, and tried to duck back inside the lab.

"And sometimes," he continued, "the truth has to be enough."

She looked back at him, and faintly, almost imperceptibly, she smiled. That pleased him. He felt he'd said the right thing. In fact, she was considering Ginsburg with all his honors and awards, his chair at Harvard, and she was wondering whether the truth—which should have been enough for her—was also sufficient in itself for him.

"But it's not just a triumph for us," Sandy was telling a reporter on the phone. "In fact, it's not for us at all. It's a triumph for open inquiry all across the nation."

Across the nation, Marion thought. Such a grand, almost quaint phrase. He spoke in newsreels. That was just one of the things she loved and hated about Sandy.

He had been busy all day, racing down the stairs to speak to Hawking, talking constantly on the phone, arranging interviews, spreading the news. He had been gloriously busy, almost giddy. Gleefully he scooted in his swivel chair between desk and file cabinet, and she had to move fast to keep out of his way. This was almost like old times. And she knew this was when she had to speak.

She waited until he got off the phone, took a breath, and said, "Sandy, I need to talk to you."

He turned toward her quickly, eagerly. "No, wait, there's something I have to tell you first."

She felt herself caught out then, and off balance. She had thought so long about what to say, and how, that she was nearly paralyzed to lose her rhythm like this.

"I've accepted a new position," he said, and he was beaming. "I'm going to be the head of a new private cancer facility in Wellesley. It's an entirely new enterprise dedicated to combining research and treat-

ment. It's called the Stoughton Clinic and we're breaking ground next
year."

"A private clinic!" She forgot everything she'd planned to tell him,
she was so startled and dismayed.

"And what's so shocking about that?"

"You'll spend all your time fund-raising," she blurted out.

"Don't you think I'll be good at it?" he challenged her.

"But . . ."

"But what?"

"You could do better," she said, looking away.

"And you're a snob," he reminded her, and added carelessly, "I held
out against them as long as I could."

"You did not. You did not hold out against them. You never hold
out against anything," she said.

He shrugged. "They made me an offer I couldn't refuse."

This was all a little too slick, a little too devil-may-care, even for
him. And she understood, then, that he had known exactly what was
in her mind, and what she'd been planning these last days and weeks.
He was too proud to endure the speech she had prepared. He would
not listen to her talk about how they had to go their separate ways.
Typically, he'd decided to act first. That was just his way: chivalrous
and selfish at the same time. He'd leave the lab for untold sums of
money, preempting her painful valediction. He'd saved her that. She
should have been relieved, and in a way, she was. Why, then, did she
feel he was abandoning her and selling out? It was just like him to steal
her thunder this way, to snatch the decision from her own hands—and
then make her suffer for it.

"You could have asked," she said, "before you decided to take this
position."

"What? Asked your permission? Given notice?" Now he bristled at
her. "I beg your pardon. I didn't realize I had to ask leave to go."

"You could have raised the issue," she said, "and discussed it
with me."

"Isn't it interesting," he told her, "that after all these years you still
think of me as your employee?"

"I don't," she said.

"Yes you do, Marion. You do."

Wounded, she turned on him. "You were my equal partner, and we shared everything alike."

"Not true. You know it's not true."

"You always got what you wanted," she retorted. "You got everything. Do you think you'll have more freedom over there?"

"Yes," he said cheerfully.

She shook her head. "They'll work you into the ground," she said. "And you'll be at their beck and call. They'll have you traveling constantly and holding meetings every day."

"We'll do clinical trials of our own," he said.

She looked at him reproachfully. "You'll be an administrator." She spoke the words as if they were a death sentence.

"That's right," he shot back. "I'll be an administrator; I'll be a doer. I'll manage people and money and equipment and projects, and I'll get things done. I'm not afraid of that. Wake up and look around you, Marion, and maybe you'll finally realize that if you want to get something done in this world, you—yes, even you—have to be an administrator too."

"Do you really think you're going to get research done at a private clinic?"

"Absolutely. Far more than you."

She threw up her hands at that, because they both knew it simply wasn't true.

"And do you know why?" He pressed on. "Because I have a plan."

"You always do," she said.

"I have a plan—but here's the difference between us, Marion. When I have a plan I carry it through."

"This is a plan? To start up some little clinic?"

"Little? Ha! Did I mention our endowment? We're gonna buy the Philpott and sell it for scrap." He held up his hand. "No, don't speak. You can't afford me."

And already she missed him, his bravado, his joy in competition, his sense of fun. She already missed fighting with him. She missed their constant arguments, their incessant lunchtime conversations. She missed what they had been to each other, before the inquiry. Their partnership had not been perfect, but she had respected him, fully.

And he had been wonderfully disrespectful in his turn. He was the only person in the world who'd ever teased her. Jacob and Aaron weren't teasers, and no one in the lab would dare.

"Sandy," she said.

He searched her face and saw her annoyance, her disapproval, and underneath, her sorrow. He saw all of that, but he knew her too well. He knew there would be no second chance with her. She wouldn't ask him to stay.

That weekend, Jacob surprised Marion with dinner reservations at Upstairs at the Pudding. "What's the occasion for all this?" she asked, glancing around the expensive candlelit restaurant.

"A successful appeal, to begin with," Jacob said, lifting his glass of wine.

"Oh, that," she told him. "That's more cause for embarrassment than celebration."

"Then there's the interview for Feng."

"He'll be going out to Houston on Monday," she said.

"And he seems to stand a good chance there."

"We'll see," she countered superstitiously as she picked at her smoked pheasant salad.

"And there's the job offer for Prithwish at Genentech."

"That was very nice," she said, slightly more cheerful.

"They're well on their way," Jacob told her. "Even Cliff. What did you say he was doing?"

"Well, apparently he has a possibility in Utah."

"You see how they all land on their feet," said Jacob.

"I suppose they do." She didn't want to sound ungrateful. She was profoundly grateful the NIH appeals board had spared her lab, tremendously relieved to be done with ORIS and its suspicious inquiries—the politics and gamesmanship of the past two years. Still, the thought of starting over pained her. She would have to develop five-year plans for funding. How good Sandy had been at grandiose plans, and how she hated the idea of projecting her work into the future, assuring others that results would come to pass where as yet there were none. He had done all that for years, so that she had not dirtied her hands. And the whole thing was dirty, the whole dirty game. She would have to go to the dog and pony shows and talk up the lab, and she would never get any work done because she would be traveling and on the phone and always, always interrupted. Desolately, she thought about all this while she sat with Jacob at their table high above Holyoke Street.

But Jacob was not desolate at all; he had never been happier, his dark eyes never so loving or so bright. "Try to see it the way I do," he told Marion. "It's an opportunity. Try not to underestimate yourself—because every time, you rise to the occasion. You know you do." If he could only make her see how much better off she was at that moment than she'd been for years—how much richer she was now without Sandy's flashy talents and questionable resources. She had cast off an entire line of research, a universe of empty possibilities. Now the world was all before her. His wife was free—liberated from half-truths and spectacular data. She was free of the windmills of publicity. Free of puffery and free of scandal, and what was more, he had played his own small part in liberating her. He could not help congratulating himself that he had been right about the virus from the beginning. He was happy, truly happy. He loved the rack of lamb on the table, he loved the wine, he loved that what he had foreseen and dreamed had come to pass. He was discreet by nature, and inward-turning in his practice, nearly self-contained—except at this moment of celebration. Then it seemed the prodigy in him slipped out, the brilliant child he had been danced with righteous satisfaction, and joy loosened his tongue.

"I always knew Cliff's work was too good to be true," he told Marion. "I said as much to Robin."

She set down her fork. "What are you talking about?"

He froze for a second, then collected himself. "I said as much to everyone who would listen," he reminded her, "especially you."

"What do you mean?" she demanded. "When did you speak to Robin?"

He knew he had said too much. He should never have mentioned Robin's name.

"When did you speak to her?" Marion pressed him.

"It's not important. It was a long time ago," he said. "Before any of this ever happened. It doesn't matter."

"You told her you thought the results were too good to be true?"

"I gave her my opinion. You know I hated the R-7 paper. That was no secret."

"But you told Robin you hated it?"

"Of course not," he said. "I would never say something like that directly."

No, she thought, looking at her cunning husband.

"I would never betray a confidence to someone like her," he insisted.

"But you might hint," she said.

"No, no. You misunderstood me. Forget everything I said."

But she could not forget. Nor could she sit there with him and go on eating, as he celebrated the end of false research, and flawed inquiries, and boasted of his own insinuations.

"Marion," he said, "let me explain."

She left the table. She made her way through the velvety restaurant and out the door, past the ladies' room and the coat check in the hall. She didn't have the ticket for her coat, but she didn't bother with that. She hurried down the stairs, and without hesitating for a moment, she began walking home.

The wind was bitter, but she was wearing a good wool suit, and told herself she didn't care. She walked straight through Harvard Yard and then out the gate to Quincy Street before she even felt the cold. How pleased Jacob had been at dinner. How pleased with himself. That was the thought she couldn't bear. He was delighted she had failed. No, that wasn't right. He was thrilled that Sandy had failed her. That was it; he was ecstatic to see Sandy vanquished. Because, of course, he hated Sandy with all his heart. Sandy was quick and worldly; he was a clinician, and not a real scholar. He was a player. And Jacob hated Sandy for always wanting something from science: new treatments for his patients, glory for himself, money for the lab. That was blasphemy, to come to science wanting to make and take, to enter into research so impatiently, to try to bend an inquiry for personal and social gain. He hated Sandy for treating the publication process like a joyride, and taking her along. Above all, Jacob hated Sandy for that—for capturing her imagination, tempting her into his irresponsible, irrepressible funhouse world. He was only a distraction and a magician, to Jacob's mind. He was an expert at wishful thinking and public relations: parlor tricks and sleight of hand, and yet she and Sandy had been inseparable. Jacob could not bear that.

Her husband had not been jealous. Not in the ordinary way. He wasn't so primitive, but he had been quite willing to play on Robin's jealousy. To whisper doubts into Robin's ear. To encourage her to act where he could not. She knew even Jacob could not have planned what Robin had done, or foreseen an entire inquiry. But the fact that he was glad of the results; the idea that he could have imagined even some of what had come to pass! Almost without thinking, she crossed Quincy Street and turned away from Inman Square and home.

She strode instead into the institute and walked down the well-lit empty corridors and rubbed her cold hands together. He loved her. She knew that. He would give up his life for her. In fact, in many ways, he had. He had sacrificed for her, sublimated his imagination for her. And yet, how much had Jacob really given up, and how much had he transferred onto her shoulders? He'd bestowed on her every pressure to succeed, and his professional ambition and all his pain, the sharp hunger for perfection. He'd cast upon her his hope and his determination, and all the fury of his relentless mind.

The office was quiet. Sandy's side was stacked with papers and jottings on yellow pads and crumpled messages, and photographs of his girls and Ann. Marion's desk, of course, was neat and clean. The amber cursor on her computer monitor winked at her. Sandy had been insisting that she needed a fancy Spark Station, but Marion was too frugal.

"He loves to spend grant money," Jacob had caviled once.

"He's good at getting it," she pointed out. "Why shouldn't he spend it?"

Of course Jacob had been right about Sandy; he was right about everything. How difficult it was for her husband, always to be right. Certainly it was difficult for everyone around him. He was too true to be good. How tragic to see inside people, straight through all their pretenses. She opened up her desk drawer and took out her knitting. There, in a plastic bag, were the two pieces for the front of the cardigan, and also the sleeves. The big piece for the back was almost done; she smoothed it out on the desk and examined her work.

Her mother, Alice, had taught her to knit, and taught her well. When Marion was a teenager she'd knitted herself a powder blue angora sweater. One evening, when she'd almost finished, she set the sweater on the chair next to her bed. In the morning, when she woke up, the sweater was gone, and a mess of blue yarn lay on the chair next to her knitting needles. "What happened?" she asked her mother frantically.

"I found a mistake in it," her mother told her, and then, as if she had done Marion a tremendous favor, she explained, "It was all the way at the bottom, so I ripped down to the third row for you."

Even years later, her mother had no idea why Marion had been so angry with her for this. "If you make a mistake," she'd told Marion, "you have to rip it out."

But the sweater had not been her mother's. The experiments had not been Jacob's to revoke. Marion picked up her long silver knitting needles chained with tiny loops to months of work. She slipped one needle out, and then the other. Delicately, she pulled her wool and watched two stitches disappear. She plucked further at her yarn and an entire row of stitches vanished, then another. Slowly, meticulously, stitch by stitch, she began to unravel Jacob's sweater.

Fifteen minutes later, Jacob found her, and the sight of the crimped ecru wool on Marion's desk stopped him in his tracks. He had intuited where she'd gone, and thought to bring her coat as well, but he stood stricken in the doorway of her office, almost afraid to cross the threshold.

She said nothing to him, but kept on pulling at the wool. With a weird, meditative fascination she watched her stitches disappear.

"Forgive me," he said.

She didn't even want to look at him. Nevertheless, she let the knitting go and sat back in her chair. Ann had been partly right when she'd considered Marion unforgiving. Marion did not have an easygoing nature. She did not take the world lightly, or bend easily to other people. Still, she forced herself to consider her husband where he stood in the doorway. She understood his belief in her—his dark, fraught, critical faith, so different from Sandy's. Even in her anger, she understood his ambition for her and his restless, unacknowledged jealousy.

"Forgive me," he said again.

She sighed and stood up and took her coat from him and said, "I'm sure I will."

4

SANDY DID not go to the annual cancer meeting in San Francisco that May, but he pretended he didn't care. He went so far as to tell Ann he'd regretted all the time he'd spent away from the family in the past several years, and this was one of the main reasons he'd given up the lab and its attendant conferences. And she accepted the explanation with only the slightest quirk of an eyebrow.

Once, at night, he turned in bed and wrapped his arms around her. He held her tightly, and she kissed and tried to comfort him. She didn't need to ask what was wrong. She knew he simply missed the lab; he missed playing the research game. More than anything, he missed Marion.

"She can't be having an easy time of it," he told Ann as she flipped pancakes for Sunday brunch. "She isn't really a good collaborator—for most people."

"No," Ann said.

"It's not in her nature," Sandy said. "She's too quiet, and secretive, and . . ."

"Selfish," Ann supplied wickedly.

Sandy stared at her for a moment, shocked, and then chortled. "That's right, just a little too selfish."

Ann's birthday often fell on the weekend of the conference, and this year, because Sandy was home for it, the girls came in from school and cooked a grand family dinner. Louisa prepared poached salmon, and

Charlotte served up new potatoes and perfect asparagus. But Kate ran into trouble with the cake and threw away her first attempt in despair. Dessert was delayed, and served at last as a trifle layered with strawberries and whipped cream, and much teasing on the side.

"There was probably a time when they taught baking at Hill," said Sandy.

"I'm sure they did in the nineteenth century," said Kate.

"Well, maybe they should reinstate the class," said Sandy.

"Very funny," Kate said coolly, although, in fact, she'd shed a few tears in the kitchen.

"You picked an ambitious recipe," Ann murmured.

"We tried to talk her out of it," said Louisa.

Kate shrugged. "It looked interesting."

Ann leaned over and kissed her, and pushed the hair out of her eyes. She itched to brush it and tie it back. There was a boyfriend now, a tall, gawky kid Ann had met exactly once. From what Charlotte said, Ann gathered that Stephen was very smart, and very rich, and very wild. Kate couldn't deny these first two accidents of birth, and had tried to explain about the third. The facts were, however, that Stephen had been suspended a couple of times from school. It seemed he would be graduating, but he was taking the year off afterward to travel in Italy. Ann was delighted that Kate's friend would not be going with her to Brown. Theirs, Ann thought, was a separation devoutly to be wished. Of course, Kate felt differently about the matter, but like her father, she tried not to let her disappointment show.

Sandy was in good form. He had just accused Charlotte of cowardice for not applying to medical school, and was now laughing at Louisa for taking intensive Russian.

"What happened to Robert Hooke?" he demanded. "What happened to early modern English biologists?"

"I'm not doing Hooke anymore," Louisa said.

"That's a shame."

"Why? You told me Hooke was a waste of time."

"Weasel, it's all a waste of time," Sandy told her. "At least with Hooke you knew the language."

"But I know what I want to do now," Louisa said. "I know what I want to study."

"And what's that?" Ann asked her.

"Lysenko," she announced triumphantly.

"Jesus," her father groaned. "He wasn't even a scientist."

"Yes, he was."

"He was Stalin's tool."

"That's the whole point!" Louisa's eyes were shining. "He set back plant genetics a hundred years, not to mention ruining the Soviet agricultural economy and causing—"

"I thought you were looking for scientists to admire," Ann said.

"But I think corrupt scientists are far more interesting—from a policy point of view, don't you?" asked Louisa. "You can look at the interplay of science and politics, and you can watch the corruption of the scientific process. And now the Soviet archives are really starting to open up—it's virgin territory! Once I know the language I can go to Russia and I can get into stuff no one has even looked at for forty years!"

"Or you could actually do some science yourself," Sandy said. He could not understand why anyone would turn down that opportunity—to engage in scientific problems firsthand. His own hours in the lab and in the office with Marion had been the happiest and most important of his life. He'd understood she could not keep working with him; he'd broken off with her himself. And yet, strangely, he still had trouble understanding that their partnership was over. He actually dreamed that they were working together still. Wonderful, detailed dreams. He was eating his sandwich in the office, and she was stirring her blueberry yogurt with a plastic spoon. She was carrying her umbrella, just in case, and they were walking up Oxford Street in the sun. They were debating the language in a new grant proposal, puzzling over unexpected results, celebrating a new victory, scooping Agarwal.

But Sandy was not going to collaborate on great discoveries; he was going to tend rich patients instead. He was not going to know the thrill of the chase anymore; he was going to raise money. He knew all that as soon as he woke up.

He had hoped for so much better. Now he was left to himself, where he had wanted to surpass himself. Caught short. And he grieved for Marion. He put up a good front, but he missed her more than even Ann would ever know. He wondered when he'd pass a day without thinking of her. He was fifty-two years old and he'd seen more of death than most people. Still, despite all his experience, he'd never felt a loss like this before. He'd been unsinkable. As an oncologist he'd counted on his ability to do much and reflect little. Now, suddenly, he saw that he was not invincible, that he could not achieve everything he desired, that his opportunities were finite, that death would come to him too.

And they had just begun. After twelve years, they had really barely started. He had never imagined that their time would end. He was not accustomed to ending anything that he enjoyed. If he delighted in one concert at the symphony, he would go to others. He had season tickets; he would hear great music endlessly. If he ran once in the Boston Marathon, he would run again. He ran each year and gloated as the qualifying times for his age group grew easier. He was accustomed to succeeding, and he had succeeded. He'd fully expected to marry a lovely, brilliant woman, to live in an exquisite house, and to send his daughters to the finest, most expensive schools. It had never occurred to him that he might not realize all his plans. He had achieved everything he had imagined, except great science. That had been his best dream, and he could not make that dream come true alone. Now, without Marion, he saw before him an ocean of possibility, but no vessel to carry him; he could only stand helplessly, looking out to sea.

Later that night, he went to see Kristen Braverman in the hospital. The new treatments were not working; she had been readmitted, and she was afraid.

She told him she had trouble falling asleep because she was afraid she would not wake up again, and he reassured her, telling her many other patients had trouble sleeping. He told her this difficulty was natural, an altogether common complaint. Then his voice choked up. The words came out in a hoarse whisper. He coughed and pulled himself together. He would not break down there next to Kristen's hospital bed; he owed her more than that.

These conversations were harder now. His optimism, once unassailable, was now not quite so grand. He could still rely on his ego and his arrogance, but he could not scoot from one bedside to the next quite as fast. The trouble was, he looked at his patients and he saw he was like them. He was waiting, as they were, watching and hoping for some progress, some new breakthrough. He was no longer a researcher

himself, no coinvestigator, and he sat, instead, with the ones suffering.
Like them, he had to put his faith in other people. He had always been
good at motivating patients to accept the protocols of treatment, the
pain, the complex and sometimes useless procedures. It was far more
difficult for him to accept his own limitations, to express an optimism
once removed and faith in research no longer in his power.

Still, that night he tried not to let his sadness show. He pushed the
heavy hospital curtain to one side, and the night sky pressed in upon
the glass. Curving streets and city lights glittered impassively below.

He gave Kristen his speech—the same speech he'd given her husband months before. He pointed at the picture window, in the general
direction of Cambridge, and he began to tell Kristen in the grandest
terms about the cancer research being done. "They're working on the
problem," he told her. "They're working on the problem all the time."
And he tried to sound confident, defiant even. He tried to banish
death from the room. But he did not use the royal *we* anymore when
he spoke about research. A wistful quality, a most ineffectual humility,
had crept in. "The smartest person I have ever known is working on
these problems," he told Kristen. "If anyone can find a new therapy,
she can. In fact, I know she will."

He knew Marion was not missing him in the same way. She had the
work. She'd have no time for mawkish thoughts, and he was glad of
that. He imagined her, far away in San Francisco, in the white and gold
ballroom of the Fairmont Hotel. The room was crowded with colleagues and competitors, and she was about to overturn all the accepted theories about breast cancer. She was going to unleash glorious,
dazzling, saber-rattling results.

In fact, her talk was not nearly so well attended. This was no
keynote address. She was speaking in a small conference room to an
audience of forty-five researchers, among them Art Ginsburg and his
posse. Marion noticed Ginsburg, and then Robin on his left. She saw
them both instantly. Ginsburg had deeper pockets than Marion, the
more formidable reputation, the more aggressive approach. Still, he
was not above competing with her. He often set his students to work
on problems she and her own postdocs were pursuing. An omnivore
and magpie of a scientist, he collected anything that glittered. Now he

sat in wait for her in the audience. She worried her results were unimpressive, and at the same time feared her work was good enough for him to steal. How he must have enjoyed taking Robin under his wing, bringing Marion's own researcher over to his side. Robin sat primly with her notepad on her lap, and she looked right at Marion, daring her to meet her eye.

What do you want? Marion asked Robin silently. You had your hearing and your media coverage. You had your claims examined thoroughly, proved and disproved, and then corroborated by other labs. What do you want now?

Robin did not know exactly what she wanted, but she knew what she wasn't going to get. Marion was constitutionally incapable of apology.

Robin would not be forgiven for turning against the lab, for showing Marion such disrespect. She had always known that. You were with Marion or you were against her, and Robin couldn't help enjoying her position next to Ginsburg, flanked by students from Ginsburg's huge lab. She couldn't help feeling a slight rush, in the moments before Marion's talk, as she joined the others with their longbows raised, Marion's new data in their sights. And then, of course, Robin felt ashamed of such bloodthirsty thinking, and annoyed with herself for such pettiness.

Marion looked tiny behind the lectern. Her voice was small, her manner stiff. She had trouble with her transparencies, and Ginsburg rolled his eyes. Five minutes into the talk, he was looking at his watch. Robin felt almost protective of the woman up there in the navy suit. She wanted to run up and adjust the overhead projector. She wanted to cup her hand behind her ear and signal Marion to speak louder. She wanted to save her former mentor somehow. She saw how much Marion hated public speaking; she knew Marion wished Sandy were standing there in her place.

Marion was forcing herself to slow down and speak clearly, pale with the effort. Robin felt a tenderness toward her, even though Marion had been entirely unfair to her. There was a kind of triumph in that, too, in being strong enough and independent enough to feel charitable. She had idolized Marion once, and wanted to emulate her. Now she saw Marion through Ginsburg's eyes, and she looked fussy and nervous. Robin had never detected in her what Ginsburg could smell a mile off; she had never understood Marion's fear.

How much more dramatic then, how stunning when Marion came to her new results on metastasis. Suddenly, as she unveiled her new data, she cast all her uncertainty off. Now Ginsburg sat up and listened, and the conference room hushed. All the researchers in the room seemed to draw closer. And now Marion's quiet voice grew stronger; her detailed disquisition resolved itself into three main points. She was not charismatic, but her ideas were. And when she launched her propositions, she was the archer, shooting arrows into the audience; each of her statements incisive, brilliant, and characteristically self-critical.

Ten hands flew up as soon as Marion finished speaking. A hundred questions seemed to fill the air, Ginsburg's among them. Robin was jotting down a small query of her own. She was so absorbed, her hand shot up in front of everyone.

And Marion viewed her audience with some satisfaction, although she did not forget the poor beginning she'd made in the first half of her presentation. She glanced at the raised hands and enjoyed the interest in her work, although she still begrudged the lost days she'd spent traveling. She took a sip of water and watched Ginsburg scribbling furiously, and then gazed at her former postdoc, her rebellious child with her hand raised. What do you need now? Marion asked herself. Strange, she'd never posed the question that way before. She'd always considered what her postdoc demanded, what she did or did not deserve. What did she need? That was the puzzle, but as was so often the case, framing the question properly went a long way. What did she need? In that calm, clear, nearly joyous moment after her talk, the answer began to come to Marion. Ah, yes, of course, she thought with some surprise. And she called on Robin.

Acknowledgments

I am indebted to several scientists for sharing their expertise with me. Many thanks to Annie Penn for her historical perspective and incisive questions, and to Paula Fraenkel for brilliant advice in matters both literary and scientific. Special thanks to Tom Schwarz for his detailed and insightful comments. Philip Standel drew upon a wealth of experience to answer queries about the care and breeding of mice. Jonathan Singer, Lisa Spirio, and Jeanne Winsten allowed me to watch them work at the Whitehead Institute. I am deeply grateful for their generosity.